WITHDRAWN

No longer the property of the
Boston Public Library.
Sale of this material benefits the Library

Praise for
SEVEN NIGHTS TO SURRENDER

"Jeanette Grey has become a must-read author in romance. SEVEN NIGHTS TO SURRENDER is lyrical, stunningly sexy, and brings swoons for days."

—Christina Lauren, *New York Times* bestselling author

"A must read! I couldn't put it down. Jeanette Grey's writing is so refreshingly honest. SEVEN NIGHTS TO SURRENDER is intensely emotional and sexy as hell. I need the next book ASAP!"

—Tara Sue Me, *New York Times* bestselling author

"With its sexy setting and sensual story, Jeanette Grey's SEVEN NIGHTS TO SURRENDER sparkles!"

—J. Kenner, *New York Times* and international
bestselling author

"Achingly sexy and romantic—I couldn't put it down!"

—Laura Kaye, *New York Times* bestselling author

"Sensual, sultry, and exquisite, SEVEN NIGHTS TO SURRENDER will sweep you away and seduce you on every page! Crackling with tension and steamy with sensuality, it's a feast for the senses you don't want to miss!"

—Katy Evans, *New York Times* bestselling author

D1547033

"With her unique flair, Jeanette Grey delivers a deliciously sexy and irresistible romance that keeps you turning the pages for more. You'll savor every word so you don't miss a single sizzling moment."

—K. Bromberg, *New York Times* bestselling author

Praise for
WHEN THE STARS ALIGN

"I couldn't put it down! I loved every sentence! The writing is outstanding, the setting entrancing, and the characters stole my heart. Fresh, flawed, and instantly lovable, you'll root for Jo and Adam at every turn."

—S. C. Stephens, #1 *New York Times* bestselling author

"The heat of the island has nothing on the off-the-charts attraction that sizzles between its feisty and fiercely unique heroine and idyllic hero. The journey to being the best you is often equal parts beautiful and tragic, and Grey sets the scene perfectly. A sassy and sexy read full of heart and adventure. This romance is like a breath of fresh air."

—Jay Crownover, *New York Times* bestselling author

Confessions
in the Dark

Confessions in the Dark

JEANETTE GREY

FOREVER
YOURS

New York   Boston

This book is a work of fiction. Names, characters, places, and incidents are the product of the author's imagination or are used fictitiously. Any resemblance to actual events, locales, or persons, living or dead, is coincidental.

Copyright © 2016 by Jeanette Grey
Excerpt from *Seven Nights to Surrender* copyright © 2015 by Jeanette Grey

Cover images by Shutterstock. Cover design by Elizabeth Turner.
Cover copyright © 2016 by Hachette Book Group, Inc.

All rights reserved. In accordance with the U.S. Copyright Act of 1976, the scanning, uploading, and electronic sharing of any part of this book without the permission of the publisher constitute unlawful piracy and theft of the author's intellectual property. If you would like to use material from the book (other than for review purposes), prior written permission must be obtained by contacting the publisher at permissions@hbgusa.com. Thank you for your support of the author's rights.

Forever Yours
Hachette Book Group
1290 Avenue of the Americas
New York, NY 10104

forever-romance.com
twitter.com/foreverromance

First published as an ebook and as a print on demand: March 2016

Forever Yours is an imprint of Grand Central Publishing.

The Forever Yours name and logo are trademarks of Hachette Book Group, Inc.

The publisher is not responsible for websites (or their content) that are not owned by the publisher.

The Hachette Speakers Bureau provides a wide range of authors for speaking events. To find out more, go to www.hachettespeakersbureau.com or call (866) 376-6591.

ISBN 978-1-4555-6269-5

To my writer friends. I'd be a puddle on the floor without you.

This book wouldn't be what it is without the help of a lot of people. My thanks to:

My editor, Megha Parekh, for finding all the ribbons I'd laid out and seeing how to tie them into the tidiest of bows.

My agent, Mandy Hubbard, who's gone to bat for me more times than I can count.

My critique partners: Heather McGovern, whose fangirl pictures have provided an endless source of inspiration and whose sage advice has talked me down from a hell of a lot of ledges; and Brighton Walsh, who's the foul-mouthed, extroverted yang to my yin and the genie on my shoulder telling me I can do the thing.

The beautiful blogging ladies of Bad Girlz Write, for always raising a glass, and the amazing folks at Capital Region Romance Writers of America, for lending an ear and a helping hand.

And my incredible husband, family, and friends, who continue to support me on this crazy adventure, no matter where it leads.

CHAPTER ONE

Sometimes, Cole could still hear her voice in his mind.

He squeezed his eyes shut hard against the torrent—like that could ever make it go away. Like he would even want it to. The memories were full of soft words and gentle hands, kindness and warmth, and he hadn't deserved a bloody shred of it.

An ugly laugh tore at the back of his throat. He'd proved that well enough.

She hadn't deserved...

Forcing his eyes open, he gazed out across the tracks, at dingy rail ties and the ugly concrete of the platform, but he couldn't blink away the afterimage burned into his memory. The train station around him threatened to dissolve, stuttering out into crimson spatters on the snow, and he gripped the strap of his bag for something to hold on to.

Christ. What had he been thinking, going out today? He should've stayed in his apartment, should've celebrated all alone.

Taken down that bottle of the good stuff he'd been saving. The library would've kept for another day—for another year.

But her voice had told him to go.

A roaring in the distance drew his focus back to the present. His vision resolved, and he took a deep breath. The hardest part was done at this point—he'd put on proper clothes and gathered up the papers he wasn't even sure why he bothered with anymore. He'd made it through his front door. Tempting as it was, he was too stubborn to turn back now.

Nodding to himself, he strode to the edge of the platform. The inbound train was still three stops away, twin pinpoints of light piercing through the early April gloom. Uncivilized, a city as frigid as Chicago laying its tracks aboveground, but a decade of missing the Tube wasn't going to put him back in London anytime soon. He was too stubborn for that, too.

Stepping away from the edge, he glanced in the other direction, at a pair of lights that was even closer. And then his gaze caught on something else.

Two men. Flat-brimmed caps and too-large coats, standing idly beside a boy who radiated tension. They weren't with him, then. Cole narrowed his eyes. Crossing his arms over his chest, he shifted his weight.

Chances were that it was nothing. Strangers could be rude, and the "L" wasn't exactly a sanctuary for personal space. He was reading too much into things.

Unless he wasn't. He'd seen that look on blokes before. God, but had he ever. Seen them sizing up their targets, probing for weaknesses. His own shoulders ached, remembering standing like that boy was, every muscle held so tightly, this vain effort to look unassuming and unthreatening until it all boiled over.

Until bone was snapping and his fist was bruised and hot, and his whole life was spinning out of control with the force of this *anger*—

And they moved so fast.

With a roar of sound and wind, the outbound train swept into the station, blowing the boy's scarf across his body, and it was all the opening they needed. One tapped his arm and the other had his bright green rucksack in his hand and then they were both tearing down the length of the platform toward a pair of opening doors.

Cole didn't so much as stop to think.

"Hey!" Between one breath and the next he was in motion. Around him, gazes darted up from mobiles and magazines, but neither of the men slowed their pace a bit, and he shouted, louder this time, "Hey!"

Sometimes cowards only needed to be called out on their actions, to have some kind of attention brought to them before they withered and retreated. But not these arseholes. One cast a glance back over his shoulder. Caught sight of Cole as he took another step toward them and another. Instead of stopping, he nudged his partner and they broke into an outright run.

And Cole was right behind them. His vision went crystal clear, the echoes of the past that had haunted him all morning receding into background noise in his mind. But they didn't disappear. Grief and anger fueled him, the tangled mess of memory that had clogged his chest expanding. Every time he'd not fought back and every quid he'd lost.

Everything he'd lost, and this useless feeling he'd been living with for so long.

And always, always, that voice in the back of his mind. The one that had pled with him and sobbed, and it was telling him to stop. That this was madness and he'd get himself killed, but he was past the point of listening now.

The men ducked into the train just as the doors began to close, and an ember of rage turned to fire inside Cole's lungs. They were going to get away with it if he didn't hurry, if he didn't—

His blood sang as he leapt a bench, hurtling forward to shove an arm between the sliding doors. As they stuttered back, he shouldered his way through, reaching up to yank the cord for the emergency stop. He caught the eye of a dumbfounded girl standing by the intercom and pointed at the speaker. "Two men in black. Sixth car. Nicked a handbag." He gestured out the window at the boy still staring in shock at the chaos on the train. "From him."

The men were still two cars ahead. Cole didn't wait for the girl to acknowledge him. He took off even as the loudspeakers blared, the conductor barking out a demand for an explanation. And people could be so bloody stupid. Oblivious and inattentive and he had to force his way past them. He pushed into the space between the cars and on into the next one. He was gaining on them; he had to be.

But there was movement outside the window, dark coats and the bright green of that bag, and *bollocks*. Bastards had jumped the train, just as the inbound one pulled in on the other side. If they got on that train, he'd lose them.

Cole swore out loud and caught himself on one of the poles,

slowing his moment enough to change direction. As he launched himself through the door and pounded across the platform after them, parting the crowd like the sea, he had this moment—this teetering sense of vertigo.

This was past the point of sanity, past the point of what anyone could have expected. Past what even that boy could have hoped that anyone would do.

The fire in his ribs flared hotter, blanking his mind to anything else. How hard had *he* hoped, back when he'd been that defenseless? How deeply had he wished and prayed? If only someone had stepped in...if only anyone had seen...

How could they *not* have seen?

With one last burst of power, he tackled the man with the bag. The bastard crumpled, clearly caught by surprise, and Cole reared back his arm, balled his hand into a fist, and it would feel so good. The satisfying smack of bone on flesh, the coppery tang of blood on the air, and he could do it.

But he hesitated. There was a flash, and for a flickering instant, all he could see was Helen's face. The naked fear in her eyes, because she'd seen it. This ugliness inside him, and he was just so *angry*—

A hot, bright burst of pain lit the back of his skull. Oh Jesus fuck, there had been two of them. He reeled, swung off-balance, and the bloke beneath him took every advantage, throwing him off. Cole landed on rough concrete, no time to catch his breath before a hard kick landed against his ribs. Another leg rose, and he twisted.

He screamed when a foot came down on his knee. A sickening pop rent the air, fire shooting up all the way to his spine.

The man with the rucksack made to rise, his friend helping him up, and Cole saw red.

He lurched to rise, and a fresh wave of agony crashed over him, his leg buckling. But he got a hand on the belt of the guy closest to him and yanked him backward, even as his buddy started running, and shite.

Shite, shite, *shite*, how was he going to pull this off?

"Fucking psycho." The guy in Cole's grip spat right in his face, and Cole would kill him. Violence was this humming thing in his hands, buzzing through his every nerve, and he finally had a place for it to go.

He had something to *do*.

He kicked out with his good leg even as the bad one shrieked, tangling the man's ankles, pulling him down to his level, and he'd crush his skull. Feel the shatter of bones beneath his fists—

Except then there were hands on him, and he was still swearing, still swinging. He'd take this one, too, he'd take them all, every one of those sniveling little shits who'd been tormenting him for years, picking on the little nerd who'd always been taught to not fight back, but he was sure as hell fighting now. He'd make them sorry they'd ever—

He was turned over onto his back, the belt torn from his grasp as he stared up into a ruddy face. A furrowed brow.

"Whoa, whoa, easy there."

And there was something about the tone. The accent. American, not English. And Cole was thirty-five instead of nine.

All the heat bled from his face at once, the haze pulling back from his eyes.

Bloody hell. A police officer stood over him, while another

had the man he'd been ready to murder pinned down to the floor. Two more approached with the second man in tow.

Dangling from one of their hands was the bag.

The fight drained out of Cole, and he went limp. His foot skidded out against the concrete, and he choked on the sound of pain forced from his lungs as his knee flexed. God*damn* it all.

Time went blurry for a little while after that.

Witnesses were collected and statements given. Somewhere in the midst of it all, the boy came forward to claim his bag. Cole squeezed his eyes shut tight. He was even younger than he'd looked. Thirteen. Fourteen, tops.

After it was over, the boy came up to him. Cole was sitting on the ground still, waiting for an ambulance. He couldn't put an ounce of weight on his knee, and the back of his head throbbed. His ribs ached. The hot flow of adrenaline in his veins had faded, leaving him exhausted and shaking, and the last thing he wanted to do was talk.

The last thing he *ever* wanted to do was talk.

And sometimes, he longed for it so desperately it hurt in his bones.

Staring at the ground, the boy addressed him with a cracking voice. "That was pretty crazy what you did just now."

"I know."

"Thank you. For getting it back for me." He fidgeted with the strap of his bag. "You really shouldn't have, though."

As if he didn't know.

Cole shook his head. "I had to."

And it scraped at the back of his throat. Because that was the truth of the matter. The ugly fact he'd never been able to escape.

When his blood was up and his lungs got hot, it took him over. It blinded him to reason, to sanity, even. The anger was a force inside of him, and he was powerless to stop it.

His mind floated back to another night. Another fight and another life, and the horror in Helen's eyes.

And God, he wished that he could *stop*.

"It's not a problem, Mom, I swear." Serena Hartmann tucked her phone between her shoulder and her ear as she bent to reach the bottom of the hamper. She tossed the last, offending, escape artist of a sock into her laundry basket and stood, pushing her hair back from her face.

On the other end of the line, her mother still didn't sound convinced. "Are you sure? You're not too busy?"

"Not at all."

Okay, that wasn't completely true. She had her lesson plans to get ready for next week and those books she'd promised to bring her neighbor who was in the hospital and that résumé she needed to edit for her friend. Laundry to do. But all of that could wait.

It wasn't as if Serena minded picking Max up from practice. She liked watching him play, and she'd been meaning to talk to him some more about his application for Upton, anyway. See if he'd gotten around to asking his teacher about finding a tutor for math.

But her mother kept on fretting. "You just spend so much time shuttling him around and looking after him. A single girl shouldn't have so many responsibilities."

Something grated behind Serena's ribs. She'd never been the type to run from her responsibilities. Hadn't she proved that the last time Penny had gotten sick? Hadn't she been proving that pretty much every day for the last twenty-something years?

Taking a deep breath, she insisted, "Really, it's fine."

"You should be off doing something for yourself..."

Serena huffed. "Who says I'm not? An aunt can't enjoy spending time with her nephew?"

"I know you love Max. I just..."

Ugh, they could be at this all day. Serena appreciated her mother's concern, but it was time to move things along. "Listen, Mom, I got it. Can I let you go, though? I need to get this load started."

"Oh, wait, just one last thing, sweetie..."

With fond exasperation, Serena rolled her eyes. Her reception always cut out in the basement, but she could take her mom along at least to the bottom of the stairs. Balancing her laundry on her hip, she grabbed her keys from the hook by the door, nodding and *mmm-hmm*ing at all the appropriate places as her mom rambled on. She bit off a curse when she nearly knocked over the little bowl she kept spare change in, reaching out to steady it before it went toppling to the floor. She frowned as she readjusted it, spinning it so the messed-up spot on the glaze faced the wall.

Double-checking she had everything, she let herself out of her apartment. Only to stop dead at what might have been the longest, most creative string of swear words she'd ever heard in her life—and she taught middle school, so that was saying something.

Alarmed, she tossed her keys in her basket and gripped her phone with her free hand, taking a step forward and peering up in the direction of the sound. The cursing intensified in both color and volume, and Serena's pulse kicked into high gear.

"Sorry, Mom," she interrupted. "I really do have to go. Talk to you tonight."

She hung up, wincing as she did. She might pay for that this evening. But the muttering from the stairwell cut off to the sound of a clatter, like something was falling and hitting every single step on the way down, and that made her wince even harder.

Pocketing her phone, she called out, "Hello?"

Another low grumble filtered down to her, clearly not meant for her to have heard. Treading lightly, she took the first couple of steps toward the second floor.

"Is everything all right up there?"

"Brilliant," the voice said, louder this time. It was a man's voice, deep and rumbly, the edges of the word rippling with just a touch of a British accent. She tried to ignore the way that *did* something to her. Because for all that whoever it was seemed to be striving for disaffectedness, there was a twist to the tone. And the huff that followed, accompanied by a sharp thud, was pained.

She frowned, climbing higher. "Are you sure?"

"I'm *fine*," the voice stressed.

She hesitated. This person sure didn't seem to want her help. But as she reached the landing between the first and second floors, she spotted something lying on the ground.

A crutch.

She stopped, peering around the corner. The guy was sitting at the top of the next flight, one leg stretched out in front of him. All she could see from here were a blue running shoe and the loose cuff of a pant leg. Darting her gaze between that and the crutch, she bit at her bottom lip, considering.

The smart thing to do right now would probably be to walk

away. Bald-faced lie though it might be, this person had effectively rebuffed her twice now. No one would blame her for taking him at his word.

But her heart gave a little pang. She had more than enough experience with people who refused to admit they needed help. She knew what it sounded like when they tried to push her away.

She had to at least *try*.

Setting down her basket on the landing, she picked her way forward. "Okay, well, if you're sure you're fine. I'd hate for somebody to trip on this, though." All exaggerated movements, she bent to grab the crutch, then finally turned to face its owner.

And nearly swallowed her tongue.

It wasn't that she didn't recognize her third-floor neighbor. She'd seen him in passing a handful of times in the year she'd lived here, and she'd appreciated him in an idle sort of way. But the man had always held himself so tightly, like he was marching off to war every time he went to check his mail.

He was barely holding himself together at all right now. He'd traded out his neat jeans and tailored shirts for sweatpants, and his close-cropped dark hair looked like he'd been raking his hands through it all afternoon. Bruiselike shadows hung beneath the piercing, deep brown of his eyes, and the sharp line of his jaw was dark with stubble. She swallowed hard. It looked delicious, like it would be rough against the palm of her hand, and her throat went dry just looking at it.

Then she had to mess everything up by glancing downward at his mouth. Tilted into a grim line, it was tight and angry. And there, at the top right corner of his lip—the harsh, pale slash of a scar.

He coughed pointedly, calling her out on her staring. Her gaze rose to the angry set of those stormy eyes, and her breath caught.

"Well, then," he said, tone dry, words sharp. "Do you plan to take it with you?" He nodded toward the crutch in her hands.

"Oh. Right." Jolting into action, she climbed half the flight of stairs before a remembered warning tickled the back of her mind.

She might've only run into this man in passing, but some of her other neighbors hadn't been so lucky. When she'd been new to the building, there had been vague mutterings about the man in 3A. Mostly, he seemed to keep to himself, rarely coming or going, never accepting invitations. But once or twice...

Well. Suffice it to say that the guys in 3B didn't listen to their music too loudly anymore.

She took a step back, suddenly wary, but the thin thread of the man's patience had apparently run out. With one hand on the banister, he rose to his feet, and Serena's gaze raked him up and down.

Holy crap. His usual clothes fit him well enough, but the tight gray Henley he wore today draped over the dips and curves of lean, pure muscle, highlighting the broad expanse of his chest and shoulders. She had to stop herself from licking her lips at the sight.

But then he rearranged the crutch he'd managed to hold on to, tucking it under his arm, and started to take a single, purposeful step forward.

And almost buckled right in front of her.

"Cocksucking son of a—"

Without thinking, she narrowed her eyes at him. "Language."

Catching himself between the crutch and the banister, he

jerked his head up, mouth agape as he stared at her. "Excuse me?"

A fresh wave of heat washed across her face. Sure, it'd been a while since she'd had the chance to interact with a grown-up who wasn't another teacher or her mom, but scolding a grown man for his cursing was a whole new level of not-smooth. Still, she lifted her chin, planting the foot of his crutch on the ground and bracing her other hand on her hip. Pushing her embarrassment aside the best she could, she shrugged. "I just don't see any need to talk like that."

"And I bloody fucking well do." His right leg was held at an odd angle, and he raised it higher as if to make a point.

Oh. Now that she wasn't letting herself be quite so distracted by the rest of his physique, it struck her how loose-fitting his sweatpants were. The offending leg was unnaturally straight, something bulky making the fabric of the pants bunch around mid-thigh. Maybe a brace?

"What happened?" she asked, nodding toward his leg.

"Does it matter?"

"To me it does."

All at once, something in him seemed to crack. His posture, puffed-up and stiff, crumpled, and he bowed his head. When he looked at her again, pain and fatigue were written across every line of his face, and her heart stuttered.

"Look," he said, the exhaustion bleeding into his tone. "I understand that you mean well. But I have had a very, very difficult couple of days, and if you would simply hand me my crutch..."

Her mortification only grew. "Oh my goodness, I'm so sorry." Here she was, practically holding the man's walking aid hostage while she interrogated him. What had she been thinking?

She took the rest of the steps at a jog, but before she passed it to him, she paused. "Wouldn't it be easier without it?"

She'd broken her leg when she was ten, and going down the stairs had always been the worst. Having the banister to hold on to really helped.

"Please." The word was hollow and aching, like it cost him so much more than the air in his lungs to get it out. "Simply—"

"No, really," she insisted. "Isn't that how you lost your balance in the first place?"

He visibly bristled. "I didn't—"

"Then what, did you throw it?" She meant it as a joke, but the pinch to his brow made her wonder if that wasn't exactly how things had gone. She boggled.

Boys. Honestly. It didn't matter how old or how gorgeous they were, or how good they smelled up close like this...

Mentally scolding herself, she leaned away, giving him back the space she'd had no right to barge into. Still gripping his crutch, she glanced toward the landing above them. "Here, let me help you get to your apartment."

He let out a low, dark laugh. "I'm trying to *leave* my flat."

Seriously? "To go where?"

"How is this any of your business?"

God, this was one of Penny's episodes all over again. Instinct had her digging in her heels.

She wiggled his crutch at him, all her compunctions about holding the thing hostage bleeding away.

Exhaling a sigh that was pure frustration, he reached for it, but she held it just beyond his reach. Only to gasp in horror when he lunged.

And she saw the whole thing coming a million miles away, but there was no preparing for a couple hundred pounds of male teetering into her. On instinct, she threw herself into his fall, trying to take some of his weight, to shore him up, but he just dragged her down, too.

The next thing she knew, they were both on the ground, draped across the stairs, his body hot and hard above hers, and God, he really did smell incredible. Warm and rich and with a hint of something woodsy mixed in that made her insides melt.

The portion of her insides that weren't being crushed, in any case.

"Oof." She shoved at him, and he heaved himself away like he'd been burned. Except when his gaze met hers, it wasn't angry or disgusted or anything like that.

It was *hungry*. Deep in her belly and in the points of her breasts, a warmth bloomed, awareness crackling in her skin at how close they still were.

"Shite," he swore, and okay. Maybe he was a little angry, too.

The desire she could've sworn she'd seen in his eyes faded as he struggled to sit. Propping his leg in front of himself, he raked a hand through his hair. Gingerly, she sat up, too, checking herself over to see if anything smarted or pulled. From the feel of it, she was going to have one heck of a bruise on her hip tomorrow from where she'd landed, but other than that she seemed okay.

She turned to him to find his face twisted away. A curl of dread opened inside her. She reached out a hand, almost stopping herself before she pushed on through, settling her palm on the broad muscle of his shoulder. He flinched but didn't push her off. She sucked in a shaking breath. "Are you all right?"

For a second, she wasn't sure what the sound falling out of him was. Unless— Oh crap, was he *crying*?

But then he shifted to look at her, and no. Not crying. The man was laughing, and the bare hint of a smile on those lips transformed him. For a second, she could scarcely breathe.

Scrubbing a hand over his eyes, he let the laughter trail off. He forced out a long, slow sigh.

"No worse than I was, I suppose."

With a grin on her own lips, she found herself squeezing his shoulder. Feeling the firm shape of it before she pulled away. "Well, that's something." Testing the waters between them, she knocked her arm lightly into his. "And, hey, you're three steps closer to making it out of the building."

"Fantastic."

They sat there together in silence for a long minute after that before he started making motions to stand. She did likewise, holding out her hand to help him. He gave it a considering look. And, yes, fine, he was clearly a proud sort, but his hesitance was officially ridiculous.

"I won't bite. Promise."

Finally, he placed his open palm in hers. Tingles ran all the way along her arm at the warm press of broad fingers against her skin, and she swallowed hard as he levered himself to stand. When he let go, she missed the touch immediately. Trying to hide her re- action, she bent to pick up his crutches, passing him the one. He tucked it under his arm, gripping the railing with his other hand.

And he just looked so tired. She chewed at the inside of her lip for a second. There wasn't any harm in offering, was there?

"Hey," she said. "If you won't let me help you get back to your

place, maybe come and sit down in mine for a bit? Take a break."
And it struck her. "Is someone waiting for you outside?" Surely
he couldn't drive like this. He had to have somebody coming to
get him. "You can call them, or I can go down and tell them..."

A whole new wave of darkness twisted his features. "No. No
one. I was...My doctor's office. It's only three stops on the 'L.'"

Wait. He had to be kidding. "You're planning to take the
train?" In his condition? When he could barely make it a dozen
steps down the stairs? The station was a full two blocks away, and
it didn't have an elevator. "No. Absolutely not."

"It's hardly your concern." His gaze had softened since they'd
taken their little tumble, but it went hard all over again.

"It kind of is now."

He scoffed. "Hardly."

But she was weirdly invested at this point. And besides, if he
didn't want her helping him, she was looking out for everyone
else around him, too. The next person he fell on might not take it
so well.

"At least let me call you a cab or something."

Between her sister and her students, one of the things she'd
learned over the years was that sometimes even arguing was a sign
you'd already lost. It was time to stop talking and act.

Ignoring the way he sputtered, she grabbed his crutch and
started off down the stairs. He'd either follow or he wouldn't.

But at the landing, she slowed. Flipping her hair over her
shoulder, she cast a backward glance at him. Cocked a brow and
fixed him with a level look.

"Well?" she asked. "Are you coming or not?"

CHAPTER TWO

Routine. For three miserable years now, Cole had clung to it. Early morning runs and cups of tea, weekly visits to the library to catch up on the articles he didn't have access to anymore. Equations worked by lamplight and the same dozen recipes repeated over and over, and all of it he did alone.

When was the last time he'd talked this much? The last time he'd been touched?

A low shiver worked its way through his body, but he breathed through it.

Now here he stood, perched on one leg while the swollen mess of his injured knee throbbed. His shoulders ached from just the hobbling he'd done around the shoebox of his apartment, not to mention the disaster that had been his efforts to leave it thus far.

Fuck, he must've been high as a kite when he'd climbed these stairs the other day. It was all a haze of ambulances and X-rays and narcotics, the diagnosis of a dislocation and a sentence of weeks of immobilization and impeded movements.

And now this woman. This infuriating, nosy, kind, beautiful woman who had overwhelmed him with her efforts to help. He'd made a bloody fool of himself in front of her already. It hadn't been enough that she'd guessed about the fit of pique that'd had him hurling his crutch into the wall. She barged right into his space, surrounding him with the sweet cloud of her scent, and she'd questioned him. Challenged him. Until like a clod he'd lost his balance and taken her down with him, the press of her body beneath his warming him in places he'd been so cold.

Reminding him of pleasures he'd lost. Ones he could never, ever allow himself to have again.

Gripping the railing harder, he narrowed his eyes at her. Mischief danced in those pale green eyes, her invitation practically taunting him, and did she have any idea how close she was to getting burned? His temper—that hot, uncontrollable thing—was too close to the surface already, and he didn't trust it. Didn't trust himself. He hesitated there, muscles coiled, throat tight.

Until finally, with a shrug, she turned away from him, her hair bouncing, loose curls the color of warm gold settling around her shoulders, and his stomach churned.

Helen's hair had been just as brilliant. Just as soft.

And just like Helen had, this woman was asking him in. He was almost ready to take her up on it, even. She paused on the landing to retrieve the laundry basket he'd caused her to abandon, and he gripped the railing harder to keep himself from following after.

This was a terrible idea. But what else was he supposed to do? Even with the insane amount of time he'd allotted himself, his idea of getting to his doctor's office by train had been a fantasy.

A taxi was the most logical next option, and the notion of climbing the stairs to his apartment again only to have to descend them when the car arrived made a cold wash of sweat break out on the back of his neck, his shoulders and knee both screaming at him.

It would be fine. He could rest in her apartment for a few minutes before continuing. It wouldn't have to mean anything or break any of the promises he'd made. When he was ready, he'd go. Get in a cab and make it to his appointment and then haul himself back up these steps. There was no reason he had to leave again for at least a week. He could live on leftover birthday cake and bourbon until he could get to the grocer's by himself.

For a long moment, he closed his eyes. Helen's voice in the back of his mind pushed its way to the surface, calming his breath and his stuttering heart. Laughing at him, all warmth and gentle teasing as it asked him what on earth he was so afraid of here.

When he opened his eyes again, it was to stare at the same brown carpeting on the stairs and the same scuffed, green paint on the walls. The only thing changed was his resolve.

Nothing for it.

Gritting his teeth, he fumbled as he hunched to walk the crutch another step down. He shifted his grip on the railing and filled his lungs. Raised his bad leg a fraction higher in the air.

The strain on his shoulders as he pushed off to land on his good leg made him shake, but he clenched his jaw and did it again and again. Slowly but steadily, he made his way to the landing, and damn that woman if it wasn't easier this way, not having to juggle the two crutches at once, being able to use the banister for balance. He kept going, hopping his way around the corner to the next half flight. At the base of it was a spill of light.

And her. She stood in the open door to her flat, leaning against the jamb. As he neared, she stepped forward to hand him his other crutch, and he released his death grip on the railing to accept it.

"Your cab will be here in twenty minutes," she said. Leaving the door open behind her, she turned to head inside.

A whole different kind of tension gathering behind his eyes, he crossed the landing to peer in after her.

At its essence, her flat was a mirror image of his own. A tiny entryway opened onto a larger living area. A small but serviceable kitchen to the left, most likely, and then a hallway leading off toward the bedrooms and the bath. But it might as well have been a photo negative. She'd painted it all a warm yellow, and the sweet scent he'd caught the barest whiff of in the stairway mixed with something earthy—cinnamon, maybe—and the aftertaste of heat. Like candles that had recently been burned.

Homey. Soft and light. And an emptiness curled inside him sharp enough to cut his fingers on.

Restless, anxious energy crawled beneath his skin, but before he could give in to the instinct to back away, she reappeared from around the corner, popping her head out of the kitchen.

"Come on in, if you like. I can make you a cup of tea?"

Tea. He almost laughed. Back home, it would be insane to offer anything else, but it was so rare here. "Yes," he said, hobbling forward. He twisted to close the door behind him. "Please."

"Coming right up." Her retreating footsteps were followed by the sound of running water and the *click-click-click* of her lighting the stove. When he made it to the doorway, she shooed him away. "Sit."

He all but collapsed into the closest chair available, an over-stuffed thing that welcomed him with a sigh. Shifting one of the pillows she'd piled there out of the way, he leaned back.

"Here." She'd snuck up on him without his noticing to scoot an ottoman across the floor. Grunting, he lifted his leg and settled it atop the stool, and it was the most comfortable he'd been in days. Maybe years.

His gaze fell on the overflowing basket she must've set down as she'd been calling for his cab. Guilt twisted his stomach. "I'm keeping you from your chores."

She laughed at him, heading back into the kitchen. "No one will notice if I wear the same skirt three days in a row, will they?"

He would. He craned his neck to follow her with his eyes. If it was the skirt she was wearing today, he *definitely* would. It wasn't obscenely short by any stretch, going nearly all the way to her knees, but the fabric was soft-looking and draped across her thighs, making her calves look shapely and strong. And paired with the thin sweater that hugged her breasts...

Making a noncommittal noise, he turned back around and scowled, digging into his pocket to check the time on his phone. Twenty minutes. He could handle twenty minutes. More like nineteen by now. He settled in to wait in silence.

Ha.

"So," she said, raising her voice to be heard from the other room, "you avoided my question before about what you did to yourself."

Of course she'd be back to that again. The way she phrased it got under his skin, and he snorted. "I didn't do it to myself."

Except he had, hadn't he? Not for the first time since it'd happened, he cursed himself. A moment's hotheadedness, his damn prickly sense of injustice. If he'd ignored them, if he'd just stuck to his routine and not gotten involved...

The back of his throat burned. He never could manage not to get involved, could he? Even as isolated as he was these days, he couldn't seem to look away.

"Did someone do it to you, then?" The bemusement in her tone got to him all over again.

He crossed his arms over his chest. "If you must know, yes."

"Really?"

"Really."

"Well, that sounds like a story."

One he'd already told to the police. But he clearly wasn't going to be able to avoid telling it again here. "I caught two blokes nicking a backpack." He shrugged. He didn't have to make it a good story. "The thieves didn't like being confronted." Or chased down, or tackled. Or nearly punched. He gestured at his knee. "One of them gave me this as a thank-you present."

"Wow. So you're like a hero, huh?" And it could've been so flippant. But coming from her...it wasn't.

But it should've been. A hero. That was the last thing he was. If she knew...

"Hardly," he said, and the darkness to his thoughts colored his speech.

After a moment, she cleared her throat. "I don't know. You sound like one to me."

That was *not* what Serena had been expecting. Her own story of breaking her leg had involved more klutziness than crime-fighting, and she'd figured this man's situation would be much the same. But he'd interrupted a mugging? Something inside her gave a little shiver at the thought.

To keep her breathing even, she focused on arranging the remainder of a bag of Oreos that had been left from Max's last visit on a tray. The kettle gave off the first hint of a whistle and she flipped off the heat, then poured the water into the teapot with the crooked handle that she never got the chance to use. After adding a sampler box of tea to the tray, she carried it all out into her living room. He sat up straighter as she approached.

Damn. He hadn't gotten any less attractive in the handful of minutes she'd been in the other room.

She turned away from him as she set the tray down on her coffee table. "Can I fix you a cup?" She started to rattle off the half-dozen options, but he stopped her on the first one, voice clipped. Frowning, she placed the tea bag in his cup and poured. Leaving it to steep, she settled into the chair opposite his. He seemed more than content to watch the tea brew in silence, even going so far as to pull out his phone.

But she was still way too preoccupied by the whole running-down-a-mugger thing.

Even as his gaze darted toward the screen, she shifted forward, crossing her legs in front of her. "So, are you, like, a cop or something?"

That would be some sort of an explanation, at least.

"What?" The space between his eyes crinkled with what seemed like genuine confusion before he collected himself. "No. Not at all."

Oh. "A firefighter?" Or a mixed martial artist, maybe?

"I'm—" He cut himself off, a shadow flickering across his features. "I used to be a professor." He hesitated before adding, "Of mathematics."

Definitely not a cop, then.

A dozen questions rose to her lips about what on earth a former professor was doing chasing criminals, but then her mind caught on that statement. "Wait, did you say math?"

And there were those lines between his brows again.

"I did."

Oh hell, this was probably weird, but the question spilled out all the same. "You don't do any tutoring or anything, do you?"

She'd been pestering Max about finding someone for weeks now, but he kept forgetting—or more likely, he was too embarrassed to ask. Her own efforts had come to nothing. So late in the year, all the best people were already booked.

"Tutoring?"

"Super basic stuff." She stopped, stumbling over herself to explain. "It's for my nephew. He's only in fifth grade, but I'm trying to help him get into a private school for next year. The rest of his grades are great, but he needs to score really high on his entrance exams, and the math stuff is his problem area. I just need to get him caught up. A few hours a week, maybe."

As she'd been talking, he'd shifted in his chair, his posture going more rigid and his hands tightening against the arms. "Fifth grade."

She hesitated. "Is that a problem?"

"I..." His jaw flexed, the sharp point of it moving beneath the shadow of his stubble. "Children. I don't have much experience."

"But you have taught before, right?" Sure, different ages were different, but the principles were the same.

"Adults. College students."

"Then a ten-year-old should be a piece of cake."

Protests seemed to form on his lips, discomfort written on every line of him.

So she leapt to the first inducement she could think of. "I can pay you." Not much. Her own job as a teacher offered all kinds of rewards, but monetary ones weren't really among them.

And then it struck her.

"In services," she said, perching closer to the edge of her seat. Oh, this was perfect. "I'll call and cancel your cab and take you to the doctor's myself. Wherever you need to go. You're stuck on those crutches for how long?"

"Weeks."

There was a deer-in-the-headlights element to him, and it probably should have made her slow down, but she pressed her advantage instead.

"You'll need rides all over the place. Doctor's appointments, trips to the grocery store. You name it. A cabbie isn't going to help you get down the stairs, you know."

At that, he bristled. "I don't need help." He practically spat the last word.

She waved him off, because who was he kidding. "Tell me it wasn't easier getting down the stairs with only one crutch."

As if swallowing glass, he narrowed his eyes at her. "I was managing. I don't need charity."

And there was her trump card. "But it wouldn't be. Not if you helped me. It'd be an even trade."

That had always been the key with Penny. Make it out like her sister was doing her the favor, allowing her to help.

"Come on," she said. "At least give it a try. I'll take you to your appointment today either way." Depending on how long it took, she might have to run to pick Max up from practice right after. But that made this even better. "You can meet Max on the ride home. You'll love him." How could anyone not?

"And if I don't?"

Ugh. Please. "Then we call the whole thing off. But he's a sweet kid. I promise."

He was wavering; she was sure of it. She held her breath as he seemed to mull it over.

And it didn't make much sense, why she was suddenly so invested in this. She didn't know this man. He could be lying to her about his qualifications, and even those were sparse. But she was desperate to get Max into that school, and this was the best lead she'd gotten so far.

And there was more to it, too. Not just the dark beauty to his eyes or the full lines of his mouth. The way his shirt draped across the musculature of his chest. There was the way she'd found him, defeated at the top of the stairs. The pride with which he'd tried to turn her down.

He *needed* help. And help was the one thing she always had to give.

Her heart in her throat, she stood. Took the two steps toward him and held out her hand. "So? What do you say?"

What Cole wanted to say was, "Are you completely insane?"

But he stared at the open palm extended toward him, the

brave set to her jaw, and the kindness in her eyes.

And what he heard himself ask was, simply, "Why?"

Her half-smile faltered for a fraction of a second. Then, re-grouping, she replied, "Why not?"

Only any of a thousand possible reasons.

He gestured to the hamper and then to the overflowing messenger bag near the door. "Surely you have better things to be doing than ferrying around a...a cripple."

She shook her head. "We don't use that kind of ableist language around here."

She had to be kidding him.

"You didn't want me to say 'fuck,' either, and yet..."

Huffing, she extended her hand a little farther into his space. "Well, this time I really mean it. Now do we have a deal or not?"

He wanted to check the room for hidden cameras. This had to be a joke, or a terrible reality TV show. Something. People didn't make these kinds of offers. Especially when he had so little to give her in return. Only four square walls and a particular tragedy. The beginning of a story that couldn't possibly end well.

One last time, he balked. "I don't even know your name, and you expect me to get into your car?"

At that, the corners of her mouth turned up. "Serena," she said.

And he was running out of options here.

Everything in him screamed at him to decline. Even if her generosity were real, she wanted him to—what? Spend time with a child? Teach it arithmetic or some such nonsense? No. He couldn't possibly. His heart pounded painfully behind his ribs, memories of blood and glass too close to the surface, of raising a hand against the boys who had made him their own personal punching bag. The look on Helen's face the last time he'd seen her. He dug his nails in hard against his palm. He didn't trust himself, and she shouldn't, either. It was too big a risk.

It was too far to have fallen. All his degrees, his publications, and to be reduced to explaining the most basic concepts...

"Honestly," she said, and a sadness colored that smile. "What have you got to lose?"

His chest squeezed even harder, making it impossible to breathe.

Nothing. There was nothing *left* for him to lose.

And for a moment, she looked so much like Helen, sounded so much like the voice inside his head. Cajoling him and pulling him out of his own misery. They both should have left him there. But Helen never would, and this woman, Serena—she wouldn't, either, would she?

He wanted so badly to reach out and take her hand.

It was the briefest moment of flickering indecision, but that was all it took. The next thing he knew, he'd placed his palm in hers, and her skin was so soft. Something deep inside him melted, his blood pulsing with a life, a warmth he hadn't known in so long. Grief was an ever-present specter hovering just behind his shoulder, but for an instant, the emptiness of it cut less bitterly into his heart.

And she smiled at him. Warm and beautiful, the rosy curve of her mouth tilting upward until its brightness threatened to blind him.

He nearly faltered. That smile. It couldn't be for him. It wouldn't be—not for long. This had been a mistake. He moved to pull back, but she was stronger than she looked.

Holding firm, she squeezed his palm. "This is going to work out so great. I can just feel it."

With that, she was in motion, dropping his hand and crossing the room. His skin burned with the sudden loss of her touch, and his mind reeled. She grabbed her phone and a little blue handbag from a table near the door, swinging her hair out of the way before she dialed and held the speaker to her ear. She looked to him and motioned for him to come along. He hadn't so much as begun to rise when she turned away.

"Yes, I ordered a cab a few minutes ago. I need to cancel that."

For a blessed second, her attention was diverted, and he closed his eyes against the stinging there. He took a rough, deep breath and then another.

This woman was a storm, one he'd already walked out into without so much as an umbrella. He was going to end up soaked to the bone.

But he was a desert, and after so many years of stagnant air, her whirlwind, her rush...it was such a relief.

He opened his eyes again as she ended the call. This time, he didn't wait to be persuaded or cajoled. He got his hand on the grip of his crutch. Slow and hobbling, he crossed the bit of carpet to her door. She held it open for him, the full power of her grin still turned on him.

He soaked it in. And stepped right out into her deluge.

CHAPTER THREE

Cole?"

At the sound of his name, Cole looked up from his mobile to find a woman in teddy bear scrubs scanning the waiting room expectantly. About bloody time.

He and Serena had made it to the office with half an hour to spare, but it hadn't gotten them in any faster. One more minute of whatever ridiculous soap opera had been blaring away on the television and he'd have put his fist through the screen.

Worse, Serena had insisted on waiting with him. He didn't know what he'd been expecting. For her to have gone home, perhaps, or out for a cup of tea, since they'd left theirs sitting untouched in her flat in their hurry to leave. But no. She'd followed him in, getting doors and grating against every misgiving floating around in his heart. Sitting right next to him in an uncomfortable, pink, fake leather chair, her arm brushing his and the sweetness of her scent crowding him, setting him more on edge than the daytime television, even.

It was torture and perfection, heaven and hell, and he couldn't have gotten up out of his chair faster if he'd tried.

As he rose, something inside him unclenched. He didn't relish being poked and prodded by doctors, but at least it would be a respite. A moment away from this woman who'd forced her way into his space and his day and—it was starting to seem—his life.

So of course she followed him.

He stopped cold, and his voice was a barely restrained hiss. "This isn't necessary."

"It kind of is." She put a hand on his arm to keep him moving forward, leaning in close, and his thoughts spun. "I hate these waiting rooms. The awful TV." She dropped to a near-whisper, an exaggerated shudder shaking her frame. "And all the germs."

He swallowed his questions about why on earth she'd come in, then. What was the point? He felt the same, would've done the same.

The nurse gave them a tight smile as she showed them to an empty exam room. He sat on the table, leaving Serena one of the chairs, and recited off the particulars of his injury in response to the nurse's questions. When she was satisfied, the nurse closed her computer and opened a drawer to hand him a flimsy paper sheet. "The doc'll want to see your leg."

Of course he would.

"Naturally," he gritted out.

And then the nurse was leaving, closing the door behind her, and it was just him and this woman. And instructions for him to take his trousers off.

He swallowed hard, the back of his throat aching as he gripped the sheet, crinkling the scratchy fabric between his hands.

Color rose across her cheeks. "I can..."

"Just. I know it's silly, but..." He made a twirling motion with a finger in the air.

He couldn't be arsed about her seeing his legs, but he didn't need her gawking while he strained to unlace his bloody shoes.

"Right." Except she didn't turn around at all, just stared at him, and what if this were different? If he were baring himself for her for real. If she were going to *touch* him—

If he were allowed to touch her.

His reverie broke, shattering like so much glass. When he cleared his throat, the sound broke the air. She blinked, eyes wide, the flush on her pretty, pale skin deepening. She whirled around almost too fast.

He had to take a long, deep breath.

It was as much of a struggle getting his shoes off as it had been the day before, his leg painful and stiff, the brace unyielding. But he managed. They clunked against the tile, and then there was nothing but to untie the drawstring of the trousers he would never have worn outside his apartment, not in a million years, but he hadn't had a choice. He pushed the fabric off and away, staring down at his own naked legs until his vision threatened to dissolve.

He settled the sheet over his lap and worked his jaw. "You can look now."

And she did.

Heat bloomed through his body, an ancient pleasure humming just beneath his skin as her gaze took him in. Hungry, and God, fuck, but no one had looked at him like that in so long. He hadn't let them. He crushed the sheet in his fists, everything in him going tight.

It was too much.

"Oh." Her lashes fluttered. When they opened again, her eyes were clearer, and the iron bars around his ribs relaxed. She dropped her gaze and muttered, "Sorry."

"It's fine."

It was as far from fine as it could be.

If awkwardness were something you could drown in, Serena really, really should've brought a life jacket. Worse, it was basically all her fault. She'd been the one to insist on following him in here, and she was the one who'd frozen up when it was time for him to change. She should have left him alone for that part if nothing else, but it was as if her feet were bolted to the floor.

Even now, she kept glancing over at him. His legs were so long that the sheet only covered part of them. With his socks still on, it shouldn't have been sexy at all, but he had these lean, muscular calves, his skin faintly golden through the dusting of hair. The starchy, white drape only did so much to hide the shapes of strong thighs or the dark outline of what she was pretty sure were boxer briefs.

The black, boxy shape of the brace he wore around his knee.

A knock at the door had her jerking her gaze away from his legs.

Cole—that was the name they'd called in the lobby—sat up straighter. His voice came out strained when he called, "Come in."

The doctor was a woman, mid-fifties maybe. She shook Cole's hand and nodded at Serena before opening her laptop and scanning the screen. "So what do we have here?"

"Dislocated patella," Cole said.

The doctor went through the details of the injury with him, and Cole sighed. Huh. Maybe that was why he'd seemed so put upon when Serena had asked. He must have recited the story a hundred times by now. And yet as he told it again, he left out all the best parts, the robbers and his heroics, and she wanted to jump in. To make sure this doctor knew what kind of person she was treating.

Then again, maybe the fact that he didn't mention it spoke more to that than the story ever could.

"All right, then." The doctor stood and gestured at the sheet. "Let's see what we're dealing with."

Serena hadn't been wrong about the firm shapes of his thighs. As he hiked the fabric up, he revealed more of himself to her. The doctor undid the fastenings of the brace, and Cole sucked in a tight breath.

Serena let out one of her own. The whole area around his knee was flushed and angry, the joint swollen. A dark, purple bruise went green around the edges across the side of his leg, and his skin bore red lines from the constriction of the brace.

Whistling, the doctor leaned in to touch, and Cole's hands clenched into fists at the first hint of contact.

"Tender?"

"You could say that."

The doctor chuckled but kept going. When she was satisfied, she stepped back. "Believe it or not, the swelling is pretty much what I would expect at this stage. Keep up with the anti-inflammatories, and no weight on it for at least another few days. Maybe a week."

His shoulders stayed stiff as ever, his posture as closed, but the way his eyes shuttered and his head bowed belied that show of stoicism. "Then what?"

"Start playing with how much pressure you can tolerate. Do *not* push it. Until the soft tissue heals up, you're more likely to reinjure yourself. We'll see you back here in a couple of weeks."

"And until then there's *nothing* I can do?"

The doctor hesitated, maybe hearing the same low thread of desperation Serena did. "Well. There are some exercises to work on range of motion and preserve muscle mass, but I'd be very conservative this soon after the injury."

"Show me."

The stretches she walked him through were simple in the extreme, but even gently bending his knee made him wince. "That's plenty," she said, stepping away. Then she turned to Serena. "Are you his wife?"

And Serena would have missed it completely if she hadn't been looking at him at the time. The way his face, already drawn, flashed white, his hold on the edge of the table going punishing. "No," he said, like it were impossible, repulsive.

It stung. But she recovered quickly enough. Looking away, she even managed a smile. "Just a friend." Not even that, honestly.

Oblivious to the moment's drama, the doctor nodded. "It's your job to keep him from overexerting himself."

"I don't—" She started to protest. She wasn't his wife and she certainly wasn't his keeper.

He interrupted. "I can manage myself."

The doctor's skeptical glance showed just how much she thought of that. She looked to Serena again. "Watch him."

The weight of the responsibility settled over her shoulders like an old sweater, all frayed but worn in. Her mother had given her the same directive often enough, and who was she to refuse? She was the one who was well. She could handle it.

Weakly, she nodded. "I'll see what I can do."

"Great." She clicked at her touchpad a few times before closing the computer and tucking it under her arm. "Schedule a follow-up for a couple of weeks, and then we'll probably be ready to get you into physical therapy. Until then, take it easy. Heal. Doctor's orders."

Cole nodded, but it was all rippling, barely contained dissent in those broad shoulders of his. The doctor left, and Cole reached for the brace. He leaned forward to slip it over his foot and bit off a curse.

And Serena had half a mind to let him struggle, humiliated heat still bubbling away in her chest from his dismissal. But after another try and another fail, she stepped in, taking the thing from him.

"I can—"

She cut him off. "But you don't have to."

The brace was a heavy fabric tube, like a dive suit, reinforced with boning along the sides of an opening that seemed made to fit around his kneecap. She played with the Velcro straps meant to hold it secure around the joint before grasping it by the top. Ducking to hold it open by his foot, she paused, cocking a brow at him.

"May I?"

But he looked so sour about it all. "It's just the angle. I managed fine this morning."

Proud, proud, stubborn man. "Good for you." Then, again, she asked, "May I?"

He gave a curt nod. Together, they managed to get it onto his leg. His throat bobbed, his jaw going hard when she helped him drag it past his calf, over the angry shadow of that bruise. She muttered a quiet apology as she fastened the straps, pulling them tight across the wound.

"There." She smoothed the Velcro down.

And there wasn't any explaining it. The job was done, his brace in place. But she couldn't seem to step away. Couldn't take her hand back.

The skin of his thigh was smooth and warm, the muscle jumping as she traced her fingertips across it. A low hum of heat zipped down the center of her chest to settle lower in her belly, and her heart pounded behind her ribs.

Then his hand was on hers. Stilling it. She looked up into eyes so deep she could've fallen into them. Grasping her palm, he stroked her knuckles with his thumb, gaze darkening, breath halting.

He blinked. When he looked to her again, it was with a ragged inhalation. The haze in his eyes bled away, leaving behind something she could only categorize as pain.

He pushed her away.

She didn't hesitate this time to turn around when he reached for his pants. Arms crossed over her chest, indignation and anger and embarrassment all twisting together in her lungs, she waited until she heard the clinking of his crutches. She avoided his gaze as she helped him get his shoes. Once he had his crutches under him, she moved toward the door, only to feel the warm grasp of his palm around her wrist.

She waited, heart thundering.

Low and quiet, he said simply, "Thank you."

And she didn't know what she'd been expecting, but those two words—they were exactly what she'd wanted and a crushing disappointment all at once.

"You're welcome." She tugged her arm away and headed for the door. As she waited for him to cross the space, she checked the time on her phone. Damn. "Come on," she said, ushering him out. "We're going to be late."

CHAPTER FOUR

It probably said a lot about Cole's day that the best thing to happen to him in it so far was being allowed to wait in a car.

It wasn't even a particularly nice car. Ten years old if it was a day, rattly and rusting on the outside, though at least the interior was clean. He shifted, trying to get comfortable, but it wasn't much use. He'd already slid the seat back as far as it would go, and he still had to hold his blasted leg at this precarious angle if he wanted to keep it straight.

He took a deep breath. Everything would be fine. Serena would return with the tiny human he was supposed to make nice with and train to do tricks, and then she'd take him home. Back to the silence that sometimes threatened to suffocate him but that he'd give just about anything for right now.

Silence and solitude. No doctors belittling him or women railroading him. No one touching him. Placing the softest of hands on the bare flesh of his thigh, setting off sparks beneath his skin, making *him* reach out. God, she'd felt so good inside his grasp.

It'd been the most fleeting moment of contact, and yet his flesh burned hot at the very memory.

He should've shut it down much sooner.

Rapping his knuckles against the window, he stared off into the distance at the field they were parked in front of. Children of all sizes stood around, some of them tossing balls back and forth, and his throat went tight.

If she'd told him her nephew was an athlete from the outset, he could've avoided this whole ridiculous excuse of a farce.

He squeezed his eyes shut hard against the flash of a boy twice his size standing over him. A rugby player, that one, though all the imbeciles from the clubs were the same. Muscle-headed tormentors, and he'd been easy pickings then. Too small and too smart and entirely too keen on making certain everybody knew it.

Already incapable of walking away from a fight.

He rubbed at the jagged line across his upper lip and exhaled long and low. The hundred agitations of the day had his blood up, but he could keep it under control. He could come across as civilized for however long this took, no matter what this child looked like or how he acted—

His eyes snapped open at the sound of the car door opening. Serena slid into the driver's seat, mid-conversation with the boy currently getting in behind her.

And Cole's breath got stuck in the back of his throat.

This wasn't the hooligan he'd been imagining, wasn't one of the bullies who still plagued his nervous, sweating dreams some nights. It was a boy. Clear green eyes the same shade as Serena's staring out at him from behind Coke-bottle glasses, the thick plastic frames resting on ears that stuck out just a little too far from a narrow head. Pale skin and freckles and braces, blond hair with a fringe that was a hint too long.

The blooming blush of what would be one hell of a bruise on his arm.

Forget Cole's blood being up. It sang in his veins, memories of impact playing out across his ribs, of being down on the ground, his glasses shattered on the pavement, and his vision went red.

"What. Happened."

Whatever Serena had been saying cut off abruptly, her head whipping around. The boy's eyes went wide, and that was fear there. Fear Cole knew entirely too well.

Serena followed Cole's gaze, then scowled. "Max. You're supposed to keep ice on that thing."

Max looked away, reaching for an ice pack Cole hadn't seen and holding it to his arm.

"It's nothing," Serena said. "Just a new pitcher throwing a little wild."

But Cole watched the boy's face. The way his skin pinkened and his mouth went tight. "Is that so?"

Max nodded, but he wouldn't meet Cole's eyes.

"Come on." Serena put the keys in the ignition. "Buckle up, or your grandma's going to blame me for getting you home late for dinner."

Cole kept watching the boy as he did as he was told. Serena put the car into gear and backed them out of their space. As she turned to check over her shoulder, she caught Cole's gaze. Her brows furrowed.

"What?" she asked.

"Nothing." Cole drew out the word. He twisted to sit facing forward again, cracking his knuckles in front of him.

A wild pitch, his arse. Even if the story wasn't a complete fabrication, the throw had been intentional. And Max was pretending it hadn't been.

Cole's lungs pressed hot against his rib cage, the violence that lived in his bones changing and shifting. Howling to be let out.

It was all he could do just to keep it in.

Silence hung heavily in the air of the car as Serena steered them through the nightmare of minivans clogging the exit to the parking lot. She checked the rearview mirror before casting a glance at Cole and easing over a lane.

"Cole," she said, "this is my nephew, Max."

He released his breath and his grip on the seat. He could pretend to be under control. Twisting in his seat, he extended his hand toward the boy. "A pleasure to meet you."

Max nodded and dropped the ice pack long enough to return the gesture, frigid fingers clasping Cole's palm with a surprising grip. He looked up, not the meek child he'd been a second ago, but one with challenge in his eyes.

He knew that Cole knew, and he wanted to know what Cole would do about it.

Cole stared at him steadily, giving his answer. Nothing. Not yet. Letting out a sigh of relief, Max pulled his hand away.

Serena smiled, utterly oblivious to the conversation they'd carried out in gestures and looks. "Cole's offered to help us out, Max. He's going to be your new tutor."

Max's focus shifted in an instant. "Aunt Rena!"

"Uh-uh. This car is a no-whining zone. I've given you plenty of time to find one on your own."

"But—"

"Do you want to go to Upton next year or not?"

Sulkily, Max redirected his glare out the window. "Yeah."

"Then we need to get those math scores up. Just a couple of afternoons a week, right, Cole?"

But Cole was distracted. He'd idolized going off to university when he was Max's age, probably for the same sorts of reasons. He would've done anything for the chance to change schools right then and there.

And now he'd do anything to help this boy have the chance he hadn't. To avoid what had happened to him...

"Cole?" Serena said again, prompting him.

"Yes." The affirmation came out too strong, his throat rough with the weight of it all. "Yes, of course." He managed a tight smile, his lips scarcely remembering how.

Her shoulders more relaxed after his agreement, Serena started negotiating schedules, but it wasn't anything he had to pay much mind to. His weekly pilgrimages aside, he was at his leisure, nothing but time.

And now this boy. This woman. This circling tide of memories. Of chances that maybe, for once, he could make right.

It was some kind of minor miracle that Serena found a parking spot right outside their apartment building. She'd dropped Max off at her mom's already, declining the typical invitation to stay for dinner for once in favor of getting home. She glanced over at the man in the passenger seat and sighed.

He better appreciate her giving up her mom's meat loaf for him.

Checking her mirrors, she managed to parallel park with only a little bit of curb-scraping, then turned the engine off.

"Well. Here we are." She mentally shook her head at her own nattering.

"Indeed."

To his credit, he only put up token protests when she insisted on giving him a hand pulling his crutches out of the car. Holding the door to their building for him and pacing him on the stairs.

As they passed her door, he shook his head. "I can manage..."

"I never said you couldn't." But she kept going with him all the same.

By the time they reached the second floor, a fine sheen of sweat had broken out around his temples, making the dark tangle of his hair look black in the dim hall light. His jaw clenched, the point of it hard beneath the cover of his stubble, and the muscles in his shoulders bulged. She licked her lips before she made herself look away.

She was doing him a favor here, was all. Being neighborly and being nice. She'd help anyone in his situation, attractiveness aside.

But she wasn't sure she'd have quite the same buzzing under her skin as she did. The same temptation to reach out a hand toward his arm to steady him.

In the end, she couldn't resist.

If anything, his biceps tensed harder as her palm settled on that warm muscle through the fabric of his shirt. Her heart pounded. But he didn't push her off. Just mashed his lips together and kept his gaze directed straight ahead.

At the top of the stairs, she was perfectly prepared for a polite dismissal. She pulled her hand away and stepped aside. A low shiver worked its way along his spine, and he turned to look at her, the full power of those dark, piercing eyes pressing down on her, making her breathing speed.

"Would you like to come in?"

She boggled, blinking hard, snapped from her reverie. If it was possible, he seemed as surprised by his invitation as she was. The lines around his mouth pinched, lips parting as if to say something else. To take it back, perhaps, but after a silent moment, he squared his jaw, looking to her in expectation. Challenging.

She probably would've said yes regardless, too curious about this man to miss the opportunity, but the dare in his eyes was what clinched it.

"Sure. For a minute."

With a sharp nod, he turned his head and advanced on the door. He got it unlocked and pushed it open, holding out his crutch as an extension of his arm, motioning for her to go first.

It was dark within, only thin gaps in thick curtains allowing any of the twilight glow from beyond the windows to seep in. She took a bare handful of steps, afraid to bump into anything or trip. Closing the door behind himself, he turned, and then his whole body was coming into contact with hers, hot and hard against her spine, and her breathing sped, while his seemed to stop. The wet sound of his throat swallowing echoed in her ears, so close, and she shut her eyes, tempted to lean back into him.

But then there was rustling, the hollow sweep of a hand across plaster. The metallic *thunk* of his crutch tumbling to the floor and a click.

And all at once, the place flooded with light. Warm brilliance bloomed from behind her lids, and she snapped her eyes open, suddenly aware of herself again. Of the awkwardness of how they were standing, pressed together like this. She sprang forward, and he swayed, like he'd been leaning into her, too.

Or maybe like he'd dropped his crutch in his hurry to get the light.

"Oh." She scrambled, embarrassed heat spreading over her cheeks. She dipped to pick up his crutch. It left her still too close to him, and her face was even with his hips now, and—

A strangled sound erupted from his throat, making her face flare even hotter. God. Could she make any more of a fool of herself? Practically coming on to him in his doctor's office, and now this? What was she thinking?

"Sorry, sorry." She got his crutch and stood, too fast, looking everywhere except at him as she passed it back to him.

But then his hand brushed hers as he accepted it, long fingers overlapping her knuckles. Stilling her.

"Serena."

His voice was rough and low, and her name sounded way too good in it. She jerked her gaze to meet his. His eyes had gone even darker, and his Adam's apple bobbed, and she stopped.

Maybe she hadn't made such a fool of herself after all.

This was insane. She'd only just met this man, and he was hot and cold in turns. He didn't meet any of the many, many standards she'd set for if she ever did get around to dating again. But there was something in his gaze and in his tone, in the way his body *did things* to hers.

His fingers flexed, his lungs expanding, rib cage so close to grazing the points of her breasts.

Then, so slowly, with what seemed like painstaking control, he let her go.

The spell broke, and she stumbled backward. The instinct to apologize rose in her throat, but she'd already said she was sorry once. Besides, he'd been the one to touch her.

He took a deep breath and let it out with what seemed like staggering control. All sharp efficiency, he turned away, gait uneven as he got his crutch back under him and lurched toward the kitchen. Calling over his shoulder, he asked, "Tea?"

For a second, she gawked. "Excuse me?"

"We never got to have ours earlier." Now that he was saying more than one word, the shakiness to his voice shone through. "I can make some. Proper tea," he added.

Working to get her footing again, she nodded. "Right. Yes. Please."

She raked a hand through her hair. Maybe she should be offering to help. The rubber tips of his crutches made thudding noises against his kitchen tile as he got the water going, and it couldn't be easy, managing a kettle and keeping all his weight on one leg. But her brain was still buzzing, her hands trembling and heart thundering. She wanted to laugh. Chances were, she wouldn't manage to make the tea *properly*, anyway.

Taking the minute to herself, she hugged her arms across her chest. Now that he wasn't so close to her, she could think again. Could process and see.

And part of the appeal of coming in had been the chance to get a look around.

The floorboards creaked as she moved beyond the cramped little entryway where she had stopped on their way in. The place was...white, mostly. Stark, unpainted walls, entirely bare. Except for—

"Oh." One entire wall of his living room was floor-to-ceiling shelves, crammed nearly to the point of bursting. She lost her hesitancy, the English major in her drawn like a magpie toward those soft leather spines. Pitching her voice over her shoulder, she asked, "Did you raid an entire library or something?"

A low chuckle rang out from behind her. Had she ever heard him laugh before? "Too many degrees will do that to you."

He wasn't kidding. She uncrossed her arms to reach toward one of the rows of books, sliding a fingertip along the tops of them. The titles ran the gamut from calculus to field theory, and just trying to read some of them threatened to give her hives.

Her brows drew together as she moved on to the next shelf, though. Volumes of history and poetry took over where the mathematics texts left off. They weren't coffee table books, either. She tugged at the spine of one about the Napoleonic wars and opened it to find too-dense type staring back at her, notes scrawled in the margins in a delicate hand. "What on earth did you get all those degrees in?"

China clinked from the next room over, a bitten-off curse chasing it, followed by a heavy beat of silence. Oh hell, she'd probably overstepped again.

But then his answer came, just loud enough to carry. "Not all of them were mine."

Oh. Her heart gave a little flutter, and she shut the volume before easing it back into place. "Right."

She surveyed the rest of the shelves without comment, a picture beginning to form in her mind, but it wasn't one she knew how to put into words. The academic texts transitioned to lighter fare, novels, science fiction mingling with romances and classics. Hemingway and Austen and the Brontës. Finally, she turned away, her gaze sliding over a plain brown leather couch, half covered in books and papers. A pair of folded reading glasses perched atop a sleek, modern laptop.

And there, through the open doorway into the kitchen, Cole.

What the bloody hell did Cole think he was doing? He'd endured this woman's meddling all afternoon because it had been the simplest way to get to his appointment. Because she was beautiful and interesting, and if there was anything he couldn't seem to resist, it was the chance to get himself burned.

But it had all been with the knowledge that he'd be able to retreat. To return to the sanctuary of his home, to be alone.

Until he'd asked her in.

He stood there, fist clenched around the handle of the teapot his brother-in-law, Barry, had given them nearly a decade ago, gaze locked with Serena's from across the length of his apartment. She was touching Helen's books, was standing in this space where he never invited anyone, and he could scarcely breathe.

He wanted to cross the room to her and pick her up in his arms. Feel her body pressed to his the way he had by accident twice now, but with purpose this time. Wanted to taste the sweetness of those full, pink lips and get his hands beneath that maddening skirt, wanted to *have* her. It had been so long.

He wanted to be *able* to do that. To throw these infernal crutches away and stand tall on his own. Self-sufficient and independent, needing no one and nothing.

He wanted her to leave.

Ribs creaking with the force of his exhalation, he set the teapot down before he shattered it.

Tea. He could focus on tea.

Blanking his mind to everything else, he managed to get the little tin of Earl Grey from the cupboard without losing his balance or dropping a crutch. By the time he'd scooped the leaves into the strainer in the pot, the kettle had started to rattle. He busied himself with getting down saucers and cups.

And nearly dropped one when Serena was suddenly there, leaning against the counter, too close and not close enough, and his focus was shot. It'd been shot since he'd fucked everything up with his knee, since he'd met her. Maybe since years and years before.

Then she moved closer, and his bones trembled. "That's a pretty pot."

"Thank you," he said, all sharpness. "It was a gift."

"May I?"

He nodded, and she reached past him, arm brushing his side. With nearly the amount of care he himself tried to take, she lifted it by the handle, tilting it as she examined the spout. Raised it higher to inspect the bottom without spilling the leaves.

"Hand thrown." She set it back down.

"Oh?"

"You can tell from the signature. And from the gesture marks. The ridges on the inside." She shrugged. "I used to dabble in ceramics."

Maybe more than dabbling, based on how she talked about it.

And it was so banal, wasn't it? Having this sort of idle conversation as they waited for the water to boil. So *normal*. So far beyond his experience it ached. Like a muscle he hadn't had occasion to really work in too long.

He struggled to follow the thread of it all the same. "Used to?"

"Haven't had time to take a class in ages. There's just so much going on, you know?"

He didn't. He hadn't the slightest hint of a clue.

The bewilderment in his expression must have shown, because she faltered. "Just...work and looking after Max, and I do some volunteer stuff, too."

"Of course." So she was one of those. He should've figured. Always running around, always busy. It exhausted him just thinking about it.

And yet he'd been one of them, too, back ages ago. Before he'd cocked it all up. And now he was here, puttering, playing with equations and writing papers that no one would ever read. *Useless.*

The bubbling in the kettle rose to a higher pitch, the first piercing cry of the whistle blaring. Relieved for the distraction, he flipped the heat off, then reached for a mitt to pour.

Serena waved him off. "I can do this part. Unless there's some secret to it?"

He shook his head and stepped aside. While she dealt with the water, he looked around the barren expanse of his kitchen. She'd offered him biscuits that afternoon, but he had nothing of the sort. Only—

"Cake," he said, and his throat threatened to close.

She set the kettle back on the burner, brows drawing together. "Excuse me?"

"I have cake. If you'd like some." Neither of them had had supper, so she'd probably decline. Everything would be fine.

Except a soft, perfect smile stole over her lips. "I have never in my life said no to cake."

Right. He turned toward the fridge where he had stowed it for the sake of the icing, hobbling his way over there and hauling the door open with one hand but then stopping, a fresh wave of cursing ringing out in his head.

And it burned, but there wasn't any real way around it. "I can't..."

"I've got it." She reached in for the platter, balancing it with two hands the way he couldn't right now and taking it over to the sad little table by the window. She gestured with her head toward the chair already pulled out. "Here, sit."

He should've protested. Should've tried to at least do what he could. But a sudden wave of exhaustion crashed over him, the throbbing of his knee joining a growing ache behind his eyes and in his heart. He fell into the chair with a heavy thud, and it was only her presence that had him stacking his crutches against the edge of the table instead of hurling them to the ground.

"Wait. Is this..." She trailed off, staring at the candle he'd left in the center of the cake. Black wick burned down to the barest hint of a nub, wax frozen down the side mid-drip. "Was it your birthday?"

"No." Jagged glass littered his mouth, grated his larynx, and sliced ribbons from his lungs.

"Then why—"

"It was my wife's."

He stared at the candle. The one he'd snuffed out with his breath. With his own bloody hands. And then at this woman and her golden hair and her kind, pitying eyes.

His knee screamed at him as he shoved the chair back. He rose to his feet regardless, pitched with all his weight to one side, and his face flashed cold, but his chest was a mass of fire and ancient, impossible regret.

He couldn't do this.

"Cole—" She edged away from him. Good. She should. Eyes wide, pupils blank, she stared at him.

"I think it's time for you to leave."

CHAPTER FIVE

Hey." Serena's mom peeked her head out of the fridge where she'd been stowing some leftovers for Serena from dinner the night before. "Whatever happened to that tutor Max said you found for him?"

Serena sighed under her breath, stealing a glance at Max, who was packing his schoolbag. He'd spent the afternoon with her the way he did most days when he didn't have Little League and she didn't have any after-school meetings or clubs to supervise. Serena's mom was just stopping in for a minute on her way through to pick him up. And of course she would have to ask about that.

What had Serena been thinking, introducing Cole and Max so quickly? It had only been a few minutes' interaction, but it had apparently made quite the impression on her nephew. He'd gone from being reluctant about the whole tutoring thing to asking about it every time he saw Serena, and now he'd started bringing it up to her mother, too.

"I don't know," Serena said, hedging. Nearly a week had passed since he'd kicked her out of his apartment. All she'd done was ask him about the birthday cake that *he* had offered *her*.

The birthday cake for his *wife*.

And it wasn't even as if she hadn't seen that one coming. No way that entire book collection had all been his. Clearly, at some point, there had been a woman in his life, and it was even more clear that there wasn't one anymore. He hadn't worn a ring, and there hadn't been so much as a hint of a woman's touch to anything else in that apartment.

She hadn't anticipated the way just mentioning her would make him shut down, though. Whether she'd died or divorced him, there was a no-go zone about a mile wide around the entire subject. A wound that hadn't even begun to heal.

And here Serena had thought they'd had a moment.

Her mom frowned. "I thought you wanted him to work with someone before he took that entrance exam."

"I do." She'd stopped by Upton the other day to pick up a fresh study guide and to drop off some cookies for the secretaries—store-bought but no one needed to know that. She was going to get Max into that school, come hell or high water.

Even if it meant swallowing her pride.

Serena made up her mind. "I'll ask him about it. Today."

"All right." Her mom didn't exactly sound confident.

In the other room, Max made a show of zipping his bag. "Okay! I'm ready."

Serena met him at the door, ducking down to go through their ritual. A secret handshake and a giant hug that stole the breath from her. "See you tomorrow, tiger."

When she let him go, he flipped the lock and started bounding down the stairs.

"Wait for me at the mailboxes," her mother called after him.

"I know!"

Her mom held up in the doorway, turning back to her and lowering her voice. "I didn't want to ask in front of him, but have you talked to your sister recently?"

Serena's stomach sank to her toes. "No." But they only talked every now and then, anyway. "Is something wrong?"

"I don't know. She's just been sounding...unhappy."

Serena couldn't remember a time she did seem happy. Still, if it was enough to have her mother concerned..."What are we talking about here? Full red alert?"

They hadn't had one of those in ages, and Serena had been this close to relaxing, to believing that they'd finally gotten past that kind of thing. But the longer the good patches lasted, the more uneasy she felt. Getting complacent usually meant it was time for everything to go wrong.

Her mom shook her head. "No, nothing like that. Just...if you do talk to her..."

Serena sighed. "I'll see if I can't get the scoop."

"You're an angel." She rose onto her toes to plant a kiss to Serena's forehead.

Serena closed her eyes and soaked it in.

They said their goodbyes before Max could get too restless downstairs and make a break for it. As Serena closed the door behind her mother, she surveyed her apartment, tempted to get to work tidying the mess Max had left. Or sorting out tomorrow's lesson plan, or figuring out her volunteer schedule for the rest of the month or checking her e-mail or...well...anything, basically.

But she'd promised her mom. She'd promised Max, effectively. *Cole* had promised Max, and no matter how much he'd upset her, nobody got away with disappointing her kid.

Besides, for all that she'd been avoiding him this past week, there was this part of her that wanted more than anything to see him. Sure, he was moody and standoffish and cursed like a sailor. But he was also gorgeous and smart, and even the accidental touches they'd shared had fired off sparks. Whether or not it led anywhere, that had to be worth at least seeing the man again.

Decided, she nodded to herself and grabbed her keys.

Still, at the top of the stairs, she hesitated. She stood in front of Cole's door, staring at the number to his apartment until the twisting mess of anticipation and dread in her belly began to squirm. Ugh, this was ridiculous. Put up or shut up. Rolling her eyes at herself, she balled her hand in a fist and knocked.

Only to be met by the muted sound of yet more creative swear words from within. The clatter that followed them was a little more ominous, but presently the thumping sounds of crutches on hardwood carried toward her. She took a single step back as the labored footfalls approached the door, folding her hands in front of herself and adopting the most neutral expression she could manage.

He let her stand there like that for what felt like forever. She gazed right into the peephole, cocking one brow. God, his avoidance issues were even worse than hers.

"I know you're there," she called out. "I could hear your crutches."

A dull thud of an impact echoed through the door, and she

swallowed a chuckle, imagining him banging his head against the wood. The lock released with a metal-on-metal click, and then he was shuffling backward as he pulled the door open.

Serena frowned. He...looked like hell, honestly. Deep bruises of exhaustion shadowed his eyes, and his hair was mussed, his face pale. The same loose sweats he'd been wearing the last time she'd seen him hung off his hip bones, and—

Oh, Jesus. She all but swallowed her tongue, any thoughts she might've had rolling around in her head fading to a hissing, popping sort of static.

He wasn't wearing a shirt.

How the heck she'd managed to notice his eyes or his hair or his anything else was a mystery for the ages. Miles of smooth skin stared back at her, the dips and ridges of abdominals and pectorals. Deep black, rolling lines of ink set into perfectly toned flesh, and her mouth went dry with the embarrassment of riches laid out before her. She had to squeeze her own hands, biting her nails into her palms against the impulse to reach out. To touch.

He cleared his throat, and her gaze shot back to his face. Tired though they were, his eyes were sharp. The hard muscles of his arms and shoulders tightened, his knuckles white on the handles of his crutches.

"Well?"

Well. She'd come here for a reason, hadn't she? One beyond trying to read the band of letters and symbols around his biceps, mapping the nautical star across his heart or the lines that curved beneath his ribs.

"Um..."

"Yes?" And there was an edge of irritation to his voice now.

It helped to pierce the haze that had fogged her thoughts. A little. Enough. Shaking her head, she blinked a couple of times.

Focus.

"Hi," she said, and she still sounded like an idiot, but at least she was an idiot making actual words with her mouth.

A ghost of a smile teased at his lips, highlighting the pale line of his scar. Making the faintest hints of dimples show through the stubble on his cheeks. "Hello."

She dug her nails into the heels of her hands even harder. "I...um...I came here because..." Why was she here? Oh! Right. "Tutoring."

His brows rose on his forehead. "Yes?"

"My nephew. Max." She might be managing words, but sentences were another thing entirely. She both wished he'd go put on a shirt already and prayed he never, ever would. "You promised you'd help him. With math."

His spine straightened at that, and even with her brain cells scrambled, a part of her reared up, too. Braced and ready for a fight.

But instead of issuing a sharp remark, he sighed. "So I did."

The ready agreement almost shocked the words right back out of her. But she rallied, somehow. "Great." She opened her mouth, prepared to start rattling off their schedules, but before she could, he interrupted.

"How's tomorrow afternoon? Three-thirty?"

"That's..." She snapped her jaw shut. "Perfect, actually."

"Brilliant." He flashed her a tight smile.

And without another word, he closed the door in her face.

* * *

The next day at 3:25, Cole stood at the door to his apartment, jaw clenched, crutches propped against the wall. On so many levels, he didn't know what the fuck he thought he was doing. But there was nothing else for it. Sucking in a breath, he shifted just ever so slightly forward.

The first tentative fraction of his weight he put on his bad leg was only a dull pang, so he gave it some more. Edged forward, more and more. Until—

"Cocksucking son of a goat fucker with *leprosy*."

A sharp jolt shot all the way up his leg, and he listed sideways, barely catching himself against the wall. The coppery tang of blood seeped into his mouth. He sagged, catching his breath and closing his eyes.

Apparently, a full step without his crutches was still a little ways off.

His doctor had told him it'd be a week, at least, and he'd let that week pass, suffering it and the claustrophobia and the weight of his indolence in silence. So much silence, pressing in on his ribs and lungs, and he'd never minded it before.

He did now, though.

Opening his eyes again, he reached for his crutches and got them settled under his arms. The test hadn't been a complete waste at least. Bracing himself, he leaned hard into his hands as he took his first supported step forward.

It still drove the breath from his body to put even that much of his weight on his knee, but it was bearable. He crossed a few more feet of floor, slow and aching. It would do.

Grabbing the bag he'd set down by the door, he rearranged his crutches to get the strap slung across his chest. With a deep breath, he threw the door open, and even the sight of the dingy hallway was its own kind of relief.

It was the first time he'd left his apartment in a week.

For a moment, he breathed in the air beyond his four little walls. A hysterical echo of a laugh bubbled up in his lungs. All those years he'd spent locked away in there of his own volition, and now that his movements were restricted, leaving it felt like escaping from a prison. Like freedom.

Like descending down into his own little bowel of hell.

He tightened his grip on the handles of his crutches.

He'd almost started to think Serena had forgotten him. The first day they'd met, she had shoved her way into his life, and he'd invited her to help herself to even more. Right until the moment it had all become too much. Overwhelmed, unable to breathe, haunted by another woman's voice and another moment when he'd lost himself, lost the thread of his control...

His chuckle this time tore at his throat, a dark and ugly sound. He'd asked Serena to leave, never expecting her to return. But she had. She'd come to him and reminded him of what he'd promised.

He'd thought of the boy in her charge and the challenge in his eyes. Of his own reflection staring back at him in a mirror, lip bleeding, knuckles bruised, the memory of how it had all happened in a blur.

He'd remembered the warmth of Serena's hand on his skin.

Pulse pounding, he closed the door behind himself.

The trek down the stairs pulled at his shoulders nearly as

badly as it had the last time, though at least it was easier to keep his balance now. Two long flights, and when he finally alit on the landing outside Serena's door, he drew in a long, shuddering breath. He gave himself to the count of ten to get his bearings. Then, before he could talk himself out of it, he knocked on her door.

The person who answered it wasn't Serena.

"Hello," Cole said, drawing back.

"Aunt Rena. Mr. Cole's here." Max looked back over his shoulder into the apartment.

Serena's voice floated out to them. "Well, don't just leave him standing there."

Apparently, that was the signal the boy had been waiting for. He opened the door wide, abandoning it to scamper back inside. Cole peeked around the edge of the frame before hobbling in.

Nothing about the place had changed in the past week, except that a small hurricane might have torn through the middle of the living room. Standing from where she must've been kneeling on the floor, Serena pushed the soft, golden strands of her hair back from her face and turned to him with a sheepish smile. "Sorry for the mess. Ten-year-olds, you know?"

Cole didn't, but he nodded all the same. "Not a problem."

"Max, what do you say we move this operation to the kitchen?"

"Okay." Max grabbed a book and a pencil from the pile of detritus around her coffee table, only to be yanked right back. He accepted the additional packet of papers Serena pressed into his hands before heading off toward the kitchen.

She shook her head at his retreating back, but it was all fondness. "Wouldn't remember his head if it wasn't attached." She looked up, and her gaze met Cole's.

And they were still the whole length of the room away from each other, but the distance stretched and then yawned and then snapped, and heat shivered through his bones.

One afternoon. He'd spent all of one afternoon with this woman before avoiding her for a week, and just seeing her made it feel like something in his chest clicking back into place. The intensity of it staggered him, almost too much again and not nearly enough. He could have drowned in the mere sight of her for days.

Or for a bare handful of minutes. The moment broke, shivering to the floor with the call of, "Aunt Rena?"

Serena's gaze darted away, her chest heaving like she, too, were taking the first full breath she'd had in a while. "Yes, sweetie?"

"Does Mr. Cole want a snack?"

She laughed. "Is that your way of asking if you can have one?"

"No..."

Even Cole could see through that one.

She flashed him a grimacing grin. "I'd better feed the monkey before he stops being subtle. I bought some cupcakes—"

Cole stopped her before she could reach the kitchen, tucking his crutch beneath his arm as he reached out. He wrapped his hand around her wrist, and the warmth soaked through his skin.

As if burned, he let her go. Patting at his side, he fumbled with the strap of his bag until he could get at the flap and wrench it open. He dug around inside and came up with a Ziploc bag. "Here." He passed it over.

She stared at the bag like it held worms. "What—"

"Brownies." He cleared his throat, mouth suddenly dry. "Homemade."

Foolish. Nothing she'd needed, and yet he'd been so overcome last night. So guilty and sick with his own behavior.

So lost, with nothing to do.

She jerked her head up, eyes narrowed, brows skewed. "You *bake*?"

He forced his shoulders down. He didn't need to get defensive about this.

"It's a hobby." It was chemistry, was what it was, numbers and measurements and the proper things added at the proper times. And it had always made Helen smile.

"So it is." The lines on Serena's forehead didn't smooth out at all, but she shrugged, taking his offering with her into the kitchen. "Hey, Max, look what Cole brought you."

Max's eyes went wide behind his glasses. "Dude."

As she busied herself pulling plates down from the cabinet and pouring glasses of milk, Cole hovered in the doorway, surveying the scene.

It was...nice. Domestic and warm, and he felt suddenly, terribly out of place.

Until Serena turned to him, one hand extended toward the table. Toward a plate and a full glass of milk and a chair already pulled out in welcome. For him.

And an empty place inside his heart squeezed down so hard it hurt.

Her expression faltered. "Did you not want...I can make tea, or..."

"No," he got out, almost choking on it. "No. It's perfect."

* * *

Serena was trying not to hover. While still, you know, hovering.

Cole and Max were sitting kitty-corner to each other at the little table tucked against the wall in her kitchen, eating their brownies and drinking their milk. She wrapped a brownie in a napkin for herself, grabbing it and another glass of milk and edging toward the doorway.

"Max, sweetie, why don't you show Mr. Cole your study guide?"

He dug it out from the pile she'd sent him into the kitchen with, smudging the cover with chocolate, and she tried not to wince. Cole took it and started flipping through the pages, expression even. After a moment, he set it down decisively. "Let's start from the beginning, then, shall we?"

She gave him some credit. For all that he'd protested the idea of working with a kid, he was approaching it like a natural, talking to Max as if he were a grown-up. No dumbing things down. And no swearing, either—at least so far.

Keeping her ears half open, she retreated to the living room, settling in on the end of the couch where she could still see them without being in their way. The deep timber of Cole's voice floated on the air, the lilting quality to his accent lulling her. She wanted to wrap it around herself like a warm blanket. Could just picture a world where he sat around her apartment reading to her—or heck, explaining fifth-grade math.

Content with the fact that they seemed to have things more or less in hand, Serena pulled out her bag and the pile of essays she still had to grade and got to work.

She was on the sixth one when Max let out one of his more aggravated groans. Sitting straighter, she glanced up. Max was a good kid, smart and hardworking and destined for big things. But he could also get cranky in the afternoon, and if he was already getting frustrated...

"No, no, see," Cole interrupted, leaning forward and plucking a pencil right out of Max's hand. "There's a trick to these."

He launched into something even she wasn't completely sure she understood, scribbling as he went and pointing at the study guide.

And for a second, all she could do was blink and stare.

Gone were the sullen expression and the perpetual scowl. The man's whole demeanor came alive, eyes sparkling and voice rising. Because he was excited about reducing fractions.

"Oh!" Max threw his hands in the air. "Why don't they just teach it that way in the first place?" With that, he stole his pencil right back and bent his head to the page in front of him.

Letting out a breath, Serena sagged into the couch. Without really meaning to, she'd found herself on high alert, all ready to step in and intervene. She hadn't needed to, though. Cole had been entirely in control. He'd been amazing, was what he'd been.

As if he could feel her gaze on him, the wonder with which she beheld him, he turned his head, keen eyes focusing on hers. When he grinned, it just about took her breath away.

It could've been seconds or minutes or years that passed like that, their gazes locked across the entire breadth of her apartment. The moment held until Max lifted his head from his work and turned the page around. "Like that?"

Cole startled, maybe as lost as she had been. In an exaggerated movement, he widened his eyes and gave his head a little shake. He refocused on Max, studying his paper for half a second before nodding. "Yes. Brilliant."

Serena's pulse fluttered as she returned her own gaze to her lap and the pile of essays there. The weight of Cole's stare was burned into her, a warmth swimming through her veins, making it hard to think about anything beyond it. But somehow she managed.

Still, when her phone chirped an hour later, the air in the place carried a near-physical charge. A humming static that had her fumbling with the buttons. She stared at the screen in confusion, surprised to see so much time had passed.

"Max." Her voice came out rasping and rough, and she coughed into her hand as if the state of her lungs had anything to do with it. "Your grandma's on her way. Time to get cleaned up."

She rose from her seat as he finished one last problem and beamed with pride at Cole's approval of his solution. Cole held out a hand for him to shake. "Well done, sir."

Of course Max ate that up. He accepted the handshake and bowed to boot. If Cole wasn't careful, the kid would be asking to be knighted by the time they got to the end of the prep book. Leaning against the fridge, Serena shooed him to go wash his hands.

Cole sat back, one eyebrow raised as he directed his gaze at her.

She waited until Max was out of sight. "You were really good with him. I think he learned more in the last hour than he has in the last year."

"He's a bright boy."

"You're a good teacher."

He laughed, shaking his head, but there was something freer to him than there usually was. "Tell that to my linear algebra students."

At the mention of his old career, the first hint of a shadow returned to his eyes.

She shrugged, shifting her weight. Treading with care. "I bet they learned a lot from you, whether or not they liked the class."

"Doubtful. Teaching was fine. I enjoyed it. But I didn't have the temperament for it. The patience." He fiddled with Max's discarded pencil, twirling it absently between his fingers. "Research was more my speed. You could publish a paper and teach the world about what you were doing without that pesky interacting-with-people thing."

Serena frowned. She appreciated his recognition that teaching required a certain amount of skill, but he'd shown plenty of patience this afternoon. "Well. Your temperament just now seemed fine."

"Lucky you caught me on a good day, then," he said.

Before she could push him any further, Max returned, and the next few minutes were a flurry of chaos as he struggled to cram the contents of his schoolbag that had apparently exploded all over her apartment back in. Her mom wasn't stopping in that day, so Serena watched for her car out the window. When she pulled up, Serena paced him through their usual goodbye, made him thank Cole again, and sent him on his way.

As the door closed behind him, she sank down into the couch. She loved that she got to see her nephew most days, and with Cole doing the heavy lifting, this afternoon had been easier than most. But she'd been on her feet and dealing with preteens of one sort or another since seven that morning, and the last of her reserves was just about done.

Letting her head loll against the cushions, she spied the brownie she'd grabbed for herself but never gotten around to eating. Cole hadn't budged from his seat at her table yet, though he'd scooted his chair around and grabbed his crutches, looking more or less ready to stage his escape. She held up the brownie before bringing it to her mouth. "So you make these from scratch, you said?"

It failed to quite match the image of him she had in her mind, but he nodded in confirmation. Max certainly hadn't complained about the quality of his baking—and the kid wasn't shy about that kind of thing when Serena got the crummy grocery store ones instead of the good ones from the bakery down the street. With a shrug, she took a bite.

Her brows just about hit her hairline. "Holy crap."

"Is that a good thing?"

"That's an *amazing* thing." It was dense and fudgy and loaded with chocolate chips, and if she hadn't been attracted to Cole from the get-go, she might've been willing to overlook a whole multitude of sins with this on the offer. "Wow."

He gave her a smirking sort of a smile. "Glad you approve."

"No, seriously, where did you learn to bake like this?"

And she was starting to recognize it now—the way darkness could creep over his features. The downward tilt to his mouth that appeared when they were close to crossing one of his lines. "Recipe books."

With that, he stood, balance all skewed to one side as he got his crutches tucked under his arms.

Was she really supposed to let it go at that, though? She'd followed enough recipes in her day, and none of her results had ever been as good as this. "No no no. There has to be a secret."

"There's not—"

"Can you teach me?"

She hadn't meant to say that out loud. She'd already asked so much of him with the tutoring for Max. He had to be exhausted with the lot of them.

But he turned to face her. "Can you take me to my doctor's appointment next week?"

"Of course." She'd promised him that from the very outset. "As long as it's after I get out of school. Whenever you need."

"Then we're agreed. Baking lessons and help with fractions."

"You don't have to."

He even seemed surprised when he opened his mouth. "I don't mind."

Oh. Well, all right, then.

She grinned as she said, "Sounds like a pretty good deal to me."

CHAPTER SIX

So." There was a creeping feeling just under Cole's skin, making his hands too warm, his palms damp. "What has you so keen to learn to bake?"

A few days had passed since Serena had brought it up, and he hadn't expected her to forget it, precisely, but neither had he been prepared for her to come knocking on his door again so soon. In retrospect, he really shouldn't have been surprised. The woman wasn't afraid to ask for what she wanted.

Maybe he should've turned her away; normally, he would have. But there'd been something hopeful to her face. Something he hadn't wanted to disappoint.

He'd asked her in.

Now here she stood, surrounded by the ingredients for his mother's chocolate biscuits. He sat on a stool beside her, supervising, instructing, and it was so like that first evening they'd spent together. When he'd invited her in and made her a cup of tea. When in a flurry of foot-in-mouth disease he'd offered her a slice of Helen's birthday cake and subsequently lost his bloody mind.

He leaned forward in his seat, bracing his arms against the counter. That wouldn't be happening this time. He had himself under control.

Shrugging, Serena scanned the recipe they were working from and plucked a one-cup measure from the pile of implements he'd laid out. "It just seems like something that would be useful to know how to do. For Max, mostly. And. You know."

"I don't."

"It's a nice thing to be able to do. Bring a tray of something with you when you go to someone's house. Gifts." Her voice quirked upward, a strange pitch to that word.

He looked at her askance. "Gifts for whom?"

"Anyone." She dipped the measuring cup into the flour, then paused. "Okay, promise you won't judge me?"

"I make no such promises."

She bit her lip as if trying to hold it in. But then she told him anyway. "Sometimes I go to the bakery down the street and buy cookies or brownies or whatever. Then I put them in Tupperware and pass them off as homemade."

"Scandalous."

"I know, right? Don't tell. There are just so many domestic types where I work, and among the parents." Her expression soured. "I bet the moms at the private schools are even worse."

Ah. So that's what this is about. "The ones at Upton?"

The school where she was so intent on sending her nephew next year.

Squaring her shoulders, she nodded. "Max doesn't have all the advantages of some of the kids there. I'll even the score however I can. Baked goods for the secretaries." She glanced at him. "Private tutors. Whatever."

"Of course." A question formed on his lips. It was terribly uncouth. Nosy and awful. But she herself had brought it up in the first place. "Can I ask..."

She eyed him warily. But she didn't say no.

He worked his jaw, gulping. Best to be direct. "Max's mother."

Sighing, she placed her hands on the counter. Left the scoop in the flour and dropped her gaze. "My sister. Penny. She's...not in the picture right now."

Alive, then, at least. "I'm sorry, I shouldn't have—"

"No, it's okay. Just not easy to talk about, you know?"

Cole could only imagine.

Nothing brought out a woman's emotions like a child. Helen's face flashed hot across his vision, eyes red, cheeks flushed and damp, and if he could just...If he'd only handled it better.

If he'd only been a different man entirely.

The silence that settled over them pressed on his lungs, an awkwardness that made his fingers twitch. Serena's, too, it seemed. After a moment, she dug back into the bag of flour, fumbling with the measuring cup before hauling it out, soft white powder overflowing as she steered it toward the mixing bowl.

He reached out before he could think about it too hard.

Her wrist was so small in his grasp, the bones so delicate. Her skin was warm and soft.

She darted her gaze around to meet his, mouth twisting down.

With a soft grunt of an exhalation, he let her go. Clearing his throat, he tipped his head toward the kitchen scale he'd placed beside the mixer. "You have to weigh it. Or at the very least level it."

"Really?"

"Truly." He pointed to the mass in grams the recipe specified.

"Huh."

Together, they got the flour measured out. As she dithered around, removing a couple of extra grams, she shifted her weight, chewing at the inside of her lip.

"She was just so perfect," she said, seemingly out of nowhere.

It took him a moment to catch up. "Your sister."

Serena nodded. "She was two years ahead of me, and all the teachers loved her. Straight As, awesome at sports, the whole package. Except..." She hesitated, lines appearing between her brows. "It started when she was a teenager, I guess. She had these times when you couldn't talk to her, could hardly even get her out of bed."

"Oh."

"I mean, looking back on it now, it's so obvious she was depressed, but at the time—it's not like teenagers are never moody, you know? And she was so resistant to the idea that she needed help. We thought we got it under control before she went off to college, but..."

She trailed off, and Cole clenched his hands against some broken, forgotten instinct that had him longing to reach out. There was a heaviness to her when she talked about her sister, and he heard the burden of responsibility in her tone. Serena had been the younger of the two, but she'd been the one doing the caretaking, hadn't she?

A wry smile curled her lips. "I think it's safe to say she engaged in some risk-taking behaviors once she was on her own. Self-medicating. Unsafe relationships. And in the meantime she was putting on a happy face in her messages home. But she was avoiding phone calls until..."

"Until Max."

"Pretty much." She shook her head. "God. I've never seen her and my mom fight like that. Her boyfriend at the time ditched her in a heartbeat, and she didn't know what to do. Mom wouldn't hear of her not keeping it, but Penny had this whole bright future laid out in front of her. Even if she hadn't, though. She wasn't in any state to be taking care of herself, much less anyone else."

The picture snapped into place before his eyes. "So your mother took the child."

"Penny was in and out of hospitals for a year after he was born. Mom's basically raised him since day one."

He studied her face, watching the interplay of light across her features. The subtle, soft curve of her smile. The pride with which she spoke about this boy.

"Not without a bit of help, I suspect."

"I was still living at home when he was born. I'd watch him after school, take him to his doctor's appointments, sit with him and hold his hand when he was sick." Her mouth twisted, a wistfulness tugging the corners down. "My mom still gives me such a hard time about it."

His eyebrows rose. "About helping her?"

"About not living my life." She shrugged. "They're part of why I stayed so close to home, for college and even now. She thinks I should be out sowing my oats or something, like Penny is now, but I don't get it. I already have everything I want. I love my job and my friends, and I've got this great kid that I adore. I love my family. Is that such a crime?"

"No..." He hesitated.

Because how dare he ask the kinds of questions that were rising to his mind? After his own stagnation, his own withdrawal from anything and anyone...how could he ask?

But he did. "Maybe she wants you to have a family of your own?"

Her laughter was a sharp rush of breath. "Please."

"What?"

"I'd love that. But..." She took the basket of flour off the scale, tapping her thumb against its corner in a staccato rhythm that set him on edge. "It's not easy, you know? Finding a guy who's serious. Who would commit."

Of course. After what had happened with her sister, she had every right to her wariness.

And it burned him all the same. Made him sit a little straighter in his chair. Keep his hands a little closer to his sides.

"Anyway," she said, voice loud in the quiet of the room. "My life is fine the way it is. I'm not going to change it for a man. Not unless he can give me everything I want." She glanced at him out of the corner of her eye. "Unless he's perfect."

Cole's heart clenched, the very muscle, underused and tender, going tight.

He'd made his promises. He'd honored them all these years. And it didn't matter how lovely this woman was or how she'd barged her way into his life. How she'd made him *feel* for the first time in what felt like a century.

Promises were promises. And even if they weren't.

Perfection was a million miles beyond his reach.

Perfect. The word rolled off Serena's tongue so easily, and with good reason. She'd had this conversation with her mother so many times. Her refrain was always the same. She wasn't ready or she wasn't interested or the men she met on dating sites were only looking for one thing.

Serena was looking for more.

Only the entire package would be enough to lure her away from the life she already had.

And yet, even as she was repeating those tired lines, she was looking at this man. At the scar on his lip and the frowning tilt of his mouth. The keenness to his eyes. The slope of his shoulders and the straight line of his spine, both radiating discomfort—both practically screaming that he didn't want to be touched.

But he'd let her in. He'd taken care of her nephew and he was giving her his time, telling her these basic things she should have figured out from her mother or from any of a hundred cooking shows, but which she hadn't.

He'd been rude, and he'd been gruff, and he'd listened to her babbling on about her sister without condescension or pity, with an even voice and with interest.

He was the furthest thing from perfect she'd ever seen.

And it was strange. She'd been attracted to him from the very first instant, but it wasn't until that moment, when she was saying out loud that she would never date someone like him, that she really let herself consider it.

What would it be like? To turn in to him, reach out her hand, and press a palm against the rough slope of his cheek? Brush lips on lips and taste his accent on her tongue. What would he do? Pull her in against his chest, wrap her up in warm arms, and keep her close?

Or push her away.

Face hot, ears burning, she dropped her gaze.

"What about you?" she asked, hands unsteady as she took the basket of flour and poured it with care into a bowl.

"Me?"

"Did you ever think about a family?"

She heard what she had asked at the same time he did. At her side, he stiffened, posture winding even tighter than it had been before, and she let loose a string of curses in her mind he might be proud of.

He'd shut down on her the last time at the barest mention of his wife. She'd been bursting at the seams ever since, curiosity eating her, but she'd thought she'd tamped it down. That she could be cool.

"I did," he said, and the metal seat of his stool creaked with the force of his grip. "A long time ago."

"Oh."

She moved on to the next ingredient on the list, scanning the lines of containers just for something to do and someplace to look.

"It wasn't meant to be, though."

A hundred questions pressed at her ribs. She bit down hard on the inside of her cheek to keep them in.

"My"—he hesitated, voice rough—"my wife wanted to. She

was trying to convince me of it the night..." He sucked in a breath that could have been razors. Bleeding and sharp.

Her own lungs wouldn't work, the air in them going thin as she waited for him to let his out. To say...To tell her...

"The night she died."

Oh God. She'd known. She'd figured, at least, but it was something else to have it spoken, hanging trembling between them. A crystalline web spun from confessions, glistening brightly in the light.

Only to shatter.

He rose from his seat in a lurching motion, knee near buckling as he got his crutches underneath him. "Eggs," he said, and the word was watery. He swabbed at his eyes as he turned away from her. "We need—"

"Cole."

"I'll just get—"

"*Cole.*"

But he didn't stop. He hobbled over to the fridge and tore open the door, rebalancing himself to reach into that space, to retrieve the cardboard carton. It shook in his grip, and her heart ached.

"Here." He thrust it toward her. "I can't." He gestured helplessly at the braces beneath his arms. "Infernal things, I just—"

One last time, she spoke his name, only for him to hurl the carton at the wall. He whirled around, and the fridge door slammed shut with a clatter, the whole thing rocking, something inside it falling over. With a crash, the eggs hit the ground, but she couldn't see them.

All she could see was this man, and the bands of control with which he was trying so damn hard to keep himself together. And failing.

His ragged inhalation was a hairline fracture to her ribs. His fist hit the front of the fridge, and then his foot, and there was another, wetter, angry sound of pain inside his lungs.

She was moving before she could think.

She stepped around the mess he'd made, right up to him. Those broad, strong shoulders still radiated distance, still told her with everything he had in him to stay away, but the hurt in his bones spoke louder.

And that was something she could never ignore.

With a hand on his arm, she tugged him around, and he resisted, clumsy with the crutches and as stubborn as the day they'd met. But she managed to get a hand on his face, to touch the stubbled line of his jaw, thumb brushing against the corner of his mouth. He let out a sound that might have been punched out of him, and her own eyes went blurry as she pulled at him to look at her.

His gaze was glass and steel, both ready to break and impossibly hard. A skittering pang throbbed through her chest.

"I'm sorry," she said. "I'm so sorry."

For his loss and for asking. For everything.

Something in his expression cracked. This time, when she tried to draw him in, there was no resistance. One of his crutches tumbled to the ground, an arm going around her waist. He pressed his face into her hair and let out a breath against her ear, damp and shuddering, and she felt it like an ache inside her heart.

Closing her eyes, she curled her hand around the back of his neck. There was something so raw about him. Like he'd never said those words before, maybe not even to himself.

Like years had passed since he'd been held.

So she tucked him closer. Wrapped him up and took his weight. Took his confessions.

And tried to give him back all she had in return.

Years.

For years now, Cole had been holding himself together through sheer will. It had gotten to the point where he had scarcely recognized it anymore—the tightness in his limbs, the tension straining every muscle to just keep choosing to breathe. The strain had faded into the background, had become this barren landscape of numb forbearance that he had to trudge through, day after day after day.

Until now. Until this woman.

Serena. She'd stormed her way into his life and his home, and now she'd—what? Asked him a bare handful of questions. Refused to let him change the subject or hide his face. She'd touched him with the softest glancing brush of fingertips against his cheek, and it had all come crumbling down.

He sucked in another searing breath, and the wet raggedness, the weakness in it threatened to take him to his knees.

Fuck. Shameful, pathetic. He spat the words into the vacuum of his own mind, but even as he did, he clung to her more tightly.

Worse, she let him. Everything in him was falling, but she bore him up with quiet strength. Her hand cupped his nape, the warmth there grounding him in a way he'd forgotten it even could.

And it felt *good*. Better than good.

Too good.

He squeezed his eyes shut tight, giving himself one last moment to soak this in. The unwinding deep inside him and the luxury of letting go, of allowing himself to be touched. Tenderness and comfort, and he didn't get to have it. Wasn't allowed to keep it.

Steeling himself, he opened his eyes and dropped his arm. She let him take a scant half-step back, but then her face tilted up, and his throat went tight.

That wasn't pity in her gaze. It was resolve.

Just like that, she rose onto her toes, and she didn't let him go. She reeled him in and down, and his protest, his *shock*, died in his mouth at the hot press of soft lips to his. It was all he could do just to hold on.

His lone, remaining crutch went crashing to the ground. He got both his arms around her, pure instinct driving him. Pivoting on his good leg, he turned her until her spine hit the refrigerator door, and God, bloody motherfucking hell. He really let himself feel her this time. She was all soft curves pressed against him, full breasts and perfect hips, the subtle dip of her waist fitting to the furl of his palm.

And her *mouth*. She tasted like heaven and hell, redemption and sin, and his blood pounded in his ears as he bit at lush lips, slipped his tongue in to tangle with hers until he was lost. His mind went blissfully, impossibly blank, his thoughts going quiet for the first time in years, for the first time since—

Icy, frigid water poured into his heart.

He hadn't kissed anyone since Helen.

In one, too-fast motion, he tore himself away. He swore aloud at the wave of fire shooting from his knee. He pitched backward, stumbling, barely catching himself against the counter behind him. With both hands braced against the granite, he fought his own aching, spinning breath.

Helen. Helen whom he'd loved and whom he'd ruined, who had asked him for more, for a family and a life, and he'd known he couldn't. He'd known. There'd been that ugly, awful, untameable thing inside of him, and no one should have to live with that. No child should have to grow up with a father who didn't know his own strength, who couldn't control his fucking temper, who lost himself to the white-hot anger in his chest until he forgot what he was doing, who he was hurting.

His breath caught. No woman should've had to live with that, either, but he'd been so fucking selfish. So wrong.

And then she'd died. Because of him.

He looked up, his chest pounding, and the gaze that met his own stopped him cold.

Serena stared back at him with her lips red and bruised, her hair a golden, gorgeous mess, face flushed. But those pale green eyes of hers—they were full of compassion, full of kindness. Full of hope.

Forget falling. His stomach plummeted, taking the rest of it with him. Because he'd been down this road before. He couldn't do it now.

He couldn't do it ever, ever again.

Oh hell. What had Serena done?

Cole had been leaning on her, emotionally and physically, surrender written into every line of him, and the intimacy of it had floored her. When he'd pulled away, he'd done so with such reluctance, all stoic reserve, as if he'd allowed himself too much in that single moment of letting go. It had only made her want to give him more.

This simmering attraction she'd felt from the first moment she'd seen him had bubbled over—and he'd loved it, was the thing. She shivered, spine still pressed against the fridge he'd backed her into. He'd returned her kiss with so much passion, like a dam breaking, and her skin thrummed, glowing and perfect, his touch and lips burned deep into her flesh.

But he was on the other side of the room now. He might be farther if there was anywhere left for him to go.

And she could already hear it. Regret.

She shook her head. "Cole—"

"I can't."

He might as well have hurled the words themselves at her. They stung like tiny blades between her ribs.

"You *can't*?"

"No." Eyes haunted, expression wretched, he gazed back at her. His knuckles were white where they gripped the edge of the counter behind him, like it was the only thing holding him up.

She paused. Because that wasn't *I don't want to* or *Sorry but I'm not interested.* Maybe she should let it go, but she could taste the heat of his kiss on her tongue. Could feel his chest pressed against her breasts and the growing hardness between his hips.

"Why not?"

His mouth opened, only to snap shut again. "I just—" He cut himself off, seeming to start and stop again a dozen times. But then he drew himself up taller, flexing his jaw as he shifted his weight to his uninjured leg. That terribly broken, terribly proud look of his passed across his features again, and he dropped his gaze. "Could you hand me my crutches, please?"

She very nearly said no. She'd held the damn things hostage from him before, and she wasn't afraid to do it again.

What on earth would that prove, though? Bullying him into talking to her wasn't going to help anything, and it hurt some tender place inside her to see him stuck like that. Unable to move or get away.

Sighing, she peeled herself from the fridge, crouching to gather them up. She took a couple of steps toward him before offering them out. When he went to take them from her, she stopped short, not letting go.

"Why not?" she repeated.

He tugged harder, pulling the crutches from her hands. This time she didn't resist.

It was an awkward shuffle as he got them situated under his arms again. A pang zipped through her as he leaned his weight into them and used them to turn himself around. Showing her his back, he pulled in a huge breath that rattled his shoulders. He hung his head.

"I made a promise," he said. "My wife. What happened to her that night. I could have prevented it. If I hadn't—" He craned his neck to peer at her over his shoulder. "I can't be with anyone. I won't."

"Oh."

The ache in her heart grew and grew. How long had he been living like this? He'd told her when they'd first met that he didn't have anyone he could call. No family and no friends. The loneliness of it twisted inside her gut.

Part of her wanted so badly to try to change his mind, to show him what he'd been living without. But there'd been a finality to his statement.

He only cemented it as he faced away from her again. "I'm sorry. Kissing you back. It was a mistake."

Dropping her hands to her sides, she swallowed. It hadn't felt like a mistake to her. She wasn't about to apologize for starting it, not when it had felt so good. So right.

Gritting his teeth, he eked out, "I'll understand if you want to go."

For a long moment, she stared at him. He wasn't kicking her out this time at least, but he was pushing her away all the same. And it struck her.

How many other people had he edged out of his life?

How many times had Serena's sister tried to edge her out of hers?

She squared her shoulders and lifted her chin. It wouldn't be easy to forget the slick press of his mouth or the heat of his hands on her, but she could put it aside for now. He needed her. He needed someone.

Decided, she bent down to wrap unsteady hands around the carton of eggs he'd hurled. She rose to stand and made her way over to the counter, hoping against hope as she opened the lid.

She let out a breath. "Here," she said, voice gentle. "Look."

All the eggs on one side of the carton had smashed, thick yolk bleeding out from the shattered shells. But there were still a few intact. A few that could be saved.

"How many did we need again?" she asked.

In a slow, uneven movement, he turned to look at her. His gaze darted down to the carton in her hands and then up to connect with hers. There was something pleading to those dark, stormy eyes.

Throat rasping, he answered, "Two. Do you think we can salvage that many?"

"Yeah." A low tide of relief swept in. They were speaking the same language here. Both working to say the same thing.

She'd only known this man for a little over a week, and she hadn't been lying when she'd said she liked her life the way it was. She liked her job and her friends, and she loved taking care of her family.

But already, she liked her life better with him in it. She liked the thrills he shot through her when he looked at her. The touch of his hand and the lilt of his voice. The set of his eyes.

She liked the way he kissed her, too.

Maybe, at least for now, he couldn't bring himself to give her what she wanted. But she was patient. She could prove herself worthy of his trust.

And in the meantime...

She plucked two whole, perfect eggs from the mess they'd made of the rest of them. Meeting his gaze, she nodded. "I think we've got everything we need."

CHAPTER SEVEN

Cole could not stop staring.

Max's head was bent to the problems Cole had set him to, pencil clasped between skinny fingers, his tongue sticking out of his mouth.

The skin around his eye bloomed with a vivid, vicious bruise.

Cole dug his nails into the palm of his hand, letting out a harsh huff of a breath through his nose. At the sound, Max glanced up, one eyebrow raised, and Cole forced himself to look away.

Not that that was any better. His gaze went unerringly, instinctively to where Serena sat grading papers on the couch. His throat went tight for an entirely different set of reasons at the sight of her. The soft fall of that golden hair and the pout of her lip.

His heart squeezed hard behind his ribs. Nearly a week had passed since his disastrous attempt to teach her how to bake. In the end, the biscuits they'd made had turned out perfectly, but it didn't matter. The buttery, chocolate crumbs turned to ash on his tongue. All he could taste was her mouth.

All he could see was her face as he'd torn himself away.

Fuck, but it had been the last thing on earth he'd wanted to do. She'd felt so good beneath his hands, all her curves pressed against him. A part of him was desperate to storm right over to her this instant and lay claim to her again. Another part went icy and aching and cold.

Biting back a wretched little whine of disgust with himself, he dropped his gaze. Scowling, vision swimming, he did his best to stare a bloody hole into the surface of the table.

In the intervening days, Serena had tried to keep things normal between them—as normal as they could get for two people who barely knew each other and yet whose lives had become so suddenly and swiftly entwined. She'd taken him to his doctor's appointment and invited him down to tutor Max again. She'd held her chin high, and her voice had stayed strong, but her smile had started cracking around the edges. One more thing he'd managed to ruin.

One more reason his decision had been the right one.

Before he could belabor the point much further, Max lifted his head, stretching his arms out to the side before settling back down and turning his paper around so Cole could see. Thank God basic decimals didn't take too much of his attention. He went through the work with a sliver of his focus, nodding in approval at the vast majority of it. Clucking in his head at whatever moron had been teaching the boy these concepts in the past.

It made him nostalgic, honestly. He'd never been much good at teaching, back before his career had gone off the rails, but he'd had a success or two. Watching Max discover a talent for mathematics brought him a certain sense of satisfaction.

Made him wish his professorship wasn't another thing he'd managed to lose.

After correcting a couple of minor errors, he turned the page. "Think you've got one more section in you?" he asked.

Serena piped up. "His grandma's not coming for another half hour."

That hadn't been the question, but Cole held his tongue. With a sigh of resignation, Max folded his arms on the table and rested his chin atop his hands. "Go for it."

Cole did just that, aware all the time of the ears listening in from the other room. As he spoke, he kept having to restrain himself, to steer his gaze away from the edges of that bruise. To not glance over at Serena. To keep his thoughts about it all to himself.

As he scribbled out a handful of examples for Max to work, a harsh tone rent the air. He ignored it, pushing the page across the table. Max dug in. Over on the couch, Serena found her phone. She swung her hair over her shoulder and away from her ear, exposing the long, pale column of her neck, and Cole swallowed, looking away.

"Hello?...Oh, hi, yes."

There was a rustling of papers, and out of the corner of his eye, Cole watched as she stood. She picked her way across the room and disappeared around the corner. A second later, the door to one of the bedrooms closed, muffling her voice.

Leaving Max and Cole alone.

Cole's heart thundered in his chest. The mottled purples and blues around Max's eye faded out to a sickly green at the edge of his temple, and he remembered what that felt like. Keenly.

As if he could feel Cole's gaze on him, Max's grip on his pencil tightened, his knuckles going white, his shoulders tensing.

Fuck. What right did Cole have? He didn't know this boy or his situation; he knew nothing beyond the vague echoes of his own. There wasn't any reason for him to get involved. For years now, he'd been doing everything in his power *not* to get involved.

Except when a teen on the train had been robbed in broad fucking daylight.

Except when a boy was being beaten to a pulp and nobody was *doing anything.*

Cole set his pencil down with a solid, resonating *thunk.* Max flinched, and that alone had bile swimming in Cole's stomach, flashes passing across his eyes, but they weren't what mattered right now.

"So." He flexed his jaw, then pointed toward the boy's eye. "Another wild pitch?"

Max's whole body seemed to shrink, his spine curling in on itself. Fixing his gaze on the paper in front of him, he turned his pencil over, scrubbing the eraser across the page until it tore. "I fell."

"Did you now."

Max gave a single, jerky nod.

Cole's vision tinged with red. He wanted to tear that school apart. That playground or that alleyway. Where the bloody hell were the fucking grown-ups?

"You need to tell someone."

Finally, twin green eyes met his, fire tinging their edges. From behind thick lenses, they glared at him. "Like who?"

Cole's throat ached. "A teacher. Principal. Your grandmother."
Your aunt.

Serena was a teacher, wasn't she? Didn't she know the signs?

Max shook his head. "Teachers don't do anything. Tattling just makes it worse, anyway."

Helpless rage filled Cole's useless hands, a tide of memories welling up and threatening to pull him under. He knew the story too well.

And God. Fuck. He hated to ask, the very question punching through him like the kick that'd cracked his ribs, and for a blinding moment he was there. He tasted blood, and his breath burned, cold pavement stinging his palm.

The shattered fragment of his broken glasses slicing cleanly through his lip.

"Have you ever tried fighting back?"

Max dropped his gaze, his mumble barely reaching Cole's ears. "How do you think I got this?"

Cole would kill them. He'd smash their laughing faces in with his own bare hands. Just like he had...

He bit down on the inside of his cheek. "Running away?"

"Works sometimes."

As Cole looked on, Max bent his head back to his work, the scratching of his pencil the only sound besides the roar inside Cole's ears. Because what comfort could he offer? He'd fought his way out of a scrape or two. He'd run. But mostly he'd existed until the anger ate his very lungs away.

Until he'd escaped. But the hot, red thing behind his ribs had never left him. He'd survived and he'd succeeded, but he'd lost a part of himself.

The part that had known how to stop.

"They'll outgrow it eventually," he said, and it was the worst imaginable reassurance. All he could offer was..."Or at least mine did."

Max's head snapped up, his eyes widening. "*You* got bullied?"

"Mercilessly. For years." He tried to smile, but the tugging in his lip was a red-hot brand. A reminder.

"What'd you do?"

"The same things you've tried. But in the end, I mostly kept my head down." He'd kept his silence. He'd let resentment drip like acid in his heart. "It gets better. And worse. But by the time you get to university..." The smile came easier this time, but not much. "It doesn't matter anymore. You keep living your life."

Outrage twisted Max's features. Outrage and despair. "You have to wait until *college*?"

And Cole could just see it. The years and years spread out, never seeming to end.

"It might not be that bad." His mouth flashed painfully dry with the weight of the lie.

What was he doing here? He was cocking this up—was absolute rubbish with children. With life.

Helen had fought so hard to convince him that he could be a father, but he'd known in his heart that she was wrong. And it all came down to this. An inability to relate to people and a violence in his limbs. A keen awareness how impossibly cruel the world could be to children—what it could turn them into. What it had turned *him* into.

His torment as a boy had started him down that road. He

wanted so badly to spare Max the worst of it, to keep him innocent and sweet, but what could he do?

A spark of hope lit bright green eyes, and it fractured something in Cole's heart. "What about at a better school? Like, a really, really good school."

Cole struggled to swallow his groan. Upton. Of course.

"There aren't any promises..."

"But it'd be better, right? At least a little?"

"Perhaps."

But Cole had gone to a good school, and it hadn't helped.

It seemed to satisfy the boy regardless. He attacked the numbers with the fervor he might've liked to turn on his tormenters. Like the decimals and fractions could save him.

What Cole would give to do that himself.

Well. He'd do what he could.

"I have to tell your aunt." It wasn't quite asking permission, but it wasn't quite not that, either. It was trying not to break a child's trust.

Scowling, Max opened his mouth. But before whatever protest was twisting his lips could make it out, the back bedroom door creaked open, and it was like a rug flopping over the whole thing. Max straightened in his chair, pencil moving across the page, and Cole was struck dumb as Serena padded back out.

"Sorry about that," she said. She hesitated, pausing in the doorway to the kitchen. "You guys okay in here?"

Pleading eyes turned to Cole's. And maybe it was the bruise. Maybe the glasses.

Swallowing, Cole nodded. "Brilliant."

Relief seemed to ease Max's shoulders. Appeased, Serena

turned away, but the burning thing behind Cole's ribs didn't ease at all.

He had to say something. He had to *do* something. Before it was too late.

"Don't forget to give those papers to your grandma, now, okay?"

Max rolled his eyes. Well, eye, considering the other one was almost swollen shut. "I won't."

Serena shook her head as she leaned down, holding out her fist for their secret handshake, counting the bumps and slaps in her head instinctively. When they were done, she ruffled his hair and pulled him in for one last hug. Then she tugged open the door, and he shot through it about twice as fast as she would like. She twisted her mouth to the side. She probably should've yelled at him to go slower, considering the spill he'd taken on the stairs at school the other day.

Or at least the one he'd said he'd taken.

Frowning, she crossed over to the window to watch him pile into her mother's car, waving when her mom looked up. She returned her hand back to her chest, worrying at her necklace.

It wasn't like Max to lie. He was a sweet kid, a good kid, but he was entering those preteen years where people changed. Already, he was getting quieter, more withdrawn. And he'd been having an awful lot of accidents lately.

Not for the first time, she wished Penny were here. Serena's mom did the best she could with Max, but she wasn't as young as she used to be, and Serena only had him a few hours a day. If something were wrong, really wrong...

"He's being bullied at school, you know."

Serena whipped around. It wasn't as if she'd actually forgotten Cole was there. It was almost impossible to, what with the way his presence could fill a room. But she'd been so focused on Max.

Apparently, so had he.

While Max had been getting his stuff together, Cole had risen from the table. He'd gotten as far as the cutout between her kitchen and the living room. He leaned against the wall there now, crutches under his arms, a messenger bag slung over his shoulder. And the vision of him there, tall and proud, color high on his cheeks as he stared straight at her struck her dumb.

This past week, things between them had been strained, the memory of his kiss a weight pressing in on her skin. The memory of how he'd let her touch him and peer past that mask of restraint he wore. How he'd sagged against her and given her a fraction of his burdens to carry, at least for a little while.

In the days that had followed, they'd been as civil as they'd ever been before. But they'd both been avoiding each other's gaze, edging back from the precipice they'd been so close to going over—the one that in that instant she would have happily followed him past, tumbling off into a free fall in his arms.

But the full power of those dark, brooding eyes was focused on her now. His gaze was a brand searing into her, and a shiver wracked the length of her spine.

Her fingers tightened around the chain of her necklace, the fine metal links biting into her flesh. Her throat was dry, but she fought to think past the surge of heat deep in her bones. He was talking to her about her nephew. It was important.

She blinked hard, working her jaw. "Excuse me?"

One of his brows rose. "The black eye. The bruise on his arm."

"Oh." The haze of her thoughts cleared. "Oh."

"You didn't honestly believe they were accidents?"

She had, actually. Sort of. Her stomach sank as her suspicions returned to her. Hadn't she just been fretting about these very doubts? Hadn't there been a part of her, deep in the back of her mind, screaming at her that something was wrong?

Her knees went weak beneath her. She pushed away from the window, crossing the couple of feet to drop into her seat on the corner of the couch. Rubbing hard at her temple, she looked up at him. "Did he tell you this?"

"I suspected. When I asked, he all but confirmed it."

Oh hell. How long had this been going on? What other signs had she missed or written off? And more..."Why would he hide this?"

Cole let a beat pass before he answered. When he did, the edge to his voice was gone. It went softer. Kinder. "Plenty of reasons. None of which make much sense when you're not a ten-year-old boy."

"How did you know?"

A pained shadow flashed across his eyes. His mouth crumpled before straightening back out. "Children are cruel. In any decade. And on any continent."

For a second, she boggled. Cole was this tall, self-assured Adonis, a hero who ran down thieves, and he was trying to say...

Anticipating what she was about to ask, he sighed. "I was scrawny when I was his age. Scrawny and mouthy, and I didn't know when to walk away from a fight." Another cloud darkened his gaze. "I still don't."

It was too hard to imagine. But there wasn't any reason not

to take him at his word. He'd met Max a grand total of three times, and yet he'd seen the signs she'd missed. She chastised herself again, biting down on the inside of her cheek. God, she was a teacher, even. She should've known better. Max deserved better.

Hunching forward, she let her head fall into her hands. "What am I going to do?"

Cole said Max had "all but confirmed" what was going on. If she asked him outright, would he be any more forthcoming? Would it make her feel any less helpless if he did? Being a teacher cut both ways here. She'd seen enough bullies and enough victims over the years. There were things she could do to make her classroom a safer space, words she could say that might or might not help to change the culture of the place.

But life wasn't a classroom. Not every space was safe, no matter how hard she wanted to wrap cotton wool around every single kid who'd been forced to face that terrible truth too soon.

The quiet of her own distressed breaths was broken by the soft thuds and clinks of Cole's steps. She chanced a quick glance up before burying her face again, swabbing at the dampness around her eyes. The couch dipped, and it was too much to process all at once. Guilt roiled through her, but he was so close. His knee grazed hers, and he shifted, a tentativeness to him she never would've expected.

A shuddering breath was pushed out of her body when his hand settled, warm and broad against her shoulder.

And she shouldn't. After her impulsiveness in kissing him, she should stay stoic and strong. She shouldn't move.

But then his thumb stroked at her, the motion jerky, like he'd forgotten how to do something so simple. So basic as offering someone comfort through touch.

She gave in. Leaning into him, she took what he was offering her, clumsy as the offer might be. The solid heat of his chest burned into her side, and he stiffened as she let her head fall to his shoulder. The bobbing of his throat echoed in her temple, and she held her breath.

Slowly, bit by bit, he relaxed. His hand fell away from her shoulder, only for his arm to tug her in close. The side of his face pressed to her hair, and she squeezed her eyes shut tight.

"Be there for him," he said. "No matter how hard he tries to push you away."

The words buried themselves inside her heart. Because they were the answer to the question she had asked—the one about what she could do for Max.

But maybe. Just maybe. They were the answer to one she hadn't asked. To another kind of question entirely.

CHAPTER EIGHT

Cole had been through an untold number of personal hells in his life. Turned out, physical therapy was a whole fresh new one.

Willing the timer on the bike he was pedaling to turn over faster, he mopped at his brow. Couldn't they afford bloody air-conditioning in this place? It was as characteristically brisk outside as springtime in Chicago ever was, but in here it was a sauna, and the combination of heat and effort and the building ache in his leg had him panting.

Grimacing, he focused harder on the bright red numbers ticking by on the display. Unconsciously, his gaze kept flicking toward the waiting area not a dozen feet away. Serena had a stack of papers to grade, but she wasn't making any pretense about not watching him as he made a damn fool of himself. Every sly little smile that passed across those lips had him burning up inside, and for reasons unrelated to the heat.

Fuck, but what a picture he must make. Sweating through his workout clothes despite having hardly done a thing. At top condition, he could run or lift or swim for hours, but he'd been benched for weeks now, and he was pushing his recovery. Everything hurt.

He wasn't ready. Hell if he was prepared to admit that now, though.

"Whoa, whoa, whoa."

Cole couldn't quite suppress his glare. His therapist, Mike, an infant in a polo shirt and ill-fitting khakis, had approached while Cole hadn't been looking. Clucking, he reached his arm right into Cole's space to adjust the resistance on the bike. Cole gripped the handles even harder to keep from flinching. Or decking him.

"Take it easy there, buddy," Mike admonished as he reduced the difficulty to almost nothing. "This is just a warm-up."

The man had the gall to pat Cole on the shoulder, and Cole did flinch this time.

Mike took a single step backward, hands up in front of himself. "Sorry."

"It's fine." It wasn't.

In his isolation, so few people had touched him. It'd made his skin ache. Made it all the more grating when someone he didn't want to dared to presume.

Made it all the more exquisite when someone like Serena did.

With a weak smile that showed just how much he believed Cole's lie, Mike nodded at the bike. "Come on. I think you're warmed up enough. Let's see what we can do about getting you walking again."

Finally. With not a small amount of difficulty, he disembarked from the bike, got his crutches under him, and followed Mike to a spot that was even closer to where Serena sat. Of course.

What followed were twenty of the more unpleasant minutes of his life. Stretches and light strength training, and none of it should've been difficult, but it was. He fought to keep from looking over at Serena, to ignore the heat that crept across his face at the idea of her looking at him while he was struggling like this.

And then it got worse.

"Okay." Mike clapped his hands together. "These last ones would be better if you had a partner." He glanced to the side, then back to Cole, one eyebrow raised. "Think your lady friend over there would be okay to help?"

Klaxons fired off inside Cole's mind. No. Absolutely not. On so many levels that would never work. It couldn't.

"She's not—" he started, but it came out bumbling, the words twisting themselves on his tongue.

Before he could get the rest of the words to form, Serena's voice rose above the roaring in his ears. "You need me?"

Cole sighed, burying his face in his hand. Because if there was anything on this earth that beautiful, insane, ridiculous woman couldn't possibly resist, it was the chance to help.

"Absolutely," Mike said, ignoring Cole's barely suppressed groan.

He couldn't bring himself to look up, but every step Serena took toward them was a whisper on the air, a rattling of the bracelets around her wrists. A fluttering of a butterfly's wings, wreaking chaos with the universe he knew.

She was wearing trousers today at least, no bare calf or knee to tempt him as it peeked out from beneath the hem of a skirt as she came to join them on the mat.

"What do you need me to do?" she asked.

"Here." Mike prompted them into arranging themselves. Cole bit down hard on his tongue as he rolled over onto his stomach, an itchy feeling skittering along the back of his neck at the exposure involved. He crossed his arms in front of himself and closed his eyes as he let his brow rest against his wrist. "Bend your leg, Cole."

With a grunt, he did just that, and it pushed the air from his lungs. But then the torture truly began.

Addressing Serena, Mike said, "And if you would..."

Warm, soft hands on his calf were a jolt of electricity zipping all the way up his leg to his spine. It was bare skin on skin and the heat of her breath. She was so close, sitting right beside him, *touching* him, and the only ache wasn't in his knee.

His breath went tight, every inch of his flesh coming alive at this faintest hint of contact. The gentleness of her fingers where they curled around him. The sweetness of her scent crowding in on him.

The memory of how she'd felt pressed against him as he'd succumbed to her kiss, tasting her tongue and scraping his teeth across her lips.

And fuck. Motherfucking son of a cocksucking whore, but he was hard. Desperately so, the pressure of the floor against his hips dizzying as he lay there. Sweating and exposed as she placed her hands on him.

As his obnoxious twat of a therapist instructed her exactly how to put her hands on him.

"That's it," Mike said, "a little tighter," and Cole's brain fuzzed over. "Cole...Cole?"

"Yes?" Cole gritted out.

"Push back into her hands."

He was going to go insane. Actually, honestly insane.

A wet noise fell out of his lungs. But he did as he was told, pressure that seared him to his bones.

"Good, good. Not too hard. That's it. Now release."

He let his breath go as he relaxed the muscles in his leg. His head was spinning, his blood pounding. Then Serena stroked down the curve of his calf, nearly all the way to his knee, the softest brushing sort of touch, and he felt it in his heart.

He twisted his head to the side and opened his eyes.

It was the very worst kind of a mistake. She was right there, kneeling beside his hips, the front of her shirt dipping low as she hunched over, that soft, ripe flesh threatening to spill forth. The warm smile on her lips just for him.

And he wanted her. Wanted her to be touching him for real, to be in his bed and in his life and to be anywhere but here.

He turned his face away, clenching his hands into fists. He'd had his chance. He could've said yes.

But no. Still no.

So few things he wanted were things he ever got to have.

Life was not even remotely close to being fair.

Serena stood there, patiently holding the door as Cole levered himself into the passenger seat of her car. Despite the cool breeze outside, he hadn't bothered to put on his jacket or change from his gym shorts back into sweats. The damp fabric of his T-shirt clung to every dip of muscle on his chest and shoulders, and the tousled mess of his hair was darkened with sweat. His skin faintly gleaming, the firm shapes of his forearms and calves practically beckoned her. Made her pulse go fluttery and her face flash hot. It was all she could do not to reach out and touch.

And it wasn't *fair*. She'd more or less accepted that he wasn't ready for whatever road they'd been heading down in his kitchen the previous week. Since then, she'd kept her hands to herself and her ogling to a minimum.

But that was before she'd basically gotten a doctor's note requiring her to touch him. Before he'd placed himself in her care, lying prone before her and straining against her grip, looking at her with such heat and anguish in the darkness of his gaze.

Before he'd forced himself to look away.

But that was fine. She could do this. She could be his support and his help and his friend without pushing for more than he was willing to give.

Taking a deep breath, she waited until he was settled, seat belt fastened, before passing him his crutches. He tucked them into the side of the seat well, then gave a quick, jerky nod. The whole time, he kept his gaze focused forward, and her heart fired off a little whimper of a pang. Apparently, they were back to not making eye contact again.

Fine.

She closed his door and stalked around to the driver's side. She couldn't help the flush to her cheeks or the frustration boiling its way through her veins, but she could play his same game. Staring straight ahead, she slipped behind the wheel and got the car going, giving it a bare second to warm up before shoving it into gear.

As they pulled out onto the street, she tapped her thumbs

against the steering wheel. Chewing on the inside of her lip, she glanced at the time. She did have one more errand she'd been hoping to run today. It was kind of on the late side, but they should still be open.

Of course, accomplishing it would mean an extra twenty minutes in the car with Cole. Usually that would only be a positive, but right now she wasn't sure. Mentally shaking her head at herself, she gripped the wheel tighter. Whatever she felt about him, no matter the tension currently simmering on the air, she wasn't going to let him mess up her plans.

Checking her rearview mirror and her blind spot, she maneuvered over into the turn lane. She could almost hear his brow furrowing.

"What—" he started.

She cut him off as smoothly as she did the jerk who tried to merge in front of her. "I have a stop to make before we head home."

His hands flexed in his lap. "Oh."

It was only a mile or so, but traffic this time of day was a mess. Through the stops and starts and the lights that seemed to change just for her, she held her tongue, and he held his.

Right until they turned onto the tree-lined side street.

She'd been to the Upton campus enough times by now that she didn't have to think too much about where she was going. Rumbling past the scattered handful of Beamers and Audis parked in the back of the lot, past the other beaters in the faculty section, she made her way to the administration building and slid into a visitor slot.

In front of her, all the ivy and stone made her breathing speed.

Blocking out the man beside her, she took a moment to get her game face on.

Because the simple fact was that this wasn't her world. She was a public-school girl through and through. As a kid, she'd known this kind of place existed, but she'd only considered it in the most passing sort of way. It was where the smart kids and the rich kids went. Penny, maybe, could have gone there.

Then Serena had ended up here for some professional development class a couple of years ago. She'd gotten to see past the ivy on the façade, to meet some of the teachers and tour their facilities.

And it had left an aching feeling deep inside her chest. These people—they weren't kidding when they said they were the best.

Her ribs tightened hard around her lungs. Maybe even then she'd known. She hadn't approached Max about what Cole had told her about the bullying, but she didn't have any doubts that it was true. Some kind of intuition had been telling her he wasn't happy at his neighborhood school for a while now. She'd denied it, had told herself he was a strong kid, that he was fine.

But she'd also spent the past two years hell-bent on getting him here.

"I'll just be a couple of minutes."

She undid her seat belt and slipped out of the car without a glance Cole's way. But as she popped the trunk and reached inside, the passenger side door swung open.

What the—

She grabbed what she'd gone in there for and closed the trunk. As she stepped around to the side of the car, it was to find Cole struggling to get out of it.

She shook her head. "You can just wait here."

"Well"—with a heaving breath, he used one crutch and his grip on the headrest to haul himself out of his seat—"perhaps I don't want to wait here."

"Why—"

He shoved his whole body into the door in an attempt to shut it. It didn't latch, and she risked life, limb, and offended scowl to duck into his space enough to slam it the rest of the way closed.

He came up short. "Did you make those?"

Darn it, this was part of why he was supposed to have waited in the car. It was too late to hide the plate of cookies she'd brought behind her back, or maybe in a nearby bush, so she tossed her shoulders back and raised her chin. "That's none of your business."

"As your baking instructor, it most certainly is."

"One lesson doesn't exactly make you my 'instructor.'"

"It is if one lesson was enough to teach you *that*."

He was taunting her now. Obviously, these were from the bakery, with their perfect icing and the golden crispness to their edges. He'd been a good teacher, sure, but he wasn't a miracle worker.

She raised one brow. "And if I told you I had made them?"

He met her challenge. "Then I'd ask you for your recipe."

For a long moment, they stared at each other, neither willing to give in first. Oh, this was ridiculous.

"Fine." Rolling her eyes, she waved her free hand at him. "I bought them."

"Shocking."

"Oh, be quiet." She gave him a halfhearted shove with her elbow, taking care not to upset his balance. For the first time since the physical therapist's office, she looked up at him. Deep into dark, liquid eyes, and he didn't force his gaze away. Something in her went soft, a lump forming and sticking in her throat. She glanced toward the main building of the school, then back at him. "You really want to come inside?"

He shrugged, but he missed casual by a mile. "If this is what I'm preparing Max for, I might as well see it, hadn't I?"

There wasn't really any harm.

She nodded. "Sure."

It wasn't the quickest walk of her life. Cole's steps were labored, his exertions of the day clearly taking their toll, but he soldiered on regardless, letting her get the door for him without so much as a protest. To her relief, the main office was still open, the lights all on.

She took another deep breath before stepping inside.

Only to falter the instant she saw who was behind the desk.

Oh well. Nothing for it. Plastering on her best smile, she strode forward. "Mrs. Cunningham. I'm so glad I caught you."

The woman in question was a fifty-something-year-old nightmare of good manners and bad intentions all rolled up in a designer pantsuit. As the assistant headmistress looked away from her computer, the most withering, condescending expression pinched her mouth.

"Ms. Hartmann. So delightful to see you. Again." The derision the woman could put into one word. "To what do I owe the pleasure?"

The whole thing made Serena feel about three inches tall, but she kept smiling through it all. "I was just in the neighborhood.

Thought I'd stop in and grab the latest schedule for the entrance exams."

"Yes, it has changed so much since we printed it in February. Or since we placed it on our website."

Serena's mouth hurt from the effort it took to keep the corners lifted. "Well. Max, my nephew, you know, he'd just be so disappointed if we missed out on anything."

Sighing, Mrs. Cunningham gestured toward the display in the corner of the room with all the prospective student information. As if Serena didn't know where it was.

Right. "I'll just help myself, then."

Still clutching her plate of cookies, she headed that way, her stomach twisting low in the pit of her abdomen. Two minutes of thinly veiled dismissals with this woman had wrung her out.

Her face warmed, her eyes tingling, and she buried her gaze in the rows of brochures.

Maybe she'd been kidding herself all along. She wanted this so badly for Max. A fresh school, a better school...Serena couldn't give him his mother back—couldn't make her sister decide to be involved in her own incredible, amazing kid's life. But this was something she'd imagined she might be able to do for him. Something she could give him.

But she didn't belong here. Hell, she was probably hurting his chances just being here.

Before she could sink too deeply into her own little pity party, the dull thumping of crutches on tile caught up with her. It sent a fresh wave of annoyance humming through her veins. She'd thought Cole had been right behind her, but now here he was.

She glanced back at him, but at the sight of him, she had to stifle a groan.

Here he was in gym clothes, jaw shadowed by two days' worth of stubble and his hair a sweaty mess.

God, Mrs. Cunningham was going to throw him out on his ass. Meticulously politely, but still. And here Serena'd been trying to make a good impression.

In despair, she wanted to drop her head into her hands. But as she lifted her fingers to her temple, Mrs. Cunningham called out, "Can I help you?"

Serena's head jerked up. That was not the woman's usual tone.

In what felt like slow motion, Serena turned around. Her gaze darted comically between lean, handsome, tousle-haired Cole and old sour-faced Mrs. Cunningham, and before her eyes, the scene inverted itself. How could she have been so wrong? Mrs. Cunningham wasn't going to throw him out. From the looks of it, she might dive right across the counter and eat the poor guy alive.

And it wasn't as if she'd forgotten the experience of meeting this man for the first time. She still got shivers just looking at him sometimes. But it was another thing entirely to watch someone else going through it.

Then he went and opened his mouth, and it got both a hundred times better and a thousand times worse.

"No, thank you." The smooth rolling lilt of his accent trilled its way through her, and through Mrs. Cunningham as well. He nodded toward Serena. "I'm with her."

Mrs. Cunningham's eyes widened as she looked Serena's way. "Oh."

Serena was going to hell. Her moment of insecurity disappearing, she seized on this new development and held on to it with both hands. "Cole, this is the assistant headmistress of Upton. Mrs. Cunningham, this is Cole."

To his credit, he seemed to catch on without missing a beat. "Cole Stafford." He approached the counter and tucked his crutch against his body to offer his hand. "It's a pleasure."

"Likewise." Mrs. Cunningham gripped his palm in hers, and the hairs all stood up on the back of Serena's neck. She knew the warmth and the strength in that grip. She knew what it could do.

With a smile that somehow managed to radiate both discomfort and charm, Cole withdrew his hand. "Lovely school you have here."

"Well, we do our best."

"Serena's nephew is so looking forward to enrolling. I'm working with him to get him prepared." His mouth softened, the curve there becoming less forced. "He barely needs it, of course. Such a bright young man."

Serena just about choked on her own tongue when Mrs. Cunningham's smile deepened, too. "We look forward to his application. It's a wonderful stepping-stone, attending here. Seventy percent of our graduates go on to Ivy League schools. Harvard, Yale. Cambridge, even."

"Ah. I was an Oxford man myself. For university. Princeton for my doctorate."

Serena never would've believed it if she hadn't seen it, but Mrs. Cunningham just about swooned. "Marvelous institutions."

The whole time they'd been making small talk and showing off their pedigrees, Cole's gaze had been sweeping the room. He paused, tilting his head to the side. "Serena, dear. Did you see this?"

Dear? Serena might be about to follow Mrs. Cunningham into her fainting spell. Swallowing, she moved to join him beside the counter. "What's that?"

He pointed to a glossy placard set on a stand toward the end of the counter.

She scrunched up her nose. "A benefit?"

"Yes." Mrs. Cunningham slid the placard across the glass. "To help raise funding for our library expansion."

It was the first Serena had heard of it. Unease went rolling through her abdomen. She looked up from the fancy script of the announcement. "Are other applicants' families attending?"

For the first time since Cole had walked in, Mrs. Cunningham's jaw went tight. "Some. It's certainly not required." Her voice went a fraction gentler. "It's two hundred and fifty dollars a plate."

Serena's head spun. Not just at the number, though that was bracing on its own. But at the way the woman said it.

Of course she knew Max would be a scholarship student. Serena had asked for that application along with the general one the very first time she'd come by.

She took an instinctive step back. Only for Cole to put his hand at the base of her spine, sending heat humming all the way through her nerves.

"A small price," he said. "For our children."

Mrs. Cunningham let out a sigh of relief. "I'm so glad you agree."

"We'll take two."

Serena couldn't quite stop herself from gawking. Turning to him and asking, "We will?"

Cutting her a pointed look, he managed not to be ruffled. "Of course we will."

He dropped his hand away from her back to reach into his pocket for his wallet. As he passed a card across the counter, Serena's whole body threatened to sag. She didn't want Mrs. Cunningham to hear this, but she couldn't let it go unsaid. Leaning in, she dropped her voice. "You don't have to do this."

Everything in Cole seemed to say, *We'll talk about it later,* but he kept his smile fixed firmly to his face. "It's no matter."

Five hundred dollars was definitely a matter. But that was only the tip of the iceberg.

What was he *doing*? He seemed to like her kid, and when he wasn't telling her they couldn't be together, his body certainly seemed to like hers. But this level of investment, this swooping in and offering to help her with problems she hadn't even known she had...

Explaining all the while that this was usually the office assistant's job, Mrs. Cunningham floundered with Cole's credit card, but eventually she managed to make the transaction. She passed the card back to him with two letterpressed pieces of ivory card stock, and he accepted them blithely, only to turn around and hand them straight off to Serena.

"We'll see you next Saturday, then," Mrs. Cunningham said.

"We're looking forward to it." Then Cole gave Serena an expectant look.

It took her a minute to decipher it. When it struck her what he meant, she could've slapped herself. They seemed so irrelevant now, but her little offering of baked goods was still clasped tightly in her grip.

Swallowing her pride one last time—at least for today—she raised the plate above the level of the counter. Casually, as if she hadn't brought them just for this purpose, she asked, "Mrs. Cunningham. You don't happen to like lemon cookies, do you?"

Mrs. Cunningham paused. Cole had already softened her up so much with his shoulders and his accent and his fancy degrees. For once, she didn't bother to hide her interest. "Lemon?"

Pay dirt.

"I had extras," Serena hastened to explain. And this was the tricky part—crafting a statement so it wasn't exactly a lie. "You know how some recipes make a ton, right?"

Oh dear God. Was that actually a laugh? "I don't think my mother-in-law has any that aren't portioned to feed a small army."

Was that actually a personal anecdote?

Scarcely able to believe anything she was hearing, Serena placed the cookies on the counter and peeled back the edge of the plastic. "Please. Help yourself."

"Don't mind if I do." She plucked one out, then made as if to re-cover them.

"Keep the plate. I'm sure some of the others in the office might appreciate them?"

"I'm sure they would." It was the kindest expression Mrs. Cunningham had ever turned on Serena. "Thank you, Ms. Hartmann."

They beat a fairly hasty retreat after that—as hasty of one as Cole could beat with his leg, in any case. As they traversed the halls, questions bubbled up in her by the dozens. Questions and protestations, and she was fit to burst with the effort it took to hold them in.

How dare he? What was he after?

And maybe, more importantly...how could she ever begin to thank him enough?

Thin ice. Cole felt like he'd been treading on it for weeks now. Every single day since Serena had stormed her way into his life, the cracks had been forming. He'd been skating too close to his promises and too far from the safety of the shore, and now he'd overstepped so badly. She'd scarcely spoken to him the whole way home, and it wasn't just the tension that had pulled between them after his PT appointment. She was stewing on something, and it was probably those damn tickets. The way he'd barged into her conversation.

Could she really fault him, though? The irony of it cut to the bone. She was the one who couldn't stand to let an opportunity to help slip by. Cole had seen his chance to do the same, to maybe begin to repay a little of her kindness, and he'd seized upon it. Dreadful, snobby people like that woman weren't any stranger to him; he knew how they worked. With scarcely a word, he'd had her eating right out of the palm of his hand. He'd only done what anyone in his position would do—what he'd imagined Serena would *want* him to do.

So why did he feel like she resented him for it?

Finally, she turned onto their street. He bobbed his good knee up and down, clenching his hands and releasing them over and over as she parallel parked. Without looking at him, she unhooked her seat belt and got out, and his anxiety and his resolve wound higher.

They made it all the way to the door of her apartment before he broke.

"I'm sorry." The apology came tearing out of him, and he should have left it there. But this hot, burning center of his pride lodged up in his throat, and he shook his head. "No. Actually, I'm not."

At least that got her to turn around. She studied him for a long moment before asking, "Well? Which one is it?"

"Both." He wasn't making any sense. "I'm...I'm sorry if I overstepped, but I'm not sorry for what I did." Unless...maybe this was about his making her feel obligated? "The tickets are yours. Take whomever you want."

Her brows rose on her face, disbelief making her eyes go wide. "Are you kidding me?"

What? "I—"

"Don't think for a second you're getting out of going with me."

That didn't sound like anger in her voice.

"You want me to?"

"Seriously? You had the assistant headmistress of the school practically swooning at you. I've never gotten that woman to so much as smile before." Glancing down, she shook her head. "It was incredible. You were incredible."

Oh. "I'm glad I could help."

"Also, you were *totally* overstepping."

He was getting whiplash.

"But," she said, "that's okay." A grin played with the corners of her lips. "Did you really go to Oxford and Princeton?"

"I did." His shoulders rose in preparation for defensiveness. He should have known better, though.

"That's pretty impressive."

"Not nearly as impressive as it sounds."

"Listen, though." Her smile dimmed, her expression growing serious. "If you want me to pay you back for those tickets—"

Ah. Maybe that was it. Her self-consciousness about not having been able to afford them on her own. He cut her off before she could get any further. "It's not a problem."

"You'd have to give me a little time to get the cash together, but—"

"Serena." Her name came out sharp on his tongue. She jerked her head up, her protest dying mid-word. "I said it's not a problem."

She was a public school teacher, for fuck's sake.

She wrung her hands, and an edge of vulnerability crept into her voice, squeezing his heart. "I just don't want to put you out."

Didn't she understand? Did she have no idea? "You're not."

She'd barged her way into his life, all right, but she had *never* put him out. She'd breathed life and lightness into all the darkened corners of his endless, wasted days. A few hundred dollars was nothing.

An unhappy frown twisted her mouth. "I don't even know what you do for a living. Can you afford—"

"I can." The forceful way the words left his lungs seemed to take her aback. He drew in a deep breath.

She wanted to know what he did for a living. Fuck. It was the last thing in the world he wanted to talk about, but all at once the answer was forming itself.

What was it about her that did this to him? From his pathetic, broken confessions about his wife to this. She drew these stories out of him. These truths he rarely admitted, even to himself.

"I..." He flexed his jaw, trying to summon the words. "I don't do anything. Not anymore." And this was the hard part. He couldn't keep the bitterness from his tone. The anger, at the past and at his life and at himself. "I got let go."

"Oh, Jesus, then you don't need to—"

He cut her off again. "Right after my wife died." And for a second, he was back there, standing alone in that empty, aching house. He could still smell her on his skin, could still hear her voice.

Even today, he could taste the burn of liquor on his tongue.

"I...didn't handle it well."

He'd lost his fucking mind was what he'd done. Guilt and grief and rage had been a storm inside him, the howling winds of it tearing him to pieces.

"It's funny. You're a teacher, so you wouldn't understand, but professors—we're there for the research. I liked the teaching well enough, but I was rubbish at it. Talking to people, handling their personal problems, and after—" *Helen.* He couldn't even say her name. "After she was gone, I stopped trying. I screamed at students. Showed up drunk."

Serena's face twisted before him. Horrified. Well, she should be.

A shuddering echo of a breath tore through his lungs. "I didn't last long after that."

Administrative leave, they'd called it. When it had come time to revisit, to plead for his job back, he'd blown the hearing off. To have to face them all again...to see the looks on their faces...

In his mind, he was there. His brother-in-law, Barry, had been the dean, and he'd given Cole so damn many chances, and he'd aggressively pissed away every one. When Barry'd finally shown Cole the door, Cole had wanted to rear back, to let his fist fly in his face and give the restless anger in his bones a place to *go*.

But then he'd looked in his eyes, and he'd seen the same grief that lived in his own.

"Cole..."

The way she said his name struck straight to the core of him. The horror was still there, but there was kindness, too, and he didn't deserve a fraction of it.

He shook the echoes of ghosts from his shoulders. Refocused until his vision was clear again.

But when he tried to smile, to pretend that it was all okay, it didn't work.

"I never went back." He hadn't been able to face his own failure. He couldn't stand to look his brother-in-law in the eye and see the pity there. The disappointment. The pieces of Helen that still lived on in him. "Now I just..."

Exist. For years, that's all he'd been doing. There were the journals he kept up with on his weekly pilgrimages downtown, the calculations he carried out on scattered scraps of paper he left strewn around his space.

There was a hole, where something had used to be but wasn't anymore.

Eyes shining, Serena took a step toward him. It was all he had left not to take one back.

"Cole. I can't take your money."

A burning bark of laughter escaped his throat. "Please."

"No, if you're not working right now..." And how could she even be kind while saying that?

"I have plenty." More than he ever, ever wanted to have. "My family gave me a cushion, and then..." Fuck. His voice wavered, and he couldn't seem to bring it back under control. "The life insurance policy."

The ones she'd bought for both of them, because all along she'd been planning ahead. Because she'd been thinking, hoping that they'd—

He blinked against the stinging in his eyes. Curled his hands in tighter fists around his crutches.

"You see." His racing heart refused to slow. But he could say this. He had to. "I've been living off death for years now." Wasting what had come into his hands once everything else had slipped away. "So please."

And this mattered to him. His throat ached with the sudden desperation of it. Of how much he *wanted* this.

"Please," he said. "Let me spend it on something that matters. Let me give this tiny fraction of it to you."

As swiftly as it had filled him, whatever strength had fueled his words ebbed away. The rest of the world filtered back in. The too-worn carpet and the doors that surrounded them. This public space in which he'd made himself more naked than he'd been before anyone in years.

"Please," he said again, but it was weak. Hollow.

For a moment, Serena stood there staring at him, long lashes fluttering against pale cheeks. The soft pout of her mouth opened and closed, crumpling before flattening back out. And then resolving, lifting into a smile that hurt it was so genuine.

"All right."

Relief was a whole other kind of force surging through him. "All right?"

"God." She dabbed at the brilliance of her eyes. "Of course. Like I could actually say no to that?"

She could have. But she hadn't.

"Thank you."

She managed a shaky laugh. "Pretty sure I'm the one who should be thanking you." One corner of her lips pulled to the side. "I don't suppose you'd let me give you a hug now, would you?"

Right. That was what people did, wasn't it? After heartfelt confessions or a substantial gift of cash. A hug wasn't outside the realm of reasonability.

All the same, the idea of it set him right back on edge, his fingers twitching, skin raw with the possibility. Heart terrified.

"I don't know." He hesitated. "It was fairly disastrous last time."

One of her brows quirked up. "That's not exactly what I'd call it."

He'd blubbered on her and pawed at her and come damn near close to breaking all his vows and taking her against his fridge. *Disaster* seemed like an understatement.

But her arms were already rising, her weight shifting forward as if to close the gap.

And he'd never pretended to be made of steel.

With a put-upon sigh that was a lie against the eager thumping of his pulse, he met her halfway. He closed his eyes as she put her arms around him, and it was awkward and it was awful—he nearly lost his crutches and buckled his aching knee. But he got one arm around her, too, and it was the best thing he'd felt in days. He let the sweet scent of her soak into his bones and the warmth of her heal something that had been raw and untouched beneath his skin.

And then he pulled away.

Clearing his throat, he got his crutches underneath him, turning toward the stairs before he did something he'd regret.

"See?" she asked, voice wobbling. "Not so disastrous this time."

Her gaze on the ground, she crossed her arms in front of her chest. Like she were still holding him. Like she still needed to be held, and it hurt. Continuing to walk away.

He let a flicker of a smile pass over his face. "Good night, Serena."

"Good night, Cole."

He hovered there, waiting on the landing until her door swung shut behind her.

Then he started the long climb to his empty apartment. Alone.

CHAPTER NINE

This was a disaster.

In disgust, Serena threw yet another cocktail dress on the "no thank you" pile. She'd had some luck at this consignment store in the past, but now, when there was something specific she actually, honestly needed to find *today*, she was striking out entirely. Exhaling hard, she pinched the bridge of her nose. At this rate, she was going to be trying to impress all the fancy Upton people in a recycled bridesmaid dress. She hadn't had any illusions of being able to pass herself off as high society, but she'd thought, maybe, with the right dress...

Maybe with gorgeous, cultured, professorial Cole at her side...Maybe she could've at least made a decentish impression.

Turning from the mirror, she slipped her next-to-last option off its hanger, holding the fabric up before sighing and undoing the zipper.

A different kind of nervousness buzzed beneath her skin as she stepped into the dress. Going to this benefit was about helping

Max, and that was her first and last priority. But there were a couple of other ones sandwiched in between them.

And all of them were named Cole. Cole who could be bristly and recalcitrant at the slightest hint of an offense to his pride, who could turn on the charm like a switch when there was something he wanted. Cole who was a widower, and who had dropped his shields yet again.

He'd let her see straight through to the bleeding heart of him, and it had only left her wanting more. For the second time, he'd let her wrap him up in her arms, and what she wouldn't give to keep him there forever. To maybe show him a little of the love he'd been living without for all these years.

Squeezing her eyes shut tight, she dismissed that line of thought with prejudice. The man was clearly still grieving, and there were more secrets lurking behind his closed doors. She could almost taste them in the memory of his kiss and in the rasp of his breath beside her ear as he folded her in against his chest.

He'd said he wasn't ready. And she could respect that.

Resolved, she got the dress pulled over her arms. It was a softly draped, black, sleeveless number, with just a hint of shimmer in the fabric. It hit a little higher on her thigh than she usually preferred, but the fit felt good. Contorting herself, she reached behind her back to get the zipper. She made it almost all the way to the top before her flexibility ran out. Oh well. Close enough.

Steeling herself, she turned to face the mirror again, and—

Oh. That worked, actually. Classy and yet sexy, and maybe it was a tiny bit on the snug side, but she could work with that. She dug around beneath her arm for the tag, holding her breath.

Of course it had to be the most expensive dress of the lot. For secondhand, it was outright ridiculous—just the idea of what it must have cost full price made a sweat break out on the back of her neck.

But then she glanced at herself again. She looked *good*. Not the stuffy teacher or the matronly aunt her mother always accused her of behaving like. She looked like a single woman in her twenties should for a date. A fancy date with a beautiful, haunted, impossible, unavailable man...

Who didn't think this was a date at all.

Groaning with frustration, she went to get undressed again—maybe the last, cheaper dress would be at least sort of acceptable. Before she could so much as grasp the zipper, though, her phone sounded off from within her purse. She frowned, dropping her arms. That was Penny's ringtone.

She still hadn't managed to get a hold of her sister since the last time her mother had raised her concerns. This wasn't exactly the greatest timing, but no way she could put off answering now. Ignoring the people in the other changing booths, she dug through her bag until she found her phone, picking up the call and bringing the speaker to her ear. "Penny?"

"Hey."

Serena paused. Her sister sounded...off. A low warning tone sounded in her mind. "Hey. Are you okay?"

"Yeah, fine." A sniffle leaked across the line. "Just got a bit of a cold."

Oh. The automatically wary part of her stood down, at least a little. Nudging her pile of discarded dresses aside, she sat down gingerly on the edge of the bench tucked into a corner of the stall.

For a moment, awkward silence hung between them, but Serena pushed through it. "What's up?"

And it was ridiculous, exchanging basic pleasantries and small talk while Serena was hogging an entire dressing room, still decked out in a slip of black organza she could barely afford. But she sat through it all the same, trying the best she could to keep her voice down. But as they droned on and on without really saying a thing, it got harder to keep the real question she wanted to ask unspoken: What the heck was this about?

Why now?

Serena had spent so much of her life waiting for the other shoe to fall when it came to her sister. Penny would go years with everything under control only to spin out without warning, leaving Serena and her mom to pick up the pieces. What should just be nice chances to catch up were always haunted by the lingering specter of another episode that would send everyone scrambling, and the anticipation of it all had Serena jittery and unsettled.

Finally, it burst out of her. "Look, not that I'm not glad to hear from you, but what's going on?"

If it weren't for the quiet breaths humming across the line, Serena would've worried she'd dropped the call. Even as it was, the seconds kept ticking past, to the point where she had to bite her tongue to keep herself from asking again. And maybe she was an asshole for pushing instead of letting her sister come to whatever was behind the call in her own time. Penny had always told her she was pushy, but if there was anything Serena had learned over the years of handling her sister, it was that she *had* to push. She had to get ahead of the situation before it crashed over them all and Penny wasn't the only one about to drown.

But then, just when she was about to try a different tack—

"Are—" The single word came out on something dangerously close to a sob.

Serena sat up straight, her muscles tensing.

"Are you happy, Rena?"

Oh hell. Adrenaline flooded Serena's system in a rush. This had a hospital visit and an emergency trip out to New York written all over it.

But maybe it wasn't that bad yet. Penny didn't reach out when she was at her lowest. Maybe Serena could still talk her down.

She considered her words carefully. It was actually a more fraught question than even her sister's mental health might make it seem. "Mostly, I guess." There were always things that could be better, and maybe she was a little overly obsessed with a guy she couldn't have. But on the whole, things were fine. They were good.

But her own state of mind wasn't really the point. It never was.

Serena swallowed, her throat tightening. "Are you?"

"I don't know."

Oh, hell, that little hiccup at the end. Penny was crying.

In an instant, Serena was on her feet. "Oh, sweetie. Penny. Talk to me."

"No." Another shiver of a sniffle. "It's fine. I shouldn't have bothered you."

"Of course you should. You're my sister—"

Penny gave a sad echo of a laugh. "I haven't been much of a sister to you, though, have I?"

Gripping the phone more tightly, Serena closed her eyes. "You're scaring me."

"I'm fine. I'm just tired."

"Have you talked to your doctor? Do you need me to make you an appointment?" She still had his contact info in her phone, she was sure.

"I'm seeing him tomorrow."

"Okay." That was good. Really good. But sometimes it wasn't enough. "Maybe you need a break?" She hesitated. "You know you can always come home, right? Even just for a few days, or longer if you need it, or—"

"Why are you always so nice to me?"

The question didn't even compute. "You're my sister."

"Yeah. I guess I am." A beat passed before she said, "Listen, I'm going to let you go."

"Are you sure?" The unsettled feeling in Serena's gut hadn't abated at all. Something was seriously wrong here.

"Yeah. You're probably busy anyway, and I...I just needed to hear a friendly voice."

Serena really, really didn't want to let her go. "Penny, you know you're more than my sister. You're my friend, too."

Growing up, she'd been Serena's best friend. Serena would do anything for her. So many times, she had.

"I know. Thanks for listening."

"Anytime."

There was another, longer pause as Serena scrambled for the right thing to say.

But then Penny spoke. "Hey, Rena?"

"Yeah?"

"Take care of yourself, okay?"

"Sure."

"No, really," Penny insisted. "Do something nice for yourself, even. You never do that."

Serena's brow crinkled. "Penny..."

"I'll talk to you again soon."

With that, she was gone.

For a minute, all Serena could do was stand there. Alarm bells shrieked in the back of her mind. If this wasn't a red alert situation, it was definitely a yellow one. She tossed her phone in her purse, ready to take off this silly, ridiculous dress so she could focus on her sister and whatever had motivated that call.

She paused, zipper undone, the fabric ready to fall off her arms. Turning, she took one last look at herself in the mirror, then at the price tag.

It wasn't *that* ridiculous of a dress. And no matter how unsettling that call had been, the way it had ended...

Maybe Penny was right. Maybe Serena did need to do something for herself.

Moving fast, she stepped out of the dress and got back into her boring teacher clothes. She could do something for herself *and* worry about her sister. Both at the same time, even.

Draping the dress over her arm, she swept the curtain for the changing room aside and headed for the register.

With her other hand, she opened her contacts in her phone and placed a call.

"Mom?" she said as soon as it picked up. "We have got to talk about Penny."

Cole forced himself to slow down. To take a long, deep breath before turning around. With his eyes shut tight and his heart thundering, he shuffled in a tight half-circle until he was facing it.

How many times had he considered taking the damn thing down? Tearing it off the back of the door with his own bare hands—or worse, putting his fist right through the glass?

Tonight, though, he needed it. Exhaling, he nodded to himself and opened his eyes.

And it was just like it always was. The mirror tucked away in his closet was nothing more than a plain, flat, silvered surface. Innocuous and innocent and he *hated* it. He hated what was always there, staring back at him from behind the glass.

Himself.

The throat in the reflection bobbed, while the one inside his body ached. With as much clinical efficiency as he could muster, he took in the hundred details he'd turned to the blasted thing for in the first place. Every piece was in order, from the tailored lines of the jacket to the break in his trousers—his new, slimmer knee brace barely showing beneath the wool. His shoes were polished to a high black shine, and he'd done his tie in an elegant full Windsor. He'd pass muster at the most refined of society events.

Right until he got to his eyes. Even after he'd shaved and subdued his hair, it was his eyes that gave him away.

His lungs got tight, and just like that, he couldn't do it anymore. He swung the door shut so hard it slammed, dismissing the mirror and the sight of his own bleak countenance as one. Sagging, he dropped his head.

Less than an hour until the benefit began, and what had he been *thinking*? Buying the tickets in the first place and then allowing Serena to convince him to accompany her. He hadn't done anything like this since...since...

Fuck. Dizziness swept over him, making him sway in place.

The last time he'd worn a suit had been at Helen's funeral. Dark-eyed men in dark clothes had lowered her down, the sky bleeding rain through a sheet of steel-gray clouds, and he'd stood out in it for hours. There'd been no one left to tell him not to.

He stood there in his own downpour now, drowning on dry land. His stuffy, shut-up bedroom closed in around him, and he could stay in it forever, couldn't he? Never answer the door again or descend those stairs. Never look upon a face that broke like the sun on the horizon, echoing out in shimmering waves of brilliant gold.

Except he couldn't. Serena—she wouldn't stand for it. She'd come up here and she'd knock until her knuckles were sore, and it didn't matter how long he resisted. Eventually he'd let her in.

Grasping his crutches, he straightened his shoulders and raised his gaze. Inevitability tugged at him.

He *wanted* to let her in. That might be what scared him most of all.

And then there wasn't time to belabor it anymore. Like clockwork, a quiet rapping sounded out from the direction of his door.

The world around him lurched back into focus. Instead of a reflection in a mirror, he was staring at a blank expanse of wall, and he might not be able to fool anyone into believing he was a gentleman—not if they had the balls to look him in the eye. But there was space. Empty room in his life, room that Serena had carved out of a morass of stagnation and grief, and it was just like that wall. Blank. Ready for him to write upon it what he would.

It was faster going than it would've been a scant few weeks ago, but it still seemed to take an age for him to reach his door. Jostling his crutch, he flung the door open.

Bloody fucking hell. The idea of locking himself away in his room had tempted him for all of a minute, but in the span of a breath, it flew out of his brain entirely.

Serena was a vision. He'd found the coy flirtatiousness of her everyday attire alluring enough, but tonight she'd clearly gone out of her way to ruin him. Rich black fabric clung to her every curve, bare expanses of milky thigh exposed, and her *breasts*...

God, but he'd touched those. In the flurry of the moment, kissing her like a man possessed, he'd had that lushness pressed against his chest, his hand drawn toward those curves. The very tops of them rose above the neckline of her dress, the soft cleft between them a siren's song luring him in. He licked his lips, wanting his mouth on tender flesh.

What would she sound like underneath him? He could almost taste the sweetness of her. She'd be so hot around him, taking him into her body the way she'd welcomed him into every other aspect of her life, and he'd be so good to her. So thorough, taking the time to learn every inch, every spot that made her whimper or sigh.

Except—

Snapping his jaw shut, he forced his gaze toward her eyes. He was blatantly staring, ogling her in the worst, most objectifying way, and she'd be well within her rights to slap him for it. But no. Those soft green irises surrounded pupils gone wide with a need to match his own, and she wasn't looking at *his* eyes.

A rush of hot, male pride swam through him, filling his veins. This was dangerous territory he was wading into here. His promises, his anger, they'd been his companions all these years. They'd kept him safe. But all at once they threatened to slip away.

He cleared his throat, and her gaze darted up, her cheeks flushing with the same guilt he himself had felt. Flustered, she dug her teeth into the pout of her crimson lip, and damn it all. That wasn't helping things.

"Sorry." She waved her hand in front of herself. "You just. You look really nice."

His stomach twisted by a fraction. The woman had only really known him since he'd hurt his leg. She'd seen him in sweats and shorts and T-shirts. Of course the contrast was striking.

He channeled his annoyance at that into a quirked brow and a smirk. "You're surprised?"

"No. Of course not." The color to her cheeks only deepened. "Just. Impressed."

Something in him softened. This was a terrible idea. Just terrible. But with the hand he'd freed to open the door, he reached up. Ever so gently, he stroked a single fingertip down the line of her cheek. Color spread in its wake, and deep inside, a tension within him coiled higher and tighter. "You look beautiful."

Glancing down, she twisted her hands around the strap of her purse. "Thank you."

She didn't step away, and he didn't remove his hand. But she didn't edge in closer, either, and he didn't dare. It felt like they could have stayed like that for days and days, caught in the push-pull and the hum of static between their bodies. Promise bloomed, ripe and impossible in the air around them, and he was caught, hovering over an abyss he didn't begin to know how to cross.

But then he looked into her eyes again, and desire still shone in those depths, but there was something else, too.

They were ringed in red.

Brows furrowing, he slipped his thumb higher, stroking just beneath her lashes. "Are you all right?"

It broke the spell. One corner of her mouth twisted down, her whole expression flinching. "Fine." She drew in a breath. "Just...some stuff with my sister."

"Is *she* all right?"

"I'm not sure." A shadow darkened her gaze. "I hope so. My mother's looking into it." Before she could explain any further, a car's horn blared outside, interrupting her, and something like relief swept over her face. Catching his palm in hers, she gave it a squeeze before she let it drop away. "That'll be our cab."

"Of course." The one they'd decided to take in case she wanted to have a second glass of wine tonight.

Allowing himself to be distracted from her aborted attempt at an explanation, he followed her out into the hallway, stooping to lock his door. At the top of the stairs, she held out a hand for one of his crutches, and he passed it to her without argument. Taking the first step down, he gripped the railing with all his might to keep his balance.

But it was a losing battle. Forget his knee. She'd already thrown him and his life so far off-kilter, he didn't think he'd ever recover.

He wasn't even sure he wanted to.

Serena'd worried for a minute as she'd been getting dressed that things with her sister would distract her from making the most of the evening. She shouldn't have doubted herself.

Or more realistically, she shouldn't have doubted Cole.

Their taxi had dropped them off outside the restaurant where the benefit was being held right on time. As she'd clattered around on her heels to the other side of the car to let Cole out, her breath had already been up, her pulse racing. She'd been in confined spaces with him before, but sitting side by side in the backseat like that, his bad leg splayed out to keep it straight, their ankles brushing with every swerving motion of the cab...

Worse, with him looking like *that*—polished and dapper, and she'd thought he was attractive before. When he actually tried, it nearly took her breath away. Closed in together, he'd smelled of the richness of his aftershave, like warm male and spicy woods, and even now, sticking close by his side as they wandered their way through a reception hall, all she wanted to do was lean into him, let her nose guide her to the point of his jaw and the hollow of his throat so she could bury herself in that scent. In him.

She clenched her fingers tighter around her clutch to keep from reaching out.

So of course, he chose precisely that moment to lean in.

"On your ten o'clock," he said, the smooth roll of his voice just adding to the numb delirium taking over her senses.

She tried to be all stealthy as she took a glance in that direction, but sneakiness wasn't exactly her forte. Nothing in particular caught her attention anyway. "Hmm?"

"Blond man in a navy pinstripe suit."

She peeked over there again, and wow. Cole's eyes were sharp. "Oh."

She wasn't entirely sure how she'd missed him the first time, honestly. The man had half a head on just about everyone else there, and his shoulders were strong and broad, his jaw sharp.

"People keep going over to him. Must be important."

He had that right. "Dean of admissions."

One Grayson Trousseau. Notoriously reclusive, always staying squirreled away in his office. She'd tried a half-dozen times on her little visits to find an excuse or an opportunity to bump into him, but to no avail.

"Excellent." Without another word, Cole started off toward the man.

Serena's hand flew out before she could stop it, catching on the fabric of his jacket, and God. He was pouring off heat. She managed not to react to that as he pulled up short, glancing back at her with one brow raised.

"What are you doing?" she asked.

"We're going to go introduce ourselves." He said it as if it were obvious, and it was, wasn't it? The entire point of attending tonight had been the chance to get some face time with the people who would determine Max's fate.

But..."Can we just do that?"

"Of course."

He didn't wait for any additional comment. She found herself pulled along in his wake, and she could say that much about accompanying a man on crutches. People did tend to move to allow them through. As they neared their target, they passed a waiter with a tray of flutes, and she didn't hesitate. Slipping her wrist through the strap on her bag, she reached out and grabbed two—if Cole didn't want his, she'd drink it herself. She took one fortifying sip, then hurried to keep up, only falling back into step with him as he was inserting himself right into a conversation.

"Yes, but we don't begin to introduce quantum conceptualizations until far too late in STEM education, anyway."

A half dozen pairs of eyes all turned toward Cole as one, Serena's included. Had those even been words he'd just spoken?

One of the men recovered first, and Serena's brows only rose higher when she recognized him as the chair of the science department. "Too true, Mr...."

"Stafford. Dr. Cole Stafford." His smile was tight, but he extricated a hand to extend it toward the man. As he gripped his palm, he nodded to Serena. "And my companion is Serena Hartmann. An acclaimed teacher who's worked with some of yours in the past. Her nephew, Max, has you top on his list for next year."

"Oh, wonderful."

Gazes turned to Serena, and she was regretting taking those champagne glasses now. Shifting them to one hand, she shook with everyone in the circle, nodding at all the names she'd been stalking so relentlessly on the school's website and social media, her throat tightening up when she got to Mr. Trousseau himself. She was pretty sure some words managed to pass her lips, but she didn't hear a one of them.

How had Cole done that? The charm he'd turned on in front of Mrs. Cunningham the previous week was out in spades, an easiness to him she never saw in their day to day.

And a coiled element, too. A strain.

Like it took work to be so polite, so witty. And it struck her. This was a mask. An appealing, unreasonably compelling mask. But the man beneath it was the one she'd met on that very first day. The one he showed her again and again as he revealed even more of his story. Making cookies together or tutoring her nephew. Drinking tea out of the mismatched mugs she'd made with her own two hands.

The conversation Cole had inserted them into resumed around them—something about increasing rigor in science and math education. Not exactly her strong suit, but apparently it was Cole's. The man had told her he wasn't a fan of teaching, but he certainly had a lot of smart, insightful things to say about it. Heads around the circle nodded, considering gazes going more and more admiring.

Until a pause in the discussion, when Grayson Trousseau turned to her, his blue eyes sharpening as they focused in on hers. "You said your nephew was applying to Upton for the fall?"

Serena's heart got stuck in her throat, her tongue thick and heavy, her mouth dry. Blinking owlishly, she nodded. Cole gave that tight smile of his again, swooping in.

"Max Hartmann. Terribly bright boy."

"Well, I'll have to keep my eye out for him," Mr. Trousseau said. "Sounds like the kind of applicant we're looking for."

Dizziness swept over her. All at once her tongue came unglued. "Thank you. He's really got his heart set on it."

The man nodded. "It's been a pleasure to meet you." With that, he made his excuses, extricating himself and heading for the bar.

The group as a whole drifted apart not long after. Still a little light-headed, Serena let Cole lead her over to a high top in the corner. Shifting his crutches, he pried the flutes from her hands and set them down, taking her purse from her, too.

Concern trickled into his voice. "Serena?"

She reached out, grabbing his hands in her own. They were so warm, the strength in his fingertips and palms squeezing back as she held on.

She lifted her gaze to his. "That was amazing."

"It was?"

"You. You were—*incredible*. Do you realize what just happened? You got the dean of admissions—Grayson Trousseau. He knows Max's name now."

Then she spotted it—the smug, low-smoldering glow to his little half-grin. He knew exactly what he'd done. He knew what it meant to her.

"Why, I could—" She stopped herself before she could say it.

She could kiss him, was what she could do.

Shaky, she let go of his hands, feeling the loss of his warmth in the places deep beneath her skin, where her attraction to him simmered. And sometimes threatened to boil over.

Dropping her gaze, she reached for her flute, draining the last of it, but it did nothing for the desert of her throat.

A wariness had crept into Cole's gaze, yet when she set her glass back down, all he did was nudge the other flute closer to her.

She shook her head. "It's yours if you want it."

"You look like you need it more."

Maybe she did. She took a more measured sip from the spare glass before pushing it away. Steadier by a fraction, she looked up at him.

"Thank you," she said, and it came out too intense by half.

The smile she got in reward was so real, though. So gorgeous and unself-conscious. So free.

"It's the least I could do."

It wasn't—not by a long shot. But that he'd said it was and that he'd meant it...This man had helped not only her, but her family.

And what she was starting to feel for him wasn't simple attraction. It wasn't that at all.

CHAPTER TEN

It was a good thing they'd had so much luck hobnobbing during the cocktail hour, because it looked like at dinner they were striking out.

Stomach sinking, Serena leaned in close to Cole as they approached their assigned table, murmuring under her breath, "I don't recognize any of those people."

"It's not full yet," he said, all reassurance, and urged her on.

She smiled as she pulled out a chair. Introductions were made, names that only vaguely registered as she kept half an eye on the front of the room. The entire administration of the school was here, and nearly all of the senior faculty. All the people who would likely have a say in the admissions process—or who would at least be listened to if they happened to put in a good word. Restless, she shifted in her seat. It was too much to hope that any of them would choose to join them here. The room was practically overflowing with people who had more of a claim on their time. But they were sprinkled around, scattering themselves at different tables.

And then the sole remaining chair beside hers pulled out.

She jerked her head up, her gaze traveling the length of a navy pinstripe suit before settling on twinkling blue eyes.

She smacked her knee on the underside of the table in her scramble to rise. "Mr. Trousseau."

He waved at her dismissively, motioning for her to sit back down. "Grayson, please. Serena, right?"

"Yes." Why did the word have to come out so breathless?

He nodded to Cole. "And Dr. Stafford?"

"Cole."

Reaching across the table, he introduced himself to the other couples seated beside them.

Couples. It made a spot light up in Serena's brain. "Is someone joining you?" She stopped herself from saying wife. "We can get another chair, or—"

"No, just me." He shot her a rueful smile, like there was a story there. But clearly not one he wanted to dwell on. He addressed the table as a whole. "So what brings you all here tonight?"

As the man on the other side of Grayson chimed in about being an alumnus, Serena took the opportunity to look to Cole, not even bothering to mask her glee. Less than surreptitiously, she nudged her elbow toward Grayson as she raised her brows in disbelief. They'd already managed to make a good impression earlier, but getting to have a whole meal with this man? It was beyond her wildest dreams.

Cole smiled in reply, but it wasn't quite as unreserved in its approval as it could've been.

She let her brows lower, mouthing, "Are you okay?"

"Fine." As if to prove it, he placed his hand over hers beneath the table, giving it a quick squeeze, and for a second, she almost forgot what she was so excited about.

Worse—or maybe better—he didn't take his hand away. He just left it there, broad palm atop hers, the stroking of his thumb sending shivers of warmth shooting up the bare skin of her arms.

"Are you cold?" Grayson's voice interrupted her reverie, and she twisted around, blinking in confusion as the man tugged at the lapels of his jacket. By way of explanation, he said, "They always keep it precisely the wrong temperature at these things. Two warm for us men and too cold for the ladies in their lovely dresses."

Oh good Lord. He was offering her his jacket, wasn't he?

If anything, she was overheated, and Cole's hand clamping down only intensified it.

"No, I'm fine, thank you," she choked out.

At that, Cole's grip relaxed, and she sat there, fully waiting for him to let go the way he always did. Every time they danced too close and he made her heart soar. He always took it back, or worse, said it was a mistake.

But not this time.

Her breath went shallow. All around her, conversation resumed. She participated in it, even. But her focus just kept coming back to the impossible. The inexplicable. The hidden play of fingers against her skin.

Let. Go.

Cole kept willing his own ruddy hand to do his bidding, but it was no use.

Serena looked and smelled so good, she was sitting there beside him in that slip of a dress, and he never should've touched her in the first place. But her flesh was as smooth and soft as he remembered it. He wanted to laugh. One little touch, one moment of reassurance, and it had been the worst kind of mistake.

He didn't know how to stop. Especially not when—

Grayson laughed at some inanity from one of the other women seated at the table. Cole gritted his teeth. He was playing nice tonight. For Serena's and Max's sake, he was on his very best behavior. Charming and dapper and not punching smug, self-important blond deans of admission in their perfect fucking teeth.

Jesus. The man didn't have to just be powerful, at least to Serena's gaze. He had to be attractive, too. Educated. She was hanging on his every word, and Cole's grip on her kept incrementally tightening.

He cursed himself bitterly. Jealous, ridiculous *fool*. How many times had he pushed her away? And now he physically couldn't seem to stop holding her hand, and why? Because another man was paying attention to her? Offering her his jacket, even?

Cole's stomach shuddered and sank. He should've thought to do that. All that creamy skin left exposed by that dress—of course she had to be freezing. Had he been thinking, he could've had her wrapped up in his coat and in his scent, but that was the effect she had on him. His brain went to toffee, sticky and slow.

He forgot to think of all the reasons he needed to let go.

Finally, he was saved by servers coming around. As a salad plate was placed in front of him, his fingers unlocked. He pulled back and straightened his spine, unable to look at her for the shame of it. Every time, the loss of her touch was a near-physical pain, and he kept forcing himself to experience it. Dancing far too close to her flame. Sooner or later, he was going to burn.

By the time the entrees arrived, he'd more or less recovered his composure, though he still gripped his silverware hard enough to bend the metal. Grayson presided over the table, coaxing people's entire life stories from them as if it were his job. Maybe it was.

Cole's knife skidded across his plate with an indecorous screech as the man turned to Serena.

"And what about you, my dear?" He darted a glance at Cole. "Your companion here said you were a teacher?"

"Yes." She set her utensils down and brushed a lock of golden hair behind her ear, trailing her fingertips down the column of her throat to fiddle with her necklace. "Seventh grade. Public school, though." She said it half apologetically, as though that were something to be ashamed about.

Cole frowned. If anything, she should be proud of what she did. He opened his mouth, about to say as much.

But Grayson spoke first, neatly sidestepping the issue altogether. "And is that something you've always wanted to do?"

"Since I was in middle school myself." She glanced away, eyes taking on that particular gleam they got when she was getting worked up about her profession. "I had an amazing teacher. One of those who really inspires you, you know?"

Heads around the table nodded, and Cole leaned forward. This wasn't a story he'd heard before. Probably because he'd never asked.

"My sister, Penny." Her voice cracked by half a fraction, but she hid it well. "She was an honors student. Always the best at everything. She had her flaws, sure, but at school at least..." A ruefulness colored her smile. "Let's say she wasn't an easy act to follow. Teachers expected me to pick things up as quickly as she did, and when I didn't, they always seemed so disappointed. But not this teacher. She made me realize—" She cut herself off, throat bobbing. "Teaching isn't about the kids who could've done it on their own. It's about the ones who need you. Who need to be noticed or encouraged." She shrugged. "I want to be that person, and teaching where I do, working with the kids I do, I get to change people's lives."

The room was loud, practically rattling with all the clinking and chatter. But the silence that descended over their table seemed to wash it away. Cole swallowed, his mouth suddenly dry.

This woman. He wanted to take her hand all over again, consequences and temptations be damned. He wanted to worship her.

He wanted to give to her what she was apparently so prepared to give to everyone else.

Self-consciousness seemed to steal over her, and she dropped her gaze, picking up her fork and poking at her potatoes with the tines.

Grayson recovered first. "Noble," he said, though there was something strained to his voice.

Cole shook his head. His throat was still parched, and he grasped for words. The only ones he could find were "You're amazing."

Whirling around, she turned the full power of her vivid green eyes on him, making him feel pinned. He curled his fingers hard into a fist. It had come out too reverent, too awed by half, and yet it didn't begin to encapsulate a fraction of what she did to him.

She inspired him. She drew him out of himself—made him

want to teach and love and be part of the world again. Part of *her* world.

For a moment, the room around them receded, their gazes locked. And he could do it. He could touch her. He could let himself.

But before his hands could begin to uncurl, Grayson cleared his throat. "And, Cole, you said you were a doctor?"

Cole's mind was a haze, all his thoughts turned to this slip of a woman who brought him to his knees, who threatened to change *his* life. The moment, crystalline and perfect, shattered around him.

He tore his gaze away. "I..." He tucked his hand beneath the table, jabbing into the meat of his thigh as if that could clear his thoughts. He shook his head. "No. A professor. I was a professor."

In another life.

"Oh? And now?"

Nothing. The same, stale anger of the last few years nipped at his heels. He did *nothing*.

But then it came to him.

Strangled, his very lungs threatening to close, he said, "I do some tutoring."

And it was the most satisfying thing he'd done in years.

Grayson's brow furrowed, and Serena laughed, a high, clear sound that soothed something inside of Cole.

After that, the rest of the dinner hour passed in a blur. Small talk about careers gave way to theater and the new show at the Art Institute and the mayor's latest scandal. Finally, someone stepped up to a podium at the front of the room. With gratitude,

Cole tuned the parade of speakers and presenters out, the meaningless self-congratulation washing over him until—

"And now," a voice boomed over the microphone, "we invite you to relax and enjoy the musical stylings of the Tony Stephens Band."

Out of nowhere, the room erupted in music. Cole started, dessert fork clattering to his plate as he whipped around.

In his distraction, an entire band had set up. He recognized the tune, an old jazz standard Helen would have loved, would have forced him to dance to, and he would have gone. For her he would have.

She wasn't the only one.

He turned back to Serena, and his heart was an impassable terrain of barbed wire and mud, littered with tire tracks and blood. But her eyes were beautiful. They were hopeful.

Right until the moment they fell.

Her mouth struggled to keep from curling down into a frown. Looking just to the side of him, she said, "You probably need a few more therapy appointments before you can dance, huh?"

Bollocks. He'd been so enraptured, so consumed, he'd nearly forgotten. His hand went instinctively for the crutches resting against the corner of his chair, the throbbing ache in his knee resurging.

Whatever had been rising in him fell, too.

"Probably." He nodded, his voice strangled.

But he hadn't known how strained it could become.

"If I may," Grayson said. "I know a step or two."

Something complicated happened around Serena's mouth. She twisted around in her seat to face the man, the pretty pink of her flush sliding down her neck toward her chest. She glanced to Cole, a question to the tilt of her chin.

It was like watching their moment fall away all over again.

"Please," he said, the words acid, "don't let me hold you back."

There was reluctance in Serena's posture as she stood. As she took the hand of another man. She glanced one last time at Cole. "You're sure?"

"Absolutely."

Tethered in place in so many ways, bound to where he sat, he watched them walk away.

And something inside him snapped.

Well, at least Serena knew what it was like to turn into a pillar of salt now.

The whole way out to the impromptu dance floor set up in front of the band, she kept taking backward glances. It was futile. She knew that. But the look on Cole's face had been so miserable as he'd urged her to go. He understood how much securing Max's place at Upton meant to her, and he hadn't tried to hold her back. He clearly hadn't been happy about it, though.

Her heart tugged hard at her chest as Grayson held out his arms. She stepped into them, leaving more than enough room for the Holy Spirit, her hand stiff where it rested on his shoulder. It was so wrong to be gazing past him, staring back at their table, at the twin points of those dark, brooding eyes that she could practically feel boring into her.

To go even more rigid in this mockery of a dance when she watched that figure rise and start a slow, aching walk toward the door.

Warm fingers tightened around her palm, and she sucked in a breath as she refocused.

"Let him stew," Grayson said.

She felt like something you'd find stuck to the bottom of your shoe.

"I'm sorry, I—" She didn't even know what kind of excuse she could hope to make.

Fortunately, she didn't have to make one at all. "It's fine." Grayson's smile was kind, his eyes clear. "You clearly have a...complicated relationship."

"That's an understatement."

"I wasn't trying to show him up or steal you away."

The thought had scarcely entered her mind. It said more than she cared to admit that it hadn't—Grayson was handsome and well spoken, effortlessly charming in a way Cole had to work so hard to be. He'd been courteous and quietly flirtatious, and a couple of weeks ago, she would've been doodling his name in the margins of her notebooks. But not now.

He squeezed her hand. "You looked like you wanted to dance, and your date couldn't. That's all this is."

Her brows ascended toward her hairline. "I'm not sure if I should be offended by that or not."

"Not at all. Under different circumstances, we would be having a *very* different conversation right now." His tone flashed dark for a fraction of a moment, suffusing with a low heat, and wow. Under different circumstances, she'd be having that same conversation with him in a heartbeat. "But," he said, voice lightening as he led her into a slow circle in time to the beat, "you have an applicant in the family, and even if you didn't..." He glanced behind her, and she couldn't resist now any more than she'd been able to before.

Cole had made it to the door, but not the one she'd feared—the one that would take him out. Maybe to the street and maybe to a cab. Maybe someplace she couldn't follow. Instead, he'd headed toward a set of open French doors leading out onto a balcony.

And he stood there, silhouetted in moonlight, so alone and so beautiful she ached.

"Oh." With a wet, shaky noise, she swallowed against the pull in her throat.

The corner of Grayson's mouth flickered upward, drawing her gaze back to him. "That's exactly why I'm not trying to steal you away."

"I appreciate that."

She appreciated his saying it, too. After all the times Cole had touched her only to pull away—after the kiss that ended before it had hardly begun—she'd started to worry this was all in her head. Cole was a lightning burst of intensity, jagged brilliance that blinded her every time it struck. He was seared into her vision now, and she wasn't the only one who could see it.

This line they'd been toeing at the edges of for weeks now—they had to either step across it or back away for real. She knew which she'd prefer, but it was time for him to decide.

And she was going to confront him about it. Tonight.

"I should—" She lifted her hand from Grayson's shoulder.

Only for a strong grasp to surround her wrist, returning it to where it was.

"Like I said." His grin flickered. "You should let him stew.

Come on." The music shifted tempo, drifting into another song. "Dance with me."

"I thought I just did."

"That barely counted, and you know it."

She did. She also knew that if Cole's expression had been miserable when she'd first walked off with this man, he'd be seething by now.

Maybe Grayson was right. Maybe she should let him see her enjoying herself with someone else for a little longer.

"All right," she said, tilting her chin up.

His smile this time was unfettered, his eyes twinkling. He flexed his fingers at her waist, taking a firmer hand in leading her around the floor. "You're a beautiful, intelligent woman, Serena. Any man would be lucky to have you on his arm."

They would.

She kept telling herself that as they danced—two more songs and then three. But when he cocked a brow and offered her a fourth, she shook her head. He let her go this time, and with a little bow of thanks, she took her leave.

Then with her shoulders straight, her head held high, she floated her way across the room. And toward a man whose eyes looked like the very darkest kind of storm.

CHAPTER ELEVEN

Fuck.

Cole's stomach was a writhing mass of knots as he stood there, not quite in the room and not beyond it. The heat from within beat at his front while the cool night air buffeted him from behind, the music swirling with a looming sort of silence and leaving a cacophony inside his mind. A precipice, then, and he had but to take a single step to either side.

Or to wait.

Pale skin glowing in the dim light, hair golden, Serena approached him, and there was a new sort of stillness to her that only served to set the waiting pieces in him further on edge. The resolve to her gait made him quake.

The things this woman set into motion in him—the things he felt whenever she was near. They were foreign and familiar, a possessiveness he never thought he'd ever feel again. A hunger and a need, and not just for her body. He needed *her*.

And it was that that made him grip his crutches tighter. Take a single, torturous step back.

The fierce pang squeezing like a vise around his heart—the sick jealousy when she'd so much as looked at another man. His laughter hurt like a sob. The very signs of how he hungered were themselves the reasons he couldn't have her. He ruined everything he touched, and he wouldn't do that to her. Even if it meant never coming close to her again.

But with that same assuredness smoothing her gait, she pursued him, a relentless march that ate up the space and drove him farther back onto the balcony. A gust of wind blew through his hair, and the notes of yet another old jazz standard went muffled and low.

Then she was standing just where he had been, on that very same dividing line. She surged across it like it wasn't even there, inserting herself into his space and into his life.

His resistance crumpled. But whatever words she'd been about to say seemed to die on her lips.

He turned away.

With his heart echoing through his ribs, he made his way to the railing and looked over. They weren't particularly high off the ground—just a couple of stories. The city below pulsed, though, teeming with life, while up here, for just a moment, all was still.

Until Serena came to stand at his side. She was a silent presence in a clear and brilliant night. As he turned his head, she stole his breath from his lungs. God, she was beautiful.

And she was shaking.

It was nothing this time to shift his weight to one side, to lean his crutches against the railing. He shrugged off his jacket and held it out for her.

For what felt like eons, she stared at him. At long last, she turned to give him her back. His throat bobbed as she slipped her arms into the sleeves. He settled the fabric on her shoulders, her body swimming beneath those tailored lines, and his blood flashed hot.

"Serena." Her name felt punched out of him, a breath pulled from his very lungs. He slid his hands down her arms. Just the tips of her fingers poked out from beneath his sleeves, but when he reached them, they were nimble and strong, grasping at his palms. She drew his arms around her until he was holding her, and it was all wrong. He was barely standing, off balance even without the heat of her spine pressed to her chest, even before the scent of her hair was in his lungs. He closed his eyes. *"Serena."*

"Dance with me?"

He shook his head. "I don't know if I can."

"There's only one way to find out."

She spun inside his arms, a slow half-circle that gave him every opportunity to pull back or push her away, but he didn't. Damn him—damn his soul and his heart and this whisper of life she'd breathed into him.

The music was faint, but the pulse of it hummed through the floor of the balcony, steady enough to sway to. He winced, putting too much weight on his bad leg, and what had he been thinking? But all she did was reach to the side. She handed him a single crutch. It was a near-physical pain to unwrap his arm from around her waist. But he could stand like this. He could hold her with what fraction of himself there was to give. He could hold himself up against the force of gravity and memory.

She lifted her face to his.

They were alone on this little balcony, in this tiny pocket of time and space, and she fit so perfectly against him. He dipped in closer, and her eyes fluttered, long lashes dark against the porcelain of her skin.

The music changed.

He pulled away like he'd been burned.

His knee screamed at him as loudly as his heart did, his skin that had been aching for contact for *years*.

But the last time he'd danced, it had been to this song. He couldn't breathe.

"Cole?"

He shook his head, throwing his free hand out in a warning. She couldn't touch him—he couldn't stand to have her near. He couldn't *do* this.

"Cole?" She said his name again, and it felt like bones snapping, like blood seeping out onto snow.

"No," he breathed. The floor spun beneath his feet, and he listed wildly. She put a hand on his arm, and red washed across his vision. He flailed out, striking at nothing. He needed air, needed time, needed years. His hand connected with the metal strut of his other crutch and he got it under him, not seeing, barely hearing. His leg was a dense ache, but he surged across the floor. The door was right there. He just had to get through it, and everything would be fine; he'd be alone and fine and safe and *miserable* and—

And her voice rang out across the distance and the space. "Don't you *dare* walk away from me again."

He lurched to a stop, everything going suddenly, shatteringly still. He'd heard those words before.

Frozen, he stood at the boundary between two worlds, seeing double, two women's voices echoing back and forth across the line.

That last night—he'd tried so hard not to let the anger that lived inside him take him over. He knew all the tricks. Disengage and walk away, but Helen had been hysterical. She'd stopped him, and he'd let her, damn it all.

It wasn't anger fueling him now, but it didn't matter.

"I can't," he gritted out.

"You can't *what*? Jesus, Cole. You touch me and you walk away, and you act like you're dying when I dance with another guy, and then when I try—" Her throat made a wet, aching sound. "*You* can't. Maybe I can't, either. I can't keep *doing* this with you."

"Then don't."

If she walked away from him, then he wouldn't have to be the one to turn away from her. It would hurt him like only one thing in his life ever had before, but he'd let her go.

It'd be for the best.

But then she was so close. Her heat seeped through the thin fabric of his shirt, the searing brand of her palm at the base of his spine.

"I've been trying," she said, and it came out small but fierce. "To get to know you. And you let me in in these little dribs and drabs. I think you want to give me the rest of it, too. I don't think you want me to go."

It was the last thing he wanted in the world. Denial sat on his lips, but the lie was too much for him to bear. He kept his silence, biting down on his tongue until he tasted blood.

"So let me in." She trailed her fingers up his spine, melting him another fraction with every inch she climbed.

"I don't know how."

"I'll show you."

She would, wouldn't she? With tender hands and gentle care, she'd open him up. She'd carve out room for herself in the frozen wasteland of his heart.

But the music was still playing, the hurt still too large and too impossible of a thing inside his chest.

He shook his head. With a hitching breath, she tore her hand away, but that only made it worse. Gripping his crutches tighter, he turned around. He met eyes that were shuttering, his chance evaporating.

So many times now, he had tried to push her away. It hadn't worked and hadn't worked. If anything, she'd only managed to work her way closer, and he didn't know how to let her go. But for her sake, he had to try. One last time. Only...

"Not here," he said.

She lifted her gaze, and the hope there flayed him open.

"But when we get home..."

His breathing stuttered. "When we get home, I'll tell you everything."

And if she was smart, she'd walk away from him for good.

Serena let out a heavy sigh. Exhausted, she stared out the window of the taxi, watching the city blocks go by. Just as it had on the way there, Cole's leg brushed hers, but the kind of tension it inspired in her now wasn't the same at all.

The push-pull and the back and forth, the hundreds of mixed signals he kept sending her had worn her down. She hadn't been lying when she'd told him she couldn't do this anymore. Forget the havoc he was wreaking on her heart. It was his fault they'd left the benefit early. Instead of focusing on Max, she'd let herself get distracted.

For so long, her missions in life had been clear. Take care of her family. Take care of her students and her friends. Taking care of a broken, beautiful man hadn't been part of the equation. She'd worked him in seamlessly enough until now, but if he was going to keep her from doing the things she needed to—if she was going to give and give and give and receive nothing from him in return...

She bit down on the inside of her cheek. That wasn't fair. Cole had gotten Max caught up on a full semester's worth of math in a handful of weeks. He was the reason she'd been able to go to that benefit in the first place and make what inroads she had. He'd given her these pieces of his story.

It never felt like enough, though.

So many times in her life, she'd tried to tell herself that the nods of appreciation and the words of thanks were all she needed. But they weren't. And this was even worse somehow.

Every time Cole pulled away, it was another stinging slap of rejection, but each one seemed to hurt him as much as they did her. She didn't understand it.

But she wanted to. She was going to. He'd promised to talk, and by God she was going to hold him to it.

When they pulled up outside their building, Cole insisted on paying the fare, and she let him. She frowned as she did, though. What a waste. Stone-cold sober, she slipped out of the cab and went around to Cole's side, wordlessly taking his crutches as he passed them over to her. Handing them back once he'd gotten to his feet.

The silence held as they made their way inside, all the way to the first-floor landing, where she paused. Maybe she should follow him to his apartment, but if this went badly...She didn't know if she could stand to hear him telling her to go again. Watching him leave her place wouldn't be much easier, but at least it seemed like something she could bear.

Taking a deep breath, she got her keys out and headed for her door. "I guess you'd better come in." She made her tone firm, not brooking any argument. By some miracle, she didn't receive any. He followed her inside, letting her sweep through the space ahead of him, hanging up her keys and flicking on lights.

And then there wasn't anything else to do. Her fingers twitched, restless and empty. Maybe she should make some tea—offer him something to eat or to drink or—

Or she could quit it with the stalling already.

She turned to face him. He was standing in the middle of her living room, larger than life and so tall. So proud.

She swallowed hard. Clearly she was going to have to start this. "Have a seat." She motioned toward the chair he'd all but fallen into that first day they'd met. When she'd found him sitting at the top of the stairs, his crutches strewn around him, pain etched into every line of his face. She glanced down at the reminder. "Your leg must be killing you."

A low, awful laugh escaped his throat. "You have no idea."

She didn't.

He made no move to take a seat, and her patience—something she'd always prided herself on having so much of—threatened to fail her.

God. What was it about this man? He made her crazy and delirious in turns, and she just wanted to wrap herself around him. She wanted him to *want* her to.

She crossed her arms in front of herself. The sleeves of his jacket bunched at her elbows and around her shoulders, making her feel even smaller and more helpless, and she didn't know what to do about it.

Except take it off.

The cool air on the bare skin of her arms was a shock after the warmth of his coat. The haze of his scent faded away, leaving her thoughts clearer. Her spine straighter.

"Here." She offered the jacket to him, but he shook his head, and she draped it over the back of the chair instead. Crossing her arms again, she shivered. She was too cold and too exposed in this slip of a dress.

She'd *made* herself too exposed for him. Time and time again, and what did she expect but more silence? More charged glances and fiery touches that led to nowhere and nothing.

And he had promised her an explanation.

The thin, remaining thread of her patience snapped. "You said when we got home you'd tell me everything." Looking him square in the eye, she lifted her chin in challenge. "So talk."

Cole wanted to laugh. All the years he'd spent not talking, all the endless nights and wasted days trapped within the same four walls. He'd locked himself inside, and he'd locked his history in there with him. At some point he'd lost the key. He didn't know how to get it out.

And now this woman stood before him, this slip of a girl who was stronger than just about anyone he'd met in his life. Selfless and sweet and so damn forgiving when he disappointed her again and again. She was finally demanding answers, and she deserved them, too.

But Jesus Christ. Where the hell did he even start?

A hundred moments flashed across his vision as he weathered her stare. The tide of them threatened to sweep him away. He was a boy, palms skinned and glasses shattered against the pavement in a London alleyway. A young man trying so desperately to be *normal* for the woman who would come to bear his name.

An older man, still numb with horror as he traced those letters across the granite that marked her grave.

He was here. Now. Steadily creeping on toward middle age with nothing to show for himself but debts and years and promises he was terrified to break. Serena made him want to, though, and that might be what scared him most of all.

Maybe that was the answer, then. He didn't have to go back decades. He could start with the beginning of *their* story.

His knee gave a twinge as he took the handful of labored steps toward her window. He looked down through the glass at the pavement a half-story below. And then he turned back to look at her.

"It's funny, you know." He heard the words before he felt them pass his lips, the weight of so much silence making his voice sound twisted and strange. "The first time we met, you asked me how this"—he gently tapped his crutch against his leg—"had happened to me."

Confusion marred her brow, her shoulders dropping by a fraction. "What—"

"I told you, and you said I was a hero."

"Because you are."

The laugh he'd nearly let out before escaped him now. "I'm really not." His fingers flexed, grip tightening until the padding on the handles of his crutches creaked against the strain. "I just get so *angry* sometimes."

"You saw someone getting mugged—"

"And I lost it. You don't...You can't know." Even now, the boiling in his blood was set alight by just the memory. "The boy whose bag was stolen, he looked like such a target."

And Cole knew how that felt. That's how he had been—younger and smaller. Mouthy and smart and too perfect of a temptation to resist.

He gritted his teeth. "I used to be that target." He met her gaze, staring into the ocean of her eyes and wishing he could float away along the calmness of her sea. But he couldn't. Not here. Not now. "I told you how I knew what was happening to Max."

"So you were bullied. So were a lot of people."

"I was bullied until I *snapped*." He had to look away. "Day after day after day." The scar on his lip seared and burned. "They never stop, and I had to...I couldn't..."

And he was there. In that alley halfway between his parents' flat and school, caught and pushed—they always *pushed*. Glass sliced into his lip, and his hands were bloody, gravel ground into his knees and palms. He remembered the silent seething, the resentment, the bruises that never healed.

How it felt to let it all go. To fight back. Impact and fists, and they were his blows this time, every hurt returned, and he'd been lost. A fucking savage.

"I put one boy in the hospital." His throat went raw, the bitter taste of bile rising at the image. "I nearly ended up there myself."

He'd nearly been expelled. The classroom had been his only refuge, and he'd come so close to losing that, too. Meetings and suspensions, and through it all he'd remembered every shove. Every time they'd driven him closer to the edge, but he had been the one to throw himself over.

In the end, it was only his fault.

"They never bothered me again," he said. "But it didn't matter."

The genie had been let out. He'd crammed the anger and the bitterness beneath his skin, but it had become this living thing. It never left him.

It never stopped.

"I never had many friends." Even in the neighborhood where they lived, full of families just like theirs, he'd been the outsider. "It used to be because I was strange, but after that it was because I was mental, too."

"You're not—"

"I am. I was." Normal people didn't have this crimson current running through their veins. They didn't have to clench their fists to try to keep it all at bay.

They weren't too terrified to have children or to touch a woman for fear of what they'd do.

"Everyone knew it," he said. "Even when I went to university..."

Oxford had been a breath of fresh air, a chance for a new start. No one had known, and yet it had felt like *everyone* had. The scar on his lip may have been the only visible one, but there were others carved deep beneath his flesh. They'd shaped him. Isolation and whispers and stares—he hadn't known how to talk to people. How to be any more than he had ever been.

So he'd thrown himself into his studies and into tearing his own body apart. He'd shot up a foot in that final year of secondary. Had started to fill out, and newly arrived at university, he'd put the new mass to good use. He'd run and lifted and done anything he could to quiet the thread of his own thoughts in his brain. He'd gotten his first tattoo.

And he'd listened. He'd learned.

He shook his head. "It wasn't until I got to graduate school that anything changed."

When he'd arrived in Princeton, it had been as a whole new man, with a new attitude and a new resolve. Maybe it had been the accent and maybe it had been his looks. Maybe the careful study into how to speak and act and be.

No one had seen. No one had suspected. Least of all...

"Helen." He choked, throat squeezing, but somehow he managed to get her name out. To force those aching syllables onto the air, where they hadn't lived or breathed in years. Because he hadn't been able to utter them. Not until now. "That's where I met Helen."

And he had to look away for this part. Tucking his crutch beneath his arm, he lifted one hand to his heart and pressed his palm to the ink there. To the symbol of her he'd carved into his ribs.

A shaky exhalation sounded from behind him. "Was that your wife's name?"

"Yes. She was..."

Brilliant. Smarter than he had been, and it had been so effortless, the way she'd drawn him into the circle of their peers. They'd met at some sort of a graduate mixer, and he still didn't know how the awkward mathematics student had fallen in with the beautiful historian, but he had. Lonely nights in his own apartment had given way to drinks at the pub with one or both of their departments, and through all of it, Helen had been by his side.

And when she'd touched him...when he'd kissed her...

"She changed my life." He closed his eyes, wanting to live in that memory forever. "I thought she'd changed *me*."

But she hadn't. Beneath it all, the same fire had still burned, and it left the same ashes in its wake.

She'd started to grasp it, too, eventually. He'd kept the embers of his anger tucked safely away, but they'd found their way out more than once. Some arsehole spouting racist bullshit in a bar and Cole losing time until he was standing there, spitting and fighting against restraining arms, knuckles bruised and spattered with blood. A pickpocket trying to make off with someone's purse.

Helen, trying to tell him he could have a normal life.

He looked out the window again. Into blackness. Into nothing.

"We didn't fight all the time." They'd hardly fought at all until they'd married. But the day in and the day out—he hadn't always been able to keep it restrained. "She gave back as good as she got." God, but she'd been a firecracker. Her spirit had soothed him and it had riled him up, and it had left him turned around in every possible way. "And we always managed to work it out."

They always had. *Always.*

"Until..."

And it was there that his words failed him. His knees shook beneath him, the bad one screaming, and his palms went suddenly wet.

For the longest time, he stood there, scarcely certain how he managed to keep his feet, his vision blurring and his head a mess, the memory spinning out. Consuming him.

Finally, Serena's voice broke through. "Until...?"

All at once it was like the dam inside him burst.

CHAPTER TWELVE

She couldn't move.

Cole—this solid mountain of a man—was shaking to pieces in front of her while she had frozen where she stood, feet glued to the floor, throat thick and eyes stinging.

What he'd been through. The way he saw himself.

And, yes, there were parts of it she'd glimpsed in their time together. He swore like a sailor and didn't seem to know how to deal with his own frustration. But he portrayed himself as some sort of monster who responded to the pitchforks of his villagers with violence and blood, when all she had ever seen was him turning those very blades against himself.

Right now, it looked as though he'd pierced his own heart.

His gaze was far away, his face ashen, and her chest throbbed. She wanted to go to him. To wrap him up and never let him go. Even if he never wanted what she did, surely there was some kind of comfort she could offer. There had to be something she could *do*.

But her limbs wouldn't move. She hugged herself tighter, shivering against the pain etched into his face.

And then it got worse.

"She never lied," he said, the words breathless and harsh. "She told me what she wanted in all these little ways, but it never seemed like the time. She never seemed serious."

Serena's mind raced. "She wanted..."

"A child." Just like that, his gaze snapped into focus, and all the power of that stare fell squarely on her. "Can you imagine it?"

The vision of it came to her in a rush. Cole was all rough edges and tight restraint, but the idea of him holding a baby—a little boy with his shock of dark hair and his deep, black eyes...A pang squeezed her heart until it threatened to burst.

Because he didn't want that. He couldn't even fathom it.

"I can't." He shook his head, and his throat clicked, his voice stuttering. "She didn't understand. She didn't see. I can't. I can't bring a child into a world that preys on the weak, a world that's this ugly, and even if I could...*I* couldn't..."

The urge to comfort him swept over her anew. "Cole..."

"I tried to explain it to her, but she wouldn't listen. I can't be trusted. When I get angry, I lose control. I'm not...I might..."

Before her eyes, the entire image inverted itself, until he wasn't a man whose edges were softened by the son or daughter in his arms. He was *this* man. Lost and floundering and caught in memories of lashing out.

He thought he'd hurt a child.

He thought he'd hurt *her*.

It was like a bubble expanding and popping inside her lungs.

Was that the answer, then? The step she'd been missing in this dance of theirs—the one where every time they brushed too close he pulled away?

If it was possible, he'd flashed even paler, his knuckles bone-white around the handles of his crutches. As he took a swaying step, she finally snapped out of her trance. She unwrapped her arms from around herself, holding her hands up in front of her chest like she could catch him. Like she could do anything at all. "Maybe you should sit down."

But he just kept pressing on. "You don't understand." His voice dipped lower, tearing at his throat, the sound of it raw like blood. Hollow eyes turned to her. "I killed her."

Everything in her went cold.

Oh God. No. He wouldn't. She refused to believe it. "You didn't—"

"I might as well have."

Relief flooded through her. Whatever he'd done, whatever he was blaming himself for, it couldn't be as terrible as that. She dropped her arms and opened her mouth.

But he spoke right over her. "She just—she was upset. We'd been going round and round, and I got so *angry*." So scared. Unspoken terror underlay every word, making him shake. "I needed to cool down; she knew how I got. She knew and she still thought she still wanted...She pushed me and called me a coward, all because I wanted to keep a child safe, and I *lost* it. Because I was. I was terrified." His eyes went red and damp. "So I screamed at her. Called her naïve, idealistic, stupid, when she was only being kind. When she was trusting me. I proved her trust wrong." His Adam's apple bobbed, and it was like something brittle in him shivering.

Cracking. "I should have let her win. I should have stopped my-self. I should have stopped *her*."

They were nearly at the end of the story now. They had to be, and Serena braced herself.

"She was still sobbing when she got in the car. She was just go-ing to her brother's house, but it was snowing. Ice everywhere, and I begged her to stay, but she couldn't—" He gritted his teeth, his pulse beating out of his skin beside his throat. "She couldn't stand to be in that house with me another second."

Serena's own eyes spilled over, hot drops splashing over her cheeks. God, this man. What he'd been through—the guilt he lived with every day. "Oh, Cole..."

His voice went far away, nearly as distant as his gaze. "They said she didn't feel any pain. She was already gone before I got there, but her car. The blood—"

He cut himself off, choking on the word.

And she couldn't do this. The distance between them yawned, but she crossed it like it was nothing, and then she was in his space, her hands on his face. His cheeks burned beneath her palms, his eyes flashing wild. The depths of them spiraled out into some unknown, and she was sure he'd tear himself away.

But he didn't.

"It was my fault," he rasped. "All my fault. Everyone knew. Her whole family at the funeral, her brother, our friends. And I promised, Serena. I promised I'd never do that to anyone again. I'd never let this"—he let go of one crutch to wave at his own heaving chest—"poison anyone else. I swore I'd never hurt any-one again." He leaned forward until their brows brushed, his breath washing warm across her lips. "But then I met you."

Fresh tears gathered in her eyes as she stared at him. She tried to pull them back, but it was no use.

His crutch went clattering to the floor as he cupped her jaw, the rough pad of his thumb stroking softly across her cheek. The intensity to his tone made her tremble. "And you...you make me want things I told myself I could never have. You make me want to try again, but I can't—I'm still the same person. I'll hurt you. I'll—"

Shaking her head, she pressed a finger to his lips. They were plush and warm against her skin, and he was so close. *They* were so close.

Her voice broke. "The only time you ever hurt me is when you push me away."

Because that was what he was trying to do now by telling her this story. He was giving her an out. One last chance to walk away.

Heat and hope were twin coils interlacing themselves inside her abdomen. Letting them overtake her, she dragged her fingertip down his lips until it rested on the lower pout. The wet, soft flesh gave beneath that press, and he shuddered, curling his hand around her neck. The contact burned its way straight to her core.

"I'd never forgive myself if I—"

"You won't."

Even she wasn't sure if she believed it. There was so much room for heartache here. Between his temper and his broken heart, the ghosts that lived inside him...the regrets.

And there was that deeper pang within her, too. He might kiss her tonight. He might give her so much of what she wanted, but he'd never give her a family. A good woman's love could heal so much, but it couldn't change a man. If his wife's love hadn't—if he still blamed himself for saying no to that—

Serena could never even bring it up.

She stomped down on that thought with prejudice. It was a worry for another time and another day.

For now, he was here and he was hurting, and the other things she wished for in her heart of hearts...they didn't matter. Not as much as this.

"Please," she said, trembling. "I trust you. And you're not going to scare me away."

It was too much.

Helen's voice still echoed in his ears, the weight of his guilt and the memory of blood on snow too vast for him to bear, but he wasn't alone. His knees didn't crumple, because Serena was here, holding him up. Her hands were cool and soft against his face, her skin so warm beneath his palm, and she hadn't fled. He'd told her everything, had given her the truth that had haunted him for all these years—the story he'd never dared to breathe to another person before—and nothing about her had wavered at all.

And now she was *begging* him. His heart, that frozen, broken thing lurched to life in a way he hadn't dreamed it still knew how to do, and it wasn't the only part of him waking up. His flesh hummed, every point of contact a revelation, and just like that he was starving for it. He needed her—needed her mouth and her touch and her calm that was a balm for his very soul. Needed her to exorcise his demons and bring him to life again.

Leaning hard against his crutch, he staggered that last step forward until her breasts brushed his chest.

"Stop me," he whispered, their mouths a hairsbreadth apart. She might swear she trusted him, but he didn't even begin to trust himself. He was dangerous, he ruined everything he touched, and he'd fail her. He'd disappoint her over and over again. The promises he'd made—he'd sworn them for a reason, and if she showed him the slightest sliver of a doubt, he'd go. He'd leave her and he'd never return. It would kill him, but he would.

But the sea green of her eyes flashed deeper, resolve making her mouth go firm. She pulled herself even closer, sliding the damp tip of her finger from his lip to the line of his jaw, sending fire surging in her wake. When her hand threaded through his hair and *pulled*, it was a switch being flipped in his gut.

The fierceness of her gaze met his. "Never."

And he was lost. He was found.

He caught her mouth in a kiss that shot lightning through his veins. Their last time had been so rushed, his body reacting on instinct to the sheer, reckless bravery with which she'd pressed her lips to his. He'd scarcely known what was happening until it was over, until he was reeling backward, horrified at himself for taking something he had no right to want.

His stomach dipped even as he took her now, slicking his tongue along her bottom lip to press inside, mind blanking against the pleasure of that soft, wet glide. He didn't have any right at this point either, but they were both going into this with their eyes wide open, and when it fell apart—

No. All this time he'd wasted obsessing about the past; hell if he was going to waste even more driving himself insane about the future. Here in the present, she was warm and safe and in his arms. She wanted him, and he wanted her.

Christ, he wanted her *so much*. She opened to him without a moment's hesitation, and he scraped his teeth across her tongue to swallow her moan. His skin prickled at every place it pressed to hers, and it was like a well springing open inside him. All this time, he'd been suppressing the animal, male need for touch and contact and sex—he'd missed sex so much. But he'd missed so many things. The lush curves of a woman's body and the sweet haze of a kiss that went on and on and on, and all of it was even better than he'd dared to dream, because it was Serena. Serena's sighs and Serena's taste in his mouth. Serena's fingertips working magic against his scalp.

Serena's body pressed to his where he was achingly, shockingly hard.

He shuddered, nearly losing his balance at the fire that roared up his spine. Fuck, but he had to slow down.

"Tell me what you want," he mumbled against her mouth. He skated his palm down her shoulder, skimmed the curve of her breast to the dip of her waist and gripped her hip—too rough by half but he couldn't let go. "I want to be so good to you."

He wanted to take his time with her, but the urgency building in his veins threatened to overwhelm him before they'd even begun. It had been too long; it had been forever.

He'd thought he'd never, ever have this again.

"What do *you* want?" she countered, gasping as he kissed his way to her jaw and the tender flesh of her throat.

He was babbling. He was drunk on the taste of her skin. "You. Just you."

"You have me."

And he did, didn't he? Every step of the way, she had given

herself to him, offering him her time and her patience and a forgiveness so deep it shook him to his bones. It struck him like a whiteout—like a blow to the skull—and he was just that staggered.

He didn't have much. But this was his chance. He'd give her all he had left in return.

Reclaiming her mouth, he pressed himself into her, urging her backward, and she must have been reading his goddamn mind with how her fist came to curl around his tie, tugging him along, taking him with her as she navigated their way across the room. It was an awkward dance, stumbling and shuffling, and he couldn't stop kissing her even long enough to grab his other crutch, but fuck it, fuck everything. Nothing hurt as he propelled himself forward. She flung her hand out to the side as they went, feeling along the wall until she managed to get the hallway light.

Christ, she was beautiful, cheeks flushed from his kisses, and the bare skin of her shoulders and neck smooth and pale. He slid his palm up the center of her chest this time, over the racing thrum of her heart to stroke her collarbone with his thumb, fingers stretching out across the swell of her breast.

He groaned aloud when her hand settled over the top of his, dragging it lower until he cupped her fully. She felt ripe, felt perfect where she fit against his palm, and the surge of white-hot need had him twitching inside his trousers.

Together, they staggered through the open doorway to what must be her bedroom. She missed the light switch by a mile, hand thumping against the plaster. She protested against his lips as he drove her on. "I should—"

"I don't bloody care."

He needed her *now*. Under him, legs spread, the soft wet of her open for him, and he'd put his mouth on her for days, until she was screaming and senseless with it, and then he'd drive inside, finally *feel* her—

The backs of her legs hit the bed, and he bore her down onto it, throwing his crutch to the side as he followed after, climbing on top, cock aching and mouth watering, his skin practically vibrating.

And then he put his weight on his bad knee.

What the—

Serena blinked her eyes open, struggling to fight off the haze of sex and need that had fallen over her with every crushing kiss and brush of Cole's body against hers. One second, he'd been all over her, pushing her back onto the bed with intent in his gaze, and the next he'd gone rigid, pulling his mouth away with a shocked gasp before pitching to the side.

To be fair, she'd heard longer strings of curse words pouring out of him. But it had been a while.

"Um..." She rose up onto one elbow, reaching out with the other arm. She was still panting, breathless from his touch, but the heaving of his chest seemed to be about something else entirely. She hovered there with her hand a few inches above his ribs for a moment, uncertain what she should do. Touch him? Leave him alone?

A sinking feeling settled in the pit of her stomach. Really, things had been going entirely too well. Even she had no idea how they'd moved so seamlessly from him shaking apart in front of her, recounting the worst day of his life, to them practically mauling each other on her living room floor. It was like all the simmering tension between them had hit a flash boil, bubbling over in a rush of steam and contact, and it had been too fast, too easy. Too good. She should've known something would go wrong.

She'd just been hoping that maybe they could get it right this time.

Letting out a groan of frustration, Cole covered his face with his hands. He took a couple of deep breaths like that while Serena's stomach dropped another fraction of an inch. Finally, he pulled his hands away. His gaze met hers, the tight line of his mouth tilting ever so slightly upward.

"Sorry," he said.

Her heart stuttered. "For what?"

If he said he was sorry for this, for touching her at all, she was going to...Well, she didn't know what she was going to do, but it definitely wouldn't be good.

He lifted one brow, and that wasn't regret on his face. If anything, it was a smirk. "For overestimating my recovery."

With that, he captured her wrist and tugged her toward him, getting his other hand on her waist. She shrieked, taken completely off guard as he hauled her along. The next thing she knew, she was on all fours over him, her hair falling everywhere, her breasts ready to spill out of this dress, and it was the best kind of whiplash.

Oh. It struck her all at once. His cry of pain and his sudden recoiling. They were about his knee—not about her. Not about *this*.

Her face just about burst with the force of her smile.

The curve of his mouth echoed hers, and the happiness on his face took her breath away nearly as thoroughly as the heat of his palm curling around her side again. He raised his other hand to graze her cheek, and she chased it, shy and adoring as she pressed her lips to the backs of his knuckles.

He cupped her face. "Hi," he said.

"Hi."

And it was dark, their faces both in shadow, the only light in the room that which filtered in through her blinds or seeped in from the hallway around the corner. But it was enough.

"Hi," she repeated, and then she dipped down and kissed him.

She'd loved the way he'd taken charge out in the other room, the way he'd propelled them here seemingly by the force of his will alone. But this, with her on top, with the chance to control the pace was good, too. She opened for the sweep of his tongue, letting the kiss go wet and deep, but she kept her body above his. She kept it slow and lingering as the hot spark from before got the time to spread and grow, more a smolder than a blaze. A warmth that made her insides bloom and glow.

His having two free hands to touch her with was a pretty great thing, too.

"Mmm." A soft sound got knocked out of her lungs at the heat of broad palms skimming along her sides. He smoothed all the way down her hips and over her thighs, and she was so open kneeling over him like this. She clenched inside, slickness gathering at the catch of rough fingertips on the hem of her dress.

Ever so slowly, as if giving her time to tell him no, he slipped his hands just underneath. She exhaled into his mouth, scraping her teeth over his lip, everything tensing inside her. He pushed the fabric up, and she moaned, shifting her hips into his touch.

It was all the encouragement he needed. Bolder now, he stroked his hands along that bare expanse of skin, thumbs pressing into the tenderness of her inner thighs, so close to where she wanted him. He drifted higher and higher, and her body was a live wire. Was just the wet need and the aching tips of her breasts, the fire zipping up and down her spine with every pass.

He grazed the center panel of her underwear, and her arms gave out beneath her.

"Fuck," he breathed, rasping. "You're soaked."

His hot touch pressed in harder, choking another noise from her, and she dropped her head, closing her eyes. Burying her face in the solid muscle of his shoulder as she rocked into the petting of his hand.

His voice dipped even lower. "You like me telling you that? Like me telling you how good you feel?"

And what could she say to that? It was filthy, really; it made her all hot and squirming inside, and she loved it. She nodded, and his breath caught, the sound of his swallowing echoing through the space.

He swirled a circle around her clit through the fabric. "Pretty little knickers all wet for me."

Good Lord, was he *trying* to kill her?

It was so damn tempting to just lie there, head cradled against his arm and let him take her to pieces, but she pushed up, tucking a finger into the knot of his tie and loosening it before opening her mouth against his throat. She kissed a wet line to his ear. Warm and breathy, she nipped at the lobe. "Maybe you should take them off me, then."

With a low rumble of a growl, he got a hand around her neck and tugged her to meet his mouth. He kissed her sass from her lips even as he slipped past the elastic of her panties. God, he hadn't been kidding. The glide of his fingertips was so slick, her flesh drenched. He teased along her slit, dipping just barely inside before taking a glancing stroke across her clit that had her moaning around his tongue.

"Barely need to, do I? Could make you come just like this. Greedy kitty all swollen and aching for it."

That he probably could was the worst of it. His finger slid inside so easily, and it had been so long. She'd wanted him for ages, and her head was spinning that they got to have this. That he wanted to make her come and that he was so *good* at it. His other hand slid up her side to cup her breast through her dress, and it was another sparkling point of contact.

But she wasn't done for yet. Fumbling, she let go of his tie to glide her palm all down the length of his chest, past his belt and—

"Jesus." He bucked into her touch, clicking their teeth together as she cupped him, and *damn*.

He was hot and hard and long, and she was going to have that in her. Another hot pulse surged through her at the thought, and she nipped at his lip.

"I don't know," she said, trying hard for disaffectedness and missing by a mile. "Two can play at that game, can't they? Think I can get you to go off like this? Make you come in your pants like a—"

The "teenager" part got cut off in another shriek, and this time there wasn't any pretense that the noise in his throat was anything other than a growl.

"Naughty," he groaned, slipping his fingers from her to get a hand under her thigh.

And it shouldn't be such a turn-on to keep getting manhandled like this, but it was. He tugged and bodily lifted her, and crap, she'd been so aware of his limitations on the crutches that she'd almost forgotten the pure muscle the man was carved from. There wasn't any forgetting it now. He got her knees settled to either side of his head, strong hands clamping on to the curves of her thighs, and his mouth was right there, red and sinful through the dim, and she felt faint.

"What are you—"

"If you can't keep your hands to yourself," he said, eyes darkening, "I'll just have to keep them where I can see them."

With that, he grasped both her wrists, dragging her down until her palms slapped against the mattress above his head, and she was still reeling when a hot thumb traced the place where her leg met her hips. When he dragged the panel of her underwear to the side.

And then he...oh God, he wasn't going to...he...

Her knees went weak, her whole body trembling at the first wet lick along the length of her. She pounded a fist into the mattress. This wasn't real, it couldn't be, except that he lapped at her, again and again. His tongue was hot and perfect against her softest parts, and when he found her clit, she bit back on a scream.

"No," he scolded, parting from searing flesh for the scantest fraction of a second, palm taking a barely-there swat at her rear. "Let me hear you."

He dove back in, lips surrounding her. He sucked at her clit, only stopping to take fluttering strokes of his tongue over her, and she didn't try to hold back this time. Slapping at the bed again, she choked out his name, and it was happening too quickly. She never climaxed this fast, and she wanted it to last, wanted to get naked and explore, and—

And he plunged two thick fingers deep inside, thrumming hard against her inner walls and she was lost.

She came with a shout, black fire surging through her, blanking her mind to everything except the pulsing warmth, the sweet kiss of his mouth. The fullness of having him inside, but she only wanted fuller. Wanted more.

When her vision returned to her a solid minute—or possibly a decade—later, she was straddling his face, her mouth and breasts mashed hard against her quilt. Shivering aftershocks rocked through her as he took another slow swipe with his tongue. He pulled away, slipping his fingers free, then patted at her thigh as if that were an acceptable cue to dismount.

She was still desperately needy, her blood hot, her head dizzy. But she was also filled with a sudden, indignant blaze.

In a rush, she pushed off the bed, rising to kneel over top of him. Gazing down at him through the dimness, she settled her shaking hands on her hips.

"I'll have you know"—she flipped her hair back over her shoulder—"that I put my hands wherever I please."

Without further ado, she did just that.

Really, Cole should have bloody well known. At every turn, Serena had been the one pushing and pushing in this relationship. It wasn't any surprise that she wouldn't want to lie back and let him take charge of things here, either.

Challenge in her eyes, she walked on her knees down his body until she hovered above his hips. She curled those delicate little fingers of hers around the buckle of his belt, and white-hot sparks slid up his spine, his prick jumping, heart thundering. As she pulled the leather through, he reached out, gripping wildly, but he didn't stop her.

Forget that she didn't swear or that she worked with children. This woman was a match burning bright, sexual and confident, and he wanted her so badly he was screaming inside with the ache of it. She'd ridden his face with hardly a moment's hesitation, had left his mouth slick with her. Her taste and her scent surrounded him, making him wild, and then she was tugging at his trousers and reaching inside.

"Fuck." He arched back, baring his throat, his eyes rolling up in his head at the warm touch of soft fingers on bare skin as she pulled him out. It was heaven, absolute heaven, a cool drink in the desert after years of being alone, of never being touched. Of never imagining he would ever be touched again. "Serena, please—"

What the hell was he even asking for? It didn't matter. She wrapped her fist around him and stroked, sliding her palm over the slick tip, pulling his foreskin back as she drew down to the base, and then she was—

"No, oh no—" The words slipped out, but they weren't a protest. He had to close his eyes against the perfection of wet, red lips pursing around him, of his own hard flesh disappearing inside, but it didn't matter. The afterimage was burned into him; he'd be ruined by this. He thumped his head back against the mattress, threading his fingers into the soft tumble of her hair. "Yes. Just like that."

She found the spot right under the head, flicking her tongue against it as she sucked him deep, and he right near lost his mind. Giving in to it, he tilted forward with his hips, doing all he could just to hold on, to last. His balls drew tight, and he groaned out, "Baby..."

She pulled off before the feeling could crest, and he snapped his eyes open. Ugh, mistake. She hovered with her parted lips right over his prick, sweet pink tongue peeking out. The vision alone made him throb. After one last squeeze, hard around the base, she let him go. The wet length of him fell against his abdomen, but he only had a second to lie there, bereft, before she climbed her way back up his body.

"Who's greedy now?" she asked. Her kiss was just as intoxicating as before except it was better. The faintest hint of his own taste mixed with hers, and he dug his fingers in deep against her hip. She nipped and licked all around his mouth, lapping up what she'd left of herself on his skin, and they were both greedy, apparently.

They'd *both* been wanting this for so long.

Holding her in place with his fingers twisted in her hair, he kissed her deeper, tongue chasing hers. He snuck the hand at her hip back under her skirts, and forget soaked. Her kitty and his mouth had left her wet all down her thighs. She got her own hand in there, too, pulling her knickers out of the way again.

Shifting, spreading her legs, she rubbed all her slick, hot flesh over the bare length of him, and he wanted nothing more than to claim her. To press inside and fill her up, but—

"Condom," he grunted out.

She shook her head. "Don't need one, I promise. I'm safe. I—"

His whole mind went white with static.

Bare. She wanted him to fuck her bare, and he was helpless. Nodding, he got a hand around himself to angle his cock.

The shout he made was punched clear out of him. She sank down on him like it was nothing, and she was an inferno, slick, hot silk consuming him, burning him to ash, and he didn't care.

Why had he been denying himself this?

Insane with it, he pulled her to his mouth and kissed his gratitude and his pleasure and his absolute adoration into her breath. She rose and fell over him in tiny rocking motions that kept him so goddamn deep, grinding her clit against him with every stroke, and he was breathless, wordless, *boneless*.

"What?" she asked, scraping her teeth across his lip. "Not going to tell me how good I feel now?"

Did he even remember how to speak English?

"Perfect," he babbled. "Hot and tight, Christ, you're so wet, so perfect." He bent his good knee to get his foot flat on the mattress, and it was enough leverage to thrust up into her. A whole new level of intensity burst through him with the longer slide. He slipped his hand over her breast, and fuck, why were they still clothed, but he could worry about that later. Get her naked *later* because he was fucking her now, and she was fucking him right back. He curled a possessive hand around her thigh and urged her higher. "Harder," he begged, "need it, need you."

She lifted up and he slammed into her, and then it was both of them chasing the edge of oblivion. She made the same sweet noises against his lips as she had when he'd been licking her pussy—close, she had to be close.

"Can you come again for me, beautiful? Want to feel you."

He got his thumb between them, digging at the hot pearl of her clit, rough flickering strokes that had her clenching around him. "Come on my cock, let me hear you—"

She rode him ever harder, and he held his breath. Every piece of him tightened, released a screaming pressure that beat against the walls of his restraint until with a wail she ground down into his thumb. Her whole body seemed to seize, voice breaking into a chanting of his name, and that was it.

The last thread of his control cleaved clean in two. Holding her in place, he fucked up into her, a half-dozen shimmering thrusts, her hot flesh pulsing through the echoes of her climax, and then the black haze of it was there, right *there*—

"Going to...in you..."

"Yes," she groaned, "Cole."

Pleasure burst across the closed darkness behind his eyes. His every nerve sang with it as he emptied into her. Throwing his head back, clasping her so tightly to him, like he would never lose her, like he could keep this forever, he gave her everything.

And let himself slip into a world where he could imagine that was enough.

CHAPTER THIRTEEN

Serena woke up gradually, emerging from the dreamy haze of sleep, rolling over and rubbing at her eyes. Sunlight filtered in from behind the blinds she'd apparently forgotten to close the night before, and the bed was deliciously warm. Burrowing back down, she pulled the covers around her shoulders and closed her eyes, luxuriating in the hint of soreness in her muscles.

But then it all came back to her in a rush of heat—the reason she'd forgotten to draw her blinds. The reason why she was so sore. She shot up, blinking her eyes open as the too-bright world around her swam.

Cole. She patted the other side of the bed only to find it cold, and a sliver of ice formed behind her ribs.

He was supposed to be here. He'd finally broken down, that wall he kept around himself crumbling before her eyes, and then he'd given in. He'd kissed her. Her whole body tingled with the rush of sense-memory, and she dragged her fingertips over her lips just to remind herself it had been real. He'd put his mouth on her and made her come and *made love to her.*

She dropped her head into her hands. She'd given him a toothbrush, for God's sake. Stripped down to his boxers and an undershirt and the brace around his knee, he'd curled around her, holding her as she'd drifted off into the deepest, most perfect sleep she'd had...maybe *ever.* And okay, he hadn't actually said that he would stay, but she hadn't been crazy to assume.

Unless she had been. Her heart gave a panging little squeeze. She'd pushed again, hadn't she? The man was clearly still in mourning, and— Oh God. What if he hadn't been ready? What if he regretted it—or worse, blamed her? She'd just been trying to offer him a little comfort.

And in the process, she'd taken exactly what she'd wanted from him all along.

Her eyes stung, and she punched at the mattress hard. Stupid. This wasn't about her. She should've checked in with him more, should've asked him if he'd even wanted to stay at all. He'd seemed so into it, though. He'd seemed to want her.

When her lip threatened to wobble, she'd officially had enough. Flopping back down, she buried her face in her pillow and let herself have one frustrated scream. Then she'd pick herself up and march her way to his apartment. She'd make sure he was okay, and she wouldn't press, and if he didn't want this after all, she'd...well. She'd be devastated, but she'd accept it gracefully and then she'd come back down and have herself a good little self-pitying cry.

Nodding to herself, she dragged her face back out of the pillow.

And just about went out of her skin at the soft knocking at her bedroom door. A deep voice rang out. "Serena?"

Or he could totally still be here and she could be having a melodramatic fit.

"One second," she called out, racing to catch her breath. She launched herself out of bed, skidding to a stop on the hardwood in front of her mirror. Her hair was a fright, but she raked her fingers through it the best she could. The tank top and shorts she'd gone to bed in were her least unfortunate ones, and he'd already seen her in them at this point, so there wasn't much sense freaking out about them.

Turning, she grabbed her robe off the back of the door and slipped her arms into the sleeves. Wrapping the tie around her waist, she squeezed her eyes shut for half a second to try to get some sort of composure.

Ugh, it wasn't any use. She was *giddy* as she flung the door open.

And there he was. In an undershirt and his dress slacks from the night before, cheeks dark with stubble, his always messy hair a fraction worse than usual, and she adored it.

"You're here," she said, breathless, and she could have slapped herself.

But the line of his mouth lifted into the most beautiful smile. "I am." He glanced past her toward the rumpled mess she'd left of her bed. "You looked so peaceful. I didn't want to wake you."

"I wouldn't have minded." Her face flashed warm. She wouldn't have minded at all. She was usually an early riser anyway, and waking in his arms, held safe against the warm solid bulk of his chest...

Maybe rolling over into soft, perfect morning kisses, him hard against her, broad hands sliding up her thighs toward her hips...

She was snapped out of the fantasy when his smile wavered. "Are you all right? I thought I heard..."

Right. Because instead of morning kisses, she'd woken to a big fat load of morning panic. Her flush deepened, but it wasn't a sexy flush, this time. Caught off guard, she cast about for any kind of a reasonable explanation for the noise she'd made, but came up blank.

Fortunately, she was saved when a whiff of something *amazing* reached her nose. Her eyebrows rose. "Did you cook?"

He shrugged. "I couldn't sleep."

He passed it off as casual, but the way he said it made it sound like that wasn't exactly something new for him. She paused. Her hand seemed to lift of its own accord, reaching out to touch his chest, and she almost stopped herself. But she could do that now—touch him when she wanted to. After last night, she could probably do a whole lot more. The headiness of it was a rush after so much time spent holding back.

Watching his reaction, she let her palm settle over his heart. "What about you? Are you okay?"

Her concerns this morning might have been overblown, but they hadn't been unwarranted. He'd been through a lot last night.

Curling his fingers around her wrist, he let out a long breath that made his ribs rise and fall. "I am, actually. Better than, even." The corner of his lips twitched, like there was more he had to say, but he thought better of it. Taking her hand in his, he tugged her in the direction of the kitchen. "Come on. You must be famished."

She was, actually.

It only struck her as she fell into step behind him that he was using just one crutch. "How's your knee?"

"Dreadful," he said, all cheer, and there was definitely a limp to his step, but he didn't seem to be letting it hold him back.

She frowned, but whatever protest she might have made got lost as she turned the corner into the kitchen. Her eyes went wide. "Wow."

When she couldn't sleep, she read or did crossword puzzles. Apparently, Cole power-baked. The little table in the corner was covered in what looked like scones and maybe even some cinnamon rolls and she didn't even know what else. Half a dozen batches, at least.

Letting go of his hand, she stepped forward. "When did you wake up?"

"A few hours ago. I have a hard time sometimes, and..." He trailed off.

"And?" she prompted, glancing back at him.

His throat bobbed. "And we may have dredged up a few things last night."

She turned around at that, the table full of sweets forgotten. Cole was leaning against the doorway, his one crutch tucked under his arm. There was something tired about him, though the shadows under his eyes weren't exactly new. But the signs of fatigue weren't what really stuck out to her.

He looked...looser somehow. Less weighed down.

"I...," he started, before closing his mouth and beginning again. "What happened to Helen. I've never talked about it before."

Serena's heart skipped a beat. "Never?"

"No."

He flexed his jaw, and something inside her ached. Approaching slowly, she crossed the space to him. She put her hand over his, stroking the points of his knuckles with her thumb. A little of the strain seemed to seep out of him.

"I'm glad you told me."

"I'm glad you made me." He flicked his gaze to hers, a softness creeping over his expression. "Serena, I—"

And she wasn't sure she was ready for this. Whatever he was about to say, the gravity to his tone made the air around them go silent and still. She braced herself.

"Last night. It was a gift. A treasure." He intertwined their hands, linking them. Making her hope that maybe the *but* that was hanging on the air wasn't about to come down on her head. "I don't deserve you."

"Don't—" *Don't do this. Don't walk away.*

The piercing darkness of his eyes robbed her of her voice. "But I want to. So badly."

Her throat went dry. He didn't have to deserve her. Love didn't work like that. She shook her head, only for him to slip his hand from hers and reach up, cupping her jaw to still her.

"I don't know what there is left of me to give," he said. "But I want to give it to you." He swallowed wetly. "I want to try."

It was all she needed to hear. Vision blurring, she launched herself at him, wrapping her arms around his neck and hauling him close. The heat of his palm came to settle at the small of her back, and he leaned into her. Burying his face against her neck, he held her close, and it was everything she hadn't dared to hope for.

Blinking back the tears that clung from her lashes, she laughed. "I'd like that."

She'd love that.

She'd love *him*. She'd love him until all the hurting pieces in him healed over, and then she'd just love him some more.

When he pulled back, she mirrored him, letting enough space between them so he could lean down. The touch of his lips to hers was like the sun rising inside her, and she opened to him, drinking in the light.

With a rough exhalation, he broke away. It was too intense, the way he gazed into her eyes. The grip of his hand at her side.

"I want to be so good to you, Serena."

Only she heard the doubt inside that affirmation. A shadow of a cloud passed over the sun, and she fought to suppress her shiver at the sudden chill. Dropping her gaze to his mouth, she drew him in for another kiss.

Doubt was a thing for another time and another day. For now, he wanted to give her everything. He wanted to be good to her, and that was enough. If he couldn't...

Well. At least they got to have this. For now.

CHAPTER FOURTEEN

How many times had Serena's mother warned her that she should be careful what kind of face she made, because it just might get stuck that way? Sure, she'd been trying to get Serena to stop sticking her tongue out at the time, but the phrase had taken on a whole new meaning today.

Serena. Could. Not. Stop. Smiling.

With the exception of Sunday dinner with the family, she'd spent the entire weekend with Cole. So much of their acquaintance thus far had been fraught with these confessions in the dark, but for that little, beautiful pocket of time, the shadows had receded. Maybe it was simply that they'd traumaed themselves out. Maybe they'd both been ready for some time to just *be*, watching movies in their pajamas and eating all the amazing things he'd baked in his insomnia.

Maybe it was all the sex.

A tickle of heat licked along her spine, and her smile turned positively goofy as she parked in one of the visitor spots at Upton, gathered up her bundle, and got out.

God, that man. She'd thought their first time had been incredible, and it had been. Filthy and revelatory and delicious, but he'd only just been getting started. If she'd known all the things he could do with his tongue when she'd met him...she still would've had to keep her hands to herself until he was ready. But she wasn't sure how she would have done it.

Someone else was coming out of the administrative building just as Serena was walking in. She shifted her bag to her other hand and got the door, her grin just about breaking her face. Ugh. This was going to become a problem at some point. Already today she'd let her kids get away with way more than she normally would have, but you try disciplining a misbehaving middle schooler with an idiotic sex grin stamped on your face.

And seriously, if a room full of preteens couldn't kill her smile, nothing could. Not even...

"Mrs. Cunningham." Serena waved in greeting as she strode into the office, and nope. Not even that sour grinch could get her down today. "How are you?"

Mrs. Cunningham glowered. "Not as well as you, it would seem." She glanced over Serena's shoulder. "Your friend didn't accompany you today?"

She was going to have to give Cole a hard time about that later. Apparently, he'd made quite the impression. For now, though, she shook her head as she made her way to the desk. "Just me."

"Pity." Okay, maybe this woman was going to be able to dampen Serena's mood after all. "It's a coincidence you should happen to stop by. Mr. Trousseau mentioned that he'd like to have a word with you."

Never mind. If anything, Serena's smile widened. God, her face actually hurt. "He did?"

"Indeed." She waved toward the rear of the office. "You can go on through."

Serena could have kissed that ugly mug. Somehow, she refrained.

With a whole new lightness in her step, she headed on back. Just before Grayson's door, she paused, taking a deep breath before she stepped up and knocked.

At the first rap of her knuckles, he looked away from his screen. "Serena."

Oh, this was fantastic. Maybe he'd pulled Max's file. Maybe he'd been impressed. "Grayson."

"Have a seat."

Serena hesitated. This wasn't quite the same warm man who'd danced with her half the night a couple of days ago. On the surface, nothing had changed. He was as impeccably dressed and as proper, but his expression was cooler.

"Okay." A flash of nerves skittered up her arms. She pulled out one of the chairs in front of his desk all the same, refusing to let a little anxiety blow itself out of proportion in her mind. Reaching into her bag, she pulled out her Tupperware. "Blueberry scone? Homemade."

Not by her, but technically true.

"No. Thank you."

"Oh." Deflating another fraction, she returned the container to its bag and set both on the ground by her feet. She brushed a lock of hair behind her ear. "Mrs. Cunningham said you were hoping to speak with me?"

"Yes. I didn't expect to see you so soon, though. You'll excuse me for being unprepared." The way he said it wasn't helping her unease.

"I was just in the neighborhood."

"Right." Grayson straightened in his chair. His gaze was so serious as he turned the full power of it on her. "About that."

"Yes?"

"You and Dr. Stafford made quite the impression the other night, as I'm sure you're aware. So I asked around a bit about you and your prospective. Max."

This was it. "Oh?"

"He's a strong candidate, I have to admit. We'll need to see how his admission scores come in, but based on his other application materials, I can't see any reason why he wouldn't be a good fit here."

A bubble of relief popped in Serena's lungs. "He's such a great kid, and I think his exams are going to go great. He's been working so hard. If you knew how important this was to him."

"I'm wondering how important this is to *you*," he said, and that stopped her short.

"Excuse me?"

Something in his expression softened. It was almost too kind. Oh damn. This was going to be bad.

"Serena. Did you know that Mrs. Cunningham has been keeping track of how many times you've 'stopped in' over the last few months? She's asked the other office personnel to do so as well."

"Oh." A numbness buzzed in her gut.

"They appreciate your culinary talents, and the school is grateful for your support at our annual benefit."

"Of course."

"But." And there it was. There was always a *but*. He tilted his head to the side. Oh no. Was that *pity* in his eyes? "I need to make sure this is absolutely clear. Our decision about your nephew's admission cannot be contingent on your...generosity."

The numbness spread. "Oh."

"The treats for the office staff. The visits. The benefit tickets, even. They can't have any sway."

One lone flicker of anger curled through the gray fog settling over her. Generosity? If she'd bought them a new building, this would be a very different conversation, indeed. "I understand."

"Then you'll understand if I insist that you refrain from additional visits in the future."

Her stomach sank into her toes. "You're banning me?"

"Not at all. In fact..." He reached over to pull a business card from the holder on the corner of his desk. "This is my direct number. If you have any questions about the admissions process or about the status of Max's application, I invite you to contact me personally."

"But you don't want me to come by anymore."

"Not without a reason. Not if your intention is to sway our decision." He extended his hand with the card a little farther until she moved to take it. He clasped her palm in his. "I'm sorry to put this so bluntly. It's nothing personal. But we need to remain impartial. Surely you understand."

Her throat threatened to close. "Of course."

An ugly sort of a laugh clogged her lungs. And here she

thought she'd been helping. She'd thought she was doing so well.

She closed her fingers around the card, pulling her arm back as she rose. As an afterthought, she grabbed the bag of baked goods from the floor. Heaven forbid he thought she had left it on purpose. One last-ditch effort to bribe him into letting her kid in.

"I'm sorry to have taken up everyone's time," she said, hating the edge she couldn't quite keep out of her tone.

Grayson stood as she retreated to the door. "It was lovely to have the chance to see you again, Serena."

She wished she could say the same. The smile she hadn't been able to get rid of deserted her entirely now. All the acknowledgment she could manage was a nod and a little wave.

She was just so embarrassed.

With her head down and her shoulders tight, she took a back set of hallways out of the building. The last thing she needed right now was Mrs. Cunningham's gloating.

She retreated to her car and locked her doors before giving up. She slumped forward until her brow touched the steering wheel. A helpless, useless feeling made her clench her hands hard.

There was just so little she could do for Max. That kid deserved the world, and he'd gotten the short straw so many times. Between his absentee mom—who Serena still hadn't heard from since that awful dressing room phone call—and his apparently terrible math teachers and the kids who were giving him such a hard time at his neighborhood school, he was due for something good.

Serena'd been doing her best to give it to him. But it seemed she couldn't do anything right for him at all.

* * *

Cole was going to tear his bloody clock off the wall.

Scowling, he refocused on the columns of figures he'd scribbled out across the page. He was close to something, he was sure. For nearly a year now, he'd been chewing at this theory of his, and he'd had a breakthrough that morning. If he could only concentrate, he might even have something publishable soon. That'd show Barry—it would show everybody at his old university who'd written him off as washed up and done.

Except, for the umpteenth time, his gaze strayed back to the minute hand as it crept closer and closer to the twelve, and this was *ridiculous*. Serena wasn't due back at any particular time. Yet here he was, sitting by the window like a damned spaniel waiting for her to come home, watching the seconds tick by in his overeagerness to see her. It was embarrassing was what it was.

It took his breath away, it felt so good.

His routine, the rigid timetable of meals and work and exercise that he'd relied on for all these years—it had gone out the window the moment he'd hurt himself, and then the shattered remains of the fall had been set on fire in Serena's wake. She'd given him something to care about, injecting life into his days. And into his nights now, too.

His pulse picked up, and he drummed the end of his pen against his knee at the coiling that seemed to happen in his blood. It was arousal at the thought of her, of how she'd felt rocking over him in the pale, damp light of dawn that morning. The feel of all those curves beneath his hands.

It was a sense of foreboding so strong he could scarcely breathe.

The plastic casing of his pen creaked beneath his grip, and he exhaled roughly as he let it go. He knew better than to let his thoughts wander down that road. Even if he was still harboring doubts about what kind of partner he could be for her, he'd been honest, at least. She knew he wasn't a whole man or a safe man. She wanted him anyway. And that was probably the hardest part of it all to believe.

Outside, the sound of a car door slamming drew him back to the here and now. His gaze went again, unerringly, to the clock—nearly a quarter to five. Well within the range of when she usually got home on days she didn't have Max. Twisting around in his seat, he glanced out the window, down at the street below. And there she was.

He was up and grabbing for his crutch in a heartbeat. It was the height of rudeness not to call or text before heading straight down. She'd just had a long day at work. She might be tired, might want to unwind. Might want a bloody minute to herself before her fucked-up hermit of a lover went stumbling down the stairs, near-mad for her presence and her touch.

Selfish. But even that rebuke didn't slow him down.

The stairs did, though. Gripping the banister with one hand and his crutch with the other, he gritted his teeth. His bad leg had been getting stronger, and even more rapidly in just the couple of days since he'd started adjusting to the single crutch. It still protested taking his whole weight, but he was able to give it more and more every day.

He stopped short before hopping down the first step. Maybe...

Recalling how he'd practiced this with his therapist, he tested stepping down with his bad leg leading. Leaning into the railing and his crutch before shifting forward, and...Huh. It barely gave a twinge. He took the next stair a fraction faster, and this was still a snail's pace to the way he'd used to storm down half a flight at a time on his way to his morning runs, but it was better. He grinned as he turned the corner of the landing.

The front door to the building creaked as it swung open and closed, and it was followed by the jangling of keys, the snap of a postbox. At the echoing thuds of footfalls on the stairs, Cole quickened his pace. But even with his head start, Serena beat him to her apartment. He rounded the corner to find her searching through her keys. She looked over her shoulder, and his heart sped, all his doubts falling away. Except...

He frowned, pausing halfway down the final flight. The woman he'd seen off that morning had been *giddy*, practically glowing from within.

A cloud formed over his head. "What happened?"

Sighing, she turned away. She got her door unlocked and stepped on through without a backward glance. For a second he worried she'd close the door behind her, shutting him out. But she didn't. He descended the last few steps and limped his way into her apartment. Still not speaking, she hung up her keys and dropped the contents of her pockets into the little ceramic bowl on her entryway table. She set down her schoolbag. And then, right beside it, a paper shopping bag. The same paper shopping bag she'd left with that morning. His furrowed his brows as he peered into it. The container he'd packed at her request was still full.

He glanced at her in question. "Serena?" His throat bobbed. "Love?"

All the fight seemed to go out of her at once. Casting her

jacket aside, she collapsed into a corner of her couch and draped her arm across her eyes. Her chest heaved with the force of her sigh, and he wasn't going to be distracted by that. He wasn't.

Swallowing back the prickle of heat thrumming under his skin, he closed the door behind himself and crossed the half dozen feet toward her. Tension radiated off of her. Tension and disappointment, and once upon a time, he'd known what to do about that kind of thing. Gingerly, he dropped down to sit beside her, placing a questioning hand on her knee.

She slid her arm lower, peeking at him through one half-open eye. Blowing out a breath, she covered it again, hiding herself from his vision. "It's nothing. Just a bad day."

"Bullshit."

"Language."

"I call it like I see it." She hadn't tried to push him away so far, so he ventured a little farther. With care, he reached out, lifting her hand and pulling it away from her face. "Something happened." He hated the way his voice wavered. "Tell me about it?"

He could offer comfort. He scarcely remembered how, but he could try. She deserved that much after all the times she'd offered it to him.

For a moment that dragged on and on, she stared at him. Then she twisted her hand in his, entwining their fingers and holding on. Closing her eyes, she asked, "Just, have you ever felt really helpless? Like no matter how hard you tried, you couldn't do what you needed to? For the people you love?"

His ribs squeezed in, and he tightened his hold on her hand. "You know I have."

Opening one eye, she winced. "Oh, crap. Sorry."

He pushed away the guilt that had crippled him for so long. This wasn't about him. "Don't be. Go on."

At her hesitation, he lifted their hands to his lips and laid soft kisses along her knuckles. He could wait her out if he had to.

Finally, she broke. "You know how I was going to bring some of your leftovers to Upton?"

"I do."

"Well, let's just say they didn't go over so well."

"What?" He'd tried those scones himself. They'd been perfect, exactly the way Helen had preferred.

"Ugh." She visibly braced herself. "You remember Grayson?"

Cole stiffened, dropping their hands from his lips. "How could I not?"

Giving him a chiding look, she continued. "Well, he called me into his office." Her eyes went bright, her jaw flexing. "And he told me I shouldn't come around there anymore."

"He *what*?" It came out too harsh. Too angry, and he fought to reel himself back.

"Shh." She stroked her thumb across his as if to soothe him. It halfway worked. "He was right. He basically called me out on try-ing to bribe Max's way into the school."

"But you haven't..."

"Please. Of course I have. I called it 'buttering them up' in my mind, but it's a pretty fine line." The dampness to her gaze flashed in the light, and her cheeks flushed hot. "I thought I was helping. I just wanted to do this thing for Max, you know? He deserves ev-erything, and I..." She trailed off, but he heard what she was saying.

What she'd already said about feeling helpless and trying so hard to do right by the people she loved.

And it was a whole different kind of tightness behind his ribs. Not rage but righteousness. Indignation. And the softest, most tender impulse.

She took such good care of *everyone*. Her nephew and her family and even him. Didn't she see that?

When was the last time anyone had taken care of *her*?

"Serena." Leaning forward, he lifted his free hand to cup her face, drawing her gaze to meet his. "You do so much for him."

She squirmed. "I try."

"You do," he insisted. "He loves you terribly."

"But there are just all these things he doesn't have. Penny left him, and my mom does her best, but I just want to fix it all."

"Some things you can't fix." He of all people knew that. "You went above and beyond with this. You've given him his best possible chance."

"Or maybe I just messed it all up for him."

"Did they say that?"

"No, but—" A low hiccup cut her off. A drop of moisture beaded at the corner of her eye, and he wanted to kiss it away. So he did.

"You," he said, pressing his lips to her cheek, tasting salt, "have done every single thing you could." He kissed her forehead and her other cheek. He kissed her nose and then leaned in farther. Until their mouths were nearly brushing, bare breaths apart. "And I am so proud of you for getting him this far."

She let out a wet chuckle of a laugh, then curled her hand around his neck. "How did you know exactly what I needed to hear?"

He hadn't, but he'd done his best. It was all anyone could really do.

With no words left to describe how amazing she was, he closed the gap between them. Her lips were soft beneath his as he gentled them open. The kiss was slow and sweet, and it reached into his chest. He'd missed sex all right, but he just might have missed this more. The connection warmed him to his bones, zipping between them, and he shut his eyes against the well of feeling opening inside him.

For the longest time, they stayed just like that. The lingering tension in her body bled away, and she trailed her fingertips down his spine, firing off sparks. He shifted, leaning them back into the couch. He was hard—how could he not be with her touching him and responding to his kiss? But it was an idle arousal. One he could take his time with.

Still, he darted his tongue out to lick between her lips, and she moaned, opening wider for him. The low heat within him deepened with the kiss, and he drifted his hand down her throat. He ran it through the valley of her breasts.

Only for her to catch his wrist.

She pulled away, eyes dark, lips wet and red, the same low desire written on every inch of her. But she dropped her gaze and shifted back, an apologetic smile to her lips. "I have a bunch of planning to do for tomorrow, and there's still dinner to figure out—"

"It's fine," he interrupted, knowing a request for a rain check when he heard it. All the same, he stole one last kiss.

It pinched to stand in his condition, but he managed it, rearranging himself in his trousers as he did. When she made a halfhearted effort to get up, too, he shook his head, urging her back.

"I'm just going to grab my bag," she protested.

"No. You're not." He didn't know when the last time was that someone took care of her, but the next one was going to happen right now.

"Excuse me?"

He grabbed her remote control and her e-reader off the end table and tossed them both at her. "You, my dear, are going to sit right there, and you're either going to find something to watch or pick a book to read."

She raised one brow, but a soft curve colored her mouth. "I am, am I? And what will you be doing?"

"I"—he got his crutch under him and made for the kitchen—"will be ordering takeout." He paused, waiting for an objection.

All he got was a hopeful, "Sushi?"

"I will be ordering sushi," he clarified. "And then I'm going to make you a nice cup of tea, which you will sip at your leisure while you take a little bit of time for yourself. Good plan?"

She nodded, a warmth to her gaze that was new—that was everything. "Great plan."

He was as good as his word, too. He called the Japanese place down the street he'd had delivery from before. As he got her kettle going, he glanced around the corner to find her scrolling through her Netflix queue. She'd tucked her legs up under herself, and his heart gave a little lurch just to be able to look on at her like this. To see her happy and relaxed and in his care.

By the time the tea was ready, she'd picked something out to watch. He managed to carry two mugs over at once. He set them both down on her coffee table before falling back into the seat beside her.

She made a face as she reached for the closest mug and curled her fingers around the handle.

"Is something wrong?" he asked.

She shrugged. "I never use this mug."

It had been one of the only ones left in her cupboard; with everything else they'd gotten up to this weekend, doing the dishes hadn't ever been top of the list.

"Is there something wrong with it?"

"The handle's crooked. See?"

Now that she mentioned it, he supposed he could see it. He made to take it from her. "I'll trade you."

"It's fine."

"Why don't you just get rid of it?"

She looked at him like he was crazy. "I made it."

How on earth had he forgotten? "Oh."

And it was irrational, the fond, protective warmth he suddenly felt for a misshapen piece of pottery. An imperfect piece this woman kept around because of sentiment—because it was the labor of her own two hands.

He kept glancing at it as they settled in, the gears in his head slowly turning. She tucked herself against his side and hit PLAY, and he tried to focus on the program she'd picked out.

But he circled around again and again to that mug.

She'd told him once before how much she enjoyed the pottery class she'd taken, and clearly she'd been good at it. She'd let it go, though. There hadn't been enough time.

She never made enough time. Not for herself.

Maybe...

Maybe she needed someone to make the time for her.

CHAPTER FIFTEEN

You sure you don't want to come for dinner tonight, sweetie?" Serena's mom had her head in Serena's fridge. That not-so-subtle edge crept into her voice as she poked around. And okay, fine, there were some proverbial flies buzzing around in there it was so empty, but that wasn't her fault. She'd been *busy*. In fact, she was running late right now.

Not that she knew what she was running late *for*, mind you. Cole had been more cryptic than usual, just telling her he had something special in mind and that she should let him know as soon as Max was gone.

It had her skin humming with anticipation, her gaze returning again and again to the clock on the microwave, and she didn't want to rush her mother out or anything, but...

Fighting not to fidget, she crossed her arms over her chest. "Not tonight. Thanks, though."

Her mom closed the fridge and turned around, brows raised. Oh, crap. Serena knew that look.

"You have plans or something?"

No sense beating around the bush. Her mom knew all her tells. "Yeah. Actually, I do."

"With a boy?"

Ugh. Did this ever get less embarrassing? "Maybe."

"I didn't know you were seeing anyone."

"It's...new." That wasn't a lie. It wasn't entirely true, either. She and Cole had been darting around this since the moment they'd met, and they'd been sleeping together for a week and a half now, seeing each other nearly every day.

She chewed at her lip. It wasn't like her to keep something like this from her mother. Her mom's opinion was important to her—the most important, really. She'd considered bringing Cole around for Sunday dinner that weekend even, but something had stopped her. What she had with Cole—it was heady and intense and exhilarating. But it was fragile, too. She couldn't help the roiling feeling in her gut telling her the whole affair would crumble if exposed to too bright of a light.

Introducing him to her family. Telling her mom. It made it feel too real.

It made her remember all the reasons this thing between her and Cole would probably never last.

Leveling her with the kind of gaze that'd had her confessing all kinds of sins back when she was a teenager, her mother tilted her head to the side. True to form, Serena squirmed, but she held her tongue.

Finally, her mom rolled her eyes and sighed. "Fine. Keep your secrets. But I want to meet this boy eventually, you realize."

"Of course." Relief made Serena loosen her grip on her own

arms. "Just let me see if there's something there first, okay?"

"All right." Her mom was giving up way too quickly. Maybe she'd sensed that Serena wasn't ready to be pressed. She'd always been perceptive like that.

Or maybe she was just too eager to change the subject.

Her mom glanced into the other room where Max was furiously swiping at the screen of his tablet, clearly not paying them an ounce of his attention. Leaning in closer, she asked, "Have you heard from your sister again?"

Serena's stomach dropped.

She'd been trying not to think too much about that last awful phone call she and Penny had had while she'd been dress shopping, and Lord knew she'd had plenty of distractions to keep her mind off it.

"No. I tried her doctor in New York, but he wouldn't tell me anything except to stay calm and be supportive." She made a face. How long had they been hearing that line now?

"I can't stop worrying. She's been sounding off for a while now, and after that call she gave you, it's almost like..."

Serena swallowed. "I know." Like the worst years, back in high school before they'd had any idea what this thing was. Like when she'd ended up in the hospital again right after she'd had Max. "But what do we do?"

"If she doesn't call home soon, I'm getting on a plane."

It wouldn't be the first time. Serena understood why her sister chose to live so far away. She and her mother could be stifling, and she hadn't been wrong when she'd accused them of treating her with kid gloves for years.

She wished all the time that Penny lived closer for Max's sake.

But she wasn't so selfless that she couldn't sometimes wish she'd stayed closer for the rest of their sakes as well.

"Well, here's hoping it doesn't come to that. I'll try her again tomorrow, promise."

"You're so good to your mother." Her mom leaned in and planted a loud, smacking kiss on her cheek.

And, yeah, that was about right. As much as she said Serena should be off enjoying her youth, her mom was never as affectionate as she was when Serena pitched in and helped take some of the load.

With a pat to her other cheek, her mother stepped back. "Okay, we'll get out of your hair so you can get ready for that date." Louder, she called, "Max? Time to go."

Narrowing his eyes in concentration, Max made a few more motions on the screen, then nodded, grabbing his bag as he hauled himself to his feet. Still unsettled by the whole conversation, Serena went through the motions of getting Max packed up and out the door, ducking down for their secret handshake and his hug.

She could nearly set a timer between their making it to the curb below and Cole's knock sounding on her door. Still gazing out the window after them, she raised her voice to say, "It's open."

Cole let himself in, his uneven gait as familiar as her own pulse now. He came up behind her, wrapping an arm around her waist and nuzzling into her throat, breath soft. "I thought they'd never leave."

She hummed in halfhearted agreement, but her gaze was still on the car below. Her mom pulled out of her parking spot, and Serena closed her eyes.

Cole felt so nice, the soft line of kisses he lay beneath her ear sending a warm buzz humming through her skin. His scent surrounded her, and that should be all she needed. But she couldn't quite seem to bring herself to relax.

He hesitated, lips parting damply from her skin. "Serena?"

She opened her eyes. "It's nothing. My mom was just asking me again about my sister."

"Oh?"

"Yeah. We're both worried about her."

"Do you want to talk about it?"

Yes. No. Maybe. It was too much to put on him, wasn't it? Eventually, she shook her head. "Not really."

He didn't quite seem to believe her, but he didn't press. She wasn't sure if that was a disappointment or a relief.

For a while, they stayed there just like that, him holding her and her letting him. If only she could really lean back into him and let him take her weight. For now, though, this was enough.

Finally, she pushed her worries away. Releasing a long breath, she turned to face him, lifting her arms to lock her hands behind his neck, and it was still a little awkward. A little tense. But she shook that off and managed a smile.

"Hi."

"Hi yourself," he said. He ducked in for a peck of a kiss and then another. His hand at her side tightened and he touched his tongue to her lip like a question.

She welcomed him in without hesitation, happy to lose herself in this. Drawing closer, she angled her head to deepen the kiss, and his breath came out rough, palm sliding higher on her ribs. A blooming heat unfurled in her abdomen and in her breasts, a little of her tension leaving her at last.

But just as she really gave herself over to it, he inched back. He bit down hard on his own lip, and his voice came out shivery. "As much as I'd like to continue this..."

"I'm not stopping you."

He exhaled hard through his nose. "We need to go."

Go? That made her pull back.

It probably shouldn't have come as such a shock. He'd told her he had plans, after all. But outside of the benefit and his appointments, they never really left the building together. There was his mobility and the sheer convenience of staying in. Everything they needed was here, and anything they wanted was easy enough to have delivered in a neighborhood like this.

She arched a brow. "Any chance you're going to tell me where we're going?"

"Slim." With one last, reluctant pat to her waist, he stepped away. The tilt to his mouth was all mischief, and that was new, too. New and intriguing and sexy, honestly. "After all," he said, grinning, "I wouldn't want to ruin the surprise."

"Take a left at the light."

Serena cast him yet another suspicious glance, but he didn't respond to it. No way he was giving away the game now.

He'd forgotten how difficult it was to keep a secret from someone you cared about—a good secret made it even harder. All through dinner, he'd nearly opened his mouth to let it out a hundred times. There was a restless excitement humming through him. It had his heel bouncing up and down, had him worrying the edges of his nails with his teeth.

He wanted her to know. He wanted her to like it.

But he wanted to see the look on her face when he revealed it even more.

Finally, they turned off Lincoln and onto the side street. They circled for a while looking for someplace to park, but it wasn't as bad as it could have been.

"I would have dropped you off, you know," she said, falling into step beside him, looking pointedly at his crutch.

"Nonsense." He'd been getting even stronger in the past week. Using the leg still smarted, but it was the path to recovery, and he had incentives to get better faster now.

Walking in his city with a beautiful woman, for example.

Or being able to really pin her to his bed for another.

A jolt of heat zipped through him at the thought. They'd found plenty of creative ways to make love in the past week and a half, but soon...

Soon he was going to climb on top of her and press himself inside. Take her hard and fast—or maybe slow. So slow, until she was begging for more.

He quickened his pace. Damn, but she had better *love* this surprise, because if she didn't he was going to be cursing himself for refusing to let her talk him into staying home.

She kept looking around as they walked, and his pulse thrummed faster the closer they got, anticipation winding him higher and higher.

They were nearly upon it when she smiled. "You know, we're actually super close to my old...pottery...studio..." Her words slowed until she trailed off completely, and then she stopped dead in her tracks. The lightbulb that appeared over her head was bright enough to light the block. She turned to him, eyes wide. "No."

And suddenly, it wasn't just anticipation making his heart pound through his ribs. A rush of nervousness blindsided him.

Fuck. What if she *didn't* like it? What if he'd cocked it all up or overstepped? He hadn't tried to do something like this for anyone in years. He could've misread the situation entirely.

Shrugging, he swallowed past the tightness in his throat. He didn't have a backup plan. For better or for worse, he was committed now to see this through. "You always talk about it like it was something you loved."

"I did. I do. But—"

"You do so much for other people. All day long, you're taking care of them. You take care of Max and your students and your mother. And me." And this was the crux of the matter, really. "You should do something nice for you." He nodded, squaring his jaw. "Since you clearly weren't going to, I figured I had to do it for you."

She blinked, thick lashes fluttering. Her gaze pierced straight through him, and there was nothing in it he could read.

Shit. Maybe he really had cocked this up.

He took a deep breath. "Look. If you don't want to, we don't have to."

"Of course I want to." She came back to life, the stillness falling out of her limbs as she stepped into him. Her hands rose to settle on his waist, and even that small touch was magic. Her smile was transcendent. "Cole. This is amazing. It's too much—"

"It's not even close to enough. You deserve everything." It came out raw, too honest by half, and he cleared his throat.

"Just...Let me give it to you."

There was that look again, intense and wondering, and it seemed to reach its way into his chest. Instead of saying anything, she brushed soft fingertips against his cheek, lifting onto tiptoes.

This, at least, he knew how to handle. He dropped his head to meet her lips, trying to pour the things he didn't know how to put into words into the kiss. Her mouth was hot and wet and too perfect of a counterpoint to the cool night air around him, and he could drown in this. He could.

But they were on a public street, barely a dozen paces from the gift he'd chosen for her. When she pulled away, he let her go, even though the soft, shy press of her shining teeth against her lip had him hard inside his pants.

"Thank you," she said, fervent in a way he couldn't look at right now.

He shook off the haze of lust and emotion welling up in him and found the strength to put a little more space between their bodies. Gesturing down the street, he fought to make his breath even. To not betray the way he'd be more than happy to sack the entire thing and find another way to show his admiration.

"Don't thank me yet." He managed a crooked smile. "You've never seen me try to do arts and crafts before."

It was funny—sometimes you had no idea how much you'd missed something until you had it back.

The studio had changed a little in the couple of years since Serena had been there. The girl manning the sign-in book for open studio hours and restocking the kiln was different, and they'd put in a mirrored wall between the two rows of throwing wheels. But the clay-spattered walls were the same dingy white. The block of clay in her hands felt the same as she smacked it into a ball.

It felt *good*, was how it felt. There was a specific kind of satisfaction to making something out of nothing—just dirt and water, fire and heat. So what if she didn't need another bowl or vase or mug? She used to love this.

And the smooth texture of the clay wasn't the only thing she adored.

"You're *glowing*," Cole said. He was riding an edge here, his tone so close to mocking without quite stepping over the line.

"Whatever." She dipped her fingers into the tub of water beside her wheel, not even looking at him as she flicked the droplets in his face.

"Hey!"

Smirking at him, she dried her hand on her jeans. She was still a tiny bit sore he hadn't clued her in to what they were going to be doing so could have at least changed, but who cared? Laundry had been invented for a reason.

She spun her wheel up to test it out, getting a feel for the speed again. She waited until she had the measure of it, and then without another moment's pause, she slammed the clay down.

Cole flinched. "Jesus."

She grinned. "If you don't want to get messy, you better back away now." She leaned forward, bracing her elbows on her thighs, muscle memory kicking in as she started forming the clay into a mound.

"Please," he said, and he was too close by a mile, the warm scent of him destroying her concentration, and she wouldn't trade it for anything. "You know I'm not afraid of getting dirty."

The way he said it was more than dirty—it was *filthy*. She shivered, rolling her eyes at him before shrugging him off. "This isn't like they show it in the movies, you know. It isn't sexy. It's hard work."

"Never said I wasn't willing to work hard." And there was that tone again, sending thrills of heat moving through her. God, the things she was going to do to him when they got home. He'd done this for her to show his appreciation, he'd said. Well, she had some appreciating of her own to do later.

She paused, working her throat to fight the lump that wanted to form.

Because he'd been right. She didn't always make time for the things she liked to do, and his setting the time aside for her? It was one of the nicest things anyone had done in a really, really long time.

Hiding her face, she bent to her work again. She wet her hands and ramped the speed on the wheel to warp nine. "Don't say I didn't warn you."

With that, she leaned in. She didn't have all the strength she'd had back when she'd been doing this regularly, but she'd taken that into account when she'd weighed out her first hunk of clay. It all came back to her as she bent to it, the power involved in coning the material up before mashing it back down to center it. The rhythm felt like a perfectly broken-in pair of shoes or a warm robe on a cool day, meditative and soothing.

Letting out a breath, she eased up on the throttle and checked her work. The once uneven lump was a smooth cylinder now, even and symmetric. She dragged the back of her wrist over her brow.

"You make it look easy," Cole said.

Grinning, she nodded at his wheel. "It's not. Just wait until your turn."

"Oh, I believe you." A tiny fraction of the haughtiness he usually projected slipped away. "Walk me through what you're doing?"

Really, he should be taking a class if he actually wanted to try this for real. But she was pretty sure he was only here for her.

Nodding, she shifted to the side to give him a better view. It wouldn't hurt the piece any, so she coned and centered again, narrating as she did. She checked over her shoulder a couple of times, half expecting polite disinterest, but Cole was attentive. He leaned into her space, maybe too close—not that she was going to complain.

"Then—and this is the tricky part..." She trailed off, giving all her focus to the clay as she made the divot in the center and then dragged hard to open the form, creating the hollow that would be the bowl's interior.

As she started to thin the walls, he edged in ever closer, and she had to pause with her hands slick with clay, the bowl incomplete. The scent of him overtook her thoughts, blanking them, making it hard to think about anything else.

"It's funny." His voice came out husky and strained, and it lit the warm ember inside her, stoking it until it caught. "You said this wasn't sexy."

Her protest stuck in her throat. "It's not."

His hot fingertips brushed the bare skin at her elbow, and she closed her eyes. She was going to drop this pot, and she didn't care. The clay spun and spun inside her hands, a slick, cool glide that was the counterpoint to the rough stubble of his cheek against hers.

"You really have no idea, have you?" He dragged his knuckles higher, grazing them along her arm, and even through the rolled-up sleeves of her shirt, it was electric. "The grace you move with. The way the water glistens on your skin. It's sensual." And he was playing with fire, caressing down her arms again until his fingers skated over the backs of her palms. He dropped his voice. "You don't know how hard you make me."

Oh God.

"You're going to make me mess up," she said, shaky.

"Then mess up."

But she didn't. Opening her eyes, she got lost in the wet glide of their hands together against the clay. He followed her every movement, neither guiding nor inhibiting, just tracing. Joining them together as they took this raw bit of earth and sculpted from it something entirely new.

Before she knew it, she was staring down at a bowl. Uneven and maybe a little small, the base too thick for sure, but she didn't care.

Cole pulled his hands back slowly, settling one warm, broad palm on the tremoring line of her thigh. "It's beautiful."

"It's all right."

"It's amazing."

His foot nudged the side of hers, applying gentle pressure. She lifted her hands from the clay as the wheel spun down. No sooner had it come to a stop than his fingertips were on her face, tugging her into him and into a kiss that made her head whirl. Slow and lingering, he claimed her mouth, and she gave it freely.

Her heart ached in her chest.

Was there anything she wouldn't give him?

Behind them, a throat cleared.

Serena jerked away, a mortified flush creeping up her face when she spotted the studio manager giving them an amused if pointed look. Ugh, Serena had caught her own students making out enough times. Being on the other side of the equation made her feel like a heel.

It clearly had no such effect on Cole. Twisting to look over his shoulder, he just nodded to the girl with a self-satisfied, "Cheers."

The girl rolled her eyes and kept walking, and Cole turned back to Serena with a smug tilt to his mouth. "Now where were we?"

He had to be kidding.

"*We* were about to see how you would fare with a pot of your own."

With a wicked crook to his eyebrow, he grinned. "You are going to regret that. Mark my words."

CHAPTER SIXTEEN

W ell, that was an eye-opening experience." Serena flicked on the lights in her apartment as she went.

"I did warn you."

"You did." She wasn't arguing with him on that. "I just thought you were exaggerating."

He'd stalled and stalled when she'd insisted it was his turn to give the wheel a shot, but he had paid for open studio time for the both of them. She'd have been remiss in her duty if she hadn't gotten him to at least try once.

Turned out, he'd been underplaying how bad he was.

And there was something endearing about that, really. He was so good at so many things, was intimidatingly handsome and smart. He was capable of such tenderness and strength. Apparently, the only thing he wasn't capable of was anything remotely involving art, and she wasn't sure what she liked more—that he wasn't perfect after all or that he'd trusted her enough to let her see him fail. That he'd prioritized what she liked to do over his own discomfort.

She got her jacket hung, then turned to him. A round of flutters went off inside her chest just looking at him.

All night long, they'd scarcely been able to keep their hands off each other. From the kiss that had taken her breath away before they'd even left the apartment to the one that had nearly gotten them kicked out of the studio, they'd held the connection between them at a low simmer. Now that they were home, they could finally give it the fire to let it reach that rolling boil her body had longed for.

And yet, here he was, standing a half-dozen feet away. He'd draped his leather jacket over the back of one of her chairs. His shirt and jeans were both streaked with white and brown spatters of clay, but he looked just as intimidatingly sexy and confident as ever. As unapproachable.

She knew better now. Unwinding her scarf, she crossed the space to stand before him. Transcribing every movement, she looped the fabric around his neck and used it to haul him in. The corner of his mouth flickered up, a soft smile that made her go warm and melty inside. When they were nose to nose, she let her gaze dart between those sinful lips and the penetrating darkness of his eyes.

But her voice stuttered, abandoning her. What was she supposed to say? Tonight had meant so much to her. *He* meant so much. Too much. Swallowing, she opened her mouth to try. But with a subtle shake of his head, he shushed her, and her throat went dry. The air around them crackled, charged with things they had yet to say. Touches they had yet to share.

And *there* was that heat. Molten liquid bubbled beneath her skin, the quiet attraction of the rest of the night finally hitting a crest.

Maybe they didn't need words at all.

Adam's apple bobbing, he lifted a hand to cup the side of her neck, rubbing his thumb beneath the point of her jaw. "You have a little something..."

Her abdomen dipped, a well of need unfurling inside her, hot and clenching. Letting go of one end of her scarf, she dragged her palm down his chest, over the thick planes of muscle to rest against his heart. Her voice came out deep and rasping. "Funny." She stroked a fingertip along a line of clay that stood out bright against his shirt. "You've got a little something, too."

"How embarrassing."

"It really is." She met his gaze, only to find the same fire burning there that she felt in her own. "Guess we'll have to get these off you before you come to bed."

Even as he spoke, he leaned in. "If you insist."

All pretense fell away as his lips met hers. His mouth was hot against the chill that clung to her skin from the cool night air outside, warming her just as surely as the brush of his chest against the points of her breasts. She opened to him, swallowing his moan as his tongue swept inside.

She had the advantage here with two hands free. She put them to good work. Letting her scarf fall to the ground, she slipped her fingers along the placket of his shirt, undoing button after button. The plain cotton undershirt he wore beneath clung to his pectorals, the dips and ridges of his abs rippling the fabric and making her breath go tighter. She slipped her hand beneath the hem to press against that smooth, warm skin. The muscle beneath her hand twitched, and a noise of pure need fell out of his lungs. It wound her even tighter—she loved the sounds he made, the reactions of his body to being touched. Every time she got skin on skin, he acted like it was a miracle. A revelation.

Maybe because he had gone without it for so long.

Her heart panged, and she curled her fingers against the trail of hair leading from his navel down. He'd done something so nice for her tonight, and it had meant the world to her. He was right that she rarely put herself first. Someone putting her first—someone concentrating on what she needed, what would make her feel good—it *had* been a revelation.

A whole new sort of resolve pressed her closer to him. He was hard in his jeans, the long ridge of his erection grinding into her as she tugged them flush. He exhaled roughly, palm curling around her neck to hold her still for his kisses, and she wanted that. She did. But she wanted other things more.

She wanted to thank him. She wanted to give him something and to put him first, too.

She pulled herself away. The loss of his heat against her left her shivering, but she could bear it. Walking backward toward her bedroom, she hooked her hands in the fabric of her top and tugged it up slowly. "Take off your clothes."

He groaned, but he wasted no time shedding his oxford, managing to balance his crutch as he did. He stalked after her, pausing in the doorway to her room to haul his undershirt over his head.

Thank God she'd managed to remember to get the light this time. She was struck dumb by the vision of him standing there, perfect chest rising and falling with every breath. The black lines of ink cut across his musculature, a sharp contrast to the warm glow of his skin, and she wanted to learn every one. Even the two that were unintelligible, just symbols and letters carved into his flesh, were beautiful.

Shaking with anticipation, she kept on backing up until her legs hit the edge of her bed. He licked his lips, gaze dark as he watched her strip. She dropped her top to the floor, shaking her hair out so it fell in waves around her shoulders, and if it were possible, the desire in his eyes etched deeper. Without looking away, she reached behind herself to undo her bra.

She shivered as the tips of her breasts flashed harder in the cool air. He reached his free hand out to grasp the frame of the door. His biceps strained as he braced himself there, and the point of his jaw flexed.

"What are you doing to me?" he asked.

The same thing you're doing to me. It was too much to hope that that was true, and yet there was this part of her that dared.

Nothing for it. She skimmed out of her pants, taking her underwear with them, stepping out of the little flats she'd probably never get clean after their night in the studio, and she didn't care. Naked, she sank to sit at the edge of the bed.

He staggered the last couple of feet to stand before her. His crutch clattered to the ground, and he was uneven without it, weight shifted to one side, but it didn't matter. He combed her hair back from her face, tracing the curve of her cheek before brushing his thumb along her lower lip. She opened her mouth, and he slipped just inside, the pad of his thumb sliding along her tongue.

His nostrils flared. "You like that, do you?"

Heaven help her, but she did.

Holding his gaze, she brought her hands to the waistband of his jeans. His belt gave beneath her fingers, and a rushing heat flowed from the stiff points of her breasts to her pussy. When she stroked her hand over the length of him through the denim, his thumb pressed deeper. She pursed her lips around it, and he swallowed hard.

At least he didn't try to pretend he didn't see what she was offering. "You don't have to."

She waited until he pulled his thumb away to lick her lips. "I want to."

It was the work of a moment to get him free. He made another one of those delicious noises as she wrapped her hand around the silky, searing flesh, smoothing the foreskin back. God, he was big. Perfect and achingly hard. The tension coiling inside of her wound higher. She was soaked with wanting, and it would be so easy to pull him down onto this bed with her. To climb on top and get the deep stretch, the fullness and the satisfaction of his body thrusting hard into hers.

Instead, she pushed his pants and boxers farther down, then took another long, slow stroke with her hand. Patience was a virtue and restraint would be rewarded. And this wasn't about her; it was about him.

She'd never had a chance to take her time with him or to try to learn exactly what he liked. How he shuddered when she rubbed her thumb through the fluid at the tip. How he closed his eyes and tilted his head back as she drew that slickness down to just beneath the head.

How he moaned her name when she slipped off the mattress

to fall to her knees. When she replaced her fingers with her tongue.

"Serena." His voice came out choked and rough, and he threaded gentle fingers through her hair as she let him slip between her lips. "Oh, that's perfect."

She hummed around him before pulling back. She wasn't going to be rushed here, either. She licked and kissed and explored, breathing against the base of him and mouthing at the tender flesh of his sac. His warm, male scent invaded her senses, the salty, slightly bitter aftertaste of him thick on her tongue. Staring up at him, she skated her hands along his thighs, over lean muscle and coarse hair before bringing them to rest at his hips, dragging her thumbs over the grooves of the V that led her exactly where she wanted to go.

And this was cruel, but she placed one more soft kiss to the very crown of him before leaning back. She wanted him desperate, wanted him insane for what she was about to give him. Her heart thundered and her pussy throbbed as she waited.

Untouched for a moment, his cock bobbed on the air, liquid beading from the slit. His breath came faster and faster, his rib cage expanding and contracting furiously, and the hand in her hair clenched, nails raking against her scalp.

Finally, he broke. "Please."

She wet her lips with her tongue. "Please what?"

"Please." His eyes were practically black. "Suck me."

Hot tremors of arousal raced up and down her spine, making her skin feel like it was too tight, and maybe she was cruel, maybe she had both patience and restraint, but even she was helpless against his plea.

"Happily," she murmured. With that, she opened her mouth and swallowed him down.

"Fuck." His legs shook, and his whole spine arched over her as she took him in as deep as she could. His other hand slammed against the edge of the mattress behind her, and he leaned into it like it was the only thing keeping him up.

Maybe it was. Maybe he needed his crutch or to sit or lie down.

Except when she made to slide off of him, he let a growl build low in his throat. Cupping the back of her head now, he urged her to take him in again, and that was all the answer she needed to dispel her doubts.

Closing her eyes, she slid him back inside, triumph a brilliant glow within her chest. On an upward stroke, she curled her tongue to flick it over that spot beneath the head that had made him groan before, and the noise it pulled out of him this time was unreal.

"Serena. Christ. You look so good with my cock in your mouth."

Her every nerve was alight as she moved into a nice, slow pace. His hips answered her, making gentle, shallow thrusts in time with the motions of her lips. The shaking in him deepened as he got closer and closer.

"Faster," he begged. "Nice and deep, yes—"

His voice cut off as she wrapped her hand around the base. He slid slickly through the circle of her fist, the wet sounds of her going down on him and him fucking her mouth obscene and delicious on the air. He sped up, taking control, and she let him.

Because maybe that was what he'd needed.

A dizzying desire made her head spin. Someday, she wanted that. When his leg was healed, she wanted him to pin her to the mattress and take her hard, fuck her for hours with all the strength that was in him. Claim her and make her his own.

She wanted him to keep her.

Groaning around the thick flesh in her mouth, she squeezed her eyes shut tighter. God, she wanted that so much.

Finally, the shaking in his legs hit a tipping point. He sped the pace of his hips, and every muscle in his abdomen clenched hard. He drew in a harsh, sucking breath.

"Shit, Serena, you take it so perfectly. Take it, take it all...I'm—"

His jaw clamped shut, the hand at the back of her head snapping suddenly away. It was warning and permission, but she opened her eyes and pulled him in deeper.

"Serena—"

He came in surging pulses over her tongue, and she swallowed it all. Every rasping gasp, every line of strain was a hot punch to her core. Her slickness coated her thighs, and she could barely breathe past how badly she needed him, needed this, needed it to never end.

She whimpered as he took one last thrust past her lips and stilled.

God. She was in so deep with this man, and he'd never promised her anything—he'd explicitly told her that he couldn't, even. There were obstacles and land mines lurking in the scattered landscape of his past. But as he stared down at her, shuddering through the aftershocks of his climax, this ember of hope ignited in her.

Maybe. Maybe.

The ember only grew as he drew back. He slipped free from her mouth with a wet *pop* that sent another lick of heat on a live wire to her clit. She stayed there on her knees, panting, her entire body tight and on edge with the depths of the ache he left in his wake.

His body seemed to give out.

Alarmed, she reached to try to steady him, but he shook his head. It was a controlled descent that brought him shuddering to the floor. Landing on his good knee, he reached out for her, and she went. They twisted and turned, arranging themselves until he had them how he wanted them. He sat with his back against the footboard of her bed, legs splayed out in front of him, his jeans still at his knees. Straddling his hips, she was even with his face, eye to eye and mouth to mouth.

With an intensity in his eyes she couldn't read, he pulled her in.

She groaned as he licked his taste from her tongue. The kiss was deep and wet, his muscles lax from orgasm while hers still felt taut, every inch of her begging for touch. He settled a hand on her hip, thumb edging down toward where she was slick and soft for him, and she rocked into him, silently begging.

Scraping his teeth over her lip, he delved deeper. Two fingers traced along her opening, and she clamped her thighs tighter around his hips.

All that time she'd spent trying to figure out exactly how he ticked, and apparently he'd already mastered her.

"There," he said as he pressed inside, curling his fingers up and rubbing deep within. Firing off sparks.

She nodded, wrapping her arms around his neck in some vain effort to be closer—to breathe his air and to surround him. To live in this moment when he was surrounding her. Filling her.

His thumb touched so gently at her clit. "And there."

"Yes." She sucked in a shattering breath at the wave of blistering heat, and it only flared hotter when he brought his other hand up to her breast.

And it took so little. He stroked and rubbed, making soft circles around her clit and firm, curving motions inside. Cupping her flesh, he pinched her nipple between his finger and his thumb, kissing wetly at her mouth until she was panting for it. All too soon, the heat was an inferno, making her tingle all the way to the curled toes of her feet, but she resisted. She wanted more, wanted everything.

But he shook his head, fighting the resistance in her body.

"Let go," he urged. "I've got you, love." And that endearment tugged at something that hurt too much inside of her, even as his fingertips pressed exactly where she needed him, as he rolled her clit just right.

Her climax washed over her all at once, dragging her under. The flames broke into cool, cool water, relief and ecstasy, and he did have her. He did.

But even as she fell into his lips, succumbing to the boneless aftermath of pleasure, that word echoed and panged inside her mind.

Love. It was such a casual endearment, such a British thing to say. But it was what she wanted, what she wasn't sure she could ever have.

And it was exactly what she felt for this man.

CHAPTER SEVENTEEN

Y ou know, there's a perfectly good bed like two feet away from us."

Cole craned his neck in the direction of said bed, even going so far as to reach a straining hand toward it before collapsing back again. "Much too far."

Serena rolled her eyes, but the curve of her mouth against his chest betrayed her smile. "Suit yourself."

"I will."

He hugged her closer, shifting to press a too-intense kiss to the center of her brow. He shut his eyes, just breathing her in for a moment. Finally, he loosened his grip, prepared for her to swat at him or get up or make some vague effort at putting on her clothes. But she didn't pull away at all. A light inside him glowed. Apparently the floor suited her as well as it did him.

Honestly, though, no one could expect him to move after *that*. He'd managed to strip the rest of his clothes off, but that was as much as he had in him. In the aftermath of climax, they'd collapsed to lie together, tangled naked on the hardwood, and it was cold and it was uncomfortable, and he didn't give a damn. All he cared was that he was here. With her.

His heart gave a restless pang, and he ducked to hide his face in her hair.

He didn't deserve her. Not the playful way she flicked clay at his face or made fun of his fumbling attempts to keep up with her at the pottery wheel. Not the tender way she touched him or the quiet intimacy that seemed to enshroud them every time they kissed.

The grace with which she'd sunk to her knees and practically worshiped him with her mouth.

Christ.

He didn't deserve her. Fuck him if he wasn't going to try to, though.

She shifted, tilting her head to look at him. A little line appeared between her brows. "I can hear you thinking, you know."

Forcing a smile, he smoothed the crinkles between her eyes with his thumb. "Sorry."

"Don't be. Just...anything in particular on your mind?"

So many things. His racing thoughts were the reason he could rarely sleep, why he had such trouble staying present. Focusing on the pleasure of holding a beautiful, naked woman in his arms instead of obsessing over all the things that would eventually go wrong.

For the time being, he pushed all those other competing ideas away. Ever so gently, he dragged a fingertip over the curve of her lower lip.

"At the moment, I'm mostly thinking about your mouth." The

soft, wet heat of it and the dark, seductive tease of her tongue on his flesh.

Her eyes flashed, and his prick, soft and sated, gave a waking twitch against his hip. Just as she had earlier, she parted those sinful lips and took a kitten lick at the pad of his finger. Fuck, could she taste herself on his skin?

"Funny," she said, voice husky. "Because I can't stop thinking about your hands."

"Is that so?"

"It is."

Arousal was a slow, lazy hum radiating between them. A part of him wanted to ride it right into a second round of lovemaking, but a bigger piece was content to let it take its course. She seemed to sense that lack of urgency, pressing one more kiss to his fingertip before letting him draw his hand away.

Resting her face against his shoulder again, she trailed her hand across his chest, gentle arcs that left soft trails of heat in their wake, keeping the fire alive without stoking its flames. In the silence, his mind started to drift.

But it was her thoughts that beat too loudly this time.

"What?" he asked as she traced the bottom of his ribs again.

"I like these," she said.

It took him too long to catch up, but when he did, the ink sewn into his skin flashed hot. "Oh."

Her fingertips swept smoothly from the symbols at his abdomen to the star over his heart, then over to the lines that curled around his arm.

"Tell me about them?"

Warning sirens blared inside his mind. She asked the question so casually, as if it were nothing. If he deflected, she'd probably back off. The temptation ate at him. They'd already tread the burned out landscape of his past enough—couldn't he have one evening to lose himself? To ignore the echoes of the ghosts in his heart?

With a deep breath, he grasped her hand in his, too hard, and she startled, frowning.

"You don't have to—" she said.

And it was that very assurance that made him realize he did.

No matter how much of himself he revealed to her, she never pulled away from him. She'd coaxed out story after story until she had the most complete picture he'd ever allowed anyone to have of his life.

She didn't have to coax him anymore. Whatever she asked for he would give.

Loosening his grip, he swallowed. He intertwined their hands and dragged her back to the inscription just beneath his ribs. "This was the first one. I got it my second term at Oxford. Right after I accepted that I would always be alone."

Her breath came out in a rush. "Oh." She darted her gaze to his. "What's it mean?"

"It's an equation. It's for..." How did he explain it in a way that might make sense? He gave up and did the best he could. "A single particle, vibrating on a string. Unaffected by any other force or object. I...I thought that was how life would be for me."

"But it wasn't."

He shifted until he was looking her in the eye. "No. It wasn't."

It wasn't as if she could have forgotten that he had been in love before. Serena's calm and Serena's hands and Serena's unrelenting, unforgivable, blessed, wonderful tenacity had been the things to pull him out of his patterns this time, but she hadn't been the first.

He pulled her fingers back to his arm. The lines of ebony ink were crisper where they wrapped around his biceps, the letters and symbols a part of him now. A reminder—one he'd forgotten for so very long.

"This was the second."

"And when did you get it?"

"Princeton. My third year of my doctorate. After—" He stuttered, the name refusing to come to his lips. "After I wasn't alone anymore."

"They're equations, too?"

"Yes." It had seemed fitting, after all. He tightened his grip on her hand. "The ones for light."

Four simple series of letters and symbols that taken together explained how every bit of brightness and color in the universe had come to be.

Because that's how it had been. A new start in a new country with a woman who had drawn him out of his shell, surrounded by the friends she had pressed him to make. It had felt like all the darkness in his life had been banished, like everything was different now. And it had been.

Everything except him.

He twisted his neck to stare at the ceiling, blinking hard. "After she died, I nearly blacked them out."

Her touch against his skin went heavier, her fingers pressing in. "I'm glad you didn't."

"So am I. Now."

Because there was still light in his world. It had taken him so long to understand it, but there was. Serena had shown it to him again.

Closing his eyes, he brought her hand to rest against his heart. "Instead, I got this."

"Oh."

She didn't push and she didn't prod. Instead, she lay there, waiting, and he could have kissed her for it.

Because this was the hardest tattoo to explain. It was the reason he'd had to try.

"It's a nautical star," he said, looking up into soft, kind eyes the very color of the sea.

Still so patient, she flexed her fingers beneath his hand, tracing the outline of the star.

The sting of the needle came back to him, nearly as violent and precise as the fire of his grief.

Throat raw, he pressed her palm in harder against his skin. "It was an inside joke." Such dramatics they'd been prone to, way back then. Evoking an orator's tone, he began, "Is this the face that launched a thousand ships?"

And Serena was so smart. Those brilliant eyes of hers went wider. "Helen."

At least she could say his late wife's name. It felt like his face was cracking. Serena's gaze fell. She moved as if to pull her hand away, but he held fast, keeping her there. Exactly where he needed her, where he wanted her, where she lived now.

"I spent some of the best years of my life with her." But not the only good ones he'd ever have. A part of him was just beginning to understand that. "She's written on my heart. She always will be."

"Of course, I would never—"

He shook his head, and her words cut off. Her gaze shuttered, though, and the idea that she didn't know this—that once again she could be putting herself and her happiness so low...

His voice broke. "But she's not the only one."

There was more room in his heart than he had ever known. The empty, aching, hollow spaces, the ones he'd thought he'd never fill in the wake of so much loss...maybe they were for her.

"Cole..."

"You're in here, too," he said, because no matter how this turned out—whether they pulled this off or he ended it in ruin—that much at least would always be true. "Serena. I told you, I can't promise you much."

"I'd never ask you to."

He soldiered on, refusing to let her derail him or interrupt. "I still don't trust myself."

He probably never would. After the way he'd lost control, first as a child with his tormentors and then again and again. With the men on the train.

With Helen.

But Serena was so bloody insistent. "Do you trust me?"

He came up short.

"Of course." More than he trusted himself.

"Then *trust me*." The heat of her palm seeped deep into his heart, melting layers of ice and scar.

Maybe she didn't only fill the empty places there. Maybe she was making new ones. Better ones.

Maybe he'd thought that once before.

The seed of doubt came out of nowhere, but before it could take too deep of root, Serena pulled him back to her. She drew her hand from his heart to rest against his cheek, directing his gaze until he was staring, lost, into her eyes.

"Cole, I—" She cut herself off, words hanging heavy and unspoken in the air.

He could imagine them, though, and she was right to keep them in. Some things he still wasn't ready to say or to hear.

Desperate, he covered her lips with his own. In the span of a breath, she caught right up with him, and he could nearly taste the relief in her kiss.

Without hesitation, she opened for him, dragging him in closer. He rolled into her until they both lay on their sides. The cold press of the floorboards bit into his shoulder and hip, and fuck, shite, he should have listened to her after all about hauling themselves onto the bed, but it was too late now. He let his hands roam over soft skin, and his body couldn't help but respond. Her breasts pressed against his chest were tight, her mouth lush, and when she hitched a leg over his, he groaned aloud.

There were things they still couldn't say, but they could communicate all the same. He kissed her with all the passion she awoke in him, all the hope she had taught him he could feel again. The head of his cock grazed the hot flesh of her thigh, sending lightning up his spine until he had to pull back.

Desperate to give her at least some fraction of what she gave him, he slipped a hand between her legs to find her soft and slick. He rubbed at her clit and probed inside, devouring the sounds of need falling out of her lungs. He chased her pleasure, stroking faster and harder. Soaking his fingers, she tightened around him, so close, and he was blind to everything. Could think of nothing but taking her past the edge once more.

"Come on, beautiful," he all but growled, "give it to me."

But she shook her head, nudging his hand away. He missed the hot clench of her immediately, wanted more of her little whimpers and the tensing of her body, the rhythmic pulses as she squeezed him.

Until she curled her fingers around his cock.

"Serena," he groaned. She'd made him come so hard not an hour ago, but it felt like days, he needed her so badly. Her touch felt so good.

She gazed clear into his eyes as she directed him home. "I want you."

How could he resist?

Poised at her entrance, the head of him snugged up against wet heat, he threaded his fingers through her hair. Angled his neck to kiss her deeper.

He pressed inside in one long glide that stole his breath away. She accepted him so easily, took him in so readily. She gave him things he'd thought he'd never have again.

She was a miracle.

With all the reverence and awe a miracle deserved, he moved inside her. She met his every thrust, one hand at his jaw and the other at his hip, urging him on. With pleasure a brilliant ember, a glowing coal, they rocked together in rolling motions of spines and hips. He couldn't stop touching her, couldn't seem to keep himself from falling into her mouth, and it was too intense. Too much like those words she'd scarcely stopped herself from saying.

And it was impossible to picture—far-fetched to the point of insane—but it came to him all the same.

What if, someday, he said those words to her?

His heart threatened to pound clear out of his chest. As if she knew, she pressed her palm to the aching center of his ribs, and his gaze went blurry and damp.

Because she didn't try to cover that star. That symbol and that reminder that was sewn deep beneath his skin. She touched him right beside it. On clean and untouched flesh, and for a moment, he felt just that innocent. That clean.

He sped the pace of his hips, her name a prayer on his lips as the feeling threatened to crest over. She ground against him harder, and he snuck a hand between them to touch her where she needed it. On the precipice, he hovered, staring deeply into crystal eyes as her whole body went taut, spine arching.

"Cole, I—"

She clenched around him, slick pulses that dragged him right down after. As she shook apart in his arms, he let the pleasure take him. The connection to this woman who accepted him. Who *loved* him. He thrust deeply into the hot, wet clench of her until it overwhelmed him, fire spreading from his balls through every inch of his skin. He emptied himself into her with a force that left him shattered. Gasping against her mouth, he drove home one final time and stilled.

When he came back to himself, his breath was ragged, his heart racing. Serena's chest heaved as she lay there surrounding him, as close to him as a person could possibly be.

He forced his fingers to uncurl, letting go of the grip he had on her hip. Then slowly, trying to say the things they hadn't yet, he placed his palm flush over hers, right next to his heart.

He still didn't know if he could give her what she deserved. But with all the strength he had left, he held on.

CHAPTER EIGHTEEN

At first, Serena thought it was her alarm. She groaned, half sitting up, but the warm, heavy arm draped across her waist had her pinned. Blinking against the darkness, she furrowed her brow. Huh. For once, Cole was passed out in the bed beside her as opposed to wandering her kitchen. She nudged at his shoulder, but he just snuffled deeper into the pillow, tightening his grip. It would be adorable, except the alarm was still blaring.

Only...She tilted her head, craning her neck to listen better.

That wasn't her alarm.

Confused, she glanced toward her clock.

"Crap."

She was used to getting up early, but this was ridiculous.

"Cole?" She swatted harder at his arm this time, and he finally budged, sleep-heavy voice mumbling something unintelligible as he rolled off.

Funny—she'd never pegged him for a cuddler, but in his sleep, apparently he clung on like a limpet.

Free to do so, she sat up and rubbed at her eyes. The blaring of the buzzer for the door downstairs didn't so much as pause. With a sigh, she threw off the covers and rose. She gave a full-body shiver when her feet touched the floor. Going to bed naked had seemed like a good idea at the time, but it was freaking freezing now. She grabbed her robe off the back of the door and drew it on.

Cole's voice followed her as she stepped into the hallway. "What—"

Beyond what had been necessary to extricate herself, she'd tried not to wake him—he got so little sleep as it was—but apparently, that was a lost cause.

"Heck if I know."

If this was some jerk randomly pushing buttons, he was getting a piece of her mind.

Flicking on the hallway light, she made her way to the intercom and pressed the buzzer. "For God's sake, what?"

"Serena?"

Not some random idiot, then. "Yeah?"

"It's Penny."

Serena's eyes snapped the rest of the way open. An icy hand reached its way into her heart. "Penny?"

What on earth was her sister doing here?

"Can I come up?"

"Of course." Scrambling, she stabbed at the button to unlock the door downstairs. She heard it unlatching and made a beeline for her own apartment door, throwing the bolt and tugging it open. An even colder gust of air met her on the landing.

Too late, it struck her that she was naked under this robe. Her hair was probably a bird's nest, and she was freezing in her bare feet. She saw her sister so rarely these days, and there was just something about your big sis. Serena had looked up to her for so long, even after she'd fallen apart. There would always be this part of her that craved Penny's approval. That wanted to impress her. For half a second, she seriously considered running back inside to try to make herself presentable.

But then Penny was there, trudging her way up the stairs.

"Oh my God." The words just came out, much louder than she'd intended, considering she hadn't meant to say them at all. She slapped her hand over her mouth.

Back when they'd been kids, people had often commented on how similar the two of them looked—the same blond hair, green eyes, and pale skin. Most of the time, when Penny was healthy, she'd worn her looks with grace, caring more about style and clothes than Serena ever had. But now, Penny's hair was dull, the ends ragged against her shoulders. Her eyes were bloodshot, and dark circles made them look sunken. Her paleness pointed more at blood loss than a northern European heritage.

One corner of her bitten, chapped lips pulled upward. "Well, if it isn't my baby sister."

With that, she stumbled and nearly went careening down the stairs.

Snapping into action, Serena threw the door wider and hustled down the couple of steps to meet her. Penny fell into her arms, and Serena's stomach sank further. She smelled like two days on a bus—and that wasn't really all that far-fetched, was it? Beneath the leather of Penny's jacket, Serena could feel ribs.

"Come on." She fought to steer her toward the apartment.

Together, they managed to get to the top of the stairs and

through the door. Serena led her to the couch, where she all but collapsed. Serena stood up straight again, chest tight.

She could handle this, though. She'd get some coffee going and definitely some food—even she could scramble a couple of eggs. And then she'd sneak into her room to get dressed and call her mom.

It was the first idea to offer her any consolation at all. Mom. Mom would know what to do.

Resolved, she turned. Only to find Cole standing in the doorway, looking all of his six-foot-something.

And suddenly she could imagine what it must have been like to be one of those muggers he'd chased down—to have all of *that* glowering at you from across a crowded train station.

He'd warned her about it so many times. But for the first time, she felt this tiny, shivering tickle of fear.

She shook it off. But that didn't mean she had any idea what to say. Lost, she glanced from Cole to Penny and back again, hoping the uncertain expression on her face said it all.

Cole deflated by a fraction. He was still clearly on high alert, but he softened his shoulders, cutting slightly less imposing of a figure. He'd dragged on his clay-spattered jeans from the night before, but other than that, he was naked, too, those bold, beautiful, painful designs on his chest and arm on stark display.

Leaning into his crutch, he stepped to the side. "I'll get some coffee going."

A warmth lit off inside Serena's chest, nearly as bright as the spark she'd had remembering her mother.

She didn't have to figure this out alone. Whatever *this* was, she had her family to lean on. She had Cole.

Then one member of her family groaned. "Shit. Rena. I didn't know you'd have someone—"

"It's fine." It was pretty darn crappy timing, was what it was. After the intensity of last night, Serena had drifted off with *plans* for what she was going to do with Cole this morning. But that was all right. She angled herself so she could see them both. "Penny, this is..." God, it was so middle school to be stuttering over a word like this—and she would know. She rolled her eyes at herself and soldiered on. "This is my boyfriend, Cole. Cole, this is my sister, Penny."

"Charmed," Cole said from the other room, managing a tight smile.

It was way too early for any of this.

She sighed. "Look, let me go get dressed real quick. Just—" A little bit of the desperation clawing at her chest leaked through. "Don't go anywhere, okay?"

The wry tilt to Penny's mouth made her look at least a little bit more like herself. "Like I have anywhere else left to go."

Serena cast one last glance Cole's way. He nodded at her, and she mouthed a silent *Thank you* at him before retreating. He hadn't signed up for any of this, and yet here he was. Gratitude had her blinking hard.

With her bedroom door closed behind her, she headed straight for her phone to text her mom. It was too early for her to be awake, but she'd kill Serena if she kept this to herself.

Don't panic, but Penny just showed up at my apartment.

Setting her phone down, she shucked her robe. If she was planning to go to work, she'd have to change again in an hour, but for now, she tugged on jeans and a sweatshirt and called it good.

Her phone buzzed.

WHAT???

Serena's thoughts exactly. She texted back quickly: *I don't know what's going on yet, but I knew you'd want to know.*

She'd barely fired it off before her phone vibrated in her hand. *I'm coming right over.*

No, she replied, *you're not. She came to me for a reason.* She bit her lip as she glanced toward the door. *I'll let you know as soon as I have a clue, but for now sit tight. Get Max off to school and then we'll talk.*

Heck. Max. What a mess would it be if her mom showed up with him in tow?

Switching her phone to silent, she stuffed it in her pocket and headed back out.

It shouldn't have been such a relief to find Penny still on her couch, but she let out a deep breath all the same.

Penny had curled in on herself while she'd been gone. She fluttered her eyes open as Serena approached and flashed her a weak but all-too-familiar smile. "What? Did you really think I'd disappear?"

"No." Not really. But maybe a little.

In the other room, Cole was a silent presence manning a couple of frying pans, and the well of gratitude burned even brighter in Serena's chest. He caught her eye as she glanced in on him and gestured with his head toward her sister.

And it wasn't really that Serena had been stalling, but maybe, just a little bit, she had.

She took one last detour, stopping to fill a couple of mugs with coffee and doctoring them up before taking them over to the couch. She passed one to Penny, who took it with that same exhausted smile.

Serena second-guessed herself, hand still outstretched. "Do you actually want that? If you just want to crash or something..." She gestured toward the bedrooms, but Penny shook her head.

"Nah, I'm gonna need it before Mom shows up anyway. Is she on her way?" The look she shot Serena this time was pointed.

Serena swallowed, but she refused to feel guilty. "I think I convinced her to wait until she gets Max seen off."

Penny closed her eyes, cradling her mug close to her chest. "Well, that's something at least."

"I couldn't not tell her."

"No," Penny said. "I guess you never could."

Serena was *not* going to get defensive. "What's that supposed to mean?"

"Nothing." Penny opened her eyes again. "Just you and Mom. Always in cahoots."

What? They'd been close enough, sure, but Penny had always been her favorite.

She stopped. This was her letting herself get distracted *and* defensive.

Forcibly relaxing her shoulders, she perched on the other end of the couch. She hesitated, entirely too aware of Cole listening in from the other room, of the distance between her sister and her.

She ignored it all, though, and reached out to rest a hand on Penny's ankle. "What's going on?"

Penny's eyes shone. Her coffee threatened to splash over the side with how hard her hands shook. "Rena. I think I made a really big mistake."

CHAPTER NINETEEN

The first time Penny got sick, she was thirteen years old. Serena had been just shy of her tenth birthday—just a little bit younger than Max was now. Amicable as it was, her parents' separation had still been fresh. Her sister had been a moody teenager, dealing with honors classes that actually challenged her for the first time, way more stressed than a kid her age should really be. Between that and the divorce, everybody had ignored the signs.

So many times, later, they'd wished that they hadn't.

Penny had woken Serena up the day after her birthday, crying uncontrollably, the floodgates opening. She'd been so stressed, she couldn't focus, she couldn't sleep, she was worthless and she wanted for it to all be *over*.

And Serena had felt like she'd been the one watching her life flash before her eyes.

She still wasn't sure how she'd managed to talk her sister down enough to get their mom involved. But suddenly, sitting there on her couch with a much older, more bedraggled Penny before her,

Serena felt like she was right on the cusp of being ten years old all over again. And just like then, she didn't have a clue what she was doing.

Struggling to keep her voice even, she asked, "What do you mean?"

The misting in Penny's eyes spilled over, twin droplets trickling silently down her cheeks. "Everything, Rena. My whole life. I think it was a mistake."

Oh, God.

The thing was, Serena had done all the reading back when she was a kid. She'd done even more as a teen when things had hit a crisis point again. You couldn't rationalize with depression. You couldn't just tell someone to cheer up or to look at all the good things in her life.

Wishing she'd managed to get a little bit more of the caffeine into her bloodstream before they'd started this conversation, Serena set her mug aside, scooting closer on the couch until she could tuck her sister under her arm. Penny went easily enough, resting her head on Serena's shoulder and curling into a ball.

"I'm so glad you're here," Serena said. A fierceness overtook her as she pressed a kiss to her sister's brow. She was glad Penny was here in this room, glad she was still here and breathing on this earth. "You were right to come." She blinked hard at the shudder of a sob that racked her sister's frame. "Now tell me *everything.*"

And it was as if something melted in Penny's spine, as if maybe she'd been waiting for someone to ask her that forever.

"I don't even know. It just...It got bad again, you know? And I've been handling it. I've been doing everything right. No skipping appointments or doses or anything, but it just got worse. I

feel like I'm at the bottom of a pool, and I can't breathe, and—"
Her voice ratcheted higher and higher, coming faster with every
ragged inhalation.

Serena clutched her close, stroking her hair and mumbling
nonsense, the words of comfort she'd been practicing for what
felt like her entire life now.

Movement at the corner of her vision drew her gaze up. She
met Cole's eyes across the room. Concern crinkled his brow, an
unspoken question on his lips, but she gave a tiny shake of her
head. She was fine. She had this.

Looking away, she ran her hand over Penny's back. "It's okay.
It's all okay."

"Just...remember when I was smart?"

"Shhh. You're one of the smartest people I know."

Her sister gave a choking laugh. "You wouldn't know it. I lost
another job. I thought I'd find something, but the insurance ran
out, and I don't know how I'm going to pay for any of it."

Serena swallowed. That was a problem, but they'd figure it out.
"We'll take care of it. Your only job right now is to get well again."
Maybe it would be something simple like switching her meds.
Maybe it wouldn't. Either way..."As long as you're here, we'll take
care of you."

How long would that even be? Penny hated having Serena and
their mother clucking over her—she'd made that perfectly clear
the last time she'd left.

Even now, Serena was probably holding on too tight.

She forced herself to loosen her grip. "And then when you're
better," she said, shaky, "when you're well enough to go back
home, we'll get you all set up. Get everything in place."

A treatment plan and the right doctors. Maybe they could even get Penny to give them the names of some of her friends so they could establish a decent network this time. That way, when things went wrong, she and her mom wouldn't have to sit here, halfway across the country and going out of their minds with worry.

Except before she could say any of that, Penny pulled free, sitting straight. The coffee she still had clasped between her hands sloshed dangerously, but Penny didn't pay it any mind.

"No. No, Rena, don't you get it? I—" Something in her face broke. "If you don't want me to, it's okay. Fuck, you'd have enough reason to. I—" She almost looked like she was about to get up, and Serena had this teetering moment where she imagined her sister heading straight out the door, maybe never to be seen or heard from again.

Serena reached out, getting a hand on her wrist and holding on tight. "What are you talking about?"

Hazy green eyes the exact same shade as her own focused in on her. "My *life* is a mistake, Rena."

"I—"

A fresh wave of tears streaked down her face. "I spent all this time running away. I thought it was better for you and better for Max and Mom, and just better. For everyone. But I can't—I just can't anymore."

"Okay." Serena took a steadying breath, but her mind was spinning.

Better? Nothing was *better* when Penny wasn't there.

Penny shook her head. "I didn't want to be the broken sister or the useless mother or the fucking burden anymore. But instead..."

Her voice cracked, and Serena's heart did, too. "I ended up not really having a family at all, and I'm tired. I'm so tired."

"Penny..."

"Please." She twisted her wrist, flipping it around so she was grasping Serena right back. "Please. Rena. I want to come *home*."

Cole didn't belong here.

His throat tight, he flipped the eggs and turned off the stove. Out in the other room, both Penny and Serena were crying now, and the whole thing had his heart feeling tender and his neck hot. This was between the two of them, and as much as he wanted to help, to support, he didn't really have any place here.

He didn't have any place *anywhere*. Just seconds ago, Penny had been talking about not having a family. Cole had one, distant as they were, both emotionally and geographically. For a brief, shimmering moment, back with Helen, he'd had another. He'd had siblings, if only in law. Nieces and nephews. But he'd lost them along with everything else.

Watching Penny be accepted back into the fold made something inside him ache.

But this wasn't about him.

The toaster popped, pulling him out of his circling thoughts. He placed a slice on the first two plates, then set another couple of pieces going. He trained his ears toward the other room, waiting for a lull. When it came, schooling his expression, he turned.

"Breakfast is ready, ladies."

Serena smiled her thanks, letting her sister go. "I'll get it."

As she approached, the tender spots on Cole's heart bloomed into bruises. The instant she came within reach, he caught her up with his free arm, tugging her close and breathing in her scent. "You're amazing," he whispered.

She'd been so kind and patient and loving with him. He should've known it came from practice.

With a soft, wet laugh, she shook her head. "Hardly."

"You are. You don't even know." He released her, cupping her face as he did and swiping his thumb at the traces of tears left on her cheeks. "What can I do?"

"You've already done so much..."

He fixed her with a stern look. "I've made breakfast."

"My point exactly. Thank you."

She expected so bloody little from people. If he could, he'd give her the world.

He opened his mouth to tell her just that, but she kissed his knuckles, then ducked under his arm, effectively giving him her back. It left him on the outside all over again. Useless.

Opening the silverware drawer, she grabbed a couple of forks, then pitched her voice higher as she picked up her and Penny's plates. "After this, we're probably going to get cleaned up. If you want to go back to your place to shower or whatever..."

She probably didn't mean it that way, but it felt like a dismissal all the same. "Do you want me to? I'm happy to stay. To help."

"My mom'll be here eventually." She shrugged.

So she *did* want him to go. A part of him itched to protest. It wasn't just the early morning wake-up call that had originally had him on edge, prepared to throw out anyone who meant Serena harm. He couldn't quite put his finger on it, but there was still this feeling of unease that made him hesitant to leave.

But he'd do as she asked.

He wasn't sure who he was comforting as he tugged her in again, fitting his chest in tight against her spine. He pressed a hard, too-intense kiss to her temple, closing his eyes for the span of a breath. "If you need me..."

"I know where you live," she said, all quiet resolve.

She'd asked him once to trust her. Part of that was trusting her to be able to handle this the way she wanted.

So even though it killed him, he let her go.

There wasn't any warning. One second, Serena and Penny were sitting huddled on the couch, distracting themselves with reruns on Netflix, and the next the door crashed open, slamming into the doorstop with a crack. Serena started, jumping to her feet.

Her mother was a fright, hair undone, the buttons on her jacket misaligned. Wild, crazed eyes scanned the apartment, racing back and forth. They skated right past Serena, and Serena's stomach gave a hint of a twist.

It twisted harder when they found what they were looking for. Her mother's gaze homed in on Penny's face, and with scarcely another breath, she was stalking across the room. Her nostrils flared, her pointer finger coming out, jabbing wildly toward the ground, punctuating every word. "Do you have *any* idea what I have been through this month? Do you want to kill your mother? Do you want me in an early grave?"

"Jeez, Mom—"

"Don't you 'jeez' me. What were you thinking scaring us like that?"

Penny crossed her arms over her chest, squirming as she slumped down deeper against the couch. "I didn't mean to."

At least this put them back on familiar ground. Penny's frustration with being *handled*, as she put it, had sometimes led her to acting out. The aftermath had usually ended up like this, with their mother channeling sheer terror into screaming while Penny quietly stewed. Serena watched on, stuck in place the way she always was, all secondhand terror and this wrong, irrational envy.

Penny was *sick*. Mental illness was just as serious as any other kind. Of course she got the lion's share of the attention. Of course their mother had been scared.

And yet, Serena couldn't seem to beat back the tiny curl of wistfulness inside her.

When had her mother ever looked at *her* like that? With that kind of ferocity and desperation to her love?

Letting out a deep breath, their mom crossed the final feet of space to the couch only to drop to her knees. She set her hands on Penny's shoulders, eyes brimming over. "Don't you ever do that to me again, you hear me? My heart can't take it. Not after everything else."

Lip trembling, Penny hugged herself tighter. "I'm sorry, Mom."

"I thought I'd lost you." With that, their mom hauled Penny into her arms. Penny resisted for the barest fraction of a moment before melting into it.

"I'm sorry, I'm so sorry."

Mom just clutched her harder, rocking them back and forth, cheeks wet.

Serena's own eyes stung, vision blurring. The lump in her throat threatened to choke her as she swallowed again and again.

Finally, their mom let Penny go. She clasped her by the shoulders, holding her at arm's length, physically shaking her. "Things get bad again, you call me, okay? You don't disappear and you don't scare your sister. You call *me*."

"I know." Penny curled her arms around herself, like she was trying to make herself smaller. "I thought I could handle it myself, but..."

She trailed off, and the nervy anticipation in Serena's chest made her lungs squeeze tight. Their mother looked set to launch right back into another lecture, and Serena couldn't take it anymore.

"Penny," Serena broke in. "Tell Mom what you told me."

Penny's mouth pinched as she looked to Serena. But she gave a little nod. "I...I want to come home."

And Serena watched it all happen. Their mom froze, everything in her going deathly still except her eyes. Her gaze bounced back and forth between her daughters. "Don't play with your poor mother's heart."

"I'm not," Penny said. "I promise. I already told Serena. I just...I want a new start. I don't want to have to do it alone anymore."

A pale shred of hope fought its way into their mother's eyes. "You mean it."

Penny's voice seemed to catch, so she just nodded, throat bobbing. Weak and small, she managed, "Mom, please. Can I come home?"

"Oh, baby girl." Her mouth cracked. "Of course you can."

They fell into each other's arms again, and Serena's tears spilled over.

They were going to be a family again. It was like this glowing bubble in her chest had formed, and it expanded, growing and growing until it felt like it would burst. Penny had left, and there'd been this hole in all their lives ever since. It was finally going to be filled, and she couldn't be happier.

Yet there was still this twisting feeling in her gut.

She swiped at her eyes. Crap, why had she sent Cole away? She'd thought this would be a family moment, and it was, but she suddenly wanted so badly to be sharing it with him. To have someone to turn to, someone to hold her like her mother and her sister were holding on to each other.

She bit down on the inside of her cheek.

In front of her was everything she'd thought she'd ever wanted in this world.

So why did it feel like it was slipping through her hands?

CHAPTER TWENTY

Don't forget to thank Mr. Cole," Serena said, shuffling Max toward the door.

Hefting his backpack higher on his shoulders, he twisted around to wave back at Cole. "Thank you, Mr. Cole."

"You're very welcome."

Serena glanced over her shoulder at him. He stood in the doorway between the living room and the kitchen, barely leaning on his crutch at all. She gave him an uncertain smile.

It was kind of amazing how fast he was getting better now. He still swore a blue streak at his physical therapy appointments, but he'd been doing all of his exercises, both with her and on his own. The lack of strain—the lack of pain—shone on his face. Who knew? He might not even need the crutch anymore before long.

His brows furrowed, an unspoken question in his eyes, and she worked a little harder at smiling. There was an uneasiness in her chest, but she couldn't quite place it.

Probably just the fact that it was her sister downstairs instead of her mom.

She paused at the door. This was usually where she and Max stopped to do their handshake and get their hug. She hesitated, shifting her weight. This really wasn't necessary, but—

Ugh. Catching Cole's eye again, she gestured down the stairs and ruffled Max's hair. "I'm just going to..."

"I'll be here," Cole said.

Yeah. He would, wouldn't he? The warmth of that reassurance pushed away a little of the disquiet twisting her up inside.

With a grateful nod, she opened the door and shooed Max through it. He hopped his way down the stairs while Serena took them one at a time. At the base of them, she glanced through the window by the door and frowned. Her mom always did a U-turn while she was waiting for Max to come out, but Penny was still idling on the other side of the street. Max opened the door and spilled out onto the sidewalk.

"Look both ways," she called.

"Duh."

Okay, maybe Serena deserved that. Max had been crossing the street on his own for years, and there wasn't even any traffic or anything. That didn't mean she couldn't worry, though.

Penny rolled the window of their mother's car down as Serena approached. "Hey."

"Hey." She ducked down to look through the window at her.

About a week had passed since Penny's dramatic return, and on the whole it had been good. She'd gotten back into therapy with her old practice, and they'd started her on some new medications that sure seemed to be helping. Already, it looked like she'd made up for a solid year's worth of sleep—maybe more. The dark circles under her eyes were all but gone, and there was some color in her cheeks again. It was good to see.

Still. Serena hadn't been expecting her to be on car pool duty yet.

Going for casual and probably missing by a mile, she lifted a brow. "Where's Mom?"

"At work. I had an appointment in the burbs, so she let me have the car for the day. We're picking her up next, right, Max?"

Settling himself in the backseat, Max pulled his seat belt across his chest. "Right."

He didn't seem to see anything amiss with any of this, so Serena wasn't going to, either.

A lump formed in the back of her throat. So many times, she'd wished that Penny would come back, for Max's sake if for no one else's. Still, she hadn't entirely realized how it would feel to see the two of them acting so easy around each other. They'd never tried to keep the kid in the dark about his admittedly unconventional family. His mom had him really young and hadn't been able to give him the life he deserved, so his grandma and his aunt Rena took care of him instead. Penny popped home for the occasional visit, and Max was always happy enough to see her, but he'd never questioned their arrangement or why he was better off with things the way they were.

When Penny had ridden back into their lives, he'd taken that in stride, too, and Serena was so proud of him she could burst.

Smiling more genuinely now, she shifted to the side to peer in at him. "I'll see you tomorrow, okay, buddy?"

"Actually..." Penny waited until Serena darted her gaze back to her. "I was thinking I could pick him up after school tomorrow."

Serena flinched back. "What?"

"I want to spend some more time with him. And besides"—squirming slightly, she pitched her voice lower, as if that would keep Max from listening in—"all this free time. My therapist thinks it'd be good for me to have some more structure. Responsibilities, you know?"

Of course. Serena had just been thinking how great it was that the two of them would get to bond. This was good.

So why did it leave her with this sinking feeling in her gut?

Pushing it aside, she rifled through her mental calendar. Max had practice the day after, so she probably wouldn't see him, unless her mom ran late and asked her to pick him up last minute again.

Except...with Penny at home, their mom really wouldn't need her to do that anymore, would she?

With a strange numbness settling over her, she said, "So Thursday, then."

Penny looked guilty. "Max and I were planning to go shopping Thursday. Did you know he's outgrown all his summer clothes already? Mom had him try a bunch of them on the other night. He's growing like a weed these days." She paused, seeming uncertain. "I mean, you can come along, too, if you want?"

Serena's ears were ringing.

"No." She took a step back from the car. "No, that's okay."

Penny's eyebrows drew together, and she tilted her head to the side. "Are you all right?"

"Yeah. Fine. Just—" Just what? Her whole calendar for the week had cleared itself like magic. She wasn't just fine—she was thrilled.

And at the same time, that little pit of uncertainty was threatening to turn into a yawning chasm.

"Just...I talked this through with Mom, and I've got all this free time right now. It's making me a little...restless." Beneath the steering wheel, her knee bounced up and down. Being at loose ends had never been a good thing for Penny. Serena knew that. "You do so much for him, but Mom told me how busy you are. And I know you're seeing that hot British guy with"—she gestured toward her chest—"the tattoos and all." An uncertain, hopeful smile ghosted her face. "I thought I could take some of the load."

Suddenly off balance, Serena blinked.

Yeah, she did have a lot going on right now. Her schedule had been packed before Cole had come into her life, and everything was so new with him. She wanted to spend every waking moment with him.

But not at Max's expense. Her time with her nephew was the last thing in the world she would have wanted to give up.

Only...*her* time was just one part of the equation. Between baseball and his social life and the growing mound of homework his teachers had started assigning, Max's schedule was pretty packed, too. Penny deserved a place in it. She came back here with the intent of a fresh start, of being part of their family again.

She was his *mother*. Of course Max should be spending time with her.

Serena just hadn't expected it to hurt so much to be pushed aside.

Swallowing against the tightness in her throat, she waved it all off. "It's fine." She scrambled. "I guess I'll see you for Sunday dinner, then."

"Yeah. Absolutely." Penny grinned, maybe the first real honest-to-goodness *grin* Serena'd seen on her in years.

Serena let out a wavering breath. "Okay. Have a good night, then. Bye, Max."

"Bye!" Max said distractedly, his tablet already in his hands.

She wanted to scold him. He made himself queasy if he played too much in the car, but it was a short ride. Penny could handle it.

She took another step back from the car, only to be honked at. She scurried out of the way, over to her side of the street, to let a truck go by. Rolling up her window, Penny gave her one last little wave.

By the time Serena realized she hadn't gotten her handshake or her hug, they were gone.

The door slammed just a tad too hard.

Cole glanced away from his mobile. He'd settled himself on Serena's couch while she'd been downstairs seeing Max off, his bad leg resting on the ottoman. Maybe if he made himself comfortable enough, she wouldn't feel like she had to invent some sort of excuse to kick him out.

Not that she'd done that very often. But there'd been something distant to her just of late. She was all wrapped up in her sister's recovery, of course, but frustration still gnawed at him. She was probably trying not to burden him with her problems, but it felt an awful lot like she was keeping him out of her life instead.

She didn't say anything. Didn't so much as step away from the doorway. He glanced at her again, only to find her eyes unfocused, her face pale.

Setting his phone aside, he sat up straighter. "Are you all right?"

She blinked, gaze sweeping the room like she'd forgotten he was there. "Yeah. Fine."

Her tone was distracted, though, and he half expected her to deflect, to start talking about dinner or any of the hundred things she probably had to do tonight, when all he wanted was to hold her. Miracle of miracles, she blew out a breath instead, deflating before his eyes. Without another word, she trudged across the room to throw herself down on the couch beside him.

Well. He could certainly work with that. Leaning back into the sofa, he draped his arm across her shoulders, pulling her in, and she went, resting her head against his chest. He twisted his neck to press a kiss to the part in her hair.

"Did Max get off all right?"

"Yeah. It was actually...it was Penny who picked him up."

"Oh." That didn't sound too terribly strange.

"She's really stepping up."

"That's...good?" He couldn't tell.

"It's great."

He held her tighter, waiting for more. When it didn't seem to be on offer, he rubbed at her arm. "Then why do you sound like she killed your dog?"

"Don't have a dog."

Obviously.

Before he could make another dry remark, she shrugged, slumping farther with the force of her exhalation. "She said she's going to pick Max up the next few days after school."

"Okay..."

"So." Her voice stuttered. "So they don't need *me* to."

Oh.

A low red haze filled his vision, but he pushed it down. Didn't they know?

Loosening his grip, he shifted in his seat, turning them until he could look her in the eye. "You know she can never replace you, right?"

Because that was the issue, he was sure. Serena's kindness had its own sort of rhythm to it. He'd never seen her so upset as she had been when the twits at Upton had told her not to come by anymore. When they told her she couldn't help.

She *needed* to help. With her family and with him, it was the common thread. When someone told her that she couldn't...

It left her like this, limp and listless and sad in a way he didn't know if he could fix.

"It's funny," she said, looking down, "ever since she left, after Max was born, it's the thing I always worried about, you know? That I would never be able to replace *her*. A kid needs his mom, and I was just..."

She trailed off, but he wasn't having that.

He gave her shoulder a little shake. "Just his aunt who's been there for him every second of every day while his mother was off God even knows where."

Serena went defensive immediately. "She had her reasons." But her voice was tinged with doubt.

"I'm sure she did. But she still wasn't here. *You* were. He adores you, Serena. You have to know that."

"Sure." She shook her head. "But that doesn't change the fact that she's here now." Taking a deep breath, she grasped his hand in hers. "It's okay. I'm glad they're going to get to know each other. I know she's just trying to help. Only...I just wish..."

He bit his own tongue, forcing himself to give her the space to finish her thought.

Her gaze darted up to meet his. "I wish she would have *asked* me. Before she and my mom decided to rearrange my schedule for me."

He squeezed her palm too tightly. "They don't deserve you, love."

Did anyone? *Could* anyone?

Laughing it off, she brought his hand to her mouth. "I don't know about that." Kissing his knuckles, she sighed. Then, tone lightening, she said, "Oh well. Look at the bright side."

"And what's that?"

She raised a brow, all casual flirtation. Letting go of his hand, she draped her arms over his shoulders, easing herself closer to put them nose to nose. "I'll have a little bit more free time this week."

It didn't take much for him to catch up with her. "Oh? And whatever will we do with that time?"

"Whatever we want to."

With that, she leaned in. He met her in the middle, covering her mouth with his own. The kiss was as sweet as ever; he didn't think her touch would ever stop being a revelation.

But there was that same distance to it, too. That distraction.

He brushed it off the best he could. But for all she said she'd do whatever she wanted to, he couldn't quite forget that there was someplace else she'd rather be.

CHAPTER TWENTY-ONE

So, just you today, huh?" Cole's physical therapist, Mike, scanned the waiting room.

Scowling, Cole gripped the handles of the infernal warm-up bike and gritted his teeth. One more minute of the ten Mike had programmed in. He nodded. "Just me."

Serena had been disappointed about her sister eating into her time with Max last week, but it had turned out to be bloody convenient. Parent-teacher conference season had come upon her out of nowhere, and both today and tomorrow, she had meetings scheduled well into the evening. Penny had basically *had* to look after Max.

And Cole had had to take a cab.

He rolled his eyes at himself as he pedaled out the last few seconds. It hadn't been that difficult. He probably should've done it weeks ago, only Serena had kept insisting, and he'd given up on trying to resist her. When she offered him something he wanted these days, he took it with both hands and held on.

The final second ticked over, and Cole slumped back against the seat.

Mike slapped his shoulder. He scarcely recoiled at all.

"See, that wasn't that bad."

"No." It was never *that bad*, but he hated it all the same. Before the injury, he'd been one of the masochists who ran outdoors even in the winter. He wanted to go places; he had no need for standing still.

"All right. Well, let's see if we can't make that girlfriend of yours proud today."

Cole leveled him with a look, swinging his leg over the seat of the bike to dismount and reaching for his crutch.

Except Mike grabbed it first and held it out of reach.

"Excuse me," Cole said.

Mike gave him a smirking grin. "Let's see how you do without it, yeah?"

Cole leaned back like he'd been burned.

Oblivious, Mike soldiered on. "You've been depending on it for too long. Go on. Take a couple of steps."

It was the most innocent of invitations, and it felt like a slap to the face. He hadn't been *depending* on it. He'd needed the bloody thing. Even switching down to just the one a couple of weeks ago had left him sore and exhausted. To go without any kind of support now—he felt naked. Like he could totter off into a free fall at any moment, alone, unmoored.

He shook his head. "I don't think—"

"Come on. At least give it a try. I'm right here." When Cole hesitated, Mike heaved a sigh. "Seriously, I can't believe you haven't given them up already. The first time you came in here, you were champing at the bit to get done with them as fast as you could. Now suddenly you're dragging your heels?"

And he had, hadn't he? He practically begged the orthopedic doctor for exercises, he'd been so eager to get better on his own. The crutches had been shackles, and they'd tied him to his apartment. He hadn't been able to do anything or go anywhere, hadn't been able to run or lift; he'd been stuck in his own damn head and those four square walls. He hadn't been able to *breathe*.

Until Serena.

His heart stuttered hard inside his chest. Was that the answer, then? Was that the reason why he'd stopped pushing himself?

He'd lost his independence that day on the train. He'd bent his will to getting it back, right up until the moment it had become a reason for Serena to take care of him.

The back of his throat tore open.

She needed so desperately for people to need her. The worst thing in the world to happen to her in all the time he'd known her had been being told she *wasn't* needed or that she couldn't help.

What would happen when he didn't need her help? He was still an emotional cripple—and he'd use all the ableist language he wanted to, thank you very much. But when he got his body back under control, when he could manage on his own...

What on earth would she do with him then?

"Cole? Hey. Buddy. It's okay, if you're really not ready. We can wait—it's cool."

Cole's gaze refocused. He found himself still sitting on the edge of the seat of the bike, the leather giving beneath the clench of his fist. A couple of feet in front of him, Mike stared at him with concern in his eyes, holding out his crutch.

Cole shook his head. He waited until Mike backed off. And then, with his jaw clenched, leaning hard into the seat, he pushed himself to standing.

Nothing happened. No fanfare and no cannons. He stood of his own power for the first time in months.

"You're doing great, man." The voice came from terribly far away.

Bracing himself, he took a step. His knee twinged, but it was a bare flicker. Nothing he couldn't ignore—nothing he couldn't have been ignoring for days or maybe weeks. The second step was just as easy, and his head spun, his ears rung.

He could make it on his own, much the same as he had been for years and years.

He didn't want to. But he could.

"Remember that you can check his assignments online anytime. I'll let you know if he starts getting behind, but it's up to him to stay on top of things."

"Thank you so much, Ms. Hartmann."

Serena held out her hand to shake. "Don't you worry. We'll get him through."

After a couple more pleasantries, she got yet another concerned parent out the door. She glanced at the clock, then let her shoulders slump. Parent-teacher conference season was great for a whole host of reasons, but it left her wiped, and she still had a few hours left to go.

Well, at least that last meeting had been an easy one. With a solid ten minutes until her next appointment, she headed back to her desk and collapsed into her chair. She twirled back and forth in it a handful of times, then dug into her pocket for her phone. Jeez, when was the last time she'd had a chance to check it?

The whole screen was blinking with alerts. Her pulse immediately ratcheted up a notch, only kicking higher when she saw she'd missed a call from Penny about an hour ago. There was a text from her, too, but all it said was to call her back. Her stomach did a somersault as she hit the button to dial.

Penny answered the instant it started to ring, her voice filled with relief. "Oh, thank God."

"What?" Serena's heart beat straight through its cage. "What's going on? Penny, are you okay—"

If she wasn't, what was Serena going to do? She was stuck here all afternoon. Maybe they could call their mother, or if she really had to she might be able to reschedule—

"Serena. Rena! I'm fine. I swear. Calm down."

A few of Cole's more colorful phrases came to mind, but she bit them back as she slumped in her chair. "Don't scare me like that."

Penny sighed, and Serena immediately felt guilty. She and her mother had both been using that phrase a lot of late. If they didn't want to chase Penny away again, they could probably stand to lay it on a little less thick.

"Sorry," Penny said, "but listen. I need a favor."

"Anything."

"Can you please, please, please watch Max today after all?"

Serena groaned. Crap. Anything but that. "You know I would." She'd always take Max if she could. "But I can't today. I told you, I have conferences."

"Shit." There was the vague sound of impact like her sister

hitting something. "Fuck. I forgot." She drew in a deep breath. "Okay."

"Why? What's going on?"

"I just ran into Becca. You remember Becca?"

"Vaguely." One of Penny's friends from back in high school maybe? Serena scrunched her face up.

"Whatever, it doesn't matter. Just, she works at this place downtown, and they're hiring a new admin, and it might be an in for me, but they have to make their decision by tomorrow. She said she can sneak me in between a couple of other interviews, but it has to be today—"

"Okay, okay, slow down." Serena almost didn't want to slow her down at all. This was the most animated she'd heard her sister in years.

Penny sucked in a long, deep breath. "I just...I think it could be really good."

The problem was, Serena did, too. Penny needed things to keep her occupied, and apparently losing her last job in New York had been a big factor in things spiraling even further out of her control. Getting back to work again would probably make her feel a lot better about herself.

A tiny niggle of doubt hummed at the back of her mind. If she could *keep* the job, it would make her feel a lot better about herself. Her illness was unpredictable, and while she was doing so much better than she had been a couple of weeks ago, she was still fragile.

And if Serena brought that up to her now, it really, really wasn't going to help.

"Okay," she scrambled. She really couldn't sneak out of these conferences for anything less than an absolute emergency, but there had to be something she could do. Someone she could turn to...

It came to her in a flash.

She had someone in her corner. Someone who'd been trying over and over to prove that he was here for her for anything. This was asking a lot, but...

She combed a hand through her hair and tugged. "I may have an idea. Give me three minutes."

The hope in Penny's voice echoed out across the line. "Okay. *Thank* you."

Hanging up, Serena clasped her phone against her chest, squeezing her eyes shut tight. This was probably a terrible idea, but for Penny she'd try anything.

Cole picked up on the second ring. "Serena?"

"I have a huge favor to ask."

"Okaaay...?"

There was something off about his voice. It made her pause for half a second, but she shrugged it off, rising and starting to pace. "Penny's got a job interview, and I'm still stuck in conferences for another couple of hours. You know I wouldn't ask if it wasn't important, but..."

She trailed off, because it was obvious what she needed, right?

Dead silence rang across the line. A pit of dread opened up in her gut, and she gripped her phone so hard she feared she'd crack the screen.

Crap. This really had been a terrible idea. From day one, when she'd basically conned him into offering to tutor Max, he'd been hesitant. He might have warmed to the kid in the time since, but he'd never lost that deer-in-headlights look around him.

And why would he? The man blamed himself and his unreadiness for children for his wife going off the road that night. The pain in his voice came back to her, a shallow knife slicing cleanly across her ribs.

Still, she had to ask. "Please. I know it's a lot, but I don't know who else to call."

"I don't...Serena..." Desperation leaked into his voice.

"Just pretend I'm there. Take him to my apartment and get set up at the table the same way you always do. There are cookies and milk in the fridge. Just...do some math stuff with him. The same as always."

"And after?"

Right. He'd never spent more than an hour or so working through problems with Max. Serena stabbed out wildly. "It doesn't matter. Let him play video games if you want, or turn on some cartoons." Max never got screen time until he was done with his homework, but she wasn't going to bring that up—not when Cole was doing her a favor. When he was stepping about a million miles outside his comfort zone for her. "Please."

She held her breath.

But then, finally, he sighed. "Bloody hell. Fine."

All the air rushed out of her lungs in a whoosh. "Thank you, thank you. I swear I will make this up to you."

She'd make him a whole set of china, or take him out to dinner, or—well, she had a variety of ways of showing her appreciation these days, didn't she? He seemed unreasonably fond of her mouth in particular...

Before she could go on about all her plans for paying him back, a knock sounded on her door. She jerked her head up, stilling her pacing. Oh man, she hated when parents were early. Tilting the phone away from her mouth, she smiled at them, welcoming them in. "I'll be with you in just one second." Returning to Cole, she said, "Sorry, I need to go. You've got this, though, right?"

"Have them ring me when they're here." It came out strangled, and her heart panged.

Fervently, she said, "Thank you."

Without another word, he ended the call. Something was still off there, but he was doing this for her. It was all she could ask.

Hoping for the best, she fired off a quick text to Penny to let her know what was going on. Then she pocketed her phone and put on her best, most reassuring smile as she moved to shake her next set of parents' hands.

She had a job to do, and she would focus on that as opposed to the drama that might be playing out at her apartment any minute now.

Besides, who knew? This could be good for everyone. Penny might get the job, and Cole might see that hanging out with a kid alone wasn't really that bad. He'd see she trusted him.

What was the worst that could happen?

CHAPTER TWENTY-TWO

Come on up." Cole's voice came out raspy and raw, and a cold shudder of anxiety made its way up his spine. Releasing the button for the intercom, he shifted to press the one beside it. He waited until he heard the door downstairs swing open before letting go.

He stood there for at least another thirty seconds, eyes closed and hands numb. When he lifted his head, his vision spun.

He sucked in an aching breath.

He could do this. He *had* to. He'd promised Serena, and Max was charging up the stairs to her apartment right now and would beat Cole even if he left his own apartment this very instant. He had to go. Now.

Mechanically, he forced his legs to move.

At the threshold to his apartment, he leaned down to grab his bag, fingers death-grip tight around the strap, and with the other, he reached instinctively for his crutch.

Except—

Except he didn't need that anymore, did he? His therapist had told him he'd let himself be dependent on it for too long. Relying on it had held him back, and so what if his knee was killing him? Twenty-four hours without the thing, and it had felt like a week, every step more labored than the last. Now he was supposed to make it down the stairs, even though those last few dozen steps had nearly pushed him over the edge after his appointment the day before.

His free hand twitched again. His crutch was *right there.* Would it be admitting defeat so much to lean on it for just one more trip?

He curled his fingers into a fist. Yes. It would. He wasn't going backward anymore; he wasn't standing still.

He was going down to Serena's flat, and he was letting Max in, and they were going to study math. It would all be normal. The boy was nearly a teenager already—even Cole couldn't cock this up too badly.

Pulse pounding, he let his hand uncurl. He opened the ruddy door.

Jesus. Each step he took down the stairs sent sharp jolts of pain shooting through his leg. It'd been achy enough before, but there was a low fire building now. He very nearly turned around. But clenching his jaw, he soldiered on.

By the time he made it to the final flight, it felt like bone grinding on bone. He turned the corner to find not only Max standing beside Serena's door but Penny as well, looking a damn sight better than she had the last time he'd seen her. Drawing himself to his full height, he fought to keep the pain from showing on his face, but at least a fraction of it must have bled through.

She stepped forward, the little lines between her brows so much like her sister's. "Are you all right?"

"Spiffing."

She didn't give him bloody space enough to breathe as he crossed the landing toward the door. Apparently that was a thing with this family. Hovering, she babbled, "Thank you so much for doing this. I can't tell you how much it means to me..."

His own irritation with himself grew and grew. He'd been short with Serena on the phone already. All this time he'd been telling her to lean on him, and this one time she did, he'd been an arse about it. But everything hurt. He'd scarcely slept and he wanted to punch his physical therapist in the throat. He was tired and aching, and she knew. Serena knew.

She knew how terrifying this was for him.

And yet she asked it of him anyway. She was inviting disaster and there wasn't a thing he could do.

Penny came a little bit too close to him, and that warning haze of crimson crowded his vision. He fumbled with his keys, dropping the whole lot of them, and he swore out loud.

Max whistled. "Does Aunt Rena make you put dollars in the swear jar, too?"

"I'd like to see her try," he muttered.

Fucking hell, it was murder crouching down. Penny bent forward at the same time, and their heads crashed together. A shock of pain spread through his skull. He shot up, biting off a whole string of curses that would've put the last one to shame, and his knee screamed.

"Sorry, sorry." Penny's hands fluttered, and she was in his

space; he couldn't breathe. He wanted to shove her away, wanted her to go.

"Don't you have somewhere to be?" he snapped.

She blinked, expression dumb. "Yes, but..." She gestured inarticulately at Max.

"I've got him."

Her brow crinkled. "Are you sure you do?"

He wanted to throw his hands up in the air. No. Of course he wasn't bloody sure. He'd tried to tell everyone he wasn't sure. But Serena had asked him to do this for her and so he would, goddammit all. "I've got it," he said, too short.

Ducking between them, Max retrieved the fallen keys and held them out for Cole to take. He plucked the little green one with the daisies that Serena had given him from the ring and finally got the bloody door unlocked.

"See?" he said, pushing it open and gesturing inside. "All sorted."

She hesitated, teeth digging into her lip. "Okay. If you need me to come back, though..."

His heart spasmed with her echo of doubt. Serena was blinded, but apparently her sister saw him for what he was. Apparently, she knew the score.

He made a choked, wet sound in the back of his throat and waved her away. Casting backward glances at him, mumbling yet more thanks, she took off, leaving Cole and Max alone.

He wasn't sure if that made him relax or if it set him even more on edge.

They went inside, and Max took off his jacket. Expression curious, he looked Cole up and down. "What happened to your crutches?"

"Don't need them anymore." Ha.

"Cool."

Cole wanted nothing more than to collapse into one of Serena's comfortable chairs, but she'd given him a job to do. Once Max had hung up his things, Cole gestured toward the kitchen table. Max groaned but went where Cole told him to.

Cole set down his messenger bag and his mobile, then got busy doing everything else Serena had told him to. A package of mediocre biscuits in the cabinet and a glass of milk for the kid. He started tea for himself, then sat down with a groan. There wasn't a decent place to rest his knee here. Perhaps they could do this somewhere else, except Max wasn't supposed to be eating anywhere but at the table.

Max gazed at him over his glass of milk. "Are you sure you're okay?"

"I'm *fine*." And it came out too sharp. He took a deep breath. "Just...I'm not feeling well."

"Is that why you're making tea?" He was spitting milk and biscuit crumbs everywhere, and the spring inside Cole's chest wound tighter. "Aunt Rena always tries to make me tea when I'm sick, and it's gross, but—" He kept babbling until Cole cut him off.

"I'm making tea because I'm *British*." What was wrong with children in this country? "And it's not *gross*."

"Yeah, it is."

"No, it's bloody well *not*." God, he was trying to argue with a ten-year-old. Was he mad? He reached into his bag for something to do, pulling out the problem sets he and Max had been going through, as well as the notebook with his own work. Later, when

Max was entertaining himself, he might be able to make some
progress there, God willing. "Come along. What did we leave off
with last time? Geometry?"

"Uuuuuugh," Max groaned theatrically, and Cole gained a
whole new appreciation for what Serena put up with every day at
her job. "I hate geometry."

"You've barely met geometry."

Things just devolved from there. Every problem elicited another round of whining until Cole was at his wit's end.

"You're not usually such a brat when your aunt's around," he
muttered.

"I'm not a *brat*."

No, not usually he wasn't, but today...

Cole's knee screamed at him as he pushed his chair out. The
kettle wasn't quite to a rolling boil yet, but it was close enough.
He got out one of Serena's mugs and the proper tea he'd smuggled
into her stash. He poured the water and turned back around toward the table.

"I need to go to the bathroom." Max set his glass down with a
clunk, shoving back from the table—straight into Cole's leg, and
Cole buckled.

His whole world went white with pain. Fuck, Jesus fuck, it was
like the day on the train all over again, like that arsehole standing
over him and slamming a foot down into Cole's knee.

The mug flew out of his hand, hot water everywhere, a scalding
splash spattering Cole's chest and his arm, more flying forward
across the floor. The ceramic hit the tile with a crash.

"Fuck, fucking fuck fuck buggering *fuck*." Cole caught himself
against the edge of the table, and there were shards of pottery

crackling underfoot, his knee was a throbbing mass, his shirt clinging to him and boiling him alive.

For a shivering, impossible second, everything was silent but for the pounding of his pulse inside his skin, the rush of a breath and another.

A tiny voice came out from beneath him. "I am *so* sorry..."

And he felt the crack. Red filled his vision.

"What the *fuck* were you thinking?" His ribs heaved, his brain spinning, and he slammed his palm against the table. Raised the other hand as if to...to...

Oh *God*.

The broken part of his mind snapped back into place, and the force of it drove the breath from his lungs. He honestly could have...He'd nearly...

He dropped his arm. His eyes leapt into focus, and oh hell. He was standing over Max, looming even with all his height and all his bulk. Bright green eyes stared back at him, wide from behind Coke-bottle lenses, and it wasn't glass underneath his feet. He wasn't stepping on a little boy's spectacles, but he could have been. In another instant he could have become those boys, the ones who had stood over him and taunted him and *hurt* him.

And how close had he been?

He curled his fingers into his palm. Max flinched, and Cole's veins turned to ice.

Christ. No. *No.*

He backed away so fast his feet slipped. His hip hit the counter behind him, and his knee was only barely holding up his weight, and he'd nearly hit a child. Not just any child, either, but this one, who had been through the same things he had—who had suffered enough. He'd raised his voice and raised his fist.

He was going to be sick.

Squeezing his eyes shut, he felt the room spin around him. He clenched his jaw shut tight around the bile at the back of his throat.

"I...I didn't mean to—" Max started.

Cole shook his head and held out a hand. "It wasn't your fault."

"I didn't know you were behind me, and—"

"It. Was. Not. Your. Fault."

It was Cole's fault. Only Cole's.

He'd known he couldn't do this. *Everyone* should have known. "But—"

Cole gritted his teeth. "Go to the living room, please." He forced his eyes open. One small mercy—at least the boy was wearing shoes. "Carefully."

"Ooookay." There wasn't any argument or hesitation. Only fear, and Cole hadn't hated himself this badly in so long.

Numbly, he fetched the broom from the pantry. It was a sodden mess of shards and water that he piled in a corner of the room. When he tried to reach down with the dustpan, his knee shot off another burst of protest, and he stopped, panting, brow pressed against the smooth coolness of the wall.

"Mr. Cole?" Max's voice was still small as he called from the other room.

Standing straight, Cole leaned the broom against the counter beside the mess. "Don't touch any of that."

"Okay." He hesitated. "Can I play with my tablet?"

Serena had told Cole to tutor him on math, but that was a dream. He couldn't. He *wouldn't*.

He'd been such a fool.

Nodding, he took one limping step toward the door. "I need to get something from my apartment. I want you to lock up after me, all right?"

"Why?"

"Just..." He took a deep breath. "Please."

Max frowned. "Okay."

It was the coward's way out, and it was the safest thing for any of them.

How many times had he tried to warn Serena? There was something inside him that should never be trusted, something angry and wrong, and she'd let him in despite his protests. She'd entrusted him with things she never should have.

He ruined everything he touched.

And he should have known better than to have ever touched her life at all.

Of course the worst parent conference of the day had had to be the last one. Serena heaved a sigh as she stepped out of her car, shaking her irritation off the best she could. Teaching was her calling in life, and she didn't shy away from taking her work home with her. But all the stresses? The bad moods brought on by difficult children and entitled, oblivious parents? They didn't get to screw with her home life. Max deserved better. Her mom. Penny. Cole. They didn't just get the dregs she had left after giving everything to other people.

She took a deep breath, closing her eyes for a moment and visualizing her grumpiness floating off like a balloon into the clear Midwestern sky. Weirdly enough, it wasn't even all that hard to do. She hadn't heard a thing from either Penny or Cole, but no news was typically good news, and a flare of optimism was a glowing ember in her chest. Penny was getting better, and she was taking steps to move on with her life, and Cole...

Cole had stepped up. He'd pushed past his fear and he'd agreed to help her out. Having someone she could lean on, someone she could depend on when she needed help...it meant the world to her.

And she was going to show him precisely how much she appreciated him tonight.

A flicker of a smile played at her lips as she climbed the stairs to her apartment. She let herself in, calling out, "Hello?"

"Hey."

She nearly would've missed Max, curled up on the couch the way he was. Setting down her bag, she said, "Hey, kiddo." She peered around the corner into the kitchen. "Cole?"

"He left."

"Huh?"

"He left. Like, right after we got here."

The hairs on the back of her neck stood up on end. "Excuse me?"

She took a few steps farther into the living room, and she'd been wrong. Max wasn't just curled up on the couch—he was curled up into himself, knees hugged tightly to his chest. His tablet game lay discarded beside him, and a hundred alarms went off in her mind.

"What happened?"

And it was like Max broke. He turned wide, glassy eyes on her, his whole face twisted. "I didn't mean to. It was an accident, I swear."

She was there beside him in an instant. He went into her arms without hesitation, and he was shaking, and something inside her trembled, too.

The story poured out of him then. How he'd been a brat and he'd made Mr. Cole mad, and he'd hit him with his chair by mistake; it had all been a mistake. She held him tighter as he pointed to the shattered pieces of the mug she'd made with her own two hands. Max's and Cole's papers were still strewn out across the table, soaked through.

"And he got really quiet, and he told me it wasn't my fault, but then he left. I thought he'd come back, but he didn't, and I locked the door the way he told me to, but..."

"But you've been alone." Serena's voice came out quiet and strained and foreign to her own ears. "For hours."

"I didn't know what to do."

How would he have? He was a big kid now, and it wasn't like they never left him by himself, but never for this long. *Never* without knowing when someone would be back. He hadn't even had a phone; he couldn't have called her or her mom or anyone. If there'd been an emergency...Her throat locked up with the mindless terror of it.

What had Cole been thinking?

More than once, Cole had tried to explain the anger that took him over sometimes, yet she'd never truly understood it until now. She'd been so preoccupied with her concern for her sister. She'd known she was pushing, but...

But she'd asked Cole to do *one* thing for her—just one thing, one afternoon, even with the promise of making it up to him later, and he'd let her down.

She swallowed around a heat that was brighter than anger and more encompassing than fear.

Max lifted his head from her shoulder. "Do you think he's okay?"

Her heart stuttered in her chest.

Oh God. She replayed the whole story Max had just told her, and it had started with Max bumping Cole, with shoving his chair into his leg. If it had been his bad leg...

That proud, stubborn man. It would have been just like him to keep a brave face and retreat to lick his wounds in private.

She had to go check on him.

She wavered, though. She couldn't leave Max alone after all of that. Torn, she rocked him back and forth.

"I'm sure he's fine." She had to believe that. Penny would come to get Max soon enough, and the second she did, Serena would go upstairs and find out what the hell was going on. "When are you getting picked up?"

"Penny said you're supposed to drop me off."

Of course. Crap. She'd said in her text that she wasn't sure how long she'd be stuck downtown. Serena would run him home right now, except her mom wasn't supposed to get off work until late, either. The idea of letting Cole stay there, stewing and alone for hours, left her cold.

Max pulled away, and Serena let him go. He looked better now, less shaken. She remembered what that felt like, too—how everything was easier when there was a grown-up around to lean on.

"Can we go see if he's okay?" he asked.

A whole different set of big, red alarm bells went off in her mind. Whatever state Cole was in, the last thing on earth she should be doing was letting Max go with her. At best he was in pain and at worst he'd turned his back on the kid, and there was no way in hell she was subjecting Max to any more of this.

She searched Max's eyes for a long second. He was a good, brave little guy, and if he was more concerned about Cole than he was about himself, then he was clearly okay.

Even though she felt about as strong as a wet noodle, she took a deep breath and put on her no-nonsense voice. "You are going to stay right where you are." She narrowed her eyes. "Have you even looked at your homework yet?"

The guilty way he dropped his gaze was answer enough.

"I didn't think so." She wasn't mad about that, but it was something to focus on for now. "Get your butt back over to that table and get to work." She grabbed her phone from her pocket and pressed it into Max's hands. "Remember: if you play Candy Crush on this, I'll know."

"Aunt Rena," he whined.

"Emergencies only," she reminded him. She tugged him close to press a firm kiss to his brow. "I'll be right back."

"Okay."

Decision made, she had to keep herself from sprinting to the door.

She climbed the stairs with her heart in her throat. Worry

and anger twisted together into a single knot of dread, drawing tighter with every step.

Finally, she stood outside Cole's door. Fighting for calm, she took a deep, fortifying breath, but it didn't help.

There was nothing else to do. Ribs squeezing in, chest aching, she curled her hand into a fist and knocked.

CHAPTER TWENTY-THREE

Cole couldn't *do* this.

A second knock sounded against his door, and he buried his head in his hands, raking his fingers through his hair and yanking until it hurt. It wasn't as if there was any doubt about who it was. He only had one person in his life, and he'd failed her. He failed everyone—whenever someone depended on him, he cocked it up. All this time he'd been pretending with this woman, playing house and making as if he were normal. The bottom had been bound to fall out eventually.

And eventually was now.

The third time she knocked, she called his name, voice high. Worried or maybe angry or maybe both, and that was the thing that finally launched him to his feet. The idea that she could be concerned about *him*...

His knee gave a cracking sort of protest, and he bit down on a curse. A restlessness crawled beneath his skin. All afternoon long he'd wanted to pace or run or just *hit* something, but he'd been tethered to his sofa, icing his knee and summoning that ice into his heart.

But as he made his way to the door, it was fire that burned inside. The hot, dense ache of his knee and the molten misery in his chest, and low, deep beneath it, that smoldering, simmering rage. It wasn't about the bullies that had tormented him. It wasn't about what he'd lost.

It was about who he was. Still.

And what he was about to do.

He threw the door open before he could talk himself out of it. Serena stood there, hand still raised, and God. She was the most beautiful thing he'd ever seen.

She only became more so as she jerked her head up. Her gaze traveled the length of his body, and when she hit his leg, took in his lack of crutches, the softness to her mouth evaporated, her jaw squaring and her shoulders rising toward her ears. The heat in her eyes set the kindling of his ruined life to ignite. She was ready for a fight. Good. He'd been itching for a fight for *years*.

"Cole."

"Serena." He didn't so much as flinch. Didn't move aside to let her in. He stood there in that doorway, looming with all his height and with all the bitterness in his heart. He blocked her way exactly how he should have since the start.

It threw her off balance, and he wanted to laugh. What had she been expecting? A warm welcome? For him to have actually turned out to be the prince she probably imagined she'd created with her kiss?

She looked him up and down again. "What the hell is going on?"

"I don't know what you mean." Of course he did.

"I mean." Her voice rose higher, until she seemed to catch herself, to remember all the prying ears in the apartments around them. She glanced meaningfully toward the empty hallway behind her before turning her pointed gaze at him. When she spoke again, it was in clipped, low tones. "I mean, what are you doing here? You said you would look after Max."

"He can look after himself."

Her jaw dropped. "That's not your decision to make."

"And yet I made it." He hadn't even stopped to think about it. The choice had been so clear. "I decided—" His throat burned. "He was better off with no one than he was with me."

Everyone was. Helen, Max, Serena. If he'd never taken her up on her offer, if he hadn't allowed either of them to get involved, they wouldn't have to be going through this heartache now.

"That's not true."

But it was. "I snapped at him, Serena. He made one little mistake, and I *lost* it. I swore at him." He could scarcely breathe against the memory of standing over him, finding his own hand raised and his mind a blur. "I was about to—"

He couldn't say it. She couldn't ask him to.

"I'm sure it wasn't that bad."

"It was worse." He'd been so close. "I told you. I can't be trusted. There's this part of me..."

One that would never be soothed. If Helen hadn't managed it, and if Serena hadn't...Two women he'd cared for, two women he'd—

God. Fuck. Two women he loved.

He loved Serena. This beautiful, kind, generous slip of a girl who'd given him more chances than he could ever hope to deserve.

He'd promised her he'd never hurt her. And yet again, he'd lied.

Choking on the ghost of a sob he'd been holding in for years, he tasted blood at the back of his throat.

And yet she was still here. She reached out, slamming a hand into the door he'd not let go of, trying to force it wider, and wasn't that just her all over? She lifted her other hand, moving to put her palm to his face, and he couldn't bear it. If she touched him, he'd go to pieces. He'd never be able to give this up.

It all fell down on him with a crushing weight. He'd already touched her for the last time. She'd brought his hands and his heart and his flesh back to life; she'd given him things he'd never thought he'd have again like love and sex and the warmth of gentle lips against his skin.

He was never going to feel that again. This had been his only chance, and it was over.

"Cole." His name tore past her throat, jagged and raw. "I told you. I trust you."

"And I'm telling you. *Don't.*"

Helen had trusted him, and he had killed her. He'd tried and tried and tried, just like he'd been trying with Serena, hoping against hope that he could be what they needed him to be. But deep down inside, he'd been the same man.

The same boy, scared and alone and lashing out, unable to tell friend from foe anymore.

"Cole..."

She reached for him again. He couldn't cede an inch of

ground, didn't dare to give her even that much of an opening. Desperate, he grasped her wrist to hold her off, to push her away, but even that amount of contact threatened to bring him to his knees. Her skin was so soft, her bones so delicate within his grip.

He let her go as if he'd been burned. He had no defense against her, no way to shut her down except with words.

It was simple in the end. He'd been living with this angry thing inside his chest for so long, ignoring it and hating it—hating himself when it got the best of him. He'd only given himself over to it willingly this spare handful of times.

He tapped into it now, and into a pit of self-loathing so deep he might never get out.

Fire rushed through his veins. He curled his hands into fists and made his voice rough and hard.

"Don't you get it? I can't be who you want me to be. I can't give you what you want."

He'd never been able to. Hadn't she told him? She wanted a family and a life, and none of it was anything she could ever find with him.

She shook her head, eyes glassy. "Cole, please. Can't we talk? It was just one afternoon. One little slip, and you didn't hurt him."

But he would.

His heart cracked open. "My wife died because she thought the best of me."

She threw her arms up in the air. "She died because it was snowing."

"I drove her out into it. My temper. Me."

"She made a choice. To walk away while you were being irrational, yes. She made the choice to love you."

"And I let her. I knew it would end in misery, but I was so bloody selfish, I let her anyway."

He'd let her love him, and he'd loved her so damn much in return.

He'd let Serena love him. It was a mistake he never should have allowed himself to make again.

"I can't do this," he said. Even the fire in his blood wasn't enough to keep him standing anymore. He leaned against the door frame like it was the only thing keeping him up, and maybe it was. His chest, his knee, his everything—it all *hurt*.

But not as much as it was going to.

Serena's face fell. "So, what, is that it? You're so much of a coward that you have one bad day and you're done?"

The whole world went sideways on him. That was what Helen had said when he'd told her he couldn't—he wouldn't—let a child be born from his defective genes. Into his house with his rage, into the world that had turned him into this.

The truth of it had sent him spiraling, screaming, and spitting into a fit that had driven her out into a night as iced and frozen as his heart.

And he knew. This was what he had to do.

"I never should have started it in the first place."

She looked like she'd been hit. "You regret it?"

How could he? These precious weeks with her—they meant everything to him. And yet, if he hadn't had them, he wouldn't have to have known.

"I do."

The tears in her eyes spilled over. "Why are you doing this?"

"Because I have to." That promise he'd made about never hurting her—he might be breaking it right now, but he'd hold to it in the one way that mattered.

Because he saw blond hair in his dreams, saw a woman walking away from him in tears. He heard her voice and he heard her screams.

He saw the wreckage that had been all that was left of her, and it was his fault.

Because it was the only thing he *could* do.

"Go," he said, and it felt like a knife between his ribs. "Please."

"I can't." Her hand was still on the door, keeping him from shutting it, refusing to let him finish this. "I need you."

"No. You don't." And this was the thing. The worst thing, and he had to force it through his lips. "And I don't need you."

The lie was poison on his tongue, was acid dripping down his throat. He needed her more than he'd ever needed anyone or anything. Even Helen, God rest her soul.

He needed her healing hands and the soft press of her lips, the light of her laughter and the heat of her embrace. The way she'd taken down his walls and put *him* back together again, turned the scraps of his empty life into a living, breathing man.

He needed her, and that was why he had to let her go.

"I don't need you," he said again.

And that was it. She faltered, everything in her falling, her hand slipping down the panels of his door. Her gaze went to his knee and then to his face, and her mouth crumpled.

She believed him.

She took one step backward, and it was the very moment he'd been waiting for. He nearly missed it, though, his heart seizing in his chest.

This was it. Goodbye. And he wanted to take it all back. He wanted to pull her into his arms and make love to her with his whole being. He wanted to give her everything.

But all she'd get was pain and ash.

So instead he turned himself to stone. With a ringing sound inside his ears, his whole body numb, he pressed his weight into the door.

His field of vision narrowed down into that tiny gap, those inches of space between him and her and a life he should have known he could never have. She stared at him through it, eyes liquid and cracking.

He slammed it shut in her face.

And then she was gone. The impact of the closing door and his closing life echoed through his bones. At long last, his legs gave out on him. He slid down the wall until he sat there, broken, on the floor.

And thought he might never move again.

It was the loudest sound in the world.

Cole's door slammed with a bang, leaving her on one side and him on the other. Closing her out, the same way he'd been trying to since the very start, except—

Except she hadn't been able to take no for an answer.

Oh *God*.

Her stomach gave a lurching twist, bitterness flooding her mouth. How many times had he tried to push her away before? Only to have her keep coming at him, refusing to turn away. So, what, had she finally just worn him down? He'd seemed eager enough at the time, but had it all been him humoring her? Him consenting to kiss her and touch her and...and *fuck* her out of pity? Out of obligation? Or—

Her gut churned harder, and she jammed her fist against her lips to keep the bile from spilling out.

His voice echoed back to her. *I don't need you.*

He didn't. Clearly. Not anymore. Her brain stuck on the image of him seared into her memory, standing in the doorway and refusing to yield. It was the first time she'd ever seen him without his crutches, and he'd looked so good. So strong.

Dizzy, she took a staggering step back and then another. His PT had been hinting at him being ready to ditch the crutches soon. Serena had been delighted by the prospect at the time. Cole was so proud—getting his independence back, being able to do things for himself again. It would be great. He wouldn't have to rely on her for rides; he'd be able to walk and take the train. He'd be able to hold her with both his arms and press her body into a wall. Into a mattress, even, hovering over her with that darkened heat inside his eyes.

She choked with the force of her sob.

Or he'd be able to close the door on her. Because he wouldn't need her anymore.

Like the last time Penny had left. After she'd stayed with her and her mother for a year, floating in and out of hospitals until she'd finally been stable again, and then she'd been gone. Leaving them with an infant who had barely gotten to know his mother, leaving them without her in their life again.

Leaving them alone.

She clenched her fist even tighter, pressing hard against her mouth until her teeth bit into her lip. It couldn't be that simple, could it? If he'd just been using her all this time, he wouldn't have taken her to a pottery class or gone through any of that crap with Upton for her.

If he didn't care about her, he wouldn't have looked at her like he was dying inside as he told her to go.

God. A fresh wave of tears blurred her vision. Just a couple of days ago, they'd been happy—maybe the happiest she'd ever been. Now suddenly he was pushing her away? Sure, he'd apparently stopped needing his crutches since then, but nothing else had changed between *them*. She'd just asked him to look after Max for one afternoon, and he'd...

He'd snapped at Max. Was that it, then?

If so, this was...this was *bullshit*, was what it was. Self-sacrificing, overprotective bullshit. So he'd lost his temper with Max. It didn't have to mean what he seemed to think it meant. He could still be a friend and a tutor to Max; he could still be with Serena. He didn't have to do this—squirrel himself away from them and from the world the way he had for the last God-knew-how-many years.

This didn't have to be what had happened with his wife all over again.

She whipped around, half inclined to go storming right back up to his door to tell him as much.

Only...if he *had* been humoring her. If he'd just been giving in this entire time...

She'd pursued him and pursued him. She'd worn him down. And if she did it now, they'd just end up in this same exact place all over again.

Reaching out, she braced her hand against the wall to steady herself. She dragged the back of her other wrist across her cheeks. Then she closed her eyes and inhaled nice and deep, holding the breath in until she couldn't take it anymore before letting it out. Controlled and slow.

He didn't need her anymore? Fine. There were other people who did. Cole could stew for a while. She still had Max to take care of this afternoon and a whole nest of issues with her family to sort out.

He was a proud, proud bastard, but she had her pride, too. She'd chased him down enough times, and if he didn't see what a giant mistake he was making...if he didn't miss her...

She shook her head against the way her ribs constricted around her heart. It hurt to even think about.

He'd come back to her. He would.

Hiccuping, she drew in another rasping breath.

And if he didn't, then apparently he hadn't ever really cared about her at all.

CHAPTER TWENTY-FOUR

Somehow, he had never entirely expected her to give up.

That night and the whole day after, Cole went about his usual routine with half an ear bent toward the stairs, anticipating the light falls of her footsteps ascending toward him, girding himself again and again. He'd said what he said for a reason, and though every moment without her was killing him, he'd stand by it. He wouldn't let her in again.

There wasn't anything for her to come in *to*.

A night and a day of icing his knee and recovering his strength and that same tightness in his lungs—that feeling of the walls closing in on him—was back, only times a thousand.

What had he been *doing* with his life before she stormed her way into it?

His papers were strewn all across his shoebox of an apartment. The ones he'd left behind at Serena's place he had to re-create, but it wasn't any difficulty to do so. He buried himself in the numbers and symbols and lines and lines of calculations the way he wished he could bury his bloody head somewhere deep beneath the earth.

She still didn't come.

On the third day, he lost his damn mind. He packed up his laptop and took himself and his new mobility down the fire escape. His bones creaked with every step, but he was fine, he was *fine*. He still couldn't run, but he was supposed to walk—he'd never get his strength back unless he did—and so he went until he was sore, for miles it seemed. At the doorway of a likely-looking café, he stumbled to a halt, panting until he got his breath back.

He went inside, and the girl behind the counter asked him what he'd like, and it was the first time anyone had spoken to him in days. He staggered against the sound of another human voice, his brain melting out his ears and his rib cage threatening to dissolve.

"Mister? Mister, are you all right?"

He opened his eyes, and it was just a girl. Any girl. With a tight smile, he gave her his order and stepped aside. When his tea came up, he retreated to a table in the corner.

And he wrote a paper.

He wrote another the next day and yet another the third. All these years' worth of work scribbled in notebooks and him with nothing to do with any of it, and it was a fucking waste. Publishing his findings had always been his favorite part about his work. It meant getting his ideas out into the world—it was a way to teach without having to talk to bloody people. He sent the articles to a half-dozen journals, but he might as well be sending them off on the wind. Without a home institution, without credentials for these lost and wasted years, no one would listen to him.

And by then, the girl behind the register knew his order on sight. She knew his name, and it was too much. He couldn't bring himself to go there another time.

So he was trapped in that apartment again. He couldn't *do* anything. He tried to bake and he thought of slender fingers gripping the mixing bowl; he thought of soft lips and white teeth and that brief sliver of time when he'd had someone to share the things he'd made with, and it didn't matter that he'd gone without before.

Serena had stormed her way into his life all right, and the lightning had left him blinded to the darkness. Her thunder had deafened his ears. He didn't know how to go back.

He got the rejections for his first round of submissions within the week. They hadn't even made it to review, and he stared at the letters on the screen.

Bracing his hands against his desk, he closed his eyes.

"This isn't *working*." He breathed it out into the silence.

He opened his eyes, and his vision blurred.

He couldn't do this. Not alone.

And it was like slipping and falling, and tossing his bloody crutch down the stairs in a fit of rage, listening to it echo with every goddamn step it crashed against. Like giving up and sitting down right there on the floor, at the top of the landing, a full flight of stairs above him and yet another below, stuck in the middle with no way to stand and no hope.

Only to have a voice call out from the distance. The most beautiful voice in the world.

A voice he'd last heard crying, begging, asking him why, and he would never hear that voice again. Because he'd told her he didn't need her, but he did. He needed her so fucking much.

When he'd lost Helen, it'd been like every star on the horizon going out. His wife had taught him how to love at all, and the next few years he lost in grief and rage and alcohol.

But he couldn't do that again. He couldn't face that emptiness, not after Serena had reminded him that there was more still in this life for him. If he couldn't have her, he needed *something*. Work, a hobby, maybe a fucking dog.

But already he knew. None of that would ever take away the ache.

He swallowed hard, throat burning.

He needed *help*.

"So." Penny pushed her hair back from her face, a ghost of a grin coloring her mouth. "I have news."

There was life in her sister's voice for the first time in so long, and it should have had Serena over the moon. As it was, she fought to muster any sort of a reaction at all. Not that it mattered much. Her mother looked excited enough for the both of them, smile positively radiant as she turned to Penny. "What's that?"

It was Sunday dinner at her mother's place, nominally Serena's favorite day of the week, but she was too tired for any of this. She'd been too tired for most things recently. But she just kept on pushing on.

Penny glanced from her mom to Serena to Max and back. "You remember that job interview I had the other week?"

Serena's fork skidded against the edge of her plate. The grating sound of it drew all eyes to her for a flash of a moment. "Sorry." She set the fork aside and picked at the edge of her napkin.

Yeah. She remembered that interview all right. She remembered her sister calling in a favor and Serena doing everything she could to lend a hand. She remembered thinking she had one person she could depend on to help her out and have her back.

She remembered him pushing her away.

A quicksilver skitter of pain squeezed her chest, and she sucked in a breath, biting down on the inside of her lip.

Nearly two weeks had passed since then, and she hadn't so much as seen him around their building. An emptiness opened up inside her heart. She'd thought he'd have something to say for himself. That he would miss her maybe. Or even that he would have to go down their shared stairs at some point or happen to check his mail or *something*, and their eyes would meet. He'd realize his mistake.

Maybe he really hadn't needed her at all.

Unclenching her jaw, she exhaled long and slow. It was what it was, and pining and moping weren't going to help her. She'd already decided not to push him anymore. Not to ask him for what he'd clearly decided he didn't want to give. It was nobody's fault that they hadn't been on the same page after all. Definitely not her sister's. Or at least that was what she kept trying to tell herself.

Across the table from her, Penny let her mouth curl even wider, her eyes bright. "I got the job!"

Serena's mom clasped her hands in front of her. "That's wonderful, baby. I'm so proud of you!" She glanced to Serena pointedly. "Isn't that wonderful?"

Serena swallowed hard and forced a smile. "Yeah. It's great. Congratulations."

"Nice," Max chimed in, though it was noncommittal. He glanced back and forth between Serena and her mom, always so perceptive when the two of them weren't on quite the same page.

Their mom ignored it, plowing straight ahead. "What will you be doing? Do you know your hours yet? Tell us everything."

It was just the encouragement Penny needed. Serena listened as she started in on all the details, but there was a ringing in her ears.

This was too familiar. They'd done this all before. Helped Penny through a crisis no matter the sacrifice it might require, applauding and showering praise on her when she got back to an even keel.

And her sister was ill. She was fighting a disease that claimed lives. She was so strong, and Serena loved her so much. She loved that she was happy.

But all she could see was the impending crash.

Penny got bad and then Penny got well, and then she left them. She went to college or she moved to New York, and they were left here standing in the ruins until the cycle started all over again, and Serena couldn't do it. Not again.

"I mean, the hours will be a little wonky at first," Penny said, "but, Serena, maybe we can work things out with Max's schedule?" She waited for a response, but all Serena managed was a nod. Uncertainty crossed her face, but at their mother's prodding, she continued on. "It has benefits, thank God. And I'm thinking, once I get a month or two under my belt, I'll be able to get my own place, stop being underfoot all the time and let you guys get back to your lives again, and—"

And the ringing in Serena's ears was deafening, everything else fading to static, the tableau of the perfect family spread out in front of her—the one she'd longed for all these years—flashing to white.

She was on her feet before she'd decided to so much as move. She was dizzy, her hands shaking, and she clenched them into fists, but it didn't help.

"How." No other words came out. She could barely breathe, could scarcely hear over the screaming pitch inside her head. "You."

All the eyes on the table were really on her now. Someone said her name, and Penny's whole face twisted up, those bright eyes that were so much like her own staring back at her, and something inside Serena cracked.

"You can't," she croaked. "You're not ready. You can't just go get your own place and—"

And push the people who loved her away.

Penny's mouth dropped. "Rena..."

"Every single time. You come back here needing us, and we drop everything. You don't even know." The words were so unfair, and they'd been building inside her for so freaking long. "We put everything on hold because there's always some...some crisis. We mop it all up, and then when you get better, you leave. You left us. You—" Her throat closed up, and her lungs were on fire. She tried to refocus, to make this about something other than herself. "You left Max. He needed you, you know. We all needed you, and you left, and now you're back, and what do you think that does to him? What do you think that does to *us*?"

Penny had been flitting in and out of Serena's life for literal decades, completely blind to the holes she left in her wake.

Ten years ago, she'd barely gotten checked out of the hospital before she'd been boarding a bus. She'd barely stopped home, barely visited until...

Until now. And two weeks ago, she'd left Max at Serena's doorstep at a moment's notice, and it had ruined the best damn thing to have happened to Serena in years. She'd made Serena push, and Serena had lost the one thing that had been just for her. The one person who'd taken the time to wrap Serena up and tell her she was worth everything, she deserved everything, deserved time and love and the chance to do the things *she* wanted to do.

He was gone.

She choked on her breath, airways seizing against the burn of time and history and words she'd never been able to say before.

"Max is amazing. He's your kid and he deserves your time, and you can't just toss him aside." The shaking in her hands traveled up her arms until it was her whole body shuddering to pieces. "You can't tell me I can't see him for weeks and then as soon as you're done with him, as soon as you decide you need something else in your life, you suddenly want us to be involved again? Life doesn't work like that. Love doesn't work like that." And Serena loved. She loved so much.

Her mother looked like she'd seen a ghost. "Serena..."

But Serena wasn't listening. Tunnel vision settled in, blacking out the rest of the world except her sister. "I don't care if you don't think you can give him what he needs. I don't care if you think you're not the right person for him. For us. You came here because you needed us, and now you need us to do things for you, and you assume we will, but then what? What happens when you have your life back and you don't need us anymore?" Her fingers went numb. "When you decide to leave again, and I can't. I can't."

"Rena." Penny's voice was so quiet it was deafening. "I left because you were better off without me."

Everything went silent all at once. Penny's expression was bereft, but she didn't make as if to take it back.

Serena's heart, already broken, cracked and shattered to the floor.

"Nothing," she said, vision fogging, "is ever better when you're not here." She sucked in a shivering, shuddering breath. "We never asked you to leave. We never wanted you to go, and I missed you. Every goddamn day. But you left. You left me." Her ribs ached. "We've been here all along. We care and we try and we do what we can to take care of the people we love, and you can't just push us away when you're done with us...You *can't*..."

Hot tears spilled down her cheeks, and she couldn't see anymore, and oh *God*. She wasn't talking about her sister anymore, was she?

She loved so much. She cared and she tried and she did whatever she could to make people care about her, too, but it never mattered.

Her sister left. Cole left.

And here she was. With nothing of her own.

She staggered away from the table, scarcely able to see. Someone called after her, but she shook her head. By some miracle, she made it to the bathroom without bumping into anything or saying anything else she might regret. Locking the door behind her, she stumbled over to the sink and turned the tap on high. Cold water on her face did nothing to ease the hot flush of embarrassment and anger and all the other emotions she usually kept so tightly under wraps, especially around her family. Random breakdowns, screaming fits, running off without listening to anyone—that was Penny's territory. Well, maybe it was hers now, too. Maybe it was time they saw she wasn't some...some doormat, someone who was quiet and caring and did whatever anyone asked of her, expecting nothing in return.

A fresh sob tore its way out of her throat. Giving in, she braced her arms against the sink, letting the tears come. She was just so tired. She'd never felt so alone.

It took a while to cry herself out. When the pressure on her chest and behind her eyes finally started to ease, she pulled in a shuddering breath and raised her head. Ugh, she was such a mess, her eyes red and her cheeks all blotchy, her makeup smudged. Cupping water in her hands, she tossed a couple of splashes over her face. Getting herself more or less under control, she turned off the tap and grabbed a tissue to blow her nose.

Of course that was when someone had to knock on the door. *Damn.* Iron bands squeezed around her chest again, and her eyes misted right back up.

"Just a minute," she called, voice breaking.

What was she going to do? She'd completely lost it on her family. They were going to look at her like she was a freak, or worse with pity, and she'd always tried to be so strong.

"Serena? Sweetie?"

And that was the end of that. What was it about her mom's voice that made her crack right open inside, letting all the soft, vulnerable parts of her out?

Hiccuping, she took another swab at her face with a fresh tissue, then went ahead and flipped the lock.

Her mom eased the door open an inch at a time. Their gazes connected in the mirror, and Serena tried to smile, but it was a watery, shivering thing.

Bless her mom. There wasn't any pity in her eyes at all. Just understanding, and whatever walls Serena had still been keeping up came crashing down.

"I'm sorry, Mom. I—" Whatever else she might've said got lodged in her throat behind another sob.

"Oh no, honey." And then her mother was in there with her, closing the door behind her as she stepped into the room. She wrapped her arms around Serena, tugging her in and melting her resistance until her head rested against her shoulder. Murmuring quiet, soothing nonsense, she petted Serena's head, and Serena shivered into it.

"I ruined dinner," she said, getting her voice back.

Her mother laughed. "You just made it a little more interesting."

"Sorry. Max—" She'd had to have her little breakdown in front of the kid and everything. She'd screamed at her sister, who was just trying to get her life together. "Penny..."

"Max and Penny both are *fine.*" She pulled away, cupping both sides of Serena's face between her hands. "The person I'm worried about right now is *you.*"

Serena's eyes brimmed over anew.

She didn't think she'd ever heard her mother say that to her before.

How much time had they spent in therapists' offices for Penny's sake? There'd been little placards with different emotions on them, and they were supposed to talk in those sorts of words.

That exercise came back to her now. "I'm just..." Her mouth crumpled, making it hard to talk. "I'm just really sad right now."

Her mother's eyes went soft. "Then be sad. It's okay."

But it wasn't. It never had been.

As if she could hear the voice of dissent in Serena's mind, her mother pulled her close again, wrapping her in a hug and rocking her side to side. "Oh, my sweet little girl." Even when Serena started to get it all back under control, she refused to let her pull away. "You know, they warn you about this kind of thing."

Wetly, Serena asked, "What kind of thing?"

"When you have a child who has these kinds of problems, they remind you over and over again to never forget that the other one has needs, too. I listened, and I looked for them so hard. But you...you never seemed to need anything. You were my sweet, strong little trouper. Always chipping in, always helping out."

"It was my job."

"You were a child." She drew away by a fraction, just enough to look her in the eye. "I put too much on you. And I'm sorry." Her throat bobbed. "You've taken such good care of your sister and your nephew. Of me, even. Now will you please, please tell me how we can take care of you?" She shifted to rub her hands up and down Serena's arms. "Serena, sweetie. I know you're worried about your sister. But what's this really about?"

The instinct was there to pretend it was nothing. She was just emotional or hormonal or something. Except that wasn't it at all. Her lip wobbled, and God, why couldn't she stop crying today? She sniffed, shaking her head and trying to turn away, but her mom caught her, one soft palm pressing gently to her cheek to keep her gaze on hers.

"Nothing," she managed to creak out. "Just. Just a boy."

And that was all it took. In fits and starts, the story of her whole affair with Cole poured out of her, how she'd found him sitting at the top of the stairs, barely able to walk and so darn stubborn he was still intent on taking the train. How she wouldn't let him, and she'd convinced him to let her help him by making it out like he was doing her a favor, and he was. He spotted Max's bullying and got him caught up on a year's worth of math in a handful of weeks.

He'd been so beautiful and so broken, and he'd sucked her in from the very first moment. And when he touched her—when he told her about the pain that had shaped his life—she'd been helpless but to fall.

"And I knew," she said, swiping furiously at her eyes, "he was terrified of kids. He knows he has a temper. But when Penny needed someone to take care of Max and I was stuck at work, I asked him to help, and he didn't want to." He'd told her as much, basically, hadn't he? "I never should have asked him to."

"That's not your fault." Her mother had guided them both to sit on the edge of the tub as Serena had rambled on and on, and she curled an arm around Serena's shoulders, holding her pressed against her side.

"He's so *good* with Max, though." It was so easy to imagine him with a boy of his own, all dark hair and gangly limbs, snuggled up with him reading or learning how to ride a bike or who even knew.

No one would ever know, because it was an impossibility. It was the last argument he'd ever had with his wife; it was one he wouldn't be willing to have again.

Her heart throbbed. Even if he did, it wouldn't be with her.

"He got mad, and he left Max all alone. I think he thought he'd actually hurt him, and I know he'd...he'd *never*."

Cole had a temper, sure, but he was the most protective, the most kind. Beneath all that gruffness, he was this lost, lonely man, loyal and true. He'd rather hurt himself than hurt anyone else.

And that was the problem.

"He thinks he'll hurt me," she said, voice cracking. "And he did. He said he didn't need me anymore. He's off his crutches, and..."

She couldn't breathe. Couldn't say another word against the hole torn anew in her heart.

Her mother hesitated for a moment, as if waiting, but when Serena held her tongue, she let out a long sigh.

"And you believed him."

Serena shook her head. She didn't know what to believe.

Her mother squeezed her tighter, pressing their temples together. "It's one lesson I never managed to get through to you, isn't it?"

"What's that?"

"You don't need to do things for people for them to love you." She said it fiercely, voice bright and crackling. "You don't have to earn it. You don't need to make people need you. They'll love you for you. For the sweet, kind, generous girl that *I* love more than the entire world."

It didn't make any sense, how much it hurt to hear those words spoken aloud and in that tone. The brutal honesty of it pierced clear into the space between her ribs.

"You've done so much for us, Rena. For me and for Max and for your sister, and we appreciate it. But we love you for *you*. Don't you dare accept anyone who gives you anything less than that."

The pain of it pressed harder against her ribs, because all those times with Cole, in her bed and in his kitchen and crammed together at a pottery wheel, she'd thought he was giving her exactly that.

But maybe she'd been wrong.

They got another minute or so together there, huddled up in that tiny space, jockeying for room with her mother's shaving cream and Max's shampoo. But they couldn't stay holed up like that forever.

The knock, when it came, was tentative. Max's voice called out. "So did you guys fall in, or...?"

Serena laughed and swabbed at her eyes. "No. We're fine." Her heart still hurt, but she was closer to meaning it than she had been in weeks.

The door cracked open, and Penny's and Max's faces both appeared in the gap. "Can we come in?"

Before Serena could offer to come out instead, her mom waved them in. "Yes, yes, of course. The more the merrier, right?"

The next thing Serena knew, she was crowded in and surrounded by her family, her mom on one side and her sister on the other, Max hugging tightly to her legs, and a part of her wanted to wave them all away. There wasn't any need to make a fuss over her.

But she'd been doing that for too long, hadn't she? They were here, offering to buoy her up. To be here for her the way she was always there for them. And so she let them, soaking in all the love and support she'd kept at bay for so damn long.

Eventually, Max must have gotten bored, because he started rambling on about something he'd learned in science class about recycling and the water cycle. Serena's mom encouraged him, maybe knowing they could use the distraction. Serena listened with half of her attention, but after a few minutes, the guilt gnawing at her stomach had her turning her head.

"Penny?"

Penny hooked her chin over Serena's shoulder. "Yeah?"

"I really am happy for you. About your job. I'm sorry I blew up about it."

"It's okay." Penny shrugged. "It was actually kind of nice that someone finally said what they were thinking for once instead of tiptoeing around."

"I should've been more supportive, though. If you think you're ready, then I believe you."

"Thanks."

And they could have left it at that, but although the words Penny had hurled at Serena might not have fully registered with her in the moment, they were sure as heck haunting her now. "You know we're not really better off without you, right? *Everything* is better when you're here."

Penny hugged her tighter. "I might know it in my head, but believing it..."

"I know."

"I'm trying, though. And, Rena?"

"Yeah."

"I mean it. I'm staying this time. I'm not going anywhere."

Serena wasn't entirely sure she believed that, either, but it felt really, really good to hear. "Okay. I'm gonna hold you to that."

She might not have everything she wanted, and the happiness in this tiny room might be too fragile for the wider world.

She might still miss Cole so much it hurt.

But this, right here...it was something. And at least for now, it was hers.

Three days in a row, Cole talked himself out of it. He made it as far as his back door and once all the way to the base of the fire escape before turning around. That he was even entertaining the idea was ridiculous. He was inviting disaster, setting himself up for failure and rejection and quite possibly a fistfight. But how much more of a disaster could he really become?

The fourth day, he put on his suit again and tied the tie that Helen had given him on their anniversary. Her voice in his head urged him on, but it wasn't the only one. If he'd ever asked, Serena would have told him to do this, too. He straightened his tie, and grabbed his briefcase and his keys. At the door and at the base of the stairs, hollow pangs of dread made his stomach twist, but he kept his head held high. He kept walking.

It wasn't until the train station loomed that he faltered.

A flickering phantom pain shot through his knee. The last time he'd been here, he'd tried to do something good, and he'd nearly done something terrible instead. He'd paid the price in any case—eight weeks of immobility and a heartache he didn't think he'd ever recover from.

With his ribs tight and his leg dully aching, he passed through the turnstile and climbed the stairs. At the top of the platform, he had to close his eyes. All he could see was the place by the timetable where those men had stood, crowding around a boy who looked like easy prey. His whole body shook with the memory of getting his hands on one of them. For just a fraction of an instant, he'd let the angry, awful thing inside his chest have the chance to run free.

After, weak and crumpled on the ground, nearly sick with himself, he'd wished that it would stop, but it never did. He never changed.

But maybe he could. Not enough to deserve what he wanted, but enough to at least be able to bear the life he had left in her wake.

A train roared into the station, and he opened his eyes.

It was strange enough, just getting on the outbound train. He'd had so little occasion to go much of anywhere these past few years, his pilgrimages to the downtown library aside. The whole ride north, he kept his gaze on the window, watching the city churn past, all red brick and graffiti and newly blooming trees. Rehearsing what he was going to say—if he even managed to make it into the building.

One transfer and half an hour later, his stop came up, and he was this close to just standing there, letting the train carry him off to the end of the line. But he'd come this far. With his heart in his throat, he disembarked, melting into the crowd of people stalking off with purpose in their lives, his hand curled into a fist so tight his nails bit into his palm.

It was strange, really, how little the campus had changed. The twisted dread inside his gut grew stronger with every ivy-covered building he passed until he was standing before the one that once had been his second home. Inside, the halls were dimly lit, and every door was a memory. They threatened to swamp him, leaving him off balance and jittery. None of the students recognized him, of course, and he refused to make eye contact with the people in their offices. But stares burned into him, and he could almost hear the whispers that had followed him out as he had left this place in shame.

By the time he made it to Barry's—Dean Meyers's—office, Cole's chest had constricted to the point where he could scarcely breathe. His legs felt like jelly, and the back of his neck was damp with sweat. Panic crashed over him. What was he thinking? He'd be laughed out of here; this was a disaster.

The door was open.

Barry had aged in the time since Cole had last seen him, but then again, Cole had, too. The reddish blond of his hair had gone white at the temples, and there were more fine lines around his mouth and eyes. He had a bit more of a paunch than he had had before. But at his essence, it was still him, and the family resemblance still brought Cole to his knees.

He looked so much like his sister. Like Helen.

Numb, the whole world tilting on its axis, Cole raised the claw of his fist and rapped his knuckles against the wood.

"Come in." Barry's gaze darted away from his computer for half a second, flitting toward Cole almost absently. Then he blinked, visibly startling. In a double take that would have been comical if Cole had air in him to laugh, he looked up again, eyes widening. "Cole."

Everything inside Cole ached, regret and fear and a loss so deep it had derailed his entire life for years.

"Just tell me to go," he ground out. He tightened his grip around the handle of his briefcase. "If you don't want to see me. I won't blame you. I won't make a scene." *Unlike the last time.*

"What?" Barry managed to look honestly confused. "Jesus Christ. No. What are you saying? Come in." He rose to his feet, and there was nothing doubtful in his expression at all. Cole didn't deserve this.

He crossed the space, held together with spit and glue, like with every step he was set to fly apart at the seams.

Barry moved out from behind his desk, raising a hand, and for a fleeting moment, Cole braced himself for a blow he probably deserved. Instead, his brother-in-law reached out, clasping Cole by the hand and holding on, and the warmth of his smile was almost too much.

"God, Cole, what has it been? Years."

"Too many," Cole agreed.

"I tried to call." He had. So many times, but...

"I never picked up." Cole's throat bobbed. "I'm sorry. I wasn't ready."

He wasn't sure he was ready now either, but what choice did he have? The irony made him want to laugh or cry or fall into a bottle again, but none of those were on the table right now. Losing Helen had driven him off the rails, and gaining Serena—having to let Serena go—it had led him here. Back to the place he'd fled so long ago.

Serena had opened his life again after Helen's death had slammed it closed. And so he was here. Now. Not ready, necessarily, but he had to try.

Too fervently, Barry grasped Cole's hand in both of his. "Damn, you're a sight for sore eyes."

The sheer generosity of it made Cole's head spin. "I thought you'd never want to see me again."

After everything he'd done. After Helen, after he'd made a mockery of his career and of the department—of the university itself. After he'd forced his own brother-in-law to show him the door.

But Barry just shook his head. "You don't know how many times we've thought of you over the years."

Cole's attempt to smile came out wobbly and awful, but it was the closest he'd come in weeks.

Their handshake had dragged on for ages now. With one last squeeze, Barry let go, then held his hand out toward the chair in front of his desk. "Sit. Please. Stay. Tell me how you've been."

As Barry retreated to his own seat on the other side of the desk, Cole dropped into the one Barry had pointed to, arranging himself. He scrubbed a hand over his face. "Shite. I don't know where to start. You saw..."

Barry had seen the worst of it, honestly. He'd seen Cole a mangled mess and a wreck of a man.

He nodded gravely, folding his hands together in front of him. "I wanted to help. I wish I could have done more."

"There was nothing anyone could have done." All Cole's will had been bent on destroying himself back then, and no one could have talked him out of it.

In all that time, no one had. Except Serena. His heart clenched hard at the thought.

An uncomfortable moment of silence passed before Cole cleared his throat. "And you? The kids? Jan?"

"All great." Barry ticked off children, half grown now. Told Cole about his life and his job and his wife.

"I'm happy for you," Cole said, and he meant it.

"You should come round for dinner sometime. Everyone would love to see you. The kids still ask about their uncle all the time."

Nodding, Cole managed, "I'd like that."

Barry's face went serious. "But you didn't just come here to ask me about my family."

"No. I didn't." He forced his fingers to unclench. His pride was a white-hot force inside him that he had to push away. Because he'd never asked for this before. He'd been offered it—had been all but forced to accept it by kind, beautiful women who'd had his best interests at heart. But he'd never asked. "Barry—Dean Meyers—I—" He cut himself off. Took a breath and licked his lips, but his throat was a desert. His *life* was.

How many times had he told Serena that she had the right to request things for herself? How sweetly had she tried to show him that he had that same right?

"Please," he rasped out. "I need help."

The words hung on the air, heavy and impossible.

And the instant they made it out of his mouth, Barry leaned forward. "Anything. If it's in my power..."

The rest of it came so easily.

"I need a job. I know I fucked up here. I burned my bridges, and I'll take my lumps, but if you have anything, or if you've heard of anything." He fumbled with the clasp of his briefcase, pulling out the papers he'd brought and handing them over. "I've been working. Three articles written and ready to go out, but no one will look at them without an institution next to my name, and I..." Fuck, this hurt. "I want to teach again."

Barry accepted the papers Cole passed over and began flipping through them, his brows rising higher with every page. But at that last bit, the space between his eyes scrunched up, and he jerked his gaze away from the lines of figures. "I thought you didn't care for teaching."

"No, I just...I didn't know how to do it back then." He couldn't pretend he was that much better now, but his afternoons with Max had reminded him of why it was worth it to try. Serena—all those times she talked about her profession with this warmth in her voice. It had reignited a spark in him he'd thought had died.

All these empty years had passed him by, and he wanted his life to be different now. He wanted to be worthy of the love he'd been given and that he'd had no choice but to throw away.

"But I've changed," Cole said. Serena had changed him. She'd woken him from his stupor. She'd made him *better*, with just a word. With the softest of touches of her hand. "I've been working at it." He grasped at the closest available straw. "Tutoring. Conferring with other teachers." *One* other teacher, but it wasn't a lie. "I'm willing to give it my all this time. Just let me try, and I'll prove it to you."

Frowning, Barry returned his attention to the pages Cole had pushed at him, and for hollow minutes, Cole sat there, waiting. Finally, when he wasn't sure he could take it anymore, Barry looked up. "This is solid work."

"You know the work was never my problem."

"No. It never was." Barry set the papers down. "This isn't a simple thing you're asking for, you know."

Cole's heart sank. "I know."

"You forced our hand. After Helen..."

"I was a disaster." He swallowed hard. "I still am. But I swear. If you give me another chance, I won't waste it."

For a long, long time, Barry studied him. Then he sat back in his chair, picking up a pen and twirling it between his fingers. "It just so happens that our Introduction to Mathematics adjunct pulled out for the summer term."

Pulse quickening, Cole sat straighter in his chair. "I'll take it."

God. If Helen could see him now. It was the worst course on their schedule, no real content, and only non-majors took it. A few years ago, he would have tried like mad to switch to anything else. But he'd spent eight weeks teaching fractions and decimals to a ten-year-old. He could do this.

"Not so fast. You'd still need to go to counseling, Cole."

Cole's throat tightened. That had been the stipulation the last time around, too, and he had laughed in their faces.

But Barry was still talking. "The board would demand it if...*if* I brought this appointment before them. But as your friend...Honestly, don't you think you need it?"

Maybe he did.

Maybe if he'd ended up on a therapist's couch the first time around, he could have avoided so much pain.

Maybe it wasn't too late. "I don't know. But I'll try it."

Just like that, the stoicism on Barry's face melted. "Really?"

"Do I have a choice?"

"You always have a choice. But I think this is the right one. Hell, I'll give you the job right here and now if it means you'll get some help."

Help. It was what he'd come here for, if not necessarily in this form.

"I thought you had to bring it up before the board," he said weakly, head spinning.

"You know they'll do whatever I tell them to."

"And you'll tell them..."

"To hire you." The way Barry said it was all conviction, and he looked so goddamn much like Helen. Like he believed in him.

Cole's chest ached. "Thank you."

"Thank you for coming to me." Something in his brother-in-law's expression broke, and all at once, it wasn't a conversation between colleagues. It was a conversation with family, and that was a feeling Cole hadn't had in a very long while. "You know none of us blame you. For what happened."

Cole huffed a hollow echo of a laugh. "I blame myself enough for all of us."

"Yeah. You do. So do me a favor, will you?"

"Anything."

"*Stop* that. She wouldn't want this for you." No, she wouldn't have. "It killed me to lose her. Killed me. But, Cole. I didn't think it meant I'd have to lose you, too."

The heat behind Cole's eyes came out of nowhere, and he shook his head to try to keep the tide of feeling in. "I'm sorry." No one knew how sorry he was.

"And I forgive you."

They were just words. But the acceptance in them, this gift of another chance...

One thread of the knot that had tied Cole up in loss and grief for all these years...it came unwound.

And it was just this tiny, tiny bit easier to breathe.

CHAPTER TWENTY-FIVE

Serena's phone buzzed at four-thirty on the dot. Sliding the pile of assignments she was grading off her lap, she stretched to reach and grab it off the coffee table. Sure enough, it was from Max's friend's mom, letting her know he was on his way.

She texted back a quick thank-you, then started gathering her things. As she did, she kept throwing little glances at the clock.

It made her nervous as hell to be letting Max walk home alone, but his buddy only lived a block and a half away. Ever since the afternoon of Penny's interview and Cole's breakdown, they'd all been trying to be a little more relaxed about letting him do some more stuff on his own. Heck, plenty of kids even younger than he was walked home from school by themselves. At his age, Serena'd done it all the time. It was just a different world now.

Besides, Max could be graduating from college and to Serena he'd still be her baby.

Before long, the place was as tidied as it was going to get. Her gaze went to the time again, and she frowned. He should be here by now. Worrying her necklace between her fingers, she went to the window and looked out, but there wasn't any sign of him.

She was being paranoid.

Taking a deep breath, she plucked her phone from her pocket and scrolled through Facebook for a couple of minutes, but the agitation in her chest grew and grew.

Okay, seriously, where was that kid? She didn't want to be that person, but she fired off another message to the friend's mom, double-checking that Max had really left when she had said he did. The reply came quickly, confirming that yes, he had. Wasn't he there yet?

Serena's hands went numb.

Crap, don't panic. She dialed her mom on instinct and grabbed her keys, heading out into the hall.

Her mom picked up after just one ring. "Oh, hey, sweetie—"

"So, I'm trying not to freak out, but Max was supposed to be home ten minutes ago and he's still not here."

"What?" She clearly had her full attention. "Have you gone out to look for him?"

"I'm going downstairs right now." Leaving her apartment made her nervous, though. What if they crossed paths or he'd just taken the long way around? The idea of him arriving on her doorstep without anyone to let him in was almost as bad as his being out there all alone.

She quickened her pace regardless. No Max in the entryway, and she pushed through the door into the bright spring afternoon and looked both ways down the street. Nothing.

A cold little curl of anxiety opened up behind her breast. "I don't see him," she said. "But I don't want to get too far away."

Crap crap crap, she'd known he was too young to walk home alone. A block and a half might as well be a mile in this city. There were alleys and creeps and serial killers. The cold little curl became an icy pit. If something had happened to him, she was never going to forgive herself.

"Okay, stay calm," her mom said. "I'm sure he's fine."

She gripped her keys and her phone both tighter. "But what if he's not?" This was a pretty safe part of town, but terrible things could happen anywhere, and Max was smart for his age, but he was also small. "Oh God, Mom, I don't know what to do."

"Deep breaths. I'm leaving now."

"Hurry." If this was nothing, Serena was going to feel like a freaking idiot, making her mom duck out of work early, worrying her like this.

"I'll call your sister."

Right. Serena should have thought to do that, too. Penny'd been really conscientious ever since Serena had kind of lost it on her. Maybe a little too conscientious, honestly, like she was the one tiptoeing around, trying to be on her best behavior, but Serena didn't have time to worry about that right now. "Okay."

"Is there anyone else who can stay by your apartment in case he shows up?"

"I don't know." None of her friends lived terribly close, and her neighbors would all be at work, except—

Oh no. No.

But what other option did she have?

"I may have an idea," she said, throat tight. "Call me as soon as you get here."

She hung up before her mother could respond. Desperate, she

took a half-dozen steps in the direction she expected Max to be coming from, but there was still no sign of him, and she didn't want to go too far away. She retreated back to her building's front door and let herself in with shaking hands.

It had been weeks now since she'd seen Cole. He'd made no effort to contact her—if anything, he had to be avoiding her, and it was a sick, twisting emptiness inside her that she lived with every day. He didn't need her, didn't want her, didn't want to see her. It ached like nothing else in her life ever had, but she could live with it. Like her mom had reminded her: she deserved someone who would give her everything and who loved her for who she was, not just what she could do for them.

But God, it grated to have to go crawling to him now. She had asked him for one thing in the span of their relationship, and it had been help with Max, and it had ruined him. He owed her nothing. Heck, he might just laugh in her face, but this was an emergency. She'd messed up so badly here. The least she could do was put her pride aside and ask.

Twisting her keys in her hands, she climbed the stairs, past her own apartment and up and up. Standing in front of his door, the angry shame of what she was about to do stole her breath away.

"This is for Max," she reminded herself, whispering it under her breath.

And then, with her heart in her throat, she knocked.

Therapy was *awful*. Cole was stomping his way around his flat, thunking things around too hard as he set about making a cup of tea to try to calm his nerves.

How many weeks had it taken Serena to pull all his secrets out of him? She'd coaxed them free with loving hands, and he'd given them to her willingly, half expecting her to abandon him at every step. Humbled and reverent every time she chose to stay.

While that bloody doctor...

He'd sat there so expectantly, judging and writing and asking these questions that twisted the very words Cole said. And so now here he was, questioning everything. Questioning himself.

Questioning his conclusion that he always had to be alone.

The whistle on the kettle blew, and he flicked it off. As the screeching died down, he braced his hands against the edge of the counter, hanging his head and clenching his eyes shut. He felt like so much wet newspaper, like someone had taken his brains out and scrambled them up and then shoved them back inside. His heart *hurt*.

And then the pounding came on the door.

Jerking his head up and his eyes open, he stepped back, scarcely breathing. No one ever came to him, no one knocked—no one had in years except Serena, and he'd made a bloody mess of that.

She wouldn't. She couldn't.

The knocking sounded out again, harder this time, and he was in motion. Ignoring the peephole, he tore open the door.

And it was a punch right to the solar plexus, a blow so hard it drove the air from his lungs.

Serena. She was really here. His eyes drank in the sight of her, every atom of his body suddenly parched. It didn't even seem possible, but she looked better than he remembered, all golden hair and soft skin, bright eyes that he could sink into and never know that he was drowning.

Her mouth was pinched.

"Serena—" he managed to choke out.

"Please." She interrupted him, crossing her arms over her chest, her whole body closed, hugging herself as if she were cold. "I know you don't want to see me, but there's no one else I can ask."

He was instantly on alert. "What happened?"

"It's Max."

Max. Christ. Another impact cracked his ribs.

Because he'd abandoned Serena when he'd pushed her away, but he'd abandoned Max, too, and the tyke had had enough of that in his life. It was another failing of his. Another brilliant, aching point of regret.

But this wasn't about him. "What do you need?"

He was already reaching for his phone and his keys. He jammed them in his pockets and stepped out into the hall, tugging his door shut behind him.

It was the first time they'd stood in front of each other in weeks, no door and no pride, no obstacles between them. It felt like so much longer. And it was so fucking inappropriate, but he couldn't stop himself from raking his gaze up and down her body all over again. If he wasn't wrong, she was doing the same thing.

But she shook her head and slid a hand up her arm to grip at her own shoulder. "He was walking home from a friend's house, but he never made it home." She barely seemed to get the words out. Her face crumpled. "I knew I shouldn't have let him go by himself, but he's getting older, and we want him to be independent. It's just a block and a half, all side streets, but I shouldn't have...I..."

Instinct possessed him. His hands were on her arms, grasping her tight, and it sent a shock of electricity coursing the length of his body. Just touching her. Even while her world was falling apart. "It's going to be all right."

She shook her head almost violently. "What if he's hurt or he got kidnapped or—"

"He's fine. And we are going to find him."

"But..." She took a hiccuping, shivering breath, but if anything it only seemed to push her closer to hysteria.

How could he possibly be expected to keep his distance? Without another moment's hesitation, he drew her in, encircling her with his arms. For a long moment, he held her tight, trying to give her what comfort there was in him to offer. When she unwound her arms from around herself and hugged him in return, something in the jumbled mess of his mind seemed to snap back into place.

It took a herculean effort to make himself let go. Clasping her by the shoulders again, he ducked down, putting his face right in her field of view.

"Tell me what you want me to do."

"Just...if you can stay in my apartment while I go looking for him. In case he shows up."

While *she* went looking for him? Over his dead body.

"Perfect, except you stay home and I'll go do the looking."

She made a sound as if to protest, and he lifted a hand, cupping the soft curve of her cheek and feeling more at home in his own damn skin than he had in so long.

"You don't have to," she said.

"I insist." He stroked his thumb across her skin. "You're going to pieces, love. Let me do this for you."

She jerked, and it was stitches tearing, the barely sewn-up wound on his heart setting back to a sluggish bleed. "I'm fine."

He pushed away the pain.

"We don't have time to argue about this." He'd stand here talking to her for days, even if it was to quibble over details. But it wouldn't help Max. "Stay here. Call me if you hear anything. Just tell me where he's coming from."

She rattled off the cross streets, and he wrote them to his memory. There were a couple of different routes he could have taken, but it was still only about four square blocks to cover.

"I'll find him," he swore.

But her eyes were damp, her lips trembling. Surrounding her face with both hands, he leaned in, pressing a dry, firm kiss to the very center of her brow. He squeezed his eyes shut tight as he lingered there.

And then he was off.

Never had he been more grateful for the freedom to move without his crutches. He still wasn't cleared to run, but he pushed the limits of it as he flew down the stairs and out the door. Calling Max's name, he ate up the pavement, glancing between houses and into the windows of cars. The chances of abduction were fairly low, all told. It was more likely he was dallying in another friend's yard or looking at dirty pictures in an alley. Buying sweets he wasn't supposed to from the corner store.

So that was the next place he went, after he'd tried his first choice of routes. It was another block out of the way, and it would've been foolish of Max in the extreme, but children weren't exactly known for their wisdom, were they? Cole poked his head inside to find it deserted. He scanned the handful of aisles all the same.

"You looking for something, mister?"

Cole nodded, speaking in distraction to the man behind the register. "Boy. Ten years old, looks younger. Blond hair, glasses. Would've been by himself, most likely."

"Haven't seen him. Had a couple other brats in here a little bit ago, though. Kids think they can distract me and get away with stealing candy, but I see everything."

Humming some vague agreement, Cole turned back around and headed for the door, muttering his thanks as he passed the register. He made his way back to Max's starting point and took a different side street home from there. He fingered his phone in his pocket. Serena would've called him if Max had shown up, but maybe she'd forgotten.

With every step closer he drew to their apartment building, the more the anxiety in him built. A fear he hadn't known before had his blood pumping faster, his breath jagged and shallow. The low throb of his healing knee threatened to slow him down, but he kept up his pace. All hope wasn't lost yet. There was still the alley back the other way—or maybe the library down the corner, though fuck knew what the hell he'd be doing there.

Cupping his hands in front of his face, he called again, "Max." Then, more frantic, "Max!"

"Help!"

Cole's blood turned to ice and fire all at once.

The word was bitten off, and he froze, listening more carefully. There were other sounds, muffled ones, mumbled words in a tone that gave the fire strength.

A wet sound and a whimper. From...

That way.

Fuck his knee and fuck everything else. It was a flat-out sprint that carried him between two buildings, down a walk and over a fence, and shit, bollocks, that hurt, but then there they were.

Max stood with his back literally up against a wall, surrounded by three older boys, each with a solid twenty pounds and the better part of a foot on him. The biggest of them had a hand pressed over Max's mouth and another on his collar, yanking hard. Blood poured from Max's nose, and his jacket was torn.

His glasses were broken.

And a lilting sense of vertigo took Cole over.

Because he'd been here before. Not in this place, but in this moment. He'd been that child, staring down another in a series of beatings.

He'd been a man, standing at the top of a train station platform, a boy's green backpack in his hand, the whole world spinning out of his control, and he would have killed those men. Given the chance, he would have *killed* them.

He was on the boys in a second. He didn't even hear the words hurtling out of his mouth. He shoved the closest boy aside, slapped away the hand of another, and then he had the jacket of the ringleader in his hand. He hauled him up bodily, until his feet didn't even touch the ground. He got right in his face, shouting, spit flying.

"How *dare* you. You...you..." Words failed him, his throat seizing up. Cole's hands were clenching, the entire world was red, and he couldn't. He couldn't.

He wasn't that man. He wasn't that scared, lost, beaten-down little boy.

Not anymore.

From behind him, the softest, sweetest voice rang out. "Cole?"

He didn't even need to turn around to feel Serena's presence wash over him. Soothing him and quieting him until he could *think* again.

A crimson tide still rushed through his veins, but all at once the world swept back into focus. The boy in his hands was shaking, his eyes wide, and he'd dropped his backpack on the ground when Cole had grabbed him.

His bright. Green. Backpack.

Cole's gaze snapped to the kid's face, and his blood flashed cold. Fuck.

This kid. This *child*. He was the boy who'd gotten mugged on the train all those weeks ago, the one Cole had empathized with, the one he'd run down thieves for, the one he'd nearly broken himself and ruined his life for. Standing on the platform, alone, the boy had done everything he could to make himself seem small, to seem less like prey.

And here. In this alley. He'd stood over Max as if *he* were the prey.

Cole's hand released before he'd even processed it. The boy fell, barely catching himself, and the rest of his crew flinched back.

Blood rushed into Cole's fingers, but his head still spun. This boy was *him*. Being taken advantage of one day and turning into a monster the next. That was what the world did to people—it was what Cole had always said whenever people asked him why he never wanted children. Why he was always so *angry* all the time.

But then, out of the corner of his eye, Cole spied Serena. He spied Max.

The world was cruel, and it made people hard.

But you didn't have to let it.

Taking a step back, Cole held out his arm. Max rushed into him, his entire body trembling, and the rage inside Cole wasn't leaving him, but it wasn't the same as the one he'd let control him in the past. The three bullies were in various states of pissing themselves there on the asphalt of the alley.

Cole let his nostrils flare as he addressed them. "If you *ever* come near him again, I will find you. I've seen your faces. He ends up with a bruise, he gets a single bloody paper cut, and I will track you down. Do you understand?"

Three heads, mouths all agape, nodded dumbly at him.

A foreign calm stole over him, like the flow of a stream, like the soft magic of Serena's hands. His shoulders dropped a fraction of an inch. "It doesn't have to be like this. You don't have to do this."

Cole never thought he had a choice in the matter, but maybe he did. Maybe they all did.

They could choose to be better.

For a long minute, the boys stared at him in mute silence, but there was nothing more he could do for them. He flicked a hand toward the end of the alley. "What are you waiting for, then? Go."

They scattered in a flurry, the ringleader casting Cole one last, conflicted glance before he grabbed his sack and ran. Standing strong, Cole watched them as they went. Boys as scared as he or Max had ever been. Tyrants and cowards, and they'd just needed to be stood up to.

And Max. He'd needed someone to protect him.

Finally, they disappeared around the corner, and the fight drained out of Cole all at once. He forced out a breath that was like his lungs collapsing, and his knee wobbled beneath him. With the trio out of sight, Max buried his face in Cole's chest, wrapping his arms around his waist and letting out a sob.

Cole tugged him in close, just as tight as he could.

As he did, he twisted around. And sure enough, a half-dozen feet away stood an angel. The woman who had tamed his beast and brought him back to sanity. Back to himself. She'd shown him that he could rise above what the world had tried to make of him.

And he loved her. God, but he did.

CHAPTER TWENTY-SIX

Okay, who wants the last slice of pepperoni?" Serena's mom held it up on offer, glancing around the table.

Max's hand shot up, but Serena batted it down. "Finish what's on your plate," she insisted.

He pouted. "But *pepperoni*."

A deep, gruff voice said, "I'll take it."

Serena's chest filled with butterflies as Cole reached past her to accept the slice. Setting it on his plate, he caught Max's eye. "I'll split it with you once you're done."

As if the hero worship could get any worse. Now he was bribing the kid with food, too.

Not that Serena was complaining. On the one side of her, Max tore back into what was left of his current slice with gusto, while on the other, Cole settled into his corner of the couch, his thigh brushing against hers, his whole side one long line of heat searing into her.

Part of her still thought it was a dream.

By the time her mother had finally gotten home earlier, Serena had been frantic, convinced down to her bones that the worst had happened. She'd torn out onto the street. Surely Cole would've already checked the most obvious paths, so she'd cut between buildings, searching everywhere she could think.

Sheer luck alone had led her to the alleyway.

To Cole, standing over a group of boys who looked like they'd seen ghosts. Serena had felt like she was seeing one, too. Over and over, Cole had warned her about his temper, but she'd never seen it—not really. His eyes had been wild, his teeth practically bared, but he hadn't scared her. He hadn't been out of control.

He'd been protecting the thing that meant the most to her in this entire world. He'd been furious, yes, but he'd been beautiful in his fury. She wasn't sure she'd ever loved him more.

The next little stretch had been a blur. Max practically had to be pried off Cole's legs, but eventually Serena had managed to coax him into letting her look him over. He'd had a bloody nose and bit of a shiner, and he was shaken up as hell. But he'd been okay.

He was here. Wearing the sports goggles he usually reserved for baseball practice, sure, but here. Safe. Surrounded by family. Serena and her mom and even Penny had managed to convince her new boss to let her out a little early for a family emergency.

And Cole.

Cole, who her mom had kissed on the face when he'd escorted Max home. Cole who'd acceded to her mom's insistence that he stay for dinner as a thank-you, barely even bothering to protest. Who'd chosen to sit next to Serena all night long, letting his presence tie her up in the most intricate of knots.

Cole who'd rejected her and told her to stay away.

She tried to take another bite of her pizza, but she couldn't seem to get it down. Giving up, she set her plate on the ground and sat back. Shifted herself a little farther over on the cushion so she and Cole didn't touch. Not until she knew what all this meant.

Fortunately or unfortunately, dinner wound down pretty soon after that. Max nearly fell asleep in his last half-slice of pepperoni, and Serena's mom sighed as she started to clear the plates.

But before she made it quite all the way out the door, she stopped. She walked right up to Cole and took his face in both her hands.

"Thank you for taking care of my grandson."

Visibly flustered, Cole swallowed. "Of course."

Without letting go of him, her mom slid her gaze across the room. "Now you take care of my daughter, too, you hear?"

"Loud and clear."

Serena's mom gave Serena a meaningful nod, and God, she wasn't even subtle when she darted her eyes pointedly from Cole to her and back again.

Serena's face felt tomato red. "Good night, Mother."

"Good night, dear."

Serena followed them all to the door. As soon as it was closed behind them, she dropped her brow to press against the wood. "I am so sorry about them."

"Don't be," Cole said, voice rough. "They love you."

"Yeah. They do."

A hot awareness that this was the first time they'd been alone together in a room in weeks settled over her. Her blood felt too warm, and it was shame and it was want and it was love, and she didn't know how it all fit anymore.

She didn't know why he was here.

Drawing in a deep, fortifying breath, she lifted her head, staring forward at the door. "Thank you. For your help with Max."

"I was glad I could help."

She'd had a lot of time in these past few weeks to think. Their relationship had ended so suddenly, and there were things she'd never had the chance to say—things that now she never would.

But there were some things he should hear. "You were just..." And she didn't want to face him, but she couldn't say this with her back to him. Hugging her arms across her chest, she turned, gaze averted, trying to stifle the shiver that ran up her spine. Trying to tamp down on the feelings that wanted so badly to break free. "You were amazing today."

The last time she'd asked for help, he'd been reluctant at best, and he'd torn himself away at the faintest hint of his temper getting the best of him. Today, though...

Today, he'd been a hero.

He started to speak, but she shook her head. She had to get this out. "I don't know what I would have done without you. I was panicking, and you were right there. You knew exactly what to do." Forget that being held inside his arms had wrecked her. The stark reminder of what she'd had and what he'd taken away had left her raw, at the same time that the warmth of his embrace—the press of his lips against her brow—had filled the hole inside her, at least for a moment. "You totally took command of the situation, and I'm just so grateful."

And then when he found Max, the way he'd handled it...She'd only arrived to see the tail end of the confrontation, but he'd been so powerful and yet so tightly controlled.

"I know—" Her throat threatened to close around the words, and crap, damn, she hated the way her eyes welled up. "I know you worry about losing it or being, I don't know, dangerous or something. But you were angry today, and you handled it. I didn't see a...a monster or whatever it is you think you are. I saw a man protecting a kid, and it—"

It made her fall in love with him all over again.

Mistiness made the floor before her blur, and she lifted her head, looking at the ceiling in a vain effort to keep the tears at bay.

"It was amazing, okay?" What more could she say?

Dull footfalls echoed across the space, and then he was there, barely a foot in front of her. Warm hands settled on her shoulders, just like they had in front of his apartment when she'd gone to him for help, and it felt too good. Too safe. She should have stepped away from the door or something, because there was nowhere to run, no way around him.

There was only him, right in her vision, fuzzy for the tears but so achingly beautiful she couldn't breathe.

"Serena." His accent rolled over her, and she shuddered.

He didn't need her. He'd told her that. He'd been completely clear.

She spoke right over him, her voice rising higher and higher, nervous babbling she didn't know how to stop. "So thank you. You didn't have to do any of it, or stay for pizza, even if my mom did rope you into it—"

"Serena." The way he said her name was hot and commanding,

and it pulled her out of her spiral. She blinked, bringing him into focus, and he was so close. He smelled so good.

"Serena. Darling," he said, and something in his voice cracked. "Of course I had to help. You have to know. You must."

She didn't know anything. She shook her head. "I—"

"It was for you. For you and for Max, but I would...I would do *anything* for you."

It was a flailing, plummeting sensation inside her chest. "But last time..."

"Last time I was a coward and a fool. Serena." His Adam's apple bobbed, those piercing eyes slicing straight through to the heart of her. "I thought I'd been through hell before, and I had, but these last few weeks without you have been a new level. When I"—his jaw flexed, his grip tightening—"lost Helen, I blamed myself. Maybe it was my fault and maybe it wasn't. But what I did to you...that was all me. It was a mistake."

Her head spun. "Then why? You never even tried, never came to apologize, or—"

"I'm apologizing now. I'm so sorry. So, so sorry." Eyes bright, movements stiff, he slid his hands down her arms until he grasped her by the hands. Ever so slowly, he lowered himself until he was kneeling before her, and the breath was knocked out of her lungs.

"Your knee—"

"It's fine." He was lying at least a little bit; the lines on his face told her that much. "It doesn't hurt half as much as it hurt to lose you. Being without you, it was like losing both legs. I can't. I...I need you, Serena."

She shook her head, the knife in her heart twisting. She fought to tug her hands free, but he held on. "You don't." Her gaze dropped unconsciously to his knee. "You said."

Her mother's words came back to her. Doing things for people didn't make them love you. Debt and obligation weren't a part of love, and she deserved better than anyone who could be bought so easily. She deserved someone who adored her for who she was.

And it would kill her, because she loved him so much. But if he couldn't give her that...

She wasn't settling for less than everything.

Squeezing her fingers tighter, he stared at her with pleading eyes. "I know what I said, and it was the truest truth and the darkest lie." A fire possessed him, deepening his tone and melting her from the inside, against her will. "There is not a thing on this earth that I need from you. Nothing you can do for me that I couldn't do for myself." His gaze shone, and it cracked her heart right through. "I need *you*. I want *you*."

It was exactly what she'd always been waiting to hear. She blinked hard, but it did nothing to stem the wetness seeping from the corners of her eyes. "What about the next time you think you're going to snap at me or at Max or..."

"Do you know what happened to me today, when I found him?"

She shook her head, her tongue refusing to form words.

"I was *terrified*. I thought I was going to lose it again, but everything was different. It wasn't like it's ever been before. I heard your voice, and I had Max behind me, and it wasn't this...this mindless rage. It was protectiveness." Something in his mouth crumpled. "It was love."

The whole world around her froze to a halt.

She'd wanted so badly to believe that he loved her. He'd shown her in enough tiny ways that he did, but when it counted...when she'd depended on him...

"Please," he said, and it was the edge to his tone that stopped her thoughts in their tracks. "It's too much to ask you to forgive me or to take me back. I hurt you, when I promised I never would. I can tell you that I thought it was to protect you, but I can't even promise you that. I was scared. You terrify me. You open me up in all these ways I never thought I'd ever open myself up again. If I ever lost you...I couldn't...Not again."

And so he'd pushed her away.

It took every scrap of her willpower to stay still. To not drop straight to her knees and welcome him back in again.

Rubbing his thumbs across the backs of her palms, he lowered his head to kiss each one in turn. When he lifted his gaze to return it to hers, the depths of the vulnerability there squeezed her heart.

So many times he'd lowered his walls to give her pieces of his tragedy. But never before had she felt like he was giving her pieces of himself.

"I've been so lost without you. I didn't know what to do. But I've been trying so hard to be worthy of you. I went back and begged for my job, and they have me teaching bloody non-majors, but I don't even care. I'm going to teach again, and it's all because of you."

She finally found her tongue again. "But you don't like teaching."

He'd told her that before, had said it wasn't suited to his temperament. That his passion was for the research.

"I know better now. After the way you talked about it. After

working with Max and seeing him *get* it, I...I understand it now."
He grasped her hands even tighter. "I'm going to therapy, and it's
awful. You can't even imagine. But it's helping. I'm getting better.
I want to get better."

This was more than she'd ever dared to dream. This man on
his knees before her, telling her he wanted to change. And yet the
parts of herself she'd ignored the last time around still hurt too
much.

"But what if we don't want the same things?"

All she'd ever wanted was to help people. To take care of the
people she loved.

And to have a family of her own.

"I'll give you anything that's in my power to give you."

Dizziness had her spinning. "You don't want children."

Pain cracked his mouth. But he didn't fly off the handle, didn't
react with the harshness and the rage he might have when she'd
brought up sensitive subjects before. Clenching his eyes shut, he
dropped his head to rest his brow against their hands.

"I'm willing to discuss it. I won't rule it out." He gazed up at
her, and then, arm shaking, he let go of one of her hands. He
pressed his open palm against her abdomen.

She gasped aloud. "Cole..."

It was too much.

He met her gaze. "You're the second woman to believe I could
be a father. I was so pigheaded, so mistrustful of myself. But
maybe..." He swallowed, licking his lips and searching her eyes.
"Maybe I should trust you."

"I'd never force you."

"You wouldn't have to. For so long, I've been so scared of

what I would do, what the world could do. But I choose my own destiny. When Max ran to me today, when he hugged me...I understood it. For the first time. I can't promise you anything, but..." Possessive heat flickered in his gaze. His thumb stroked over her belly, and her whole body flashed impossibly warm. "But the idea of it. Of you..."

Her resolve crumbled to dust.

She dropped to her knees. Eye to eye with him, she cupped his face in her palm, the bristly roughness of his cheek feeling too right beneath her touch.

"You broke my heart, you know."

"I know. And I'm sorry. I'm so sorry. But if you'll let me, I'll spend the rest of my life making it up to you. I—" He cut himself off, but when he spoke again, it was with an assuredness, an absolute conviction that soaked into her bones. "I love you. I need you. I want *you*."

And the hole he'd left inside of her filled up, up, up.

If he hadn't already been there, the glowing softness in her eyes would have brought him to his knees. He didn't dare to hope, though—scarcely dared to so much as breathe. How many second chances did a man get, after all?

But here she was, closer than he'd ever imagined anyone would ever be again. She was touching him, the warm, smooth grazing of her fingertips against his cheek firing off sparks beneath his skin. And he still didn't deserve this—he likely never would.

Just one more second chance. It was all he needed. If she gave it to him, he'd spend the rest of his life doing his best to give her the world.

"Oh, Cole." The damp sheen to her eyes grew brighter, setting off a roughness in his throat and a pressure behind his own eyes. "I think I loved you the moment I met you."

It was an ocean wave crashing in his heart. That dry, shriveled thing that she'd taught to beat again heaved, coming back to life, and he let out his breath in a rush.

"Thank God," he mumbled, and he couldn't wait another moment.

He claimed her mouth with the power of the restraint he'd relied on his entire life to try to keep himself in check; only he didn't have to anymore. This woman knew him better than maybe anyone ever had—and that thought set off a pang.

One other woman had come close, but she was gone. She lived safe inside his memory, but she didn't have to haunt him anymore.

He could let her go.

And he could allow himself to love once more.

Fully present for maybe the first time in his life, he gave himself over to the heat and the wonder of the woman in his arms. She kissed him back with a passion to match his own, like maybe she'd been longing for this as much as he had. She opened to him with the same sweetness he remembered, and he closed his eyes, licking past her lips and trailing his hands up and down her arms.

"I'm sorry," he breathed into their kiss. "I'm so sorry. Forgive me."

She shook her head, holding his face between her hands. "There's nothing to forgive."

He couldn't believe it, and yet he had to. He'd doubted her sincerity, had doubted that anyone could be so down-to-the-bones *good*, but to doubt her choice was to doubt her, and that was a mistake he'd never make again. If she forgave him for hurting her, then...

Then he was forgiven.

A ray of light burst through his chest. He clutched her closer, breaking the kiss to pull her flush against his chest, burying his face against her hair and hanging on.

All of the confessions he had told her in the dark, and now they were here. *She* was his light, a brilliance as golden as her hair, chasing the shadows from all the untouched places inside of him. A weight rose off his shoulders.

"I've missed you." His voice broke on the words. "So much."

She laughed, holding him right back. "Not as much as I've missed you."

He edged away, just far enough that he could look her in the eyes. "I am going to do everything in my power to make it up to you."

Cracking a smile as bright as the very sun, she curled soft fingers in his hair. "I think I like the sound of that."

No protestation. No insistence that he didn't have to do anything nice for her. A tide of feeling overwhelmed him, and he kissed the sunshine from her lips. Their last couple of weeks apart and his stubborn idiocy had cost them both, but maybe it had helped them, too. Maybe she'd finally come to realize that she was worth being showered with every good thing on this earth. That it was right to take some good things for herself.

He was determined to be a very, very good thing.

As he delved more deeply into her mouth, the low hum of

arousal he couldn't help but feel when she was close engulfed him. He was hard against her hip, his skin tingling and too tight. These past few weeks, his sex drive had gone all but dormant again, but it awoke with a vengeance, filling him with a whole different kind of fire.

A hint of a growl crept into his throat as he tore himself from her lips, staring down into eyes gone dark and wanting.

"Then I'm going to start right now."

And fuck, this was insane, but he felt no pain as he staggered to his feet. He lifted her up as he went, swinging her into his arms.

With a laughing shriek, she looped her hands behind his neck, holding on for the ride. "What are you *doing*?"

"Something I've been wanting to do since the moment I saw you."

A few weeks weren't close to enough for him to have forgotten the way to her bed. Instead of lumbering after her, held back by his knee and his regrets, he carried her down the hall and through the door. The twinging of his leg was no match to the freedom of sweeping her up like this. Of setting her down on the edge of her bed and climbing after her, pressing her back onto the mattress until she lay spread out beneath him.

Attacking her throat, sucking marks into the tender skin, he skated his hands along her sides, over the swells of her breasts and the dip of her waist, and it was a fucking revelation to lie on top of her. To be able to touch her as he did.

He clenched his eyes shut tight against the need storming hot inside his blood. "Stop me. Tell me you don't want this. Tell me I'm moving too fast."

"Never." A breathy noise escaped her lips, and she scratched the blunt edges of her nails along his scalp, sending fire in their wake.

He groaned into her flesh. He slid one hand to cup her thigh, spreading her out so he could settle into the cradle of her hips. He was so fucking hard for her; he needed her so much. Dropping lower, he let the line of his cock drag right over her through their clothes, and the contact shot sparks.

She whimpered, tugging him back to her mouth, and he fell into the kiss and into her. He ground down hard, and it only felt better, but it wasn't enough.

"Naked," he managed to pant out, shoving at her top. "I need you naked."

He needed her skin and her touch and the long, deep slide into her body. Needed to feel her come around him.

Or better, around his tongue.

He swore out loud, and something tore in his rush to get at her flesh, but she didn't seem to care any more than he did. She helped him wrestle her top over her head, reaching behind herself to get at her bra as he rose onto his knees to unbutton his shirt. At least one pinged off the wall, flying free, and he growled at it.

She sat up then, and her hand on his face was the only thing that could pull him from his haze. Her laughter rang out, soft and kind. "Hey." She stroked a thumb across his cheek. "Hey, there's no rush."

Everything was a rush. He'd gone so long without. He didn't want to lose a single second to buttons or zippers or his own treacherous mind again.

Her other hand settled over his, and when she spoke, this time it was firmer. "Cole. Slow down. We have all the time in the world." She paused, shifting so she could look him in the eye. "Don't we?"

It was only the faintest hint of doubt, but it was entirely too loud.

He took a deep breath, forcing himself to calm down. To get himself back under control. She was a miracle, the way she could do that for him. The way she could bring him back out of his head.

"Yes." He nodded, exhaling hard. "Forever."

Her eyes went bright, but all she did was reel him in, kissing him softer. Slower.

Better.

Together, they got the rest of their clothes off, kicking trousers and pants and shoes off the end of the bed. When they were finally both bare, she lay back, beckoning him to follow. Hovering on his hands and knees above her, he let himself really look.

God, she was beautiful. Her hair flowed out across her pillows in a cloud, and her lips were red and wet and parted, her cheeks deeply flushed.

And her breasts. The soft, pink peaks of them called out to him. His prick pulsed, leaking fluid against her hip. Shifting his weight to one arm, he slipped his knuckles down the center of her chest, gliding to the side to tweak her nipple with his thumb before continuing down. Over her navel and the little pout of her belly. He followed the line of her hip bone in.

When he traced the place where her leg met her body, she whimpered, tilting her hips toward his touch.

"Impatient," he chided, and she made another little sound of frustration. He shook his head. "You were the one who told me to take my time."

At that, she groaned, but she was good for him, lying back. Her muscles were all tense, her gaze so needful, even as she tried to relax.

Good.

He grazed his lips over hers, then down along her jaw toward her ear. "I can't decide what I want first. To be inside you or to taste you." With that, he slipped his fingers through her kitty, a teasing dip into her wetness and a glancing brush against her clit. "What do you think? Want my fingers in you or my cock? Want me to lick your pretty pussy?" Breathing wetly, he sucked at her ear. "I could eat you out for days, you taste so sweet."

She curled her palm around the back of his neck. "All of it." She nudged his head, prodding his kisses lower. "Starting with your mouth."

His prick leaked harder. So many times, he'd asked her what she wanted, but she'd never actually answered him before. She'd begged and she'd pleaded, but she'd never set the course, and it shouldn't get him so fucking hot that she was willing to now.

"As you wish."

Fuck, he was going to make her sorry she'd ever asked him to go slow. It was torture for him, too, but he bit and kissed his way down her body with all the patience he could bear. With his lips and teeth and tongue, he reacquainted himself with every inch of her. Her breasts were as soft and ripe as he remembered, her nipples as tender as he sucked them one by one into his mouth. Panting out his name, she arched her spine into his touch. Tugged at his hair, sending jolts of too-pleasurable pain to the roots and straight on a hard wire to his cock.

He nearly bypassed her pussy entirely, half tempted to fit his lips to the insides of her knees, to see what she'd do if he pressed kisses to the soles of her feet and her toes. But there was time for that—she'd said it herself. They had all the time in the world, a lifetime to spend discovering each other. And he was going to make the most of it.

For now, though, he couldn't wait another moment. The scent of her had blanked his mind. She spread her legs for him, and he braced himself on his elbows between those milky-pale thighs. He'd gotten her to sit on his face before and let him lick her out like that, but he'd never been able to lie on his stomach and worship her before. Never been able to take it at his own pace.

"Beautiful," he mumbled as he kissed right over her mound. She was all soft and pink and open, straining for it as he slid his fingers through her wetness, exposing that perfect little pussy to his gaze.

She panted and flopped an arm across her face. "Are you just going to look at it?"

Maybe he should, just to watch her squirm, but even he couldn't be that cruel.

"No," he said, gazing up into her eyes. "I'm not."

He dove in without reservation or hesitation, the way he should have entered into this thing with her in the first place, the way he was resolved he would from now on. The sweet musk of her enveloped him, taking over his senses as he licked wide stripes all up and down the length of her, dancing circles around her clit.

"Oh God." Her hand on his head told him exactly where she wanted him to be, guiding him back to the very center when he strayed, darting down to lick inside or away to scrape his teeth along her outer lips.

Only when her thighs were shaking did he fit his whole mouth to her, sucking wetly at her clit and beating a fast, strong rhythm with his tongue.

Her moan had his cock pulsing where it rubbed against her sheets. "Yes. There. That's—"

He traced a finger around her opening, and her hips tried to leap off the bed. He pressed her back down with his free hand, shooting her a stern look that was met with a desperation that only fueled his need. With two slick fingers, he fucked her deep and hard, licking faster. He couldn't wait; he wanted her to fall over, to soar. He wanted to *give* her this—to give her everything.

When she broke around his fingers, it was with a cry that tore through him, her inner walls pulsing hotly with a gush of slickness, driving him insane. He closed his eyes and chased her past the edge, but he didn't slow down when she went lax. He coaxed her up and up, until she was shivering and oversensitive and crashing through to the other side, moaning for it all over again.

But then her hands in his hair yanked hard. He parted from her flesh, meeting eyes gone needy and wild.

"Come here." She beckoned, and he had no will in him to defy.

He climbed his way up her body, smearing kisses over her abdomen and her breasts. Meeting her mouth again, he let her taste herself on his lips and swallowed her groan. His cock twitched hard against her thigh, and when she reached down to curl her palm around him, he bit down on her lip.

"Love," he moaned. "Serena, please."

She guided him down, gliding his tip through the soft, slick flesh of her, and it felt like his skin turning inside out.

Like he was inches from finally, finally being home.

"Push inside." She kissed his mouth, curling her fingers against his scalp. "Be inside me."

Fuck. He drove forward in an achingly long, slow thrust. Buried to the hilt, his hips pressed flush to hers, he squeezed his eyes shut tight. He'd never get over the dizzying heat of her, the way she seemed to be made for him, welcoming him into her.

From the very beginning, she'd been so welcoming to him. So eager and free with her love and care. He'd spent too long resisting it, but as he lost himself inside her, he swore. He'd never hold back from her again. She'd get all of him, the good and the bad, and she'd make both better with the touch of her hand. With the warmth of her kiss.

"Serena..."

"I've got you." The soft press of her palm on the back of his neck and at his hip grounded him to this planet and to her. "Cole, you're fine, you're good, you feel so good."

He met her lips again, opening his eyes to stare into bright irises the color of the sea, and he could drown in them and never ever miss the air.

For the longest time, they stayed there like that, just barely rocking against each other as the heat of their connection melted him to his bones. She felt so perfect around him, wet and tight, and to go in bare like this—to possess her so fully. It was too much and nowhere close to enough.

He needed more.

Getting his knees underneath him, he ran a hand down her side to her ass, tilting her hips up into his thrusts so he slid in that extra bit deeper, and they groaned as one. Her flesh was silk beneath his palm, her sounds of pleasure a drug. He slipped his tongue through her mouth, dragging a hand along her thigh to lift it higher, and she was right on board. Wrapping her legs around him, she kept him close, until it was like they were one, as if they could never come apart. And then her pussy *squeezed* him.

Lightning zipped from his balls to the base of his spine, his skin crackling with it, and he gasped her name against her mouth. He wanted it to last, the same way he wanted *them* to last, but it felt too good. He had to let go.

He had to trust.

Planting both his hands to either side of her head, he braced himself on his arms and sped the motion of his hips. She met his every thrust, ankles crossed and digging into his arse, urging him on. The edge was closing in faster now. Driving in hard, he ground himself against her clit, desperate to feel her come apart. Her face went tense, the soft, whining noises that escaped from her lungs reaching into the very core of him and twisting.

He let loose a deep breath, the white-hot fire gathering. His voice was a broken moan. "Can you?"

"Don't stop," she pleaded. "Don't—"

"*Never.*"

Her hands tightened against his skin, the hot clench of her pulling him in.

All his life, he'd feared losing control. But in that instant, he gave it up. He gave it to her, to have and to hold.

"I love you," he breathed.

She tossed her head back. "I love you. Cole, I—"

Her climax washed over her like a dawn across the sky. Her

pussy throbbed and pulsed, tightening around him until he tumbled after, and the black haze of need broke into brilliant light. Slamming forward one last time, he poured himself into her, imperfect and yet whole.

Complete.

EPILOGUE

Four years later

Excuse me, Professor Stafford?"

Cole glanced up, sliding his notes in his bag as he did. The young man standing on the other side of the lectern had his shoulders back, his expression tight. Cole furrowed his brow. "Yes?"

"I was hoping you had a minute."

Cole's laptop beeped, indicating it had finished shutting down. "Literally or figuratively?" He disconnected it from the projector and closed the lid before shoving it into its sleeve. "Because if the former, then you can walk with me. If the latter, it'll have to wait until office hours tomorrow."

Office hours. He'd used to eschew them entirely, threatening TAs into covering them for him or just skipping out on them entirely. Now they were one of the things he most looked forward to each week. Classes had only been in session for a few days, so he probably wouldn't have many takers, but maybe he could get a good group going again like he had last semester. Inquisitive minds who needed individual time to work through their difficulties with the material. People he could help.

"Actually..."

Cole snuck a quick peek at the time. Bollocks, he was running late.

He looked back at the man expectantly. Then blinked, refocusing on him again. There was something familiar to his features, and he struggled, trying to place him.

The man—boy—tucked his thumb into the strap of his backpack.

His bright green backpack.

Cole's eyes went wide. "You—"

"You might not remember me," he said, jaw flexing. "I never got your name, and I don't know if Max ever told you mine. But back a few years ago..."

"Oh believe me, I remember." It all returned to him in flashes. The theft on the "L"—the thundering of his heartbeat and the rush of adrenaline as he'd flown wildly, insanely beyond his control.

The moment with his nephew's tormenter when he'd very nearly done the same, except instead of losing himself, he'd been found.

He'd seen the terror in a bully's eyes and recognized it deep in his own heart of hearts. He'd seen the razor-thin line between a monster and a man, and he'd finally come down fully on the side of the man.

Swallowing against the tide of conflicting emotions, he

stroked his thumb across his ring, spinning it on his finger to calm himself. On the other side of the lectern, the young man seemed to be fighting not to squirm.

"Well. Sir." The kid shifted his weight. "I'm in this class, you see, and I wanted things out in the open. There's not another section I can transfer to, and I need the credit for my major, and—"

Interrupting him, Cole cocked a brow. "And you want to know if there will be reprisals for your having ruined my nephew's life for a year."

Cole had to give the man credit. He only very slightly flinched. "Exactly."

There was an old, bitter part of Cole that wanted to flunk the little bugger on sight.

And there was another part that wanted to thank him. If it hadn't been for him, Cole might still be stewing, grieving and angry and alone. He might've never met Serena.

He might've never gotten her to take him back. To forgive.

To agree, eventually, to become his wife.

Releasing his ring, he reached out. It was still so strange to touch people casually, but he was getting better at it. Four years of love and tireless affection could break through even the most thoroughly built of walls. Struggling for a smile, he clasped the kid's shoulder with his hand. "You are very, very lucky you never laid a hand on my nephew again."

And that he was a better man than he'd been before Serena.

Pulling his arm back, Cole returned to gathering his things. The kid's jaw flexed back and forth, his mouth opening and closing a couple of times before he stammered out, "So...so we're good?"

"We're good."

He heaved out a heavy sigh. "Thank you, Professor."

Cole waved him off, and much like he had in that alley, the guy took it as his cue to bolt. For about a minute too long, Cole watched him go.

Well, that was going to be awkward. He'd have to bring it up with Barry, either the next time he caught him in his office or when he and Serena went over for dinner the following weekend. But it was all right. Cole trusted himself to handle it. To be impartial. And to keep himself and his reactions under control.

The alarm on his phone blared out a chime, startling him back into action. Reminding him he had places to be. Silencing the alarm, he grabbed his bag and tossed it over his shoulder. If it wouldn't have been quite so unbefitting of a professor—and a newly retenured one at that—he would have outright sprinted to the "L," but as it was, he kept himself to a restrained fast walk. He lucked out when an inbound train was pulling into the station just as he hit the stairs. He ducked between the doors a split second before they closed and dropped himself into a seat.

As the train lurched into motion, he gazed off through the window. His bag was full of grant proposals that needed editing and papers to read, and normally he'd take full advantage of the downtime offered by his daily commute. But he was still rattled, still lost in memories. Still this tiny bit angry.

But mostly just so unbelievably fucking grateful for the way his life had been changed, and he would never, ever go back.

When his stop finally came up, he was so deep in thought he nearly missed it. Jolting from his seat as the doors swept open, he disembarked with his head in a fog, and the walk to the field didn't help to clear it.

Apparently, he wasn't much good at hiding his distraction, either.

It didn't take him long to find Serena in the crowd of parents and siblings and other onlookers gathered behind the fence near the dugout. Nodding to the people he recognized, he made his way over to her, sidling in behind her and tapping her on the arm.

She turned to him, all unbridled delight at seeing him, even after all these years. It went straight to his heart, making him feel as tender and bruised as he'd been back when she'd first found him. The smile on her face fell.

"What's wrong?"

Bless this woman. This joy who'd pulled him out of the mess of ashes and fire that had been his life. She knew his moods so well by now—knew when to talk him through them and when to let him stew. He'd never earn her devotion or her love, but fuck him if he would ever stop trying.

"Nothing," he said, sliding his arms around her. If he held on a little bit too tightly, she didn't call him on it. "Just had a blast from the past."

"Oh?" She tilted her head up for a kiss, and he gave it to her gladly, relishing the warmth of her lips.

"Yeah." He'd tell her the details later, talk through all the nuances of his reaction. Let her help him process it the way she always did. For now, though, he stuck to the part that was important. "Reminded me how incredibly lucky I am to have you."

The soft curve of her smile returned. "Not as lucky as I am to have you."

He didn't believe it for a moment, but he wasn't going to fight her on it. He needed her with a desperation that scared him sometimes.

Then again, maybe she needed him, too. Needed someone to remind her of how amazing she was and to shower her with all the love she deserved.

At the thought, he glanced around. "Was Penny not able to get off work after all?"

"No, she's here." Serena pointed toward first base. The twist to her tone took him by surprise.

Penny and Serena still had their moments, but recently they'd been more or less on an even keel. Following her gaze, he scanned the crowd for blond hair and a black leather jacket, and—

Ah. Yes. His sister-in-law stood a little farther down the way, her head bent in conversation with none other than the new headmaster of the school himself—one Grayson Trousseau.

"I see." Well, at least that explained Serena's tone. He mentally rolled his eyes at them both. Sisters, honestly. Refocusing, he returned his attention to the field. "How's the little slugger doing?"

"One on base so far."

"Not bad."

He glanced at the scoreboard. They were only in the second inning, and Upton was leading by two.

Just then, Max came up to bat. He adjusted his helmet and scanned the crowd. When his gaze met Cole's, Cole waved, giving him a quick thumbs-up.

Despite all of Serena's fears, Max had gotten into Upton and with a scholarship to boot. The school had been as brilliant for him as Serena had imagined it would, and the boy was flourishing, making friends and coming home with a hell of a lot fewer bruises. He was top of his class, and Cole took particular pride in how well he was doing these days with math.

Max stepped up to the plate, and they watched him as he hit a decent grounder off the first pitch. The crowd of Upton supporters erupted in cheers, none louder than his and Serena's. He made it to base, and Cole kept an eye on him even as he refocused his attentions, scarcely able to believe he'd managed not to ask yet.

Sliding his arms back around her, he rubbed a questioning hand over her belly. "And how's our other little slugger?"

"Slugging away."

He swallowed hard. The idea of becoming a parent—of inflicting all his imperfections on an innocent he had brought into the world—had terrified him for so long. It would never stop terrifying him.

But they were ready. And once their son made it out into the world, Cole would protect him with every ounce of love in his body.

Threading their hands together, Serena hummed. Their rings clinked, and for a second, the emotion of the day threatened to overwhelm him.

He pressed a kiss to the gold of her hair. "Have I mentioned today that I adore you?"

"Mmm, I think you fit it in at *some* point this morning." She ground back against him suggestively, and he growled, grasping her tighter to still her hips.

"I'm trying to be serious."

She twisted her head to look at him, reaching up with one

hand to touch his cheek. "Seriously, then. You have. You never let me doubt it."

"Good."

He let her turn her attention back to the game, but he only gave it half his eye.

A handful of years ago, he'd been lost and grieving and alone, watching his own train wreck of a life spin out and wishing to God that it would just *stop*.

Unwinding one arm from around his wife, he brought a hand to rest against his heart. The ink there wasn't new, but it still felt fresh sometimes. The nautical star was there to point him home, and beside it was a ship sailing out on clear waters. Seas that were tranquil and calm.

Serene.

The woman in his arms *was* his home now. She'd taught him how to be a better man.

And he was never going to let her go.

By day, Rylan will show Kate a side of Paris not found in any guidebook. By night, he'll introduce her to a passion beyond her wildest dreams.

In this sensuous story of indulgence and desire, Jeanette Grey delivers one of the most romantic reads of the year and proves why she is fast becoming a must-read star.

Turn the page for a preview of *Seven Nights to Surrender*, available now!

It was ridiculous, how pretty words sounded on Kate's tongue. Right up until the moment she opened her mouth and spoke them aloud.

Worrying the strap of her bag between her forefinger and thumb, she gazed straight ahead at the woman behind the register, repeating the phrase over and over in her head. *Un café au lait, s'il vous plaît.* Coffee with milk, please. No problem. She had this. The person ahead of her in line stepped forward, and Kate nodded to herself, standing up taller. When her turn finally came, she grinned with her most confident smile.

And just about had the wind knocked out of her when someone slammed into her side.

Swearing out loud as she was spun around, she put her arm out to catch herself. A pimply teenager was mumbling what sounded like elaborate apologies, but with her evaporating tenth-grade knowledge of French, he could have been telling *her* off for running into *him*, for all she knew. She was going to choose to believe it was the apologizing thing.

Embarrassed, she waved the kid away, gesturing as best she could to show that she was fine. As he gave one last attempt at mollifying her, she glanced around. A shockingly attractive guy with dark hair and the kind of jaw that drove women to paint stood behind her, perusing a French-language newspaper with apparent disinterest and a furrow of impatience on his brow. The rest of the people in line wore similar expressions.

She turned from the kid, giving him her best New Yorker cold shoulder. The lady at the register, at least, didn't seem to be in any big rush. Kate managed a quick "Désolé"—*sorry*—as she moved forward to rest her hands on the counter. She could do this. She smiled again, focusing to try to summon the words she'd practiced to her lips. "Un café au lait, s'il vous plaît."

Nope, not nearly as pretty as it had sounded in her head, but as she held her breath, the woman nodded and keyed her order in, calling it out to the girl manning the espresso machine. Then, completely in French, the woman announced Kate's total.

Yes. It was all she could do not to fist-pump the air. She'd been exploring Paris now for two days, and no matter how hard she rehearsed what she was going to say, waiters and waitresses and shopkeepers invariably sniffed her out as an American the instant she opened her mouth. Every one of them had shifted into English to reply.

This woman was probably humoring her, but Kate seized her opportunity, turning the gears in her brain with all her might. She counted in her head the way her high school teacher had taught her to until she'd translated every digit. Three eighty-five.

Triumph surged through her as she reached for her purse at her hip.

Only to come up with empty air.

Oh no. With a sense of impending dread, she scrabbled at her shoulder, and her waist, but no. Her bag was gone.

She groaned aloud. How many people had cautioned her about exactly this kind of thing? Paris was full of pickpockets. That was what her mother and Aaron and even the guy at the travel store had told her. An angry laugh bubbled up at the back of her throat, an echo of her father's voice in her mind, yelling at her to be more careful, for God's sake. Pay some damn attention. Crap. It was just— She swore she'd had her purse a second ago. Right before that kid had slammed into her...

Her skin went cold. Of course. The kid who'd slammed into her.

Tears prickled at her eyes. She had no idea how to say all of that in French. Her plans for a quiet afternoon spent sketching in a café evaporated as she patted herself down yet again in the vain hope that somehow, magically, her things would have reappeared.

The thing was, "watch out for pickpockets" wasn't the only advice she'd gotten before she'd left. Everyone she'd told had thought her grand idea of a trip to Paris to find herself and get inspired was insane. It was her first trip abroad, and it was eating up pretty much all of her savings. Worse, she'd insisted on making the journey alone, because how was a girl supposed to reconnect with her own muse unless she spent some good quality time with it? Free from distractions and outside influences. Surrounded by art and history and a beautiful language she barely spoke. It had seemed like a good idea. Like the perfect chance to make some really big decisions.

But maybe they'd all been right.

Not wanting to reveal the security wallet she had strapped around her waist beneath her shirt, she wrote off all her plans for the day. She'd just head back to the hostel. She still had her passport and most of her money. She'd regroup, and she'd be fine.

"Mademoiselle?"

Her vision was blurry as she jerked her gaze up. And up. The gorgeous man—the one with the dark, tousled hair and the glass-cutting jaw from before—was standing right beside her, warm hand gently brushing her elbow. A frisson of electricity hummed through her skin. Had he really been this tall before? Had his shoulders been that broad? It was just a plain black button-down, but her gaze got stuck on the drape of his shirt across his chest, hinting at miles of muscle underneath.

His brow furrowed, two soft lines appearing between brilliant blue eyes.

She shook off her daze and cleared her throat. "Pardon?" she asked, lilting her voice up at the end in her best—still terrible—attempt at a French accent.

He smiled, and her vision almost whited out. In perfect English, with maybe just a hint of New York coloring the edges, he asked, "Are you okay?"

All those times she'd been annoyed when someone spoke English to her. At that moment, she could have kissed him, right on those full, smooth lips. Her face went warmer at the thought. "No. I—" She patted her side again uselessly. "I think that guy ran off with my wallet."

His expression darkened, but he didn't step away or chastise her for being so careless. "I'm sorry."

The woman at the register spoke up, her accent muddy. "You still would like your coffee?"

Kate began to decline, but the man placed a ten-euro note on the counter. In a flurry of French too fast for her to understand, he replied to the woman, who took his money and pressed a half dozen keys. She dropped a couple of coins into his palm, then looked around them toward the next customer in line.

"Um," Kate started.

Shifting his hand from her elbow to the small of her back, the man guided Kate toward the end of the counter and out of the way. It was too intimate a touch. She should have drawn away, but before she could convince herself to, he dropped his arm, turning to face her. Leaving a cold spot where his palm had been.

She worked her jaw a couple of times. "Did you just pay for my coffee?" She might be terrible at French, but she was passable at context clues.

Grinning crookedly, he looked down at her. "You're welcome."

"You really didn't need to."

"Au contraire." His brow arched. "Believe me, when you're having a terrible day, the absolute last thing you should be doing is *not* having coffee."

Well, he did have a point there. "I still have some money. I can pay you back."

"No need."

"No, really." Her earlier reservations gone, she reached for the hem of her shirt to tug it upward, but his hands caught hers before she could get at her money belt.

His eyes were darker now, his fingertips warm. "As much as I hate to stop a beautiful woman from taking off her clothes. It's not necessary."

Was he implying…? No, he couldn't be. She couldn't halt the indignation rising in her throat, though, as she brushed aside his hands and wrestled the hem of her top down. "Stripping is *not* how I was going to pay you."

"Pity. Probably for the best," he added conspiratorially. "The police are much more lenient about that kind of thing here than they are in the States, but still. Risky move."

Two ceramic mugs clinked as they hit the counter, and the barista said something too quickly for Kate to catch.

"Merci," the man said, tucking his paper under his arm and reaching for the cups.

For some reason, Kate had to put in one more little protest before she moved to grab for the one that looked like hers. "You really didn't have to."

"Of course I didn't." Biceps flexing, he pulled both cups in closer to his chest, keeping them out of her reach as she extended her hand. "But it sure did make it easier for me to ask if I could buy you a cup of coffee, didn't it?"

For a second, she boggled.

"Come on, then," he said, heading toward an empty table by the window.

This really, really wasn't what she'd had planned for the day. But as he sat down, his face was cast in profile against the light streaming in from outside. If she hadn't lost her bag, she'd have been tempted to take her sketchbook out right then and there, just to try to map the angles of his cheeks.

As she stood there staring, all her mother's warnings came back to her in a rush. This guy was too smooth. Too practiced and too handsome, and the whole situation had *Bad Idea* written all over it. After the disaster that had been her last attempt at dating, she should know.

But the fact was, she really wanted that cup of coffee. And maybe the chance to make a few more mental studies of his jaw. It wouldn't even be that hard. All she had to do was walk over there and sit down across from him. Except...

Except she didn't *do* this sort of thing.

Which might be exactly why she should.

Fretting, she twisted her fingers in the fabric of her skirt. Then she took a single step forward. She was on vacation, dammit all, and this guy was offering. After everything, she deserved a minute to let go. To maybe actually enjoy herself for once.

Honestly. How much harm could a little conversation with a stranger really do?

Rylan Bellamy had a short, well-tested list of rules for picking up a tourist.

Number one, be trustworthy. Nonthreatening. Tourists were constantly expecting to be taken advantage of.

Number two, be clear about your intentions. No time to mess around when they could fuck off to another country at the drop of the hat.

Number three, make sure they always know they have a choice.

Lifting his cappuccino to his lips, he gazed out the window

of the café. It hadn't exactly been the plan to buy the girl in front of him in line a cup of coffee or to pick her up. It *definitely* hadn't been the plan to get so engrossed in the business section of *Le Monde* that he'd managed to completely miss her getting pickpocketed right in front of him. But the whole thing had presented him with quite the set of opportunities.

Trustworthy? Stepping in when she looked about ready to lose it seemed like a good start there. Interceding on her behalf in both English and French were bonuses, too. Paying for her coffee had been a natural after that.

Clear about his intentions? He was still working on that, but he'd been tactile enough. Had gotten into her space and brushed his hands over her skin. Such soft skin, too. Pretty, delicate little hands, stained with ink on the tips.

Just like her pretty, pale face was stained with those big, dark eyes. Those rose-colored lips.

He shifted in his seat, resisting looking over at her for another minute. The third part about making sure this was all her choice was necessary but frustrating. If she didn't come over here of her own free will, she'd never come to his apartment, either, or to his bed. He'd laid down his gauntlet. She could pick it up right now, or she could walk away.

Damn, he hoped she didn't walk away. Giving himself to the count of thirty to keep on playing it cool, he set his cup back down on its saucer. Part of him worried she'd already made a break for it, but no. There was something about her gaze. Hot and penetrating, and he could feel it zoning in on him through the space.

He rather liked that, when he thought about it. Being looked at was nice. As was being appreciated. Sized up. It'd make it all the sweeter once she came to her decision, presuming she chose him.

Bingo.

Things were noisy in the café, but enough of his senses were trained on her that he could make out the sounds of her approach. He paused his counting at thirteen and glanced over at her.

If there'd been any doubts that she was a tourist, they cleared away as he took her in more thoroughly. She wore a pair of purple Converse that all but screamed *American*, and a dark skirt that went to her knees. A plain gray T-shirt and a little canvas jacket. No scarves or belts or any of the other hundred accessories that were so popular among the Parisian ladies this year. Her auburn hair was swept into a twist.

Pretty. American. Repressed. But very, very pretty.

"Your coffee's getting cold," he said as he pushed it across the table toward her and kicked her chair out.

A hundred retorts danced across her lips, but somehow her silence—and her wickedly crooked eyebrow, her considering gaze—said more. She sat down, legs crossed primly, her whole body perched at the very edge of her seat, like she was ready to fly at any moment.

He didn't usually go in for skittish birds. They were too much work, considering how briefly they landed in his nest. He'd already started with this one, though, and there was something about her mouth he liked. Something about her whole aura of innocence and bravery. It was worth the price of a cup of coffee at the very least.

She curled a finger around the handle of her cup and tapped at it with her thumb. Wariness came off her in waves.

"I didn't lace it with anything," he assured her.

"I know. I've been watching you the whole time."

He'd been entirely aware of that, thank you very much. He appreciated the honesty, regardless. "Then what's your hesitation? It's already bought and paid for. If you don't drink it, it's going to go to waste."

She seemed to turn that over in her mind for a moment before reaching for the sugar and adding a more than healthy amount. She gave it a quick stir, then picked it up and took a sip.

"Good?" he asked. He couldn't help the suggestive way his voice dipped. "Sweet enough?"

"Yes." She set the cup down. "Thank you."

"You're welcome."

She closed her mouth and gripped her mug tighter. Reminding himself to be patient, he sat back in his chair and rested his elbow on the arm. He looked her up and down.

Ugh. Forget patience. If he didn't say something soon, they could be sitting here all day. Going with what he knew about her, he gestured in her general vicinity, trying to evoke her total lack of a wallet. "You could report the theft, you know."

Shaking her head, she drummed her finger against the ceramic. "Not worth it. I wasn't a complete idiot. Only had thirty or forty euros in there. And the police won't do much about art supplies and books."

"No, probably not."

The art supplies part fit the profile. Matched the pigment on her hands and the intensity of her eyes.

He let a beat pass, but when she didn't volunteer anything else, he shifted into a more probing stance. Clearly, he'd have to do the conversational heavy lifting here.

Not that he minded. He'd been cooling his heels here in Paris for a year, and he missed speaking English. His French was excellent, but there was something about the language you grew up with. The one you'd left behind. The way it curled around your tongue felt like home.

Home. A sick, bitter pang ran through him at the thought.

He cleared his throat and refocused on his smolder. Eyes on the prize. "So, you're an artist, then?"

"I guess so."

"You guess?"

"I just graduated, actually."

"Congratulations."

She made a little scoffing sound. "Now I just have to figure out what comes next."

Ah. He knew that element of running off to Europe. Intimately. He knew how pointless it all was.

Still. He could spot a cliché when he saw one. "Here to *find yourself*, then?"

"Something like that." A little bit of her reserve chipped away. She darted her gaze up to meet his, and there was something anxious there. Something waiting for approval. "Probably silly, huh?"

"It's a romantic notion." And he'd never been much of a romantic himself. "If it worked, everybody would just run off to Prague and avoid a lifetime of therapy, right? And where would all the headshrinkers be, then?"

She rolled her eyes. "Not everyone can afford a trip to Europe."

Her dismissal wasn't entirely lighthearted. Part of his father's old training kicked in, zeroing in on the tightness around her eyes. This trip was an indulgence for her. Chances were, she'd been saving up for it for years.

Probably best not to mention his own resources, then. Mentally, he shifted their rendezvous from his place to hers. Things would be safer that way.

"True enough," he conceded. "Therapy's not cheap, either, though, and this is a lot more fun."

That finally won him a smile. "I wouldn't know. But I'm guessing so."

"Trust me, it is." He picked up his cappuccino and took another sip. "So, what's the agenda, then? Where have you been so far? What are your must-sees?"

"I only got here a couple days ago. Yesterday, I went out to Monet's gardens."

"Lovely." Lovelier still was the way her whole face softened, just mentioning them.

"I mostly walked around, this morning. Then I was going to sit here and draw for a bit."

Asking if he could see her work some time would be good in terms of making his intentions clear. It was also unbearably trite. He gave a wry smile. "A quintessential Parisian experience."

"And then…I don't know. The Louvre and the Musée d'Orsay, of course." The corner of her mouth twitched downward. "Everything else I had listed in my guidebook."

Ah. "Which I'm imagining just got stolen?"

"Good guess."

Eyeing her up the entire time, he finished the rest of his drink.

She still had a little left of hers, but they were closing in on decision time. He didn't have anything else going on today—he never really had anything going on, not since his life had fallen apart. But was he willing to sink an entire afternoon here, offering to show her around?

He tried to be analytical about it. Her body language was still less than open, for all that she'd loosened up a bit. Given her age, probably not a virgin, but he'd bet a lot of money that she wasn't too far off. Not his usual fare. He preferred girls who knew what they were doing—more importantly, ones who knew what *he* was doing. What he was looking for.

This girl…It was going to take some work to get in there. If it paid off, he had a feeling it'd be worth it, though. When she smiled, her prettiness transcended into beauty.

There was something else there, too. She was romantic and hopeful, and between the story of her lost sketchbook and her delusions about Paris having the power to change her life, she had to be a creative type. Out of nowhere, he wanted to know what kinds of things she made, and what she looked like when she drew.

He kept coming back to her eyes. They hadn't stopped moving the entire time they'd been sitting there, like she was taking absolutely everything in. The sights beyond the window, the faces of the people in the café. Him. It was intriguing. *She* was intriguing, and in a way no other woman had been in so long.

And the idea of going back to the apartment alone made him want to scream.

Decision made, he pushed his chair out and clapped his hands together. "Well, what are we waiting for then?"

"Excuse me?"

"Travel guides are bullshit anyway. Especially when you've got something better." He rose to his feet and extended his hand.

Her expression dripped skepticism. "And what's that?"

He shot her his best, most seductive grin. "Me."

About the Author

Jeanette Grey started out with degrees in physics and painting, which she dutifully applied to stunted careers in teaching, technical support, and advertising. When she isn't writing, Jeanette enjoys making pottery, playing board games, and spending time with her husband and her pet frog. She lives, loves, and writes in upstate New York.

Learn more at:
JeanetteGrey.com
Twitter, @JeanetteLGrey
Facebook.com/JeanetteLGrey

CPSIA information can be obtained
at www.ICGtesting.com
Printed in the USA
LVOW12s1611200316
479963LV00001B/1/P